DAYLIGHT ON IRON MOUNTAIN

CHUNG KUO

DAYLIGHT ON IRON MOUNTAIN

CHUNG KUO

BOOK 2

DAVID WINGROVE

CORVUS

First published in hardback and trade paperback in Great Britain
in 2011 by Corvus, an imprint of Atlantic Books.

1 3 5 7 9 10 8 6 4 2

A CIP catalogue record for this book is available from the British
Library.

Hardback ISBN: 978-1-84887-831-0
Trade paperback ISBN: 978-1-84887-832-7
eBook ISBN: 978-0-85789-432-8

Printed in Great Britain by the MPG Books Group

Corvus
An imprint of Atlantic Books Ltd
Ormond House
26–27 Boswell Street
London
WC1N 3JZ

www.corvus-books.co.uk

CONTENTS

For Rose Wingrove, *née* Jackson, my loving mother,
with thanks for every year of life you've given me.
Here is another for your shelves.

PROLOGUE · Fireflies

SUMMER 2067

You who are born in decay
Dare not fly into the sun.

Too dim to light a page,
You spot my favourite robe.

Wind-tossed, you're faint beyond the curtain
After rain, you're sparks inside the forest.

Caught in winter's heavy frost,
Where can you hide, how will you resist it?

—Tu Fu, 'Firefly' AD 750

1

AT HUA CH'ING SPRINGS

It was the summer of 2067, that bright, hot summer before the beginning of the American campaign. And it was there, in the green shadow of Li Mountain, in that most ancient of places, Hua Ch'ing Hot Springs, sixty li east of China's ancient capital, Xi'an, that they met.

Hua Ch'ing was an ancient place, even by Han standards. A sprawling summer palace, built into the green of the mountainside. First built on by the Chou more than two thousand years before, then followed by the Ch'in and Han, it was a place where Tang Dynasty emperors had once bathed, surrounded by courtiers and concubines, poets and politicians; a place of culture and long history.

Here the great poet, Tu Fu, had written his reflective poems, thirteen centuries before. Poems which still had the freshness of the dew-touched dawn.

There in the moon's pale light on a clear and cloudless evening, beneath the ancient arch of the Fei Hung Ch'iao, 'the Rainbow Bridge', Tsao Ch'un floated on his back, naked as a newborn, looking up at the star-filled heavens.

From where he lay, luxuriating in the warm, sulphur-scented water, he could see the Kuei Fei, the baths of the imperial concubines, and beyond them the Lung Yin waterside pavilion. The great *Ko Ming* emperor Mao had come here once, it was said, to speak with his arch enemy, Chiang Kai-shek, whom he had captured. Since which time, history had passed this haven by.

Guards stood like dark statues beneath the locust trees that flanked the

Springs, while in a chair nearby, on the platform of the Chess Pavilion, sat the great man's friend and advisor, Chao Ni Tsu.

This was Chao's first visit to the Springs. He had spent the long afternoon dozing beside the pale green waters, in the shade of a silk umbrella, while Tsao Ch'un had climbed the steps that led up steeply through the trees, to visit the ancient temples that were hidden in the great tangle of green that was Mount Li.

It was more than fifty years since Tsao had come here last, as an adolescent, back when his parents had been alive. Then it had been packed with tourists, endless specimens of 'Old Hundred Names' who had crowded into this place designed for emperors, for calm and contemplation. The common man, smoking a cigarette and hawking up phlegm. There, six deep wherever you turned, smelling of sweat and cheap cologne. How he had loathed coming here back then. Hated the crowds, the endless gap-toothed peasants. But today...

Chao Ni Tsu smiled at the memory of Tsao Ch'un's face as he had looked about him earlier, his eyes drinking in the simple peacefulness, the pure, unchanged beauty of the place. Yes, and the emptiness. The lack of 'Old Mud Legs', spoiling things just by being there.

He had ordered his guards to form a cordon about the place for the duration, then like Ming Huang himself, had pulled on his dragon robes and gone inside, like the great emperors of old.

A long silence had fallen between the two, as if the gravity of what they had been discussing had become too weighty for further discussion. But now that silence was broken, not by the man who floated beneath the ancient bridge, like a sleeping tiger, but from the one who was prone to speak but scantly in normal circumstances. Scantly and hesitantly, afraid to commit his thoughts to utterance. Only now he did, leaning towards the dark shape in the water just below him.

'It is as you said, Tsao Ch'un. Our response must be dramatic and immediate and... *lasting*.'

Tsao Ch'un grunted. 'You think I am right then, Brother Chao? You think we should nuke them and have done with it?'

'I think...' Chao hesitated. 'I think they have made it very hard for you to follow any other path. I think... well, to be candid, I think we have two choices: To destroy them entirely, root and branch; or to license their religion. To allow it into our City in a milder, *sanctioned* form.'

'*Allow it!*' Tsao Ch'un roared, the water about him growing agitated as he turned to face his old companion. 'No, Chao Ni Tsu! Mao was right. Religion's a disease, a malaise of the brain. It makes madmen of us all! If only we could cure it, neh? Give the bastards a pill and flush it from their minds!' He sighed. 'The gods help us, Master Chao! If only they'd be reasonable.'

Chao chuckled. '*Reasonable?*'

Tsao Ch'un reached out, grasping the carved marble edge of the steps beside the bridge.

'You know what I mean. You'd think they'd see what was happening. That they'd recognize where the tide of history is taking us. See it and adapt, not fight it tooth and nail. You'd think...'

Chao Ni Tsu shook his head. 'Think what? That they'd realize that you're more *powerful* than them and that they cannot prevail? They know that, and it makes not a blind bit of difference. They would fight you to the last man anyway. Barbarians, that's what they are. Next to them we are enlightenment itself. Besides, that's not the reason why they've declared Holy War against you, Tsao Ch'un.'

'No? Then what is?'

'They do not think you have the *nerve* to nuke them.'

Tsao Ch'un laughed. 'Didn't they hear?'

'About Japan? No, old friend. And even if they did, they'd think it but a rumour. What, after all, would they have seen of it? No... they think that God is on their side. Allah, Jehovah... call him what you will... they truly believe in him. Insane, I know, but no amount of logical argument will free them from their madness. It is God's will, so they say.'

'God's will...' Tsao Ch'un spat angrily. 'And meanwhile they send their suicide bombers against our outposts!' He snorted. 'I should just do it. Get it over with and move on. Only...'

'Only what? Are you worried about the fallout?'

'Is that a joke, Chao Ni Tsu?'

Master Chao smiled in the darkness where he sat. 'You must understand one thing, Tsao Ch'un. You cannot play games with these people. You might use words, trying to get through to them, but their answer is always a bullet or a bomb. They have no time for reason. Their passion is for gesture. For martyrdom.'

'And ours?'

'Is often the same, I agree. Only where we differ is that we want the world to move forward, not backwards. We want a world at peace, where all men might be given their chance. A world without conflict. And theirs? No, Tsao Ch'un. They would have us live in ancient times, by ancient laws. And ridiculously stupid laws at that! Laws formulated by tribes of desert nomads to suit their way of life. As for how they see us... well, *we're* the heretics, as far as they're concerned!'

Tsao Ch'un was quiet a moment. Then, deciding to get out, he hauled himself up out of the silvered water in one swift movement and stood there naked beneath the moonlight, the water streaming from him.

'Do you remember, Ni Tsu, back in the early days? Back in forty-four, when the long campaign had just began? When we first sent the Brigades out to do our work? How exciting it all was. How exhilarating. Now... well, I grow jaded, Chao Ni Tsu. I grow...' He sighed, then drew his fingers through his long dark hair, combing it back. 'I guess what I'm trying to say is that nuking them would feel like a failure, somehow. Oh, I know the arguments how many lives it would save. I know all that. But *this*... it seems much too facile an answer.'

He turned as he said it, looking directly at Chao Ni Tsu.

Master Chao shrugged. But he remembered it well. 2044... Those had been hard times, difficult times; times when it could all quite easily have gone wrong. Back then, only skill and cunning had kept them ahead of their enemies.

Yes, and an untiring, unrelenting watchfulness.

My skill and his cunning, he thought, fascinated by the physical creature that stood before him. Another would have called for a towel and clothes, but he did neither. He was content to be as he was: an animal that thought. Being such gave him an edge that others simply did not have.

'I've asked Shepherd to come,' Tsao Ch'un said, seeing how Chao was watching him, but not minding. 'We're meeting him in the old city, later this evening. We can decide then, neh?'

And there it was, put off again for another hour or two. But they would have to make the decision soon. Before the great Jihad got under way. Then again, Shepherd would know what to do. He always did, unfailingly.

'Are you hungry?' Tsao Ch'un asked, his voice strangely softer now that they had decided not to decide. Not to destroy the Middle East in one big blinding flash.

Chao Ni Tsu nodded, then slowly hauled himself up out of his chair. He was getting old. His every movement told him as much. 'You know what?' he said. 'I could murder a haunch of gammon. With rice and cinnamon and...'

He smiled, seeing how Tsao Ch'un's face had lit up at the suggestion.

'No wonder you've put on weight, Brother Chao. Not that you were ever slim.'

'I can't help it, Brother Tsao. I like my food. It was my mother's fault. She fed me too well.'

'The gods bless her souls.'

'Are you not cold, Tsao Ch'un?'

'Not at all, Chao Ni Tsu. The night air's warm. You should try it. To have nothing between one and the world. To feel the air on one's skin. There is no greater delight... unless it's a woman.'

'Or a plate of gammon and rice and cinnamon...'

Two hours later, drowsy from too much food and definitely too much wine, Chao Ni Tsu settled in the corner of the chamber while Tsao Ch'un took his nightly reports.

He did this every night, though not always at the same hour, speaking to his leading commanders in the field, making sure that all was well. Right now he was talking to Marshal Wei, who had set up his command post in Tehran.

The war in West Asia had reached a strange impasse. Marshal Wei had subdued most of the territory from China to the border of Iraq, but there things had stalled, defying the marshal's most strenuous efforts to make advances.

Even so, Tsao Ch'un was pleased with Marshal Wei. He was a brilliant strategist. Without him the campaign would have lasted twice as long, for it was no easy task, fighting in such terrain. For the last six months he had rolled back his enemies mile by mile. Only now had they ground to a halt in the face of fanatical resistance.

And now there was this small matter of the Jihad.

Chao Ni Tsu smiled contentedly. It was pleasant to think that one was seated where the great Ming Huang, the Purple Emperor, had once sat. To imagine the Son of Heaven listening, perhaps, as his concubine, Yang Kuei Fei, played the lute for him or sang.

Or *bathed* with him.

He closed his eyes, imagining the sight. The old man and the beautiful younger woman, her flesh like olive perfection.

'Are you good, old friend?'

He felt Tsao Ch'un's hand pressed gently but firmly on his shoulder. Half turning, he looked up at him.

'I was thinking of the great emperor, Ming Huang and the beautiful Kuei Fei... Being here I could imagine it... could almost see them...'

Tsao Ch'un grunted. 'The old man was mad... to lose his empire over a woman!'

It was true, Chao thought. To force one's eldest son to divorce his young wife, then assign her to one's own harem. And then to promote her family, against the wishes of his court. Only a man bewitched would have followed such a course. And what was the end of it all? He had been forced to have her killed, strangled by his chief eunuch, to pacify his enemies.

Only it had not been enough to save things. An Lushan, Kuei Fei's lover and Ming Huang's general   a Manchurian of common birth   had finally overthrown him.

Tsao Ch'un came round, squatting on his haunches just in front of Chao Ni Tsu. He had put on a loose-fitting cloak of midnight blue, and combed back his long, jet-black hair. He had been up all day   since dawn, in fact   but he did not look the least bit tired.

Another might have abused his power. Might have spent his days in debauchery. But that was not Tsao Ch'un's manner. He was no holy man when it came to women. In fact he *enjoyed* women. But he had never let a woman control him, or manipulate him, or distract him. What he had, he always said, was an itch. And the only thing to do with an itch was to scratch it. Scratch it good and hard.

'Amos has been delayed,' he said, squeezing the old man's knee fondly. 'He'll be here late morning now.' Tsao Ch'un smiled. 'And he reminded me...'

Chao Ni Tsu frowned. 'Reminded you?'

'Yes, my humble friend. *Reminded* me. About your birthday. I'm sorry. I *had* forgotten. But look...' He pulled out a bright red silken package from behind his back, like a conjurer presenting a fake bunch of flowers. 'I have a gift for you!'

'Old friend...' Chao Ni Tsu sat forward, moved by the gesture, reaching out to take the package. 'You really shouldn't have...'

He opened it, let the silk fall away, then caught his breath.

'*Kuan Yin!*'

It was an ancient piece, the size of a woman's hand; a delicately carved figure of a *wei ch'i* player   just the figure and the board, in pure white marble. Marble that seemed almost soft to the touch.

Chao Ni Tsu stared and stared. It was beautiful, astonishingly beautiful. Perhaps the most beautiful thing anyone had ever given him. He put a finger to his eye, wiping the tear away.

'Your kindness overwhelms me, brother.'

'Good,' Tsao Ch'un said, getting to his feet once more. For once, his face was lit with simple pleasure at Chao's own delight. 'Then let us get some sleep. Tomorrow is a fateful day, neh?'

BENEATH THE YELLOW EARTH

The Mausoleum was huge, the great semi-transparent roof stretching away in all directions. In the shadows, down there beneath and between the slatted walkways, the life-size figures stood in formation; row after row of grey-black figures, the clay face of each one different, each modelled on the individual they had been, back when they had lived and breathed, twenty-three centuries ago.

In life the army of the Ch'in had been a million strong, soldiers of the First Emperor, Ch'in Shih Huang-ti. Their terracotta figures had followed their great lord into the realm of the dead, beneath the yellow earth; there, no doubt, to carve out an empire fit for the Son of Heaven.

Tsao Ch'un grinned, then jumped down, striding between their ranks looking first at this one then at that.

'This one, I think...'

And, raising the baseball bat he was carrying, he swung. The clay head cracked in half as it tumbled from the body.

He swung again.

'Do you *have* to, brother?' Chao queried, watching from his wheelchair on the walkway high above. 'It seems... I don't know... lacking in respect. He was a great man, our King of Ch'in.'

'A great man and a fool,' Tsao Ch'un answered, taking another swing and removing another clay head. 'Besides, this is fun. You know how much I like to break things, Chao Ni Tsu! To *vandalize* them!'

And he laughed, a great gust of laughter, before he swung again.

'You know what he believed, Chao? He believed he could be immortal. That all he had to do was build a bridge to the Isles of the Immortals, out there to the east, and he could join them, peach and all!'

Chao knew the tale. 'It's just...'

Tsao Ch'un swung again. 'Oh, leave off, Chao! Let me have my fun. What are a few clay heads compared to what we will discuss today?'

It was true. Only it seemed somehow sacrilegious. Ch'in Shih Huang-ti *had* been a great man. The great unifier of China. And it *was* lacking in respect. Unless Tsao Ch'un meant something else by the gesture.

'Immortal! I mean to say... When a man is dead, he's dead. His reputation? Well, that's different. But the flesh... the flesh decays, brave Chao. Back to dust and clay, as *these* fellows will testify!'

And he laughed again. A fierce, belligerent laughter.

There was a crack as another head fell and then another. He had 'killed' a good dozen of them by now.

'You know, Chao... I should have a purge, don't you think? Shake things up a bit. Stop my people from becoming too complacent. It's what Ch'in Shih Huang-ti would have done. He had no time for fools, you know... except himself, that is. He got conned, Chao, by a shaman. The man took him for a fortune. Riches enough to fight a great campaign. And what did he buy? A bridge! A fucking non-existent bridge! Well, you won't find me buying no fucking bridges!'

He swung. There was the crack of clay, the tumble of broken shards.

'But I do like to break things. I really do. It *annoys* them, see. All the pompous little nothings. It winds them up. Gives them indigestion. Stomach cramps... And I like that. I like seeing them all discomfited.'

Another head flew. The floor now was littered with broken pottery.

'You think me ruthless, Chao, I know. But we Han have always been ruthless. In 259 BC in southern Shan-hsi, the army of Chao   no relatives of yours, my friend, I should quickly say   was starved into surrender by the Ch'in at Ch'ang P'ing. Etiquette demanded that they give up their weapons and go home, only the Ch'in generals executed them, to the last man. Four hundred thousand men. Beheaded, every last one, their heads made into a great pile as a warning to others.'

Tsao Ch'un paused, narrowing his eyes. 'You know what? That purge...

it's a good idea, neh? You could compile a list for me, Chao... like in the old days.'

A list, Chao thought, turning his chair slightly and wishing that Amos were there so they could settle this matter. *Another bloody list.*

Back in the old days it had seemed the only way to go about things. To target one's enemies and 'reduce' them. Necessity had forced their hand. But purges. He hated the notion. Weren't they at peace now?

Only the truth was that they weren't. Not yet. Oh, America would fall, eventually. The Middle East question would be resolved, one way or another, but...

'Well, Chao? Will you *make* me a new list?'

Chao Ni Tsu looked across to where his old friend stood, baseball bat poised, ready to strike again.

'If that's what you want.'

'Oh, I do. The more I think of it... Well, imagine. When the executions begin. Think what a panic they'll be in!' He laughed, but this time it was barely a laugh. His eyes were serious, looking inward at his thoughts.

'They've grown fat and bloated, Chao. Corrupt. Not that I care too much whether they're corrupt or not, provided I see my share, but... they grow too sure of themselves. And that can't be good for me, can it now? No. We need to strip them of their power. To make them question whether they are the next to go.'

Chao nodded. 'We must make them fear you again, *Chieh Hsia.*'

Tsao Ch'un met the old man's eyes and nodded. 'Fear me... Yes. You have it *perfectly*, Chao Ni Tsu. So make a list. A long list, mind you, sparing no sector of society. And then we'll see, neh?'

Outside again, Chao let his Master push him, Tsao Ch'un quiet now, quiet and brooding. But Chao knew that quiet of old. Knew that it meant he'd come to a decision.

'Have you made up your mind?'

Tsao Ch'un spoke to his back. 'I did... and then I didn't. Smashing all those heads...' His voice softened, as if, for a moment, he was talking of something other than the murder of tens of millions.

'It's no easy thing to decide upon. Japan... well *that* was easy. There was always an animosity between us. They were always our enemies. And so I did not hesitate. I knew what I had to do. But these others... this strange alliance. I wondered if there wasn't, perhaps, some better way of dealing with them...'

A strange alliance indeed, thought Chao. Arab and Jew joining together to fight a Holy War against Tsao Ch'un. It would have been unthinkable only a year ago. But things had changed. No. When things were at their most chaotic, the Arabs and Jews had been at each other's throats. It had been a fierce and bitter war; one which seemed destined to end in mutual obliteration. Only then they, the Chinese, had arrived with their City and their settlers, and things had changed. With armageddon facing them, the two blood enemies had united, ending a hundred years and more of conflict.

Two days ago, that had been. Two days since that historic and foolhardy moment.

Tsao Ch'un slowed the chair, then stopped. 'Chao Ni Tsu? Was there ever a woman in your life?'

Chao smiled. 'There was. But that was long ago.'

'Really? I am surprised. I thought...'

'It was while I was in College. In Ying Kuo. You know, at Cambridge. Before I met you. She was a native, an English girl. A pretty young thing. We went out for a time, but I think she found me too intense, too nervous... yes, and too nerdy.'

Tsao Ch'un laughed. 'Nerdy... now there's a term I haven't heard for ages.'

'Perhaps you should google it.'

The two men laughed. Between them they had destroyed that world. Buried it where it could not be found.

'So she left you, Chao?'

'Did I say that? No, Tsao Ch'un. I wrote her a letter. Or rather, an e-mail. You remember e-mails.'

'I'm not senile, Chao. I do remember how things were.'

'Well... it was strange. You'd think I was heartbroken, only I wasn't. I was relieved. Romance... I was not programmed for romance. But I had to learn that. Had to experience it so I could understand it.'

'And move on?'

'Yes, and move on. But I sometimes think of her. She must be dead now.'

'You think?'

'Oh yes, I looked. In the records. To see if she survived. Only she didn't.'

'Ah...' Tsao Ch'un was silent a moment, then he began to push again.

'Coming here, Chao... I didn't realize it, but it was just what I needed. To get away from court and all of that incestuous nonsense that goes on. No. Let the Seven keep things ticking over. Let *them* worry and make decrees. I needed a break...'

'Yes, but why here?'

Tsao Ch'un stopped and gestured towards the horizon. Out there lay the old city with its high walls and its imposing watchtowers. And beyond it and all about, what seemed like a tiny mountain range, but what were in fact the tombs of thirty ancient emperors, dating back to the Chou, three thousand years before.

'I came here, Chao, because this is where it began. China and the dream of unification. Of one single nation ruled by the Son of Heaven. And now that we're in the endgame... well... I just thought it apt, that's all. To come and see it all, one last time. Before the game was over. Before we'd placed the last stone on the board.'

Tsao Ch'un smiled. 'And to swim, of course, and bash in a few heads and... to eat gammon and sweet chestnuts. And to talk to my oldest, dearest friends. While there was time. Before our days were done.'

CHUNG KUO

3

IN OLD CH'ANG-AN

mos, arriving, found them in the old city.

Xi'an had been abandoned twenty years back. The ancient walled city was one of the places Tsao Ch'un's Brigades had been forced to subdue, back in 2045. Though it had not yet begun to crumble, there was considerable sign of war damage. Only it was not its present state, but the great sense of history contained within its walls that struck Shepherd as he walked its empty main street, the Nan Ta Chieh, heading for the bell tower.

The Panp'o had first settled here on the banks of the Wei Ho, a branch of the Yellow River, back in the Neolithic period, almost seven thousand years past. Their villages were scattered all about this region. But it was the Chou who had first built a city, here at the end of the Silk Road, thirteen great dynasties ruling the surrounding lands from Ch'ang-an, their capital. They lasted from 1046 through to 771 BC, when they were swept away in their turn. Their successors were the Ch'in, who, after 260 years of striving against their neighbouring states, finally unified their great land; their young king, later known as Ch'in Shih Huang-ti, defeating their opponents one by one. The Han in 230 BC, the Chao in 228 BC, the Ch'i in 226 BC, and then the Wei in 225 BC. The Ch'u were defeated in 223 BC and finally the Yen in 222 BC.

Two hundred and sixty years of warfare. It seemed an implausibly long time. Yet so it had been. The 'Warring States' period, had been the last time China had been divided for any great length of time, and from its chaos had come the determination to unify the land; one that every successive emperor strove to achieve. There was of course, the *San-kuo* period, the 'Three Kingdoms' as it was known, and the *Wu Tai*, the 'Five Dynasties', but those had been mere blips   forty-four years and fifty-three respectively   since which time there had been the Tsin, the Sui, the T'ang, the Sung, the Kin and Southern Sung, the Yüan, the Ming and the Ch'ing, not to mention the *Ko Ming* under Mao and Deng. Dynasties that lasted centuries, and then fell, to be replaced by other dynasties in an endless progression.

And was that pattern broken?

Shepherd stopped, looking about him. Before its latest troubles, this had been a thriving city of ten million souls. Why, even back in the second century BC, it was said that more than a million inhabited its mighty walls   a figure, Shepherd mused, that was larger than his own country's population at that time. China had, indeed, a long and great history. He could understand just why, in its dealings with such as the Americans, it looked on them as uncultured children and their land as 'the land without ghosts'. No wonder the Chinese thought of them as soulless barbarians.

The thought amused him. He had met many Americans in the last year or two, and knew that the Chinese view of them was mistaken. Jiang Lei knew it too. But Tsao Ch'un persisted in that view. He had no time for them.

It was Tsao Ch'un's zealots, his *Pu Shou* or 'radicals', who had kept America down these past twenty years, snipping off the green shoots of recovery as they appeared. Reducing the once mighty American empire to a gaggle of contesting kingdoms. Only now those quarrelling nations were uniting. At the very last they had begun to show some fighting spirit. Some *spunk*, as they liked to call it!

It was that which had delayed him. That which, he knew, he would have to raise with Tsao Ch'un before he went from here. Raise and resolve. Because, if he was right, then America was about to become a problem.

The bell tower was directly above him now, its massive walls dominating the centre of the ancient city, pushing up into the sky. If any single structure spoke of ancient China's might, it was this. This and the city's massive walls.

It spoke of a power and magnificence unmatched in history. Why, you could run a marathon around those forty-foot-high walls, perhaps stopping at each of the great watchtowers that studded its length. Or at one of the four massive gatehouses set at the four directions of the compass, that soared into the blue, like the bell tower.

Only now, with spectacular incongruence, a dozen and more high-rise Western hotels broke up that skyline. As if here and here only, the future had collided with the past.

'Amos! Up here!'

Shepherd looked up, shielding his eyes against the early morning sun. It was Tsao Ch'un, leaning out from the upper balcony of the tower.

'Wait there! I'll come up!'

Climbing up, he wondered why Tsao Ch'un had summoned him today. And why here, where modern China   Chung Kuo   had begun? Was this meant to be some kind of lesson? Or, maybe more to the point, an explanation of events   a setting of things in their historical context. Flying in, he had found himself impressed by the great mounds of the emperors' tombs that filled the valley to the north of the city. Were they to excavate them all, he had been told, it would take a thousand years.

He smiled. It was just like the Han to exaggerate and round their figures off – 'Ten Thousand Years!' they'd cry. Only this once he was sure that they were right. This was Egypt and Rome, Troy and Constantinople, rolled into one. And then some.

Tsao Ch'un was waiting at the top of the steps, Chao Ni Tsu in his chair just beyond him, out in the open. And, at a distance, four guards. Part of Tsao Ch'un's hand-picked elite.

'Well?' Tsao Ch'un asked, grinning fiercely. 'What do you think of our little town? A monument to impermanence, neh?'

Shepherd smiled, then grasped his hands. 'I am impressed, old friend. Such a vast weight of history... one but rarely encounters something like this.'

'Which is why I let it be. Let the air get to it. Call me sentimental, but...'

Shepherd laughed. 'Sentimental? You, Tsao Ch'un?'

'Oh yes. I came here as a child. My parents brought me. We had a meal near here, at the Te Fa Ch'ang restaurant, in the shadow of the tower. Dumplings. Such magnificent, mouth-watering dumplings, based on genuine recipes from the T'ang court. I have tasted nothing like them since.'

Shepherd stared at him, surprised. He had never, in all the time he'd known him, seen this side of Tsao Ch'un. This softer side.

He looked about him. The red lacquer of the pillars and shutters was overpowering. And everywhere one looked there was elaborate decoration in the Han style, with dragons and lucky pictograms, all of them picked out in golden lettering.

Chao Ni Tsu, he saw, was dozing. *As ever these days,* Shepherd thought, walking across and then crouching in front of him.

'Master Chao...'

Chao Ni Tsu opened his eyes. 'Oh, Amos... You've come.'

'Fresh from the front,' he said, and smiling, reached out to take Chao's hands. Those clever, subtle hands that even he considered brilliant. They and the mind that lay behind them.

He released Chao's hands and stood. 'Well... we are assembled.' He looked to Tsao Ch'un. 'I saw the news. On my way here. It seems they have a death wish, neh?'

Tsao Ch'un nodded. 'I sent an envoy to them, do you know that? One of my best negotiators. And do you know what they did?'

Shepherd shrugged.

'They killed him, that's what they did. And sent him back to me. Slit open and filled with sand, then sewn up again.'

'So what did you do?'

'I sent them another. A bit of a bully this time. He was under strict instructions to let them know their options.'

'Which were?'

'To surrender or die.'

'Fine choices. And how did they respond?'

'They sent him back.'

'Slit open and sewn up?'

Tsao Ch'un nodded.

'I see.'

Amos was silent for a time, then he smiled. 'So what have we to discuss? It seems to me they've pared their options down to a single choice.'

'Maybe. And maybe not. But I wanted your counsel, Amos. I wanted to hear what you had to say before... well, before anything, really.'

Again, that was unlike Tsao Ch'un. To be so hesitant. So untrusting of his own instincts. Only it was a big decision. To destroy whole peoples. That was not something one did without reflection.

'I was wondering,' Tsao Ch'un said, staring away thoughtfully, 'how the future would see me. Whether, in better times than these   more liberal times   they would understand. All of the death, the suffering I've caused. You would have thought that I enjoyed such things. Only there is no other way. The path of blood... we must follow it, gritting our teeth, bearing the worst, knowing that what lies ahead will be much better.'

He paused, looking back at Shepherd. 'The West was weak. We all know that. Spoiled and self-indulgent. Not to speak of the waste. As for their insolence! It was quite breathtaking, don't you think? What had they, after all? A mere thousand years of history at most... and as for America, that was but an infant society. Three hundred years... it's as long as one single dynasty. Whereas China has a history that goes back three *thousand* years. Think of it! Three thousand years of unbroken culture. Three thousand years of sound government and law-making. Why, when Europe was struggling to get up off its hands and knees, still suffering the long dark ages that followed the fall of *Ta Ch'in*, the great Roman empire, this one city alone could boast a population of a million and a half souls. Imagine it. How far ahead of them we were. And they dare to call *us* backward!'

Tsao Ch'un turned, looking to Chao Ni Tsu.

'Master Chao... When you met them, these Westerners... did you like them? Were you at ease among them? And I don't mean our friend Amos here. His nature makes him an exception to the norm.'

Chao Ni Tsu smiled. 'The *Hung Mao*... they were okay. I always felt we could accommodate them in the world we planned. But as for the others...'

'So what should I do? How ruthless ought I to be?'

'As ruthless as you must,' Amos said, interrupting. 'Concede an inch and it will start unravelling. Deep down you know that, Tsao Ch'un. There *is* no other choice. You must crush all opposition, and not just in the Middle East.'

'Maybe so, but what will stop the people from rebelling? For they *will* rebel, given time. History teaches us that much. And besides, I won't live forever. What happens when I'm dead? Who will I find that is even one part as ruthless as I?'

'Then you must create a system that works. That polices itself. You have some of the ingredients already, Tsao Ch'un, in the Seven and the Thousand Eyes. But you must take it further. If it's stability you want, then you must crack down on change itself. Control is the key, and anything less than total control... Well, that way lies disaster.'

'It is so, Tsao Ch'un,' Chao Ni Tsu added, sitting forward. 'It is not enough to conquer the world. We must control it. Only, if we are to do so, then we must lock all of the doors that lead back to the past. Bolt them up and brick them over.'

Shepherd saw how Tsao Ch'un nodded at that. At his core, for all he'd done, the great man hated change. Hated the very instability he'd caused, as much as he hated drugs and their insidious effect. And insects. And the 'disease'   as he called it   of progress, which he believed was no progress at all, *morally.*

'Flying out here,' Amos said, 'I saw such scenes of devastation. Such chaos and destruction. Oh, I know it will all come good. That one day, not so long from now, people will look back on these years and say "It had to be". Only... some days, I have to admit, I fear for my soul.'

Tsao Ch'un locked eyes with him. 'Do you regret what we have done, Amos?'

'No, old friend. How could I? It *had* to be done. But I would not be a man if I did not sometimes feel for those whose lives I've damaged.'

'We have been responsible for much, neh?' Tsao Ch'un said, not flinching at the admission. 'But it is true what you say, dear friend. It *had to be.* For the world to go forward, it *had* to be unified. The only other option was racial suicide, "total annihilation", as Einstein saw it. And who is to argue with such a great man?'

'Not I,' Chao said, and all three of them laughed.

Tsao Ch'un looked down. 'As I see it, our friends in the Middle East do not want the Western world, any more than we did. They are like us in that they do not like a world they can't control. A world where the individual self has been elevated beyond the group, and where civic duty has shrivelled up and died. You'd have thought that it would have brought us together. Only... beyond those things, what do we have in common?'

'Nothing...'

Tsao Ch'un met Shepherd's eyes and nodded. 'They are a troublesome, problematic race of people, neh? Disorderly. Not at all like the Han. The Han know how to behave, how to fit in. Whereas they...' He made a dismissive gesture. 'Do you remember the question I asked you years ago, Chao Ni Tsu, when we began this venture?'

'I do, my Lord. How does one take the world without destroying it?'

'Precisely. For we knew what was to come, you and I.' He smiled. 'Oh, and you too, Amos, though you chose in your own peculiar fashion to turn it all into a game. Collapse was inevitable. We saw that. Saw that as a species we might become extinct, bones in the ground, just another evolutionary dead end. Unless we acted. Unless we tore it all down and built it up again, stronger than before.'

Tsao Ch'un paused. 'If I doubted for a moment what we have done. If I...'

He paused again, shaking his head. 'No. Doubt is a luxury I cannot afford. I must be fearless, uncompromising. I would be failing my people were I not so. To be a helmsman... few men can fulfil that role. To carry such a weight upon one's shoulders... I do not have to tell you, my friends... some days it can be intolerable...'

He laughed; sudden, unexpected laughter. 'They should fete me... they really should. Saviour of the human race, that's what I am! Only I don't delude myself. They'll call me tyrant, megalomaniac, the world's greatest sociopath. Only think. What if I had not done what I have done? What would the consequences have been? Dust, that's what. It would all have turned to dust.'

Shepherd nodded. 'So what is it to be?'

Tsao Ch'un smiled. 'It is done.'

'Done?'

'I gave the order an hour back. Before you came.'

'Then why... ?'

'I wanted to know you were still with me, my friend. Wanted... *confirmation*, I guess you'd call it.'

'But the Middle East?'

'Is ashes.' He looked into the distance, as if he could see it, then glanced back at Shepherd. His voice was suddenly quiet.

'They sent a team. Did you know that, Amos? Last night. Mossad it was. Six of their best men. Only what chance did they really have? Just getting through the screening process was impossible.' He laughed. 'Well, when did you last see a Chinese Jew?'

They were silent a moment, then Shepherd spoke up again.

'Have you considered my report?'

Tsao Ch'un nodded. 'I've looked at it. Why?'

'I just thought... maybe it was time. Before they get any stronger.'

Tsao Ch'un was emanating calm. 'That, too, is done. I am to see the Seven next week, to discuss the matter with them. But Amos...'

'Yes, brother?'

'Let us not waste any more time pacifying the Americans. Let's go for the jugular this time, neh? Let's nail the bastards, and bugger the cost!'

PART FOUR   Black Hole Sun

SUMMER 2067

When the East Wind blows
Frost ripens in the fields
Cold penetrates the thinnest of summer silks
More spider's web than cloth.

When the East Wind blows
The sickle rusts
Rain falls like an old man's tears
On hearing of an ancient lover's death.

When the East Wind blows
A castle shimmers into dust
Lives vanish with the dawn
Like mist on water meadows.

When the East Wind blows
Memory burns in the ovens
Flares bright before it blackens
Each sweet recollection given up to ash

When the East Wind blows.

—Nai Liu, 'Homage to Su Tung-p'o', 2067

CHUNG KUO

Chapter 12

AN INTERVIEW WITH THE DRAGON

Two years had passed and Jiang Lei was returning home.

It was only now, looking out across that endless, geometric whiteness, that he understood how staggeringly vast Tsao Ch'un's city had become. Operating at the very edge of things – at the breaking crest of the great wave of resettlement – he had been too close to see it. But now that he did, he grasped how different in kind it was, how transformational the idea behind it. Compared to it, all of the cities of the past had been but mud and daub. For this was *The City*, and he was returning to meet its creator.

As his craft banked to the left, Jiang saw before him the massive hexagonal gap in that otherwise unblemished surface. Down there, in the deep gloom, at the bottom of a massive well five *li* across and two *li* deep, was what remained of China's past.

The Forbidden City.

For 800 years this had been the heart of China, of Chung Kuo, the Middle Kingdom. Tsao Ch'un had made it his capital, once he had wrested power from the Politburo, taking on the mantle of the emperors and naming himself Son of Heaven in the ancient style.

It was here, beneath the Dragon Throne, that Jiang Lei was to meet the great man at noon tomorrow.

The craft descended slowly to the landing pad. From the way the banners tore at their moorings, Jiang Lei could see that a strong wind was blowing.

Welcome back to Pei Ching, where the sky is full of yellow dust.

They set down with a hiss and a shudder, the engines dying with a descending whine.

On the flight, Jiang had been reading a collection of poetry from the Sung dynasty. It was not a period he knew well and the poems of Su Tung-p'o had, before now, passed him by. But after reading them he was intrigued, both by the poems and the man. Like Jiang Lei, Su Tung-p'o, under his birth name of Su Shih, had been a government official, a conservative by nature, upholding the Confucian ideals. Unlike Jiang, however, it seemed that Su Shih had spent time imprisoned and in exile for his beliefs – mainly for criticizing government policy in his poems.

Jiang set the book down and looked across the narrow cabin. Steward Ho was sitting just across from him, staring out the window. Ho had begged to be brought along. He had been willing to pledge eternal loyalty if Jiang would but let him have a single glimpse of the ancient imperial city, and there it was, stretched out all about them, its steep tiled roofs and massive white marble stairways celebrating the grandeur and power of this most ancient of cultures.

'Master...?'

'Yes, Ho?'

'Am I to accompany you to the rehearsals later on?'

'It is certainly my intention.'

Ho smiled.

Much had changed since Jiang had last been here, among them this curious reversion to ancient imperial rituals. Which was why, before he was allowed to see Tsao Ch'un, he was to be tutored in court etiquette; taught how to behave and what to say in the great man's presence.

That troubled Jiang. Tsao Ch'un had not been like this in the old days.

But word was that Tsao Ch'un had changed. Grown more brittle with the years. Responsibility could do that to a man, even one as great – and as unpredictable in his moods – as Tsao Ch'un.

While Ho saw to his bags, Jiang Lei stepped out onto the landing pad.

A small group of officials – clearly some kind of welcoming committee – waited by the entrance to the airlock, shivering in their thin silks.

Jiang narrowed his eyes. This too was different. They could have stepped straight out of a historical drama, because no one had worn silks of this fashion for centuries. Not since the last emperor, P'u-i, had stood down.

Raising his chin proudly, Jiang walked towards them, seeing how they fanned out and allowed him room to pass between them, their heads lowered respectfully.

As indeed they should, Jiang thought. *After all, am I not a general in Tsao Ch'un's Eighteenth Banner Army?*

Only Jiang could not fool himself. He found this business loathsome. All this bowing and scraping. Oh, he would abase himself before Tsao Ch'un, but that was different. Whatever one thought of him, Tsao Ch'un was a great man. Was, without doubt, *his Master*.

Inside, still damp from the fine, disinfecting mist, Jiang took his leave of the nameless men. He knew none of them, had been introduced to none of them. Whoever they were, they were simply there to greet each new visitor.

Steward Ho appeared, minutes later, dripping wet and accompanied by a small, fussy man in a bright scarlet silk, the Chinese character *San* – three – embroidered in black on a pale cream background in a big square of silk in the middle of his chest.

'Number Three' bowed low to Jiang Lei, smiling an obsequious smile.

'General Jiang... I am Ts'ao P'i. Our Master has asked me to show you to your quarters.'

Ts'ao P'i... Jiang almost smiled at that. Ts'ao P'i, otherwise known as Emperor Wen of the Wei dynasty, had been a famous poet. Indeed, he was a better poet than a governor, if the ancient histories could be trusted.

Jiang followed, walking alongside Ts'ao P'i. Ho trailed a little way behind, struggling to carry Jiang's things, his head bowed so deeply that his chin almost touched his chest.

After a while Jiang noticed it. He stopped. 'Ho... walk straight. Lift your chin. Ts'ao P'i understands that he has your respect.'

And with this, Jiang looked to Ts'ao P'i and gave him the barest nod of his head, as if to thank him for indulging his servant.

But Ts'ao P'i's expression had changed. 'Forgive me, General,' he began hesitantly, 'but out of kindness I should warn you. The court has changed since you were last here, and such formalities as existed then have been greatly extended. It is... how should I put it... a matter of great sensitivity.'

'Are we are talking of a man's status, Ts'ao P'i? Of his face?'

Ts'ao P'i nodded, his face stern now.

'Precisely. Speaking for myself, it does not trouble me should your servant not show me his respect, but there are others who... well, let us say that to forget the outward signs of respect might be to tempt fate, even to win oneself enemies.'

Jiang took this in, then bowed to the other man. 'I thank you deeply for your advice, Ts'ao P'i.'

He turned to Steward Ho, who had witnessed this exchange about himself with open-mouthed astonishment, and smiled. 'I am afraid, Steward Ho, that you must be as you were.'

'Master...'

Ho's chin went down again.

Jiang Lei turned, looking back to his guide. 'Lead on, Ts'ao P'i. And thank you. I'll not forget your kindness.'

But before the other man looked away, Jiang saw in his eyes; the calculation there behind the smile. He wondered what deeper game Ts'ao P'i was playing and who, out of all his possible friends and enemies, he reported back to.

Court intrigues, he thought, walking on swiftly, half distracted by the beauty of the ancient architecture through which he walked. *It makes such exile as I've suffered seem almost welcome.*

At last the officials had departed.

Jiang sprawled out in the chair and summoned his steward.

'Ho! A cup of wine! Quick now!'

He let out a deep, heartfelt groan of anguish. Was this what it had all come down to? This ghastly pretence, this hellish puppet show?

Jiang Lei shook his head exaggeratedly. He would do it all. Of course he would. What choice had he? But just what was the point?

When they had said in his orders that he would be tutored in court rituals, he had thought it a small matter of which etiquettes to follow. But this...

How to stand, what to say, who to look at and bow to, who *not* to look at, when to speak, when not to speak, which way to face, how often to bow, when to prostrate oneself...

Thinking about it, Jiang Lei laughed. It was like joining a theatrical troupe. And maybe that was not so poor an analogy. Maybe he would write a poem, ostensibly about such a troupe, whereas in fact...

'Master?' Ho stood there, head bowed, holding out a silver bowl filled to the brim with Jiang's favourite red sorghum wine.

Jiang stood and, taking the cup from Ho, took a long sip from it. Setting it down, he looked to Ho with a mischievous grin on his face, turned and gave a bow. Then a deeper bow. Then put his hand to his mouth, as if he'd spoken when he ought not to have.

Ho, terrified, feeling his Master must have lost his mind, grimaced and pointed to the camera.

'But Master...'

The reminder sobered Jiang.

'Forgive me, Ho,' he said, 'only... those men. Those monkeys in silk... aiya!'

He sat again and reached for his wine, drained it at a go, then held the empty cup out to be refilled.

'Master...?'

Jiang shook the cup. 'Quick, Ho! More wine!'

But Ho shook his head. 'No, Master. You cannot...'

Jiang sat round, staring at his steward as if he'd now lost his mind. 'Cannot?'

'No, Master. You have visitors. They have been waiting this past hour...'

Jiang Lei stood, surprised. Visitors?

'Very aristocratic-looking gentlemen,' Ho went on. 'Real ch'un tzu.'

Jiang frowned. Aristocratic? He didn't know anyone aristocratic. Not these days.

'You wish me to show them in, Master?'

'Have you no names for these... these ch'un tzu?'

Ho looked puzzled at that. 'Names, Master? They seemed to know you very well, so I thought... One has too little hair, the other...'

'... too much.' Jiang Lei laughed. Now he knew whom Ho was talking about. 'Send them in, Steward Ho. And bring more wine. I have not seen my good friends these past fifteen years and more!'

Ho grinned then did as he was bid. Less than a minute later, two men stepped into the room. One was small and completely bald, the other tall, with a great lion's mane of hair that ended halfway down his back. Both were Han, and both looked decidedly aristocratic with their colourful silks and long fingernails.

Jiang rushed towards them, delighted to see them after all this time.

'Pan Tsung-yen! Hsü Jung! How wonderful to see you!'

Jiang embraced one and then the other. By the look of them, they were every bit as glad to see him.

He bade them sit, then had Steward Ho serve wine. Only then did he ask what he was burning to know.

'How is Ching Su? I thought, perhaps...'

'Ching Su is dead, Jiang Lei,' Hsü Jung said in a low, mournful voice. 'He died ten years ago. He was exiled...'

'Was he?' Jiang said, but he was still suffering from the shock of that awful news. Once the four of them had been inseparable. They had sat their exams together and, afterwards, joined Tsao Ch'un's 'Brigade' together. They had shown their poetry to one another, drunk wine on endless moon-lit evenings, and sung – tunelessly in Pan Tsung-yen's case, drunkenly in theirs – a thousand romantic songs.

As Hsü Jung told the story of Ching Su's sad fate, Jiang found him-self remembering moments from his past; seeing Ching Su vividly in his mind laughing and sharing a joke with them all. They had all been much younger then, of course, barely in their twenties. Before life had turned serious.

'Ten years,' he murmured, and shook his head sadly. Ten years ago Ching Su had died. And no one had thought to tell him.

As the wine flowed, so the talk became less sombre, more 'upbeat' as the *Hung Mao* called it. Jiang had picked up a smattering of such terms and phrases from his time on the Western Isle – in fact, he had started a note-book to try to capture them before they disappeared.

As they will, he thought. *Now that we Han are in control.*

'I read your last collection,' Pan Tsung-yen said, butting his bald head forward as he spoke, in the old familiar manner. *Like a boxer*, Jiang thought. *He uses words like punches.* Not that Pan Tsung-yen was physically belligerent.

'It was good,' Hsü Jung joined in. 'Very good. I must have read each poem a hundred times, Nai Liu. Only...'

Jiang smiled at the hesitation. Again, like Pan Tsung-yen, Hsü Jung may have aged, but he hadn't changed. Not in essence. He spoke his thoughts in parts, bringing each new aspect to the discussion like it was a parcel, espe-cially wrapped.

'Only?' Jiang coaxed.

'Only it is four years since it was published. I had hoped... well... I had hoped you would have kept on writing.'

Jiang sat back, smiling. 'I did. In fact, that's one of the reasons why I'm here. To see my publisher. I have a new collection – *Thoughts At Twilight* – that's just the working title. I'm sure to come up with something much better, only...'

Only I can't use my preferred title, The Vanishing World. *It wouldn't get past the censors.*

They talked for hours after that, catching up on what each of them had been doing, throwing in whatever they knew of old friends and acquaintances. Towards the end, however, it seemed to Jiang that they were holding something back. There was something they wanted to say, but felt they couldn't. Was it something about his wife, Chun Hua?

Finally, Pan Tsung-yen seemed to lick at his lips as if they were dry. Then, with a brief, revealing glance at the camera, he spoke out.

'It has been good to see you, Jiang Lei. It is pleasing to know that the years have enhanced our friendship. But there was a reason for us coming here tonight, and though we may get ourselves in trouble for saying so, it would have been a betrayal of our friendship to have neglected saying it.'

Pan Tsung-yen paused. 'We think you are in danger here, Jiang Lei. Things have changed. You may even have sensed it yourself. Various of our friends, whom we dare not mention by name, have died.'

'Victims of court intrigues?' Jiang asked.

'Who knows...' Pan Tsung-yen answered. 'Yet they *are* dead.'

Hsü Jung sat forward suddenly, anger in his face. 'It is a viper's nest, Jiang Lei. A foul, oppressive place. And the spies...'

Spies? Jiang Lei narrowed his eyes at the word. 'And you think I might be subject to these... *intrigues?*'

'The Han are Han,' Pan Tsung-yen said, nodding to himself. 'A nation of gatekeepers and opportunists. Corruption is rife, Jiang Lei. As to whom you can trust...'

'Trust no one,' Hsü Jung said.

'Not even you?' Jiang asked.

Hsü Jung shrugged, then smiled at the paradox. 'Least of all us... after tonight.'

Pan Tsung-yen stood. 'Come. We have said enough. We'd best leave you now, dear friend, dear Nai Liu.'

When they were gone, Jiang went and sat at his portable comset.

Who knew who was watching him? All that was certain was that someone was. Maybe even Tsao Ch'un himself. But, whoever it was, they would know he had been warned.

Unfolding the keyboard, Jiang typed in 'Su Tung-p'o' and sat back.

At once a face appeared. It looked like a photograph, but it couldn't be. Su Tung-p'o had died in 1101.

A list of options appeared. He selected BIOGRAPHY.

'Text or spoken word,' the machine asked, in its light, anodyne tone.

'Text.'

The truth was he couldn't stand that voice. Would have changed it, had it been allowed. Only it wasn't.

Su Tung-p'o had, it seemed, not been alone in his calling. Both his father and his younger brothers had been poets of some note. Su had taken his exams in 1057, at the age of twenty-one, and done brilliantly – so well that his papers were copied and circulated among students. However, before he could be appointed to a government office, his mother had died. Being a good son, he returned home to spend the next twenty-seven months in mourning for her, as was strict Confucian practice. It was thus not until 1061 that he had taken up his appointment as an assistant magistrate in Shen-hsi Province.

All might have been well, for Su Tung-p'o was a distinguished official, but he was sympathetic to the plight of the common people. Through his poetry, he made clear his opposition to the policies of Wang An-Shih, a fellow poet who was the architect of the government's plan to enforce the centralized control of the Chinese economy.

Despite various banishments and exile, Su had a long and distinguished career, including being secretary to the emperor from 1086 to 1089, but his political enemies finally triumphed. Even so, Su Tung-p'o lived on, through his beautifully crafted poems and his writings, the clarity and simplicity of which meant that they were copied many times and thus survived down to the present day.

Generally acknowledged to be the finest poet of the Northern Sung period,

Su wrote in both the *shih* and *tz'u* styles, with a fine eye for descriptive detail.

A very fine eye...

Jiang Lei sat back, stroking his beard thoughtfully. Reaching across he took his book and opened it at his favourite piece. It was only four lines; even so, it was probably the most evocative of all Su Tung-p'o's works. He read it aloud.

'Spring night – one hour worth a thousand gold coins;

clear scent of flowers, shadowy moon.

Songs and flutes upstairs – threads of sound;

In the garden, a swing, where night is deep and still.'

Jiang closed his eyes, savouring the lucidity of the poem; how it pushed aside the cloak of years and spoke to now. He himself struggled endlessly for such uncluttered beauty in his poems, and here it was. He particularly liked the way it spoke to all the senses, and then, at the very end, to mystery itself: *'where night is deep and still'*.

Reading that part again, he gave a little shiver.

I toast you, brother, he said in his thoughts, reaching for his wine bowl and lifting it to the air. *Across the long centuries I salute you.*

'Master?'

He turned. Steward Ho was standing there in the doorway, Jiang's night clothes over one arm.

'It is late, Master. I thought...'

Jiang smiled. 'I know. I should get some sleep. I have an important day tomorrow, neh?'

Only an hour before his audience, Jiang Lei was told, by the appropriate official in the correct and most formal manner, that Tsao Ch'un was otherwise engaged. Their 'meeting' was to be delayed until a time suitable for both.

Having stood there for the best part of two hours, in the unfamiliarly heavy cloth of his dress uniform, Jiang Lei could have been forgiven if he groaned. He had come so close – through six different doorways and six entirely different 'ceremonies' until he stood before the 'dragon gate'. His Master, Tsao Ch'un, sat there behind it, on his massive throne on the far side of the great hall. And now it was to be delayed.

But Jiang Lei did not groan. Nor did he show the smallest sign of impatience or disappointment. Instead, he bowed low to Tsao Ch'un's messenger and, gripping the heavy scroll which contained the papers of his appointment as general tightly against his chest, turned about and marched crisply back the way he'd come. His eyes stared ahead, passing back through the imposing doorways, past the endless uniformed lackeys and stiff-mannered officials until he was outside again, on the white marble steps, breathing in the cool morning air.

Was it a snub? If so, why summon him halfway round the world to deliver it?

No. The more he thought about it, the more he felt it genuine. Something had come up. Something more urgent than a meeting with one of his lowly generals.

So what now? How long would it be until his audience was rescheduled? He had heard that Tsao Ch'un would sometimes keep a supplicant waiting for months, even years, before he'd see them. And then only for the briefest moment. But those were supplicants. Rich men who needed a favour from their Master, the Son of Heaven. He, Jiang Lei, was not here for favours. Not that he really knew quite why he had been summoned, only that it was not at his instigation. Tsao Ch'un *wanted* to see him. He would not waste his time otherwise.

So why not make a few visits?

Jiang tried to keep calm, but his heart was racing suddenly at the thought that had come into his head. He did not even know whether it would be allowed. But surely he had to try – while he was here?

He would visit Chun Hua. Would go to see her and his daughters. *If* it could be arranged.

Jiang stroked his beard, considering the problem. This was not something Steward Ho could do. Ho was of too low a status; far more crucially, he was too inexperienced to handle this. Then whom?

The answer came at once. Hsü Jung. Hadn't Hsü always been the organizer among them – the one who had arranged things? Then why not ask him? If he couldn't do it personally, then surely Hsü would know someone who could?

Back at his quarters, Jiang went straight to his desk, not even bothering to change. If this was to be done, it must be done now, before the second summons came.

Hsü Jung had left his contact number. Jiang typed it in then waited. The screen pulsed and then a face appeared, that of a young male Han, probably from Hsü's household.

'Forgive me, but could I speak to Hsü Jung?'

The face, expressionless but for the hint of a scowl, answered him.

'I am afraid no one may talk with Master Hsü. He is currently under house arrest. But if you would leave a message...'

Jiang cut connection. Little good that that would do. They would have a trace on it for certain.

House arrest... It could be no coincidence. Indeed, it might explain the cancellation of the audience.

Jiang stood, pacing about, wondering what to do.

Just then Steward Ho came out and, surprised to see his Master there, gave a small gasp.

'Ah... Ho... I have a problem...'

'But Master, you should be...'

'The audience was rescheduled. I am to see Tsao Ch'un another time. No, my problem is this. I wish to see my wife...'

'But that is forbidden, Master.'

'No, not forbidden... but I must get permission... and, well... I do not know who to approach or how to go about it.'

At that Steward Ho beamed. 'Then you can leave it with me, Master.'

'Leave it with *you*?'

Ho nodded enthusiastically. 'I am your servant, neh? Then let me deal with such tiresome details. When do you wish to see her?'

'This afternoon?'

'I shall see what can be done.'

And with that Ho left the room. Jiang listened, heard a door on the far side of the suite of rooms bang shut.

He sat again, slumping in the chair. Hsü Jung arrested. That did not bode well. And Pan Tsung-yen?

He contacted Pan Tsung-yen's number. As the screen lit and the same stranger's face appeared, he cut at once.

Pan, too, then. Both under house arrest for seeing him.

Jiang sighed. If they had been arrested, then why not he also? What were they waiting for? Or were they on their way over right this moment?

He stood, agitated now. There was no doubt he was being watched. But at what level? Had Tsao Ch'un cancelled their meeting because of something he had said last night? Something he had overheard?

He could not think of anything seditious *he* had said, and the only things his friends had uttered that could be construed in that fashion were their final comments; their bitter warning to him to take care.

But what if this had nothing to do with Tsao Ch'un? What if this was the work of some officious minister, furthering some personal scheme at their expense? They had said it was a viper's nest, after all, and you could be sure that not everything that happened in the court emanated from Tsao Ch'un.

Besides, why would Tsao Ch'un say he would reschedule if he did not mean it? There was no reason for the great man to make excuses. If Tsao Ch'un had suspected him of treachery, he'd have been in a cell by now, a hot brand searing his testicles, making him gibber like a monkey.

And house arrest... it wasn't exactly being led off in chains.

No. But what worried him was the coincidence of events. He did not trust coincidence.

He went to the window and looked out. There were guards out there, their faces masked, anonymous. Two men – senior officials from their powder-blue gowns – walked slowly, deep in conversation.

Pei Ching. North City. The last time he'd been here had been the last time he had seen Chun Hua. Four years ago. Ch'iao-chieh had been nine then, San-chieh five.

He looked down, saying in his mind the mantra that always gave him strength, that lifted him above his weakness.

The trouble was, he didn't know what Ho could do. Very little, probably. Who did he know here, after all? And even if he did have contacts, how in heaven's name would he arrange things? If he, Jiang Lei, a general in the Eighteenth Banner could not exert sufficient influence, how could lowly Ho?

No, he was mad even to think it might work.

Jiang Lei went through and poured himself a cup of wine. It was too early in the day for drink, but for once he felt the need. It wasn't every day his friends were arrested.

He had finished his drink and poured himself a second when the comset buzzed and the screen lit up. Jiang hurried across.

It was Ho. Seeing his Master, he bowed low and then launched in, smiling as he told Jiang what he had arranged.

As he finished and the screen blanked, Jiang sat back, laughing with delight.

Steward Ho, it seems, had a cousin who knew a servant in the royal household. That servant had a friend – a very *close* friend, let it be understood – who looked after the needs of the junior minister in charge of a certain government department. A contact of the friend in that department had a brother who, at a price, would place Jiang's request before another junior minister. While *that* junior minister was unable himself to give the requisite written permission for a visit, he might, for a 'small' consideration, place the matter urgently before *his* Master, the minister himself.

In short, four small, discreet payments and it would be done. He would get to see Chun Hua.

'Ho,' he said quietly, speaking to the air, 'you are a genius.'

Maybe. But first he had to arrange these payments.

Ho returned a half an hour later, flushed at his success. Jiang greeted him, then handed him the four red packets, each marked with a different symbol, as Ho had asked.

Ho bowed low. 'It is a great deal of money, Master. Are you sure...?'

Jiang nodded. 'To see Chun Hua... I would pay ten times as much. But don't tell them that, Ho. They would only raise their price.'

Thus it was that, an hour later, Jiang Lei slid down from inside the litter. Handing his documentation to the gate guard, he waited to be passed through.

He wanted it to be a surprise, so he had not notified Chun Hua of his coming. He wanted to see the joy on her face, hear his daughters squeal with delight as they saw him enter the room.

'Is there something wrong?'

The gate guard had turned away and was talking into his handset, in a low murmur that Jiang was clearly not meant to hear.

The guard turned, gave him a contemptuous look, then turned away again.

'Soldier!'

Jiang's bark caught the guard totally unprepared. He turned back and, noticing the dress uniform for the first time, came to attention.

Jiang held himself straight, his full authority in his manner. 'Are you going to let me go inside, or are you going to keep me out here all afternoon!'

The guard bowed again. 'Forgive me, General, only I...'

At that moment there was a slamming of doors and, a moment later, the noise of several men shuffling quickly along on slippered feet. As Jiang looked past the guard, he saw five men – all Han, all wearing identical pale green *pau* – hurrying towards him down the broad, high-ceilinged corridor.

As the guard stepped aside, four of the five formed up behind the eldest, a greybeard – the number on his chest badge said 'Number One' – as if to block Jiang's way.

'What do you want?' Number One bellowed, his face sneering and ugly, clearly angry at being disturbed.

Jiang looked to the guard. 'Give him the permission.'

The gate guard handed it across, then stepped back. The look on his face seemed to suggest he was pleased to hand this over to another; that he had done his bit in stalling the stranger.

Jiang knew what this was. One last shake-down. Number One was yet another doorkeeper. He would say that the permission had not been properly verified and that it would cost a hundred *yuan*, maybe, to fix that.

Jiang dug his hand into his pocket. At once Number One stepped back, as if Jiang had drawn a gun. He yelled at Jiang.

'What are you doing?'

Jiang winced. Was their whole conversation to be nothing but a shouting match?

'I have come to see Chun Hua,' he said, trying to remain calm, not to let himself be drawn down to this other's level. 'That in your hand is the minister's permission. As you'll see, it has his chop...'

'His chop? Fuck his chop!' the man said and tore the permission in half.

Jiang stared at him, shocked. 'But you can't...'

Jiang stopped. Maybe he could. That was, if he was Tsao Ch'un's man, answerable to him alone. And that did make a kind of sense. Maybe Steward Ho had got it wrong. Maybe all that money had been spent for nothing.

Jiang took a long breath, then began again.

'Forgive me, Steward...?'

'Shao Shu... I am First Steward here. You want to see someone, you get *my* permission, *understand*?'

'Forgive me, First Steward Shao. It is *my* misunderstanding. Only I wish to see Chun Hua.'

'Chun Hua?' The man's face had a faint flicker of mockery in it that Jiang found troubling. He stroked his beard, as if considering. 'Well, I don't know, I...'

'Is there a problem? She is here, I take it?'

'Ah yes... only...'

How much? he wanted to ask; only he knew he could not be that direct. Men like Shao liked to wrap their corruption up in the guise of necessity.

'I understand,' Jiang said. 'There are expenses, neh? The preparation of the rooms... the attendance fee for your clerks...'

First Steward Shao smiled. 'I am glad you understand, General. I will have my assistant draft an agreement.'

'Oh...' Jiang Lei frowned. 'I thought maybe...'

'We have your details, General. You have only to authorize the payment.'

Jiang blinked. *The bastard was tipped off. He knew I was coming.*

But what could he do? Turn about and march away from there? Leave the odious little prick without his 'fee'? But that would mean he'd not get to see Chun Hua, and that was worth a great deal to him right now.

He waited. Five minutes passed. Long, wordless minutes that stretched his patience, and then finally the clerk appeared.

As one of the younger servants knelt, his head bowed, to make a back for the document to be rested on for signature, Jiang looked to Shao Shu again. Shao was watching him intently now, to see how he'd react.

Even forewarned by that, the figure written on the sheet shocked Jiang Lei.

Fifty thousand yuan!

The involuntary intake of breath he took betrayed him. Even so, he kept his face blank, signing his name in both Mandarin and English, then appending his thumb print over Shao Shu's chop.

Another of the First Steward's men took the document at once and whisked it away. He was gone in a moment.

It was a full month's salary. And though he could afford it, even though he was willing to pay twice that to see his beloved wife and daughters, Jiang was angry now. It was a clear abuse of Shao's position.

The junior stewards stepped back to allow Jiang passage, while First

Steward Shao, all charm and smiles now that he'd been paid, bowed low and put out an arm, indicating to Jiang that he was to step through.

Inside, beyond the security gate, five whole levels at the very top of the stack – First Level as it was known – were occupied by a massive three-storey mansion built in the northern style. Its steeply sloping red tile roof was lit from overhead by panels that resembled the open sky. That was an illusion, of course, but it was a striking one, strengthened as it was by the call of birds in a nearby copse of trees, the branches of which swayed gently in the artificial wind.

Jiang caught his breath. The house and its surrounding gardens were beautiful. He could imagine Chun Hua and the girls enjoying life here.

'Come,' Shao said, walking towards a doorway to their right, which was accessible by a short flight of pale grey steps. 'I will have them brought to you.'

Inside it was opulent, with an elegant, almost luxurious decor. The high-ceilinged rooms – all of them in a traditional Han style – had a spotless look to them.

'Through here,' Shao said, steering Jiang through a doorway framed with black lacquer, and into a small suite of rooms that were slightly more informal than those he had just passed through. 'Take a seat,' the First Steward said. 'We will attend you shortly.'

As Jiang sat, he frowned, noticing how the furniture in these rooms had a much less elegant, more worn look to it than elsewhere. The massive rugs seemed frayed, the wall hangings older, dowdier, *cheaper* than outside.

His heart was beating fast now, his palms damp. He sat, then stood again, needing to pace, rehearsing in his head what he would say. Only he knew that the mere sight of her would make him wordless. It always had. And he the poet of his age.

As the door at the far end of the room creaked open, he started forward, then took a step back as six dark-cloaked Han – scribes or clerics of some kind – entered the room and, without acknowledging his presence in any way, took their seats on either side of the room.

Jiang looked down. So this was how it was to be. Everything tightly scrutinized and written down. Every word and gesture copied into a report.

Fifty thousand *yuan*, and he was not even to be allowed a private audience. Jiang swallowed bitterly. So *this* was the new China!

It was First Steward Shao who appeared first, backing into the room and speaking as he did, his voice a rapid murmur which had the slightest edge of annoyance to it.

Shao turned, looking to Jiang, and smiled. 'General... your wife, Chun Hua...'

The look of shock on Chun Hua's face could not have been faked. She stared at Jiang in disbelief, then put her hand to her mouth, stifling a cry.

As for Jiang, he stood rooted there, unable to take his eyes from her, his mouth dry, a pain in his chest at the sight of her.

Oh, how she had aged. Like twenty years had passed, not four. But she was still his beloved Chun Hua. Still the woman he loved beyond all words.

Yet even as he put his hands out to her, even as he took a step towards her, so he was aware of his daughters in the shadows just behind her, a stern-faced female murmuring to them before pushing them forward.

Jiang caught his breath. They had seemed so young the last time he had seen them. Now the eldest, Ch'iao-chieh, was a young woman of thirteen, and her sister San-chieh was nine, almost ten. Seeing their father they began to run to him, meaning to rush into his arms, but even as they made to, Steward Shao called them back.

'Girls! You will approach your father sedately now...'

The girls stopped and, lowering their heads, did as they were told.

Jiang watched them come to him, the moment strangely dreamlike and unreal. As the two stopped just before him and made to bow, so Jiang's restraint broke. Stepping towards them, he bent down and embraced his daughters to him, hugging them tightly, ignoring the frown on Shao Shu's face.

'My darling girls... my pretty ones...'

Tears were in his eyes now, and as he looked up past them at their mother, he saw that she too was crying, sobbing like a child even as her eyes drank in the sight of him; eyes that were filled with an undiminished longing.

Chun Hua, he mouthed. *My darling girl. My love.*

To either side the clerks wrote furiously. Steward Shao, watching from the corner of the room, gave a scowl and turned away, shaking his head,.

Steward Shao had insisted that they sat facing one another formally, like at a proper audience, on hardwood benches placed a good ten *ch'i* or more apart. Chun Hua sat centrally, her daughters to either side. A forlorn sight it was, for now that he saw them clearly he saw how their dresses were also frayed and worn. It made Jiang wonder what had happened to all the presents he had sent them over the years. 'Well?' he said, smiling determinedly. 'Do you want to show me your rooms?'

Chun Hua looked down, as if ashamed. 'These *are* our rooms.'

'But I thought...' He looked about him again, and as he did, so understanding filled him. His girls were prisoners here, given this shabby little suite of rooms while First Steward Shao – and all his extended family, no doubt – had the run of the place.

'And the gardens...?'

San-chieh, his youngest, made to answer. 'Sometimes we—'

Shao Shu interrupted her harshly. 'You will not speak! Chun Hua... you will tell your daughter...'

Chun's head went down. 'San-chieh,' she said quietly, 'it would be best if you did not speak.'

Jiang Lei turned, glaring at Shao Shu, stirred to anger once more. He could see it now. See how they were bullied, day in, day out; how miserable an existence they were leading.

'Steward Shao...' he began, standing, meaning to confront the man. But even as he did, he saw how Chun Hua looked at him, pleading with him not to make a scene. He sat again, furious and frustrated, his anger making a muscle in his cheek twitch violently.

Jiang bit his lip, drawing blood, knowing he could do nothing. After all, this must be Tsao Ch'un's bidding.

Maybe so. Only did Tsao Ch'un know what Shao Shu was up to?

It was a stupid question. Tsao Ch'un knew everything. Shao Shu would not have dared act in this fashion unless he had his Master's blessing. Only what did Tsao Ch'un mean by treating his guests, his hostages this way? And why had Chun Hua not said?

The last was easy to answer. They would have censored every letter she wrote to him; maybe even destroyed most of them. But now he knew. Now he had seen with his own eyes.

In that regard it was 50,000 well spent.

As they parted, he held Chun Hua's hands, smoothing the backs of her palms with his thumbs. Steward Shao had warned him not to kiss her. Such contact had not been agreed in their contract. But it did not matter. Just seeing her again, just holding her hands was enough. Knowing she loved him still. It gave him the strength to go on.

As he bowed to his daughters and they bowed back to him, Jiang Lei saw it all clearly. It was his path to suffer. To be in exile. Even here, where he was loved the most, there was a vast distance about him.

Later, standing there in the lift, descending, the first line of a poem came to him. Crisp and clear, its simple, elegant shape suggesting a second. By the time he stepped out into the great hallway where his litter waited, he had it all, complete in his head. A poem about emptiness and loneliness and fear. A poem that burned with indignation. A poem he could never possibly set down on paper.

That evening, Jiang Lei sat at his desk and cried.

What started it he could not say. He had thought himself inured against it. But how could he be? How could any man who called himself a man escape unscathed from such an ordeal? To have one's heart ripped out through one's eyes – it was not possible that such a thing would not affect you!

And so he cried, sobbing his heart out for the lost years and for what he'd seen that afternoon. For his daughters' anguish and his wife's tragic bravery.

To be the subject of one such as Steward Shao. Jiang Lei could not imagine it. It would have driven him mad. Or to murder.

All these years he had borne it. Had counted it the cost he had to pay, thinking that he alone was suffering. But now he knew.

He had it easy. He could see that now.

Not that he'd abused his so-called 'freedom'. He might have had any number of women in his bed, keeping him warm at night, but he had chosen not to. He had been faithful to his darling Chun.

At his lowest ebb he had even thought of suicide, but even death was no escape, for Tsao Ch'un had made it plain that the family of a suicide would share his fate – to the third generation. No. The only real escape was to die in Tsao Ch'un's service.

Jiang Lei wiped his eyes. It was true what they said – that crying did no good. And yet a man needed to cry sometimes, to purge himself.

Or so he told himself. Because he did not *feel* purged. What he felt now was unclean. How could he criticize others when he acted as he did? Wouldn't a truer, more honest man defy his Master?

Perhaps. But it would make that man the murderer of those he loved. And no amount of shifting blame to he who organized it thus – Tsao Ch'un, whom many called a tyrant – could make it otherwise. No. It was simple. To defy the great man would mean the death of Chun Hua and his darling girls. And only a pedant would say that he, Jiang Lei, was not to blame.

What was the phrase the long-noses used? Ah yes... It was a 'devil's bargain'.

'Master?'

Steward Ho stood in the doorway, a bowl of steaming soup resting on the tray he held.

'Come...' Jiang said, beckoning him over.

Halfway across, Ho slowed, his face showing surprise.

'Master? Are you all right?'

Jiang nodded. 'I am fine now, Ho. Just that the meeting...'

Ho gave the faintest bow, as if he understood perfectly, then set the tray down next to Jiang.

'And thank you, Ho. You will find your Master grateful for your arrangements.'

Ho kept his head lowered, but he was smiling now. 'It went well, then, Master?'

'As smooth as silk. The mansion was... well, everything I imagined it would be.'

'That is good, Master.'

Ho waited a moment longer. 'Is there... anything else?'

'No. You can retire now, Ho. I have a few things to do, then I'll see to myself.' He paused, then: 'If there's any message from the court...'

'I will wake you at once, Master.'

Jiang smiled. 'Good. Then go. And again, thank you, Ho.'

'I am my Master's hands...'

Surprisingly he slept well, waking late, to find he had a visitor.

As he dressed hurriedly, Jiang scolded Ho for once. 'Why did you not wake me, Ho?'

'Forgive me, Master, but your visitor expressly forbade me to. He was most insistent that you got your sleep. He said he was more than happy to wait.'

'And where is he now?'

'Waiting, Master. Pacing in the garden, I do believe.'

Jiang finished dressing, then hurried out to greet his guest, wondering who on earth it might be.

And stopped dead, astonished once again.

'Hsü Jung! I thought...'

Hsü Jung came across and embraced him, then stood back, holding his old friend at arm's length and looking into his face.

'But you were under house arrest!'

'I was,' Hsü said, his deep voice resonating, 'but now, it seems, I'm not.'

'And Pan Tsung-yen?'

'He too, it seems, is free.'

'Have they explained why?'

Hsü Jung laughed dryly. 'You are clearly a stranger to Pei Ching, dear friend. If I had any inkling whatsoever who "they" were, I might begin to understand why. Besides, power does not explain, power simply acts.'

'But surely you must *know* who your enemies are?'

'Must I?' Hsü Jung smiled a smile of infinite tolerance. 'Do you know how many factions are at war, here at the centre of it all?'

'At war?' Jiang laughed. 'Your words are surely too extreme, brother Hsü.'

'Oh no, Jiang... quite literally *at war*. Assassination is a courtly art, much practised in these parts. In the light of which... well... a mere house arrest... What's that? It might even have been a friend. Someone who wished to see us protected overnight. To make sure some other faction did not do away with us.'

'But why should they wish *that*? What possible harm could you or I do *them*?'

'I would have said none... yesterday... but someone clearly thinks you important enough to have you watched closely. And not just Tsao Ch'un. Whoever those guards belonged to, they weren't Tsao Ch'un's, nor were they from the Ministry.'

'Which leaves...?'

Hsü Jung smiled. 'Too many options to consider. A minor family prince, maybe. Or some rival of yours?'

'A rival? I have no rivals!'

'Not that *you* know of.'

Jiang sighed. 'This makes no sense, Hsü Jung. No sense at all. It's all a chasing after shadows...'

'So it might seem, but consider how much power is concentrated here, at the court. More than half the world is ruled from here. All those people. All that wealth. And everyone wants a share.'

'I can easily believe. But what has that to do with me? I am but a humble general in Tsao Ch'un's service. I have no influence upon events whatsoever. I can't even influence the fate of my own family.'

'And yet your presence here at court has set alarm bells ringing. However mistaken they might be, *someone* considers you important.'

'Perhaps Tsao Ch'un needs a poet?'

'Perhaps...'

Jiang Lei hesitated a moment, then: 'Hsü Jung... could I ask you a favour?'

'My dearest friend. Of course. Whatever I can do, I shall.'

'There is a man, the First Steward at the mansion where my wife is being held. His name is Shao Shu. I wondered... is it possible to find out more about this man? Where he comes from? Who he is allied to? What kind of man he is?'

Hsü Jung frowned. 'I take it he is Tsao Ch'un's man?'

'He reports to him, yes.'

'Then it might be difficult. To make such enquiries... it could not be done without alerting someone.'

'Then leave it... if it's too dangerous. I just thought...'

Hsü Jung smiled. 'I did not say too dangerous, Jiang Lei. Only difficult. But not impossible. I have a friend... well... enough said... Leave it with me, neh?'

Jiang was about to thank his friend, but right at that moment Steward Ho appeared, breathless from having run from one end of the suite to the other.

'Master... You are summoned! Tsao Ch'un has sent his craft!'

'His craft?'

'Yes, Master. You must pack at once. It seems that you are going to Tongjiang.'

★

Tongjiang was 2300 li south-west of Pei Ching – 1160 kilometres by the old measure – in Sichuan Province.

In the very middle of nowhere, the grey, heavily misted mountains of the Ta Pa Shan dominating the skyline, was an ancient palace. It was the home of Li Chao Ch'in, advisor to Tsao Ch'un and one of his Council of Seven, whose task it was to enforce Tsao Ch'un's decrees throughout his great City.

Touching down on the massive hexagonal pad, Jiang Lei felt a shiver of anxiety pass through him. What was he doing here? This place was both elegant and brutal, the very thickness of its walls exuding power and privilege. Some ancient warlord must have had this built for him against his enemies.

But beautiful as well, the aesthete in him acknowledged. Truly the epitome of Han style.

Servants met him, bowing low, showing him the utmost respect. From their midst, and slightly out of breath, stepped an elegantly dressed five-year-old. In the sweetest, high-pitched voice, he introduced himself as Li Peng, Li Chao Ch'in's eldest son.

'Master Jiang,' he said whilst bowing low, the oversized sleeves of his pale blue silken robes sweeping the flagged floor, 'you are most welcome. If you would follow me... my father awaits you.'

Jiang smiled broadly, delighted by the boy, then followed him down the steps and across the formal garden. There, on the far side of a huge ornamental pond, two servants waited. As the visitors approached, the servants put their shoulders to the massive slatted door, sliding it back on its runners.

Inside Tsao Ch'un awaited, his arms folded across his bull-like chest. He was standing beside a massive table, upon which was the biggest map Jiang Lei had ever seen. A map of the North American continent.

Standing about that table were seven others, dressed in splendid silks, all of them in their late forties or early fifties.

These were Tsao Ch'un's most trusted men. The Seven. It was said by some – if quietly – that the great man would not have been able to function without them. If Tsao Ch'un was the head, these were his hands, and looking from face to face, Jiang Lei found himself impressed by the strength and experience he saw in their eyes.

As Li Peng withdrew, facing Tsao Ch'un all the while, his head bowed low. Li Chao Ch'in stepped forward, welcoming Jiang Lei formally to his house. As he did so, Tsao Ch'un looked on silently, his black, hawk-like eyes taking in everything.

Tsao Ch'un was, as Jiang had observed before, a small man. He had the look of a street fighter; of a man who had long lived off his wits to survive. Only standing there, surrounded by seven of the most impressive men on the planet, he nonetheless dominated the room. Was somehow more alive than they.

Intelligent as he was, Tsao Ch'un was also brutal, elemental, *visceral*. Where others might have been measured and calculating, Tsao Ch'un was direct. He trusted his instincts and did what others would not have dared to do. Hence his success. Only he was no administrator. Others could consolidate what he had won. And those 'others' were the Seven.

The formal welcome complete, Li Chao Ch'in stepped aside. Only then did Tsao Ch'un step forward and, standing before Jiang Lei, put out his right hand with its great black iron ring – token of his power – resting below the thick knuckle of the forefinger.

At once Jiang Lei knelt, bowing his head, and took the offered ring, kissing it in fealty.

'Jiang Lei,' Tsao Ch'un said warmly, taking his arm and steering him towards the map, as if they were old friends. 'We have been debating all morning how best to go about the task. The new campaign, I mean, against the North Americans. Tsu here thinks we should bomb them flat, as we did the Middle East, then wait for the radiation to die down. But I'm an impatient man. I can't wait a hundred years for things to cool off. That said, a straightforward invasion might prove costly. It might easily lose us ten million men.'

Tsao Ch'un paused and smiled. 'The question is, Jiang Lei, how would *you* go about it?'

Two hours later, Jiang stepped back, away from the map, conscious that the mood in the room had changed.

Surprised as he'd been by Tsao Ch'un's request, he had done as he'd been asked and given his considered answer to all the questions thrown at him. As Jiang turned to Tsao Ch'un again, he saw how the great man looked about him, meeting the eyes of his advisors one by one, each giving him a single nod.

'Then it is done,' he said, looking to Jiang once more. 'You, Jiang Lei, will organize and lead the campaign.'

Jiang stared back at him, shocked. He had, in that instant, been promoted to marshal.

He fell to his knees, touching his forehead to the floor before Tsao Ch'un. 'But *Chieh Hsia*... I am not a soldier. I am but a humble poet.'

'That may be so,' Tsao Ch'un answered him, grinning now and enjoying Jiang's surprise, 'but you will have guidance in the task. I am giving you an advisor.'

Jiang Lei looked up, puzzled. Tsao Ch'un was clearly not talking of the Seven.

'Shepherd,' Tsao Ch'un said, then laughed, his laughter taken up by the others. 'You will go and see him, Jiang Lei. He is expecting you. But first you will stay here for a day or two. Li Chao Ch'in needs to brief you. And besides, there are things I wish to discuss...'

Jiang bowed again, but he was shocked. A mere hour ago he had been but an unimportant general. One of hundreds in Tsao Ch'un's service. Now he was confidant to the Son of Heaven and leader of a campaign to conquer the territories of the old American empire. And it had happened in an instant.

'Forgive me,' he said, conscious of the others listening, 'but why me?'

Later that evening, finally alone with Tsao Ch'un, he got his answer.

'I have had my eye on you for some while, Jiang Lei,' he said, handing Jiang a large glass of the finest French brandy. 'I have long been impressed by you... by your integrity and your staunch refusal to use your position for personal gain.'

Tsao Ch'un raised his glass, saluting Jiang, then laughed. 'You are by far my poorest general, Jiang Lei. But that is no criticism. On the contrary. Such a trait is almost unique among my servants, and there are many of them. Like the ancient Greek, Diogenes, I have been searching a long, fruitless time for an honest man. But now I have found one.'

Jiang sipped from his glass, then nervously asked, 'Are you sure I am up to such a task, *Chieh Hsia*?'

The instinct to get up from his seat and abase himself was overpowering.

Tsao Ch'un had insisted on informality, but to be informal with such a one as he... it was impossible. It was like being informal with Genghis Khan.

Tsao Ch'un smiled, then drained his drink. 'I have no doubt of it at all, Jiang Lei. In fact, it reassures me to have you in charge. But tell me... how many Banner armies will you need for the task?'

Jiang thought a moment. 'Ten... maybe fifteen?'

'Then you shall have thirty.'

Again Jiang Lei was astonished. A single Banner was half a million men. At a stroke Tsao Ch'un had put him in command of fifteen million troops. It was very different from the 10,000 he had commanded as a general.

Jiang shook his head, then, aware that he had Tsao Ch'un's ear, 'And my family?'

Those dark, bottomless eyes stared back at him.

'You want them with you?'

Jiang swallowed, then nodded.

Tsao Ch'un studied him a moment, then smiled.

'Then so it shall be.'

Early that next morning, as the sun slowly edged its way above the distant peaks, a craft set down on the pad at Tongjiang. As its engines shut down and the door hissed open, a man in the uniform of a marshal stepped forward, out of the shadows.

Seeing the stranger in his imposing outfit, Chun Hua and the two girls began to kneel and bow their heads. But even as they did so, the great man spoke, bidding them get to their feet again.

At the sound of that voice, all three of them jerked their heads up, a look of sheer astonishment lighting their faces.

'Jiang Lei?' Chun Hua said, not sure whether she was dreaming.

He stepped closer, catching her in his arms and lifting her up, embracing her, then setting her down as the girls crowded about him, tearful now.

'My pretty darlings... gods how I've missed you...'

From a window high above, Tsao Ch'un looked on coldly. It was a touching scene, if one were of that disposition. But he was not. He had not become great through sentiment. Even so, he felt a certain satisfaction at the sight. It was as he'd thought. Jiang Lei was steadfast in both loyalty and love.

He spoke up, talking to someone in the shadows just beyond him.

'Stay close to him, Hung. Be his shadow. I trust him... for now... but even those I've trusted have proved false, and power can corrupt a man... even a good man like Jiang Lei.'

There was the briefest pause and then the shadows answered.

'It shall be done.'

Chapter 13

AMOS

Amos Shepherd sat in the shade of the oak, looking down the grassy slope towards the bay. There was the faintest wind, rustling the leafy branches overhead and rippling the placid surface of the water. Out there, across the bay, you could see the peeling whiteness of the old house, embedded in the far side of the valley. Beyond it, the City climbed the sky, so tall it seemed a natural border to the green world of the Domain.

He was painting. Or rather, he was thinking of painting. The easel was set up nearby, his palette set down beside it. But as yet the canvas was untouched, the colours unmixed, for this was the crucial part. The part that took the time. The technical act of painting was secondary. He could do that without thought. It was this that was all-important.

It was late morning, and the sun was almost at its zenith. It was the best time of the day, when the valley was flooded with light, no shadows on the green.

Amos Shepherd was a powerful-looking man, long, grey hair and a short grey beard framing his handsome, sun-burned face. He was in his fifties now, yet he had the look of a man ten years his junior: an ageless, almost biblical appearance, his sea-green eyes set deep into a face that seemed all-knowing; his powerful, aquiline nose like something carved.

In the stillness of his concentration, he was a statue in flesh.

Somewhere far off a cuckoo called. As silence fell, so a single bee drifted close and then away.

Amos narrowed his eyes, trying to pierce and penetrate the veil of appearance, trying to see beyond it. To decode it.

To outward eyes he seemed entranced, but this was the moment when it happened, when he slipped through and saw reality. Or something close. Some deeper level, anyway. Something the casual eye could never see.

The sound of the craft grew slowly. Indiscernible, at first, it grew in his head. It cut across his consciousness like a fissure in the rock.

Amos looked up.

Of course. Tsao Ch'un's new marshal.

Leaning forward, he selected a brush. Squeezing a tiny bead of black from the tube, he dipped the brush and drew a horizontal line, needle thin at one end, thickening at the other, dividing the canvas.

Skyline and surface.

As the craft swooped in over the bay, the vibration of its engines filling the air, Amos stood, watching it slowly descend to the lawn beside the cottage.

He had met Jiang Lei before, at official functions. But that had all been rather formal. There was little chance to come to know a man in such circumstances. But this time the man had come to stay for a day or two, so Amos could get to know him.

It had been Tsao Ch'un's wish.

Amos looked back at the canvas. He had laid the first stone. What followed would follow. He had no idea yet what it was, only that it was ordained. Not in a fatalistic way, but as all his paintings were, because they pursued an ineluctable yet undiscoverable logic.

They painted him, not he they.

Amos smiled. Now wouldn't *that* have sounded pretentious had he ever uttered it aloud? Yet it was true. It was all a process of surrender. He was but the channel for it.

Tearing his attention away, he walked across to his visitors. The craft had set down now and as the ramp descended, so Jiang Lei stepped out, blinking against the bright sunlight.

This would not be so strange for him as for others who had come here in the past. At least Jiang had some recent experience of the outside. Some of them had been inside so long that it startled and disturbed them. Like in that old Asimov novel, *The Caves of Steel*.

Maybe he'd show Jiang some of that stuff. See what he thought of it.

'Jiang Lei!' he hailed, walking across to greet him, offering his hand, conscious of the other's awkwardness at that – how Jiang half made to bow before tentatively putting out his own hand.

'It's good to see you again. I'm really pleased that we'll be working together.'

'*Shih* Shepherd...'

Jiang bowed despite himself. He couldn't help it. None of these Han could. It had become an auto-reflex with them. Like in the old days. And those clothes. They were like something from a costume drama.

'Amos,' he corrected him. 'While you're here you must call me Amos. You are my guest. If there's *anything* you need...'

Again that awkwardness, that slowness to respond. He liked that. This one wasn't as slick and superficial as the rest. Tsao Ch'un had chosen well in that regard.

He knew that Jiang Lei would not irritate him. At least, not in the way that so many of the others did.

He watched Jiang look about him; saw how he registered his surroundings.

'It's... stunning.'

Amos smiled, pleased. 'Yes... isn't it? There's no place like it on earth. Not now, anyway.'

Jiang Lei looked back at him. 'I'm sorry, I...'

But the words were lost in the whine of the craft's engines as it lifted again, turning and sweeping off towards the south, climbing steeply as it went.

In the silence that followed, Shepherd studied his guest.

'You want to know, don't you?'

'Do I?'

'Yes. You want to know why Tsao Ch'un chose you. I mean... it isn't obvious.'

Jiang hesitated, then, 'No. It isn't.'

'It's very simple. He chose *you* because to put any other man in charge of the venture would have been to set up a rival – Mark Antony to Caesar – and Tsao Ch'un could never countenance that.' Amos paused. 'It is not so much your qualities, Jiang Lei, as your lack of ambition that makes you his ideal choice.'

'Thirty Banners, and every last man loyal to me, their commander.'

'Exactly. So you and I are honoured. Alongside Chao Ni Tsu.'

Jiang Lei frowned. 'In what way?'

'In that we are the only *three* men on the planet whom Tsao Ch'un trusts. The rest...'

Amos laughed. A rich, deep laughter that made Jiang smile.

'But come... let me show you around. Unless you'd like to rest after your journey?'

Jiang Lei shook his head. 'No... please... I'd love to see. I've heard so much about this place...'

For the briefest moment Amos seemed to freeze, or at least to let some minuscule shard of doubt enter his eyes. Only as soon as it appeared it was gone, and he was exactly as before, charming, welcoming. The perfect host.

'Come, then,' he said. 'While the sun is overhead.'

'What's the painting going to be about?'

Amos smiled. 'I don't know. I haven't seen it yet.'

'And you *have* to see it... before you can paint it?'

'It comes in flashes. They all do. I understand it later. But while it's happening...'

Jiang Lei looked from the canvas to the man and back again. 'While it's happening... ?'

'I can't tell you. It's not something I can articulate. It's just something that happens.'

'And you trust it?'

'Yes.'

There was nothing as yet. Or as good as. Just a black horizontal line. Which could have been anything. Only he saw how Amos stared at the canvas, intently, like he was conjuring visions from the air. He had been warned about it, warned about the intensity of the man. Schizophrenic, some said, yet he seemed perfectly normal. Most of the time.

They had finished their tour an hour back, and in all that time he had seen no one except Amos. Was he genuinely alone here?

The solitary madman.

'Amos?'

'Yes, Nai Liu?'

That use of his pen name made Jiang take a mental step back. Shepherd, it was said, did nothing whimsically. So what did he mean by using it? Did he mean to suggest some kind of bond between them – that they were both artists and therefore brothers in some fashion?

Jiang asked his question.

'How did you come to know Tsao Ch'un? I mean, you two... it seems the most unlikely alliance.'

Amos smiled. 'And so it is.'

'I tried to look it up, but...'

'There's nothing there. I know. That's because it's all been erased. At the Ministry's insistence. But come... let's go inside. We can have a glass of wine, and I'll tell you everything.'

Jiang Lei sat on the bed, looking about him. He had been given a small room beneath the eaves at the very top of the house, and from the small, scuttling noises he could hear, he was not alone in inhabiting it.

There wasn't room for much – a small chest of drawers, a chair and the single bed on which he sat, tucked in beneath the tiny dormer window. On the chest of drawers was a wash jug in a bowl. Behind it, propped up against the wall, a large oval mirror stood, the backing silver blackened in places so that small holes seemed to be punched into the returning image of Jiang's face. The rafters were exposed and the bare walls of the room had been whitewashed, but some years ago now, for it was flaking in places.

The room had a damp, woody smell, added to which was a sharp, under-lying scent he could not recognize.

Jiang was not one to remark upon the quarters he was given, but this was strange. It had the feel of a child's room, not the kind of room you'd place an honoured guest in.

Chun Hua, for one, would not have liked it. But then Chun Hua had not been invited. For this was business. Serious business.

He looked down, for that brief moment letting his mind stray back to their one snatched night together at Tongjiang. How awkward that had been. Not at all how he'd imagined. But then, why was he surprised? They had been strangers these past four years. To expect things to be as they were...

Even so, the warmth of her body beside his in the night had unsettled him.

Like the room, the furnishings, the bed, it had all been too much. Some part of him had drawn back, rebelling against the physicality of it. So unexpected. So... He would adapt. In time it would be as it had been. Or so he hoped.

Jiang stood, then took the slip case Amos had given him from his pocket and looked at it again. How strange – how wonderfully strange that tale had been.

As a teenage boy, Amos had designed games for the computer market – games that had made his reputation. Yet the one which had made his fortune – the very last of them before the Collapse – was a game called *World Domination*.

The selfsame game Jiang now held in his hands.

According to Amos, a rival company had been busy mapping the globe, street by street, building by building, replicating it in their virtual world. It was a bold and wonderful idea, but also an expensive one. When they went under, Amos stepped in, raising the capital to buy their replicated world and using it as the foundation – the detailed underpinning – for his own game; a game in which rival players strove to destroy the old earth street by street and build a new one over it. A world of mile-high cities.

It was, so rumour had it, Tsao Ch'un's favourite game.

They had met in 2040, five years before the Collapse. Tsao Ch'un, it seems, had flown halfway round the world to meet him – here, in Dittisham.

It was then that it had all been conceived. Root and branch.

Jiang turned the cover over, noting the date of publication. 2039. Amos had sold over one hundred million units worldwide, making him enough money to buy his parents' old house, Landscot, along with 500 acres of surrounding land. It was back then that the notion of a Domain had begun, long before the City had appeared over the horizon.

Jiang yawned. The wine had made him tired. That and the meal, which Amos himself had cooked, using vegetables picked from his own garden.

He set the game aside, then, unzipping his travel case, took out his nightgown.

It was a year and more now since he had last worn it. Back when he was still a general, rounding up the last few natives – Welshmen, they called themselves – and processing them.

That was all done now, finished. Until they started on America.

He had peeled off his silk *pau* and was pulling the gown up over his head, when he heard footsteps on the gravel path below.

He finished dressing, then, leaning across the bed, looked down through the window at the darkened lawn.

There, in the light of the half moon, just a yard or two beyond the kitchen garden where the oak tree was, stood Amos with his back to the house. He was standing very still, hunched forward slightly, as if something had caught his attention.

Jiang looked past him, down to where the land ended on the shore of the bay.

No one. There was no one there. Only suddenly there was. Two of them, moving slowly, laboriously, climbing the slope, their long gowns hitched up about their ankles.

Two women, Jiang realized, seeing how the moonlight caught in their long, dark hair.

Jiang wondered where they had been. Whether Shepherd had, perhaps, sent them away while he was there, bringing them back overnight, then despatching them again once morning came, so that Jiang would not meet them.

Only why do that?

But then, Amos was strange. At least, that was what he'd heard. Only how much of that was true? What if he was just a very private man? What if he didn't want other people to know his business?

Then why invite me here? Why not just meet me somewhere neutral? Somewhere free of all these impressions?

Jiang saw Amos greet them, hugging first one and then the other. Then, the two of them on his arms, he turned and came back up the path, disappearing inside the cottage.

Jiang went over to the door and stood there, listening. There was the low murmur of voices from below. A door closed, then there were sudden, urgent footsteps on the wooden steps.

Another door closed. For a moment there was silence, and then there was the sound of water passing through the pipes.

Someone was washing.

Jiang Lei looked to the timer inset into his wrist and yawned. It was just after one. He would sleep now, then ask Amos in the morning.

★

Waking with the dawn, Amos let Jiang sleep, instead going down to his basement workshop where he immersed himself in that morning's news.

It was not the same news that was deemed fit for the general population. This was the real news, raw, uncensored. The same news that the Ministry's First Dragon saw each day. The same that Tsao Ch'un himself digested every morning with his breakfast meal.

If the content of the general news channels was meant to reassure and encourage (and, of course, to praise the Great Father himself, from whom all bounty came), this assemblage of mayhem and destruction, betrayal, murder and sheer lunacy acted as a timely reminder that things were far from settled – and very far from perfect – in Tsao Ch'un's City.

Men, after all, were still men. Nothing, it seemed, could change that.

Yet the problems could be contained. The madness could be channelled. All that was needed was an iron will and a determination not to let things get out of hand.

Among that morning's items were two which particularly caught his attention. The first involved what they called a k'uang wang – one of the 'frenzied'. These were men – for they were usually men – who snapped. In their frenzied madness, they ran amok among their fellow citizens, stabbing, slicing and causing as much pain as they could – as if to unload their own. This particular k'uang wang, however, had been extraordinarily inventive. A cook by trade, he had turned up at work that morning and proceeded to poison half the people in his deck, finishing matters off by chopping up the two Security guards who had been sent to detain him.

The second item was more sedate, less unusual, yet it still interested him; it spoke of a new phenomenon, one that was only recently emerging.

It seemed a boy had met a girl and, after a while, the two had fallen in love. In spite of the watching cameras and the even more watchful relatives of the girl, the two had managed to consummate their love. After a month or two, she began to show the obvious signs of pregnancy. All might have been well. The boy might have married the girl – he was certainly willing to – and they might all have lived happily ever after.

Only the girl was Han, the boy Hung Mao.

Just as soon as her condition became obvious, the girl's uncles, furious that their family's racial purity had been sullied, discovered who the boy was and burned the two alive in an oven.

The horrific brutality of the crime aside, it was that urge to purify the races – to mix but not to *mix* – that Amos found interesting. How did one break that chain of prejudice? Was it merely a question of time? Or had the seeds been sown when they had rid the world of the black and Asian races? Was it all doomed to fail? Would it all end in one gigantic bloodbath?

No one knew. But they were committed now. This melding of the races – this cheek-by-jowl approach to populating the levels – was what they had decided, and they must see it through now to the bitter end.

But there were signs that it was sometimes failing. Signs that, for all their efforts, humankind was not content with mere contentment. That whatever you gave them, they always wanted more.

Which, according to his mood, could be a good thing or a bad.

Why *should* mankind be content? Was *he* content?

Never. *Not for a single fucking second.*

He rarely swore, not even in his thoughts, but today...

Maybe it was Jiang's presence, for the man had quite certainly thrown him. Amos had thought to find a fraud, a man pretending to be good. But Jiang Lei was the real thing.

An anomaly, then...

Today, he had decided, they would talk, exhausting themselves with words, so that tomorrow they might be tired of debate and come quickly to an agreement when decisions needed to be made.

Not that he wanted to force Jiang into agreement. It was just that his experience had shown that to dwell too long upon such matters would more likely compound errors than solve them.

Besides, if Jiang Lei fought his campaign the way he, Amos Shepherd, had decided they should fight it, then thirty Banners would be more than enough.

It was merely a question of focus. Of learning from past mistakes.

He returned upstairs. It was there, in the kitchen, as he was cooking breakfast, that Jiang Lei found him.

'Amos... you slept well?'

'Very well, thank you. And you?'

Jiang Lei laughed. A clear, light-hearted laughter. 'You know, that's the best night's sleep I've had in years. That mattress was just so... not too soft, not too hard... and the down pillows...'

Amos smiled. 'I'm glad. Would you like some breakfast?'

They sat outside, in the garden, to eat.

'What's the schedule for today?'

Amos was sitting facing him, his back to the view. 'I thought we'd just relax. Talk about this and that. Just get to know each other.'

'It's just that... well, I thought...'

'Let's leave all that 'til tomorrow, yes?' Amos studied him, then smiled again. 'What did you think of him? Of Tsao Ch'un, I mean? You spent two days with him, right?'

Jiang Lei nodded, but he seemed suddenly defensive. 'I...'

'It's okay. It's all off the record here. No cameras. And no bugs. I don't allow it. It's part of our deal. Here I'm outside it all. My rules, not his. So tell me, did you think him somewhat... eccentric?'

'No.' There was no hesitation in Jiang's answer. 'I think it must be hard, living the way he does. I'd call it paranoid, only he has good reason to believe people are trying to kill him. Seventeen tasters dead. That's a statistic the general public would be shocked to learn.'

'And a dozen or more bodyguards...' Only Amos was smiling broadly. 'That stunt you did... throwing the cadre out of the back of your craft... that really amused him. Did he tell you that?'

Jiang looked stunned. 'No.'

'His sense of humour is... how should I put this... raw. People getting badly hurt... that amuses him. That probably makes him a sociopath, but it's not enough to label him so. He's a multifaceted man. What he's trying to do... the idea of a world state shared by both our kinds... that's rather heroic, wouldn't you say? *Visionary*.'

Jiang Lei said nothing. He was still reeling from the fact that Tsao Ch'un knew what he'd done to Cadre Wang.

'The bastard deserved it,' Amos said, reaching for his coffee. 'And it was a nice touch... good aiming by your men.'

Jiang looked to him. 'You speak as if you saw it.'

'And so I did. Tsao Ch'un sent me a copy, along with your file.'

'Oh...'

'You can see it if you want. I'm sure he wouldn't mind.'

Jiang Lei hesitated, then asked, 'The two women who arrived... last night...'

'My wife and daughter... you'll meet them later.'

'Ah...' Jiang hesitated, then, changing the subject: 'There's one thing I don't understand about Tsao Ch'un. His obsession with animals and insects – with killing them off.'

Amos nodded. 'Now that I do know. It dates back to his childhood, to the time when he was the youngest of six brothers.'

'He had five brothers? But I thought...' Jiang fell silent. There was clearly a lot he didn't know.

'The eldest, Hsiao, was something of a bully. It was Hsiao who had his brothers dig a pit and throw Ch'un into it. And then, as if that were not enough, he had them pour jars of insects into the pit with him. All manner of nasty crawly things. Things that bit and things that stung, and others – perhaps the worst of all as far as he was concerned – that merely flapped and clicked.'

Shepherd looked down. 'Three days he spent in that pit. Three whole days. Something broke in him. Trust, certainly, but more than that. One thing I'm sure of. Whatever Tsao Ch'un is now was forged in that pit.'

Jiang's voice was almost a whisper now. 'How old was he when this happened?'

'Just six. You can imagine. And when they finally came back for him and lifted him up out of the pit, he swore silently that he would kill them – every last one.'

'I see.'

'Yes. And when he learned that most animals carry some form of parasite or another, he put them too on his list of things he would kill when he was older.'

'Did *he* tell you that?'

'No. I got the story from one of his retainers. An old Han servant who had been with him since he was a child. He's dead now, but I have no reason to doubt the truth of what he told me... Anyway, years later, when finally we met, the thing that was uppermost on his mind was how we might keep his City free of infestation. To me the answer was obvious. We had to seal the City off, hence the Net, the seals, the de-infestation chambers. Especially the last, which I conceived very much as a kind of airlock.' Amos laughed. 'Spaceship Earth, I used to call it.'

'And the hexagonal shape of the stacks?'

'I took that from my hives. I've kept bees since I was four. It's such a strong shape, the hexagon. I'm astonished it never caught on architecturally.'

Jiang smiled. 'I think you had the last laugh, neh?'

'Maybe. As it is, the City is a vast recycling plant, a huge biosphere. It has to be. I used to liken it to a fish tank, awaiting its fish.'

Amos turned, looking back at the whiteness that surrounded the valley on all sides. 'It looks so permanent, don't you think? But it will all fall apart one day. Not today. Nor ten years from now. Not even a hundred years from now. But one day our descendants will wake up and it will have gone. We'll have moved on. On to another stage of our perpetual development. But don't tell your Master that. He doesn't want to know. Ten thousand years, that's what he wants.' He laughed, robustly. 'As if I could promise him that!

'Anyway,' he said, a moment later. 'Let's hunt. I'll get my gun... and one for you... in case you change your mind.'

Jiang Lei had a short nap after lunch. Refreshed, he sought out Amos again, and found him beneath the oak tree, working on his painting.

It had changed greatly. Almost a third of the large canvas was now filled. Jiang walked over, standing behind Shepherd, squinting at the painting, trying to make out what it was.

Whatever it was, it wasn't the view across the bay. It had the look of something symbolic. And the figures...

Amos's figures were tiny. They were dwarfed by the canvas, like travellers in some vast wilderness.

'Here,' Amos said, handing Jiang a magnifying glass. 'Don't you like the detail?'

Jiang stepped closer, taking the glass, then looked. And looked again, his eyes widening. 'But those...' He laughed uncomfortably. 'I don't understand. Why have you turned them into insects?'

Amos looked to him and smiled. 'Our conversation earlier suggested it. Tsao Ch'un may have kept the real insects out of his City, but the *true* insects got through. You recognize them, then?'

Jiang did indeed. As he studied them, he was struck by how clever Amos's imagination was. Here was the whole of Tsao Ch'un's court; all of his so-called friends and advisors, all of his stewards and servants, every last one of them captured perfectly, their faces pasted on to an array of verminous creatures. Faces of greed and lust and ambition. Faces stripped of their masks and revealed to the world in miniature.

He would have said it was wonderful, only it wasn't. There was something quite awful about it, something utterly repellent.

Amos seemed to sense his reaction. 'You don't *have* to like it, Jiang Lei. It's not meant to be liked. It has no *Wen Ch'a Te*, eh? No elegance. But sometimes that's a virtue. Not to be liked. That is the condition that the great man aspires to.'

Jiang handed him the glass. He was about to say something, but Shepherd got there first.

'I read those poems that you wrote. You know, the ones you didn't want published. The spiky ones. They're by far your best.'

'But...'

'You destroyed them, I know. But Tsao Ch'un had a spy-eye watching you. It was in your tent. Size of a very small bug. He used to watch you for hours. I didn't know why, back then, but now I do. He made his mind up early when it came to you.'

Jiang looked down. If there'd been a spy-eye in his tent, then it was not just the poetry Tsao Ch'un would have seen. He had been faithful to Chun Hua, true, but that did not mean he had not relieved himself now and then. When things got really bad. And Tsao Ch'un would have seen that.

He felt... humiliated.

But Amos had moved on. 'I promised you earlier that I'd introduce you to my girls. Let's do that now. They're working down by the water. We grow our own tobacco, you know.'

Jiang followed Amos down.

The slope dipped sharply at first, then rose a little. Beyond that it fell away again, ending at the water's edge. There, to one side, behind a low wooden fence, the two women were at work, their hair tied back.

Amos stopped, then cleared his throat. The two women looked up.

Both were tanned from the sun, their long hair dark and lustrous, and both had beautiful green eyes – deep, sea-green eyes. The only difference was their age.

Like twins, they were. Twins separated by twenty years.

'Alexandra... Beth... this is my good friend, Jiang Lei.'

The two climbed to their feet, then came across, smiling as each in turn took his hand and shook it.

'I'm delighted to meet you,' Alexandra, the elder of the two, said. 'I'm sorry we weren't here to welcome you yesterday.'

Beth, had looked down shyly, saying nothing.

'We'll see the girls at dinner tonight,' Amos said, stepping carefully over the fence, then crouching to examine the leathery-looking plants. 'Did you know our friend here is a poet? Probably the best Han poet of his age. His pen name is Nai Liu.'

'Really?' She seemed to look at him anew. 'Then maybe you'll read us some of your poems later, Enduring Willow...'

Jiang laughed. 'You speak Mandarin?'

'Just a little. My father, Charles Melfi, was a China scholar, back before the Collapse. He taught me the odd phrase or two.'

Jiang Lei bowed. 'Then I shall be honoured to read for you, T'ai T'ai Shepherd... I haven't brought anything with me, but I'm sure I can recite one or two from memory.'

Amos straightened. Then, stepping back across the fence, he smiled at Jiang.

'I have all your stuff, Jiang Lei... including the spiky stuff. I especially like the one you called "Voices".'

'You *have* that?'

'I could recite it for you, if you like.'

But Alexandra wasn't having that. 'Don't tease our guest, Amos. They're *his* poems and *he* should read them. That is, if he wants to.'

'Did Tsao Ch'un send them to you?' Jiang asked, intrigued now.

'Not at all,' Amos answered. 'I've been an admirer of yours for some while. I bought each collection as it came out. My favourite is *Restraint*. So understated.'

Jiang looked down, embarrassed as always, by such praise. But it was true. *Restraint* was his best, and Shepherd understood that.

'I was wondering,' he said hesitantly, 'if we could go out on the water. If it's not possible, of course, just say. Only...'

He met Amos's eyes, and saw how the man was grinning at him.

'You had only to say,' Amos said. 'Beth... help me get the boat out... let's show our good friend here how nautical we English are!'

Much later, alone once again in that narrow bed beneath the eaves, Jiang Lei found his thoughts returning to the day.

That afternoon, on the river, he had seen a different side to Amos: less intense, more relaxed, almost childlike. To think of him as the architect of their world was strange. But that was what he was. Without Amos Shepherd, Tsao Ch'un's vision of a unified world state would have remained just that... a vision. For Chung Kuo was the City and its workings. And that city had sprung, fully formed, from Amos Shepherd's head.

It was strange, being out there on the water. Amos had shipped the oars and let them drift, leaning back on the cushions, talking lazily of this and that. And, after a while, Jiang had found himself relaxing too.

He was here for a serious purpose, certainly. Next week he would meet his generals and put to them the strategies devised here in the Domain. Men would live or die according to those strategies. Many men. For the Americans, he knew, would not give up their empire without a struggle, no matter how divided they now were.

But so it would be, whether he commanded it or not. And maybe it was best that he was in charge, for another, more brutal man might have chosen a more costly approach, spilling blood carelessly.

That was not *his* way.

Jiang slept, to be woken hours later by the sound of rain on the thatch overhead.

He lay there a while, disoriented, vaguely aware that there was something he needed to attend to. Something he had to do.

Then he remembered where he was.

Slowly he sat up. Light was coming from the window to his right. He leaned forward, pulling the curtain aside, and looked.

Down in the garden, beneath the oak tree, a canopy had been set up. There beneath the awning, working by the light of an arc lamp, was Amos.

He was painting.

Jiang looked at his wrist timer. It was almost four-thirty.

What was he doing, working at this godforsaken hour? Did the man never sleep?

Jiang was tempted to go down and see what he was doing. To see what else had crawled from his mind in the night. Only he was tired.

He lay down again, turning on his side, facing away from the light.

Sleep. I need to sleep.

Only sleep would not come. Not immediately. He kept thinking about how pretty Alexandra and her daughter were. Not that he had any romantic ideas regarding them. Just that it was rare for him to find Western women attractive in that way. He had enjoyed reading his poems to them; enjoyed the way they'd applauded him.

Jiang yawned. The rain had woken him from a dream. A vague, meandering dream about Corfe and mechanical creatures that hopped and sprang and flew. A very odd dream, now that he came to think about it.

In the darkness, Jiang smiled. Maybe that was where Amos's paintings came from. Maybe he simply painted his dreams.

He yawned again. It was such a comfortable bed...

There was a rustling in the thatch above, the light patter of raindrops. Soft, soothing sounds.

Jiang Lei slept.

'Well? What do you think?'

Jiang Lei turned, watching as Amos came down the path towards him, ruddy with health and smiling.

Jiang turned back. He had been studying the canvas this past half hour, and he still wasn't sure whether he liked it or not. It was a work of genius, certainly, only...

Only it was a little bit too honest for Jiang's taste. A little bit too *real*, in its abstract way.

'I'm not sure,' he said, bearing in mind what Amos had said about not holding back; about not being polite for the sake of it. If that was what Amos wanted...

'Go on,' Amos said, his eyes holding Jiang's.

'It's brilliant, obviously... but uncomfortable.'

'Should art be comfortable then, friend Jiang?'

'No, but it shouldn't... perhaps... be quite so disturbing.'

'Do you find it so?'

'Immensely so. I've stood here trying to argue myself out of it, but I can't. This painting – in fact, this whole aspect of your work – unsettles me.'

Amos smiled. 'Well done. That didn't hurt now, did it?'

'No, but...' Jiang shook his head. 'I feel you're asking questions of me.'

'In the painting?'

'Yes. I feel... oh, I don't know... insufficiently prepared.'

Amos laughed. 'That makes you sound like an academic. It is but a dream, Jiang Lei. A vision I had. Have you ever seen the work of Samuel Butler?'

'No... is he proscribed?'

'Yes, but I have copies of all that stuff... in my vaults. I'll show you in a while. But I guess what I was trying to illustrate was the corruption behind it all... The thing is, we experience but a minuscule slice of existence. A single safe segment. If we were capable of seeing the bigger picture – of seeing, say, a thousand years of life in an instant – we would see that life is but a heaving, ever-changing flow. All of our growth stems from death, and what we call life is but an endless cycle of corruption.'

Jiang stared at Shepherd.

But Amos was not done.

'The campaign ahead... it will make you question what kind of a man you are, Jiang Lei. Whether you are intrinsically a good man or an evil one. When the bodies are piled high and the flies are at their thickest, when you can't sleep for the foulness of your dreams, then and only then will you have your answer.'

'Is that what you think?'

'Oh yes. You will be forced to become the cause of great suffering, Marshal Jiang. How you cope with that... how you maintain your intrinsic self under such pressure... that is the important question. It's one I've been seeking to answer.'

Jiang looked down, made uncomfortable by the way Amos looked at him, by the way he seemed to see right through him. He wanted to argue, only he knew at some instinctive level that Shepherd was right. That point in the future, that was when he would know. He had seen mass suffering before, particularly in Africa, but what lay ahead would top it all. He knew that. When an empire died, its convulsions could destroy continents.

'Anyway,' Amos said, turning his attention back to the painting. 'Let's have some breakfast now, okay? Then we can get down to the serious business. The stuff you came for.'

The planning of a war, Jiang thought, at the same time thinking how strange that was, that two men such as he and Shepherd should be responsible.

Beneath the simple, two-storey cottage was a cellar. Or rather, a specially excavated bunker, which could be reached through yet another of the ubiquitous airlocks.

'It's a nuclear shelter,' Amos explained, as he tapped the code into the panel by the door. 'Built to survive anything except a direct strike.'

Jiang Lei smiled, amused by that. 'You think the Americans would miss?'

'Not if their missiles could get through. Only there are two silos right here, on the Domain. They'd intercept practically anything the Americans could throw at us.'

'The Americans *know* you're my chief advisor?'

'I'd say it was a certainty. They have their spies just as we have ours. And it's an open secret what Tsao Ch'un has decided. The only thing they don't know is the date of the invasion.'

The door hissed open, Beyond was a narrow corridor and then a set of steps leading down. Amos led the way.

'I have a study upstairs,' he said, as the lights flicked on overhead. 'You may have noticed it. That's where I do most of my work. But some days I come down here. It's much more... high-tech, I'd guess you'd say.'

It was indeed. Standing in that huge cellar-room, Jiang Lei felt he was surrounded by the remnants of the old world – that high-tech glossy world that had existed before the Collapse.

'I bought it all up,' Amos explained, moving from machine to machine and turning them on, one by one. 'Or stole it. Or discovered it later on. Some of it never even got onto the market, it was so advanced. Now it never will. Not unless Tsao Ch'un changes his mind. You know, I've even got a datscape – a fully working one.'

Jiang had been studying one of the machines, trying to work out what precisely it was, but when Amos mentioned the datscape, he looked up, interested suddenly.

'Now isn't that strange. I met someone, while I was processing the intake, down in Dorset... in a place called Corfe.'

'I know Corfe.'

'Yes, well, the man used to be a *login*. He was on Tsao Ch'un's list. You know, the list of important Westerners to be killed. The Ministry wanted him, probably to finish off the job twenty years on, but I managed to get him on the programme. Reed, his name was.'

Amos was watching him intently now. 'And he was a *login*? You're sure of that?'

'One hundred per cent.'

'Do you know where he is now?'

'No, but I'm sure you could find out. Why the interest?'

'Just that it's a skill I'd like to learn. Did you ever see that immersion they did?'

Jiang Lei smiled. 'I did. That was Reed.'

'*That* was Reed... Interesting... I should locate the man, don't you think? Get him to train me up.'

Jiang was about to say something more – to elaborate on the circumstances of his meeting with Reed – only Amos had moved on. He had picked up an old-fashioned paper map of the USA. Turning, he threw it to Jiang.

'Here... Where would you like to start?'

Jiang laughed. 'What do you mean?'

'I mean... where's the bridgehead going to be?'

Two hours later they had the rough shape of it drawn up.

Much of their scheme was reliant upon the work Tsao Ch'un had done since the Collapse. As elsewhere, Tsao Ch'un's agents had striven hard to limit the re-generation of American power. They were fighting a long guerrilla campaign to suppress any sign of resurgence, or any attempt by the Americans to cohere into a single nation once more; a sly and devious war of foul rumour, slanderous lies and outright terrorism, that achieved its aims mainly by setting one group of Americans against another.

America had fallen and was to remain fallen.

The most important aspect of that campaign had been to neutralize America's atomic missile bases. To isolate their facilities and prevent them from becoming a threat.

Much of that careful work had been done long before Tsao Ch'un's time, by the agents of the Chinese Communists. They had spent the best part of three decades infiltrating America's computer systems, waiting for the day when they could shut it all down in an instant, even as they launched their own devastating counter-strike.

At least, that had been the plan. No one knew now whether they would have taken that fateful step. For on the day it all fell, it was Tsao Ch'un and not the Communists who had been in charge, and it had been Tsao Ch'un's decision to disarm rather than destroy.

It had not been totally successful. Some missiles had still flown. Chinese cities had been destroyed, more than a hundred million citizens killed. But the core of America's civil defence system remained intact, if disabled.

The long years of watchfulness had seen but a few minor incidents. Skirmishes mainly. But now the testing time lay ahead.

It was still possible that the Americans might try to use their missiles on the battlefield, against an invading force. Possible but unlikely, for Tsao Ch'un had built his own shadow network of missile bases controlled by his forces, designed to intercept at source any missiles they might attempt to launch.

Not that the Americans were a single socio-political force these days. It was many years since their President had spoken for them all with a single voice. As of that morning there were 118 separate 'states' within the borders of the original sixty-nine, with at least eighteen so-called 'Presidents', not a single one of whom was on speaking terms with another. Most of them were warlords, tinpot tyrants of the worst kind. Jiang Lei knew their sort. He had dealt with them many a time.

The biggest question was, who to take on first, and in which order.

Jiang Lei had no doubt at all where the bridgehead ought to be.

'Richmond,' he had answered; as he had answered Tsao Ch'un and the Seven nearly a week ago, on that morning at Tongjiang.

And for good reason: it was so eminently defensible, with the sea at his back and the Appalachian mountains forming a natural defensive barrier to the north and west.

'Why not Washington?' Amos had asked, playing devil's advocate.

'Because that's what they expect.'

Jiang Lei had thought about this a lot since he had first suggested it, and it made more and more sense every time.

'Washington we leave to rot. Or rather, we infiltrate and sow the seeds of its self-destruction. Were we to take it first it would become a symbol of liberty for the Americans. They would unite and throw everything at us to get it back. However, if we can make them perceive it as a den of corruption and self-interest...'

'Sodom and Gomorrah...'

'...then hopefully it will make our task much easier.'

'And after Richmond?'

'We roll back our enemies, state by state, along an ever-expanding front.'

'Divide and conquer, eh?'

'While *we* keep unified.' Jiang paused. 'Ideally we don't really want to fight them, only I'm not sure we've got a choice. Some of them, I'm certain, could be bought. Some of them, I'm sure, can be persuaded to join us peacefully. But the majority will fight us tooth and nail. Poor and broken as their country is now, they still see themselves as the natural leaders of the world, and us as the usurpers. That's where this whole campaign differs from the others. The Africans, the Europeans, even the Asians... each of them saw our coming as historically inevitable. But not the Americans. To them we're little more than thieves, come to steal away their eminence, much as we stole their industry and their wealth.'

Amos studied him a moment longer. Then he smiled broadly and clapped Jiang on the back.

'I'd say we're done, dear friend. We can leave the detail to the generals, neh? Can't have us do *all* their work for them!'

Jiang smiled at that.

Richmond it is, then. And within the month.

'So it begins,' he said, looking to Amos, seeing how his eyes seemed to glow with an unnatural excitement. 'So it begins.'

CHUNG KUO

Chapter 14

A CHANGE OF SKY

hey came for Jake that morning, two dark-suited men from the Ministry.
There was no time to pack a bag or say goodbye. Seated in the craft
– the compartment completely empty but for the three of them – Jake
began to wonder if he would ever see Mary or the kids again.

He knew what this was about. Boss Wu! Boss fucking Wu!

The silence, the sheer abstraction of the agents troubled him. Both were
Han in their mid-twenties, and both wore shades, like old-school CIA
agents. But they didn't need those to create a sense of anonymity. Their
faces, cold, expressionless and closed, served just as well.

How long the journey took he didn't know. It must have been three hours
at the very least, the whiteness of the City below them unvaried and unend-
ing. It was like some vast glacier, pierced in places by the dark, upthrusting
shapes of mountains, looking like massive shards of flint embedded in that
smoothly horizontal surface. Yet as they banked towards their final destination, so it opened up below him. There, jet black and strikingly magnificent
after the pale uniformity of the rest, was the great ziggurat itself, home to the
Thousand Eyes.

Bremen.

Jake's head went down. This was it. This was where his luck ran out. He
had had too many narrow escapes, too many second chances. They had
given him the chance to fit in – to conform to their new world – and he
had spurned it. Now he would be punished.

He felt sick at the thought. Not for himself – what did it matter, after all, whether *he* lived or died – but for those he'd left behind. For Peter and Mary and the girls. For what it would do to them.

They touched down on the landing strip amidst three, maybe four dozen other craft of differing sizes and designs, all of them the same matt black.

Just across from them was a massive glass door – glass, or was it ice? Only Jake barely noticed it, for he had looked up, awed by the sheer scale, the contrasting blackness of the building. There was something vaguely Egyptian about it all. Like its servants, it had a crisp anonymity.

The architecture of the dead, he thought, his fear given an edge by the sight of it.

'Come,' one of them said, forcing him onward. 'You're expected.'

They ascended in a massive lift, the three of them alone inside it, dwarfed by its dimensions. At the top the doors slid open. They stepped out into a hallway, sparsely yet elegantly furnished, at one end of which was another lift, its dark interior smaller than the first. They walked across.

There were no visible controls. No buttons to press, no notices to read. Even so, as it hissed open at its destination, Jake knew he was expected.

This time, as Jake made to step out, the two agents stayed where they were.

'There,' one of them said, indicating the door just in front of Jake. 'Just knock.'

The door hissed shut. They were gone.

Jake turned, looking about him. The hallway was like all the others in the building, the walls and ceiling a lacquered midnight black. Beside the door to the lift there was only the door that the agents had indicated. He walked across and knocked.

A muffled voice answered from within. 'Come in... it's open.'

Jake stepped through.

Behind an oak-topped desk, filled with clutter, was a middle-aged man, a *Hung Mao* like himself. He wore a pale blue *pau* trimmed with lavender silk, his long black hair tied back.

He was watering a tiny oak tree. A *bonsai*, as they used to be called – Jake didn't know the Chinese term. Seeing Jake, he smiled.

'Take a seat, *Shih* Reed. I'm Tobias Lahm. I won't be a moment.'

The room was dominated by a large picture window, which filled the wall to Jake's right. Through it Jake could see the plaza far below. But it was the colourful blue and red silk tapestry that hung on the end wall, the plants and the shelves of books that occupied the wall nearest him that caught Jake's attention. After the sombre black of the corridors outside, the room seemed filled with colour.

'I don't understand.'

Lahm met his eyes. 'You thought you were going to be punished, right?' He gave the tree a puff of the tiny water spray he was holding. There were tiny plants everywhere, in ceramic pots of exquisite oriental design. Lahm smiled. 'It's okay... you don't have to answer that.'

Again it was unexpected. This friendly manner of his. It had to be a trick of some kind. A means of getting Jake to drop his guard.

Jake sat, then looked about him again. On the desk, to one side, was an old-fashioned filing tray crammed full of hard-copy paper files. Just beside it were a couple of old-style photographs in silver frames; pictures of a European woman and two young boys. His family? It seemed likely. There was also a screen on the wall, set in among the shelves and, inset into the edge of Lahm's desk, a keyboard, next to which was a pile of books, Szu Ma Kuang's twelfth-century text, *The Mirror Of Government* most prominent. And finally, there in the top right corner of the ceiling, angled to look down at the desk, was a camera.

'Oh, that,' his host said, following his gaze. 'It isn't connected up. But sometimes it helps if my interviewees think it is.'

Jake met his eyes. Lahm had warm, pleasant eyes, with just the suggestion of a smile. He was not at all what Jake had expected, and if anything, that made him even more suspicious.

'I'm your *fan han*, by the way.'

Jake didn't recognize the term. '*Fan han?*'

Lahm smiled. 'The job title's from the early T'ang... from the seventh century, to be precise. It means "officers protecting the frontiers". Back then it would have entailed being stationed out at the very edge of the empire, on the Wall perhaps, facing the desert and the barbarians beyond. These days, however, the frontiers are internal. It is the *idea* of empire I protect.'

Lahm turned away again, attending to another of his plants. This one, Jake noted, was a miniature mulberry.

'Lahm... that's a German name, isn't it?'

Lahm didn't miss a beat. 'That's right. I haven't travelled far. My family used to live in Bremen, before the City. And before you ask, my father was a mercenary. He fought in Tsao Ch'un's Eleventh Banner Army as a major. I was given the chance to be educated in the Ministry's academy in Shanghai.'

'That's a while ago now...'

'Twenty years.'

'So you've had a lot of time to assimilate all of this.'

'I have, Jake. Which is why you are here seeing me, rather than some jumped-up little Han official.'

Those words almost shocked Jake. He was, after all, sitting in the Headquarters of the Ministry. The Thousand Eyes. To even suggest that some Han official might be 'jumped up' seemed well out of order. Unless this too was part of the game Lahm was playing. Part of the softening-up process.

'You must be very important,' Jake said, reassessing the man who stood before him, 'to have the freedom to say such things.'

But Lahm said nothing in reply. Instead, he took another tack.

'You've been having problems, I understand.'

'Who said I have?'

Lahm gave a smile of wry amusement. 'Do you often tell people to fuck off, then?'

'Only shits like Boss Wu.'

Surprisingly, Lahm laughed. 'He is a piece of work, that one, neh?'

Jake frowned. He still had no handle on this. Still didn't know what was required of him, nor why he was there.

He knew, of course, what he had *done*. That much was blindingly obvious. He could picture it vividly. But what they'd do to him – *that* was what concerned him now.

'Am I in trouble?'

Lahm sat back a little. 'Some might think so. Me... I think you've got a lot going for you, Jake Reed. I think you might just ride this one out. And that's why you're here. We'd not have bothered otherwise.'

Jake took a long breath. He could believe that much. In fact, he had thought about that on the way here. Why they should have bothered. Why they hadn't just taken him out and shot him, like the rest of the troublemakers. Because that was what they did.

Jake looked up. Lahm was watching him closely now, the smile gone from his face. Jake could see how intelligent the man was, how perceptive. He was certainly no ordinary inquisitor. But again that begged the question. Why should such a senior official like Lahm – and he clearly was – bother with someone as insignificant as himself? Or was it once more to do with past history? The fact that he'd been on their list. If so, then why had they put him where they'd put him? Why had they wasted his talents, making him a common clerk?

He didn't understand. You used somebody's talents, didn't you? You didn't just bury them in the levels.

'Let me ask you something,' Lahm said. 'Have you been having *dreams* lately?'

Jake looked away.

Lahm was silent for a moment, then: 'Let's make it clear. The reason why you're here is that you're valued by those in authority. They'd like to keep you in the experiment. So this is your one chance, your one opportunity to speak off the record: to say what it is exactly you're having problems with and why. So let's cut to the chase, eh?'

Lahm paused a moment. 'Look, I know how hard it is for you… for *all* our kind. Some days you feel it isn't worth it, right? That you've been cut adrift. That everything you ever valued has been taken from you. Well, maybe there's an element of truth in that. Maybe you *have* had a raw deal. Maybe it is hard, just getting through each day. Only the world is as it is. Or if you want to split hairs, as the Han have made it. It's their world and you've got to live with that fact, Jake. There's been a change of sky.'

'A change of sky?'

'Haven't you heard the expression? It's what you get when you change a system of government. China is China, unchanging, but those who rule it…' Lahm smiled. 'A change of sky means new thinking, new customs, a new way of behaving. You understand that, don't you?'

Jake nodded.

'Good. Because, you see, the problem's this… I know for a fact that you find aspects of our world – this world of levels – less exciting and less culturally rich than the world you remember. You may have a point. Only you have to ask yourself, was that world really any better than the world we are creating?'

Jake made to answer, but Lahm wasn't going to be interrupted.

'As I recall, there was great evil in that world you remember so fondly. Starvation and war and debilitating disease, not to speak of religious intolerance, greed and injustice. Whereas in ours...'

Lahm smiled. 'Don't you see it, Jake? Ours is a world *without* want, *without* endless warfare, a world blessedly *free* of disease. Surely it was worth the sacrifice of some of those things you treasured to create such a world?'

Jake looked down. What Lahm had said sounded almost convincing. Only it wasn't true. This world of theirs – this tame, safe world of half-men – how could it ever compare to the world they had lost, the world the Han had stolen from them? He missed that world. Ached to have it back, warts and all. Only...

Jake took a tiny, shuddering breath, then spoke up, his voice quiet. 'It's just that... some days I just can't bear it. I wake up and I just... Never to hear those sounds again... Never to hear any of those wonderful, beautiful songs, it's...'

He shook his head, in pain now. Even to say it was impossible. It broke him apart. It seemed such a small thing. Only it wasn't small at all. It was life itself. Like the rain and the wind and the sunlight on one's face. How could you live without those things? What kind of devil's bargain was it, giving up all of that? And for what? To be *safe*? He looked up at Lahm.

'You really *don't* understand, do you? What they took from us. The land, the political power... none of that really matters. But our *culture*... our music, our art, our writing... that's what we *are*. That's what makes us us.'

Lahm was watching him closely now, studying him intently, as one might study some rare specimen.

'You asked me earlier whether I'd been having dreams. Well, I have. I've dreamed of how it was before the crash.'

'Ah...' Lahm's eyes widened. 'Many of us do.'

'No,' Jake said, correcting him. 'I don't mean the Collapse... I mean the car crash. The one that killed my parents. Nothing prepared me for that. What happened afterwards... all of the things I subsequently lost... none of it was ever quite that bad. Not Kate's death, nor any of what happened back in Corfe. *That* was when my world fell apart. Back then. Only now I feel it's happening again... in slow motion.'

Jake looked down. He had never spoken of this. Not even to Mary. It had simply been too painful. All these years he had built a wall around those memories, afraid lest the roof fall in and he go gibbering mad, just thinking about it. But the dreams had ended that. And what had caused the dreams?

He began again, forming the words now with difficulty. 'You see, there are things I want back, and I can't have them. Either they no longer exist, or I'm simply not *allowed* to have them. And that's unbearable. A slow suffocation. The thing is, I'm an Englishman. My heart swells to the music of Ralph Vaughan Williams, to the writing of Shakespeare and Dickens, to the sight of a Turner landscape. It took me more than twenty years to discover it, but that's the truth. That was my real re-education. Not in your camps, but back there, in Purbeck. That's where I learned to be me. All this... can't you see it? It's all a fake. A hideous massive lie. We're supposed to sleep easy being part of it, happy to be safe and sound, but it's at the cost of denying what we are.'

'You think, in the bigger picture, what you *are* really matters?'

'More than anything.'

'Then I'm sorry for you, Jake. A change of sky is a change of sky. There *are* no Englishmen. They don't exist. We can't *allow* them to exist.'

Jake looked away.

'Look... I don't want to sneer at your dreams, Jake, but our primary concern is for what's best for all. If it were only a question of indulging a few... well, what harm would that do? Only it's not a few. There are many like you, Jake, and what all of you fail to understand is just how much you're victims of the old, individualistic way of thinking. You think *me* when you should be thinking *us*, and we can't permit that.'

Jake scowled. 'You make being alive sound selfish.'

Only Lahm, it seemed, had stopped listening.

'Well, it is. Each of us needs to consider what Tsao Ch'un seeks to achieve through us, and how we might help facilitate that process. His is the long vision, you see, not the short. If that takes a whole generation to achieve, then that's as it must be. If you want to be a useful citizen, Jake, you must subject yourself to the greater historical forces. You must learn to swim *with* the tide, not against it.

'It's all a matter of numbers. As each older citizen dies, so the problem is reduced... *numerically*. Each day there are, quite literally, fewer people who remember how things were. Likewise, with each *new* citizen that's born, so the number of those who accept things as they are will grow.' He shrugged.

'It's merely a matter of time. The transformation *will* be made. Have no doubt about that, Jake. There *will* come a time when Tsao Ch'un's version of the truth will be the only one that exists in people's minds. Until that day, however... well... we must be vigilant, neh?'

Lahm was smiling at him now, encouragingly. 'There's a Jorge Luis Borges story. Do you remember Borges, Jake?'

Jake nodded, his mouth suddenly dry.

'It's only a brief thing... a page at most... but quite brilliant in its way. It speaks of memory and what, in our heads, will die with us. Of the death of the last person to have seen Christ crucified, and of a bar of scented soap in a drawer...'

'The point being?'

Lahm shrugged. 'Just that there's a great deal that is good in the culture of the Han. Enough, I feel, to sustain us.'

'Us?'

Lahm nodded. 'You think I was always like this, Jake? Flushed with equanimity? Do you really think I didn't have to struggle to become what I am? No. I was very much like you, once upon a time. Which was why I agreed to take your case... to sponsor you... to be *fan han* to you and protect you on the border.'

'Is that it, then? Be a good boy *or else*?'

'Do you really want *or else*?' Lahm seemed, for that briefest moment, sympathetic. 'Look, Jake... I make no promises, but... well, maybe there's a chance of something new for you to do. A new job. Something that's more in your line. Something that'll challenge you. I can't say until I've had a word here and there, but... well, it might make things easier, more tolerable.'

'Yes?'

'Yes. Oh, and Jake... try not to hum to yourself, okay?'

'Ah... Captain Grant... I'd forgotten you were coming.'

Grant stepped inside, then sat, facing Lahm.

'What exactly is it that you want? You said it was important.'

Grant took the stub from his pocket and handed it across.

'What's this?'

'Load it,' Grant said. 'You'll see.'

Lahm shrugged, slipped the stub into a slot on his workstation, then settled back, closing his eyes as the data flowed directly into his head.

For a moment Lahm didn't react, and then he started forward, his eyes popping open. 'Shit! Where in fuck's name did you get this?'

'Interesting, huh?'

Lahm stood, then came around the desk, standing over the other man. 'You'd better start explaining, and fast.'

'Its name was Anton Pierce. It lived with its brother – its clone brother, that is – in one of my decks. Two days ago it went into a store cupboard, pulled out a chair, put a rope about its neck and kicked the chair away.'

Lahm went back round his desk and sat again.

'And?'

'And I had my forensics guy do a full autopsy.'

'Why?'

Grant shrugged. 'Because I didn't think it was an ordinary suicide. And because... well, because I have an instinct for these things.'

'So why didn't you let it drop? Why are you here now?'

'I was hoping you might give me some kind of explanation.'

Lahm laughed. 'Why, in the names of all the gods, would you think that?'

'Because you guys... and I mean the men at the very top, not your foot soldiers... like giving explanations. You like justifying what you're up to. Especially to guys like me who have to carry out your policies.'

'Yeah? And how would you know about such things?'

'I don't. Not for certain. But from what I've seen...'

Lahm sat back. 'Okay... so you tell me what *you* know, Captain Grant. It's GenSyn, right? And it's been specially sanctioned. You've worked that out, I'm sure. Beyond that, what?'

'It kept a log. A diary of sorts.'

'Go on...'

'From that, it's clear that it didn't know it was a clone. But there are numerous references to it feeling "not quite human", as if "something were missing".'

Lahm stared at him. 'Are you willing to sign a secrecy agreement?'

'Do I have a choice?'

'Between knowing and not knowing, yes.'

Grant hesitated, then nodded. 'Okay. Where do I sign?'

Lahm smiled. 'You already have. We have your retinal confirmation.'

'So what is this? An experiment, right?'

'An experiment within an experiment, if you like. We wanted to see if these creatures were stable... socially, that is. Wanted to make sure they weren't a threat.'

'And are they?'

'The results aren't in yet, but our friend Anton... well, there have been a few like him.'

Lahm removed the stub from the slot and handed it back to Grant.

'It's all there. I've updated your data. You get to read it all once, and then it's wiped, okay?'

'And then what?'

'Nothing. But you get to know. Isn't that enough?'

Going back down in the lift, Grant decided that it probably was. Even with all the secrecy, the one thing he was certain of about the Ministry was its bureaucratic nature. Everything had to be reported – often in triplicate. It was that which he'd depended on. That and what he'd said to Lahm, about how they loved to justify what they were up to, however nasty and devious it was. Men like Lahm, particularly, who considered themselves the guardians of the system.

Yet as his craft lifted away, Grant found himself thinking. *An experiment, eh?* No. Lahm had been more specific than that. An experiment *within* an experiment.

He had read a report somewhere that, in the old world, 1 per cent of the population had been diagnosed as clinically mad. In Tsao Ch'un's City, however, that figure had soared dramatically. In the world of levels that figure was almost 3 per cent. All of those poor sods who couldn't adapt, couldn't live under the new sky.

Which led where?

He let the thought go, then slipped his hand into his pocket, toying with the stub, turning the tiny data chip over and over between his fingers.

He'd not expected that. Not expected Lahm to give him what he wanted quite so easily. But then why not? What had he to lose?

Grant smiled, then slipped the stub into the slot beneath his ear.

★

As Jake stepped down from the craft, nodding to the single, silent guard, he thought again about what Lahm had said.

Here, outside, night was falling again. As it did, so the roof of the City began to glow beneath his feet, like something warm and living.

He took in a deep breath of the night air, then turned full circle, looking about him. There was nothing to see. Nothing but the City's roof, stretching off interminably in all directions, and close by, the docking port, which slowly rose up from that plain white surface with a hiss of hydraulics.

What he had felt, sitting there in the back of the craft, surrounded by all that plush black leather, was relief. He had put his head into the dragon's mouth and survived. And now the future lay ahead.

It wasn't going to be easy. Lahm had not suggested that it would. Only he knew now that someone was watching over him. *Protecting* him.

He felt chastened by the fact. He had a patron. A benefactor. Someone who valued him; who thought he deserved a better chance. Jake wasn't sure why, only it had to do with what he'd been. A web-dancer. Someone who had been important enough to be on their list.

There. It all kept coming back to that. What had been his misfortune was now the saving of him.

Or could be, if he could cut it in the weeks to come. And if Lahm came through with his promise of a new job.

As he stepped inside, he took one last, brief glimpse of the sky, which was heavy with pink and purple clouds.

A change of sky, he thought, remembering what Lahm had said.

He took a deep breath, then pulled his cloak up over his head and threw it aside, even as the door hissed shut and the mist of antiseptic spray began to fill the chamber.

Jake smiled. He would be home within the hour.

Lahm climbed the ramp, then ducked inside the craft.

'Where is he?'

The pilot scrambled to his feet, bowing low before the Eighth Dragon. 'He is in the back, Master.'

He went through.

Grant lay slumped on his back among the cushions, a look of deep surprise on his face. Lahm leaned close, putting his fingers to the man's neck.

There was no pulse. Not that he expected one. The synaptic wipe would have done its job with stark efficiency, delivering a pulse of data-poison directly into the cortex. Grant would have been dead just seconds after he slipped the stub into his neck.

Lahm straightened up, then looked about him. It was regrettable, but wild cards like Grant could not be allowed to roam freely, pursuing whatever enquiries they chose. Especially when they involved matters of such delicate sensitivity to the State.

Besides, Grant was replaceable, just as Reed was irreplaceable.

For now.

Lahm stared at the dead man. He wasn't sure yet how he was going to use Reed, nor for what purpose, but this business with GenSyn gave him an idea. One he would follow up.

The thing was, he had seen what Reed was capable of. Those operational tapes of him at work inside the data landscape were astonishing. There was no other word for it. He had been possessed of such amazing intuitive talent. Only it was like Jiang Lei had said in his report. The years had blunted Reed's edge. Had made him less dangerous.

And maybe, concomitantly, less useful.

Lahm sighed, then reached down and squeezed the stub from the slot in Grant's neck, wiping the crusted blood from it onto his sleeve.

Time would tell, when it came to Reed. There was no hurry. First they had to let him find his balance. Then, and only then, would they find out what use he might be. But GenSyn were the key. The more he thought about it, the better it felt.

'Incinerate the body,' he said, as he walked back past the pilot. 'And make sure all mention of him is removed from the record. As far as the local office is concerned, Captain Grant has been reassigned. *All right?*'

'Yes, Master!'

Lahm nodded. Then, turning away, he ducked out, making his way back down the ramp. And as he walked quickly back to the gate, his dark cloak spreading out behind him in the wind, so the men he passed fell to their knees, their heads bowed low, their foreheads touching the deck as they showed their respect to their Master, the Eighth Dragon.

Their respect, but also their fear.

The GenSyn building was a mere three stacks from Bremen Central, their administrative offices occupying the top five decks of the stack – fifty floors in all. Their laboratories and breeding facilities were elsewhere, in Milan, Nantes and even one on Mars, but this was the heart of the operation. This was where Jake would be working if they offered him the job.

They gave him quite a reception, no fewer than five of their senior managers greeting him off the craft, introducing themselves as they went down in the lift.

Jake wasn't quite sure why he was getting the star treatment, although it soon became clear.

'There you have her,' the senior HR Manager, Tim Curtis, said, putting out a hand. 'She looks familiar, I bet.'

It was a datscape. At least, the outer workings of a datscape. He hadn't seen its like for more than twenty years – since the day of the Collapse, in fact – but there was no questioning what it was. Only... did it work?

'Oh yes,' Rheinhardt, the Media Liaison Manager said, with a beaming smile. 'It works. Only we don't know how to train up operatives. Or didn't... until now.'

So that was it. Jake laughed. How strange, after all these years, to come full circle.

'I must be twenty, maybe thirty pounds too heavy,' he said, as they brought one of the suits – clearly fashioned on the original designs – out for him to see.

'It's all right,' Curtis said. 'We wouldn't expect you to go in straight away. We know you'll have to get fit again. To get used to it again. It's over twenty years, I know. But we can take it step by step.'

'We saw the thing you did,' another of them – he had forgotten the man's name – chipped in. 'You know... the training immersion. Lahm sent us a copy. Gods...'

Jake looked about him, surprised. All five were looking at him with deep respect, like he was something really special. And maybe he had been. Only that had been a lifetime ago. A lot had happened in between. He was no longer that man.

'I don't know,' he said, a wave of uncertainty washing over him. 'It's a bloody long time.'

There was nervous laughter. They clearly wanted this to work. Wanted him to pick up the pieces after all this time. Only he wasn't sure he could.

And, anyway, why was it so important? What did they want to use the datscape *for?* After all, the world of commerce had been greatly simplified since the Collapse – there was only the Hang Seng these days and that didn't need this kind of data system. This was far too complex for that. So what did they have in mind?

One tour and one talk later, Jake still wasn't sure what they'd be hiring him to do. But he did have a much clearer view of what GenSyn did now.

GenSyn was the last remaining company of the old West's biotech industry.

If it was alive, they were interested in it, from bacteria through to human beings, and all stages in between. They fine-tuned nature, as they liked to call it, giving it a tweak. What could be imagined could – generally – be achieved.

Only what was the point of it all? To make playthings for the bored super-rich?

The truth was, a great deal of GenSyn's business was of the mundane kind, producing panaceas for the multitudes, as well as the odd billion or two spare organs. Beyond being one of the City's chief pharmacists, however, their aim was to make humankind bigger and better, stronger and more intelligent. One whole department of the company was designed for that purpose, with a budget that allowed them to purchase the services of the very cream of the science academies.

While the academies still existed. For there were rumours – very strong rumours – that Tsao Ch'un planned to control research and development. That he had a scheme for slowing things down. And that, if true, was bound to affect GenSyn, who were the kings of fast-tracking ideas.

When they took a break, later that afternoon, Jake was shown to his accommodation – a suite of luxurious rooms in the company's First Level mansion. Left alone, he walked about it, pulling out drawers and looking in cupboards. Everything he might need was there. Anything he wanted could be ordered for him, no expense spared.

Jake nodded to himself. They clearly wanted him, and were going out of their way to get him. But why now? Why hadn't this happened before? Or was that Lahm's doing, too?

It made him wonder what Lahm was up to. What did *he* get out of this? Prestige? A finder's fee?

Whatever it was, Lahm clearly wanted him to take the job. For reasons best known to him, it suited Lahm to have Jake there, at the heart of GenSyn. As his man.

He went through. There was an office, just off the huge bedroom with its en suite bathroom.

Mary would love this, he thought, as he went across and sat before the comset.

It was while he was sitting there that he noticed the sound, growing slowly louder in the background. The sound of rain falling on leaves. Jake closed his eyes, a little shiver going up his spine. He could smell it now. That fresh, springtime scent of grass and flowers.

It was a fake, of course. An illusion. But a welcome one.

He keyed in. At once a face appeared on the screen. A pleasant young woman's face. *Hung Mao*, like himself. She smiled at Jake like she was an old friend.

'Can I help you, *Shih* Reed?'

For a moment her voice reminded him of something. Of the AI he had had in his apartment all those years ago.

Trish...

He let out a long sigh. It was ages since he'd thought of Trish. She was only a computer program, true, but she had been such an intimate part of his life. No human being had known him half as well as Trish.

'I'm sorry,' he said, 'only... are you real?'

The girl's smile broadened. 'I am... and my name is Hui.'

'But...'

'I was adopted,' she said quickly. 'By a Han couple. They raised me, along with my sister.'

'Ah... Look, I wanted to contact my wife, Mary... back home...'

'Then I'll connect you. Is there anything else you need?'

Jake shook his head. 'No, I'm fine thanks, Hui.'

'Then I'll call you once I have your wife on the line... If you want to you can go and stretch out on the bed, or on the sofa. I'll patch the call through to there, if that's okay?'

'That would be good. And thank you again, Hui.'

'It's my pleasure, *Shih* Reed.'

As the screen blanked, Jake stood. The sofa in the other room was massive. Like all the furniture, it was a hybrid of East and West. Which was something he'd noticed throughout the facility. A striving to combine both cultures. To make both Han and *Hung Mao* at ease. That, surely, was deliberate. A matter of policy. Unless that too was some directive of Tsao Ch'un's.

He chose the sofa. A minute later the screen lit up and Mary's smiling face beamed down at him.

'Hi, sweetheart. How're things going? They treating you well?'

He gestured to the suite that was all about him. 'It's the lap of luxury. You'd love it. And the job...'

'What do they want you to do?'

'To train people up...'

Mary looked perplexed. 'Train them up? But you don't know anything about biotech, or training, come to that.'

'They've got a datscape.'

'Ah...'

He saw how her face clouded momentarily. It wasn't something they had talked about very often – his past life – and neither was comfortable with it. But she recovered quickly. The smile returned. 'Do you think you're up to it? From what you said... it all sounded very demanding. Physically, that is.'

And mentally, he thought. Just melding the two, intellect and body, that was the trick. Not to let either side of the brain dominate the other.

Only what if he had lost that ability? What if he could no longer do it?

Then no one else could. Tsao Ch'un had ensured they were all killed during the Crash.

Jake smiled. It felt suddenly like he was the last of a species that was just about to become extinct. And GenSyn wanted to save him, in effect to *clone* him.

'They want me to stay here a day or two,' he went on. 'Get a feel of things. Meet a few more people.'

'They seem very keen.'

'Oh, they are.'

And probably monitoring this.

'They're talking ten times my current salary, Mary. If I want it.'

'And do you?'

Jake didn't answer, just gave the slightest shrug. 'Look... I'll speak to you when I'm back. When I've had a chance to mull things over.'

Mary looked a little disappointed, but all she said was. 'Okay. Love you.'

'Love you too. And give my love to the gang. Tom 'specially.'

'I will...'

The screen blanked.

Jake lay back, closing his eyes. He could still hear the rain falling, smell the clear, refreshing scents of an English garden.

Maybe they thought his hesitancy a bargaining tool – just a means of jacking up his salary. Only it wasn't. He was actually afraid. Afraid lest he'd lost it totally. Because it was the one thing in his life he had done well. Better, in fact, than anyone else in the world.

To web-dance again... He felt a shiver run through him at the thought. To be inside there once again, his senses razor sharp...

How could he *not* try? How could he possibly hesitate? And yet he did. Because to fail at this was to be condemned to a life lived at the lower level. Quite literally.

Jake stood, then paced the room, trying to see some clear way out of this. Only there was no clear answer.

Maybe one would come to him. Maybe he'd find the courage from somewhere to make the attempt. Only he doubted it. He knew himself too well.

They threw a dinner for him that evening, with thirty guests, most of them senior executives, but one or two of them potential colleagues, people he would probably be working with... *if* he took the job.

He liked them a lot. Liked the company, that feeling of being part of the future again, because there was no doubting it – GenSyn was still cutting-edge. By comparison, the job he'd been doing was sedentary, dull.

Backwater.

Only the thing was he couldn't say it. Couldn't voice his doubts. All he could do was go along with things, let them believe he was thoroughly seduced by it all.

Which, in a sense, he was.

Neither of the Ebert brothers had shown their faces yet. Gustav was on Mars, so there was no likelihood that *he'd* be making an appearance, but Wolfgang was in Bremen, so Jake was a little surprised – bearing everything else in mind – that he'd not yet met him.

And then there was Alison.

Alison still worked for GenSyn. He'd actually checked up on that. She was Head of Evaluation, and had been for the past twenty-five years, since they met before the Collapse. Unmarried still. Childless.

Again he was surprised that he hadn't seen her, for she surely must have known he was coming. From all accounts, everything to do with GenSyn's operation went through her office.

Or was her absence deliberate?

As the last dinner guests departed, sometime shortly after two, she finally arrived.

'Hi, Jake...'

'Hi...'

Alison was a lot older than he'd imagined her. She had put on weight, and her blonde hair, which had previously been long and straight, was much shorter now, curlier, and very obviously dyed. She wore a dark blue one-piece with a jacket, on which was appended a nametag. It looked like she had just come from a conference of some kind.

'I meant to be here earlier,' she said, coming across and offering her hand, 'but I got delayed.'

Her hand was small and slim and just a little cold. Just as he remembered it.

He looked up, meeting her pale blue eyes. 'It's nice to see you again.'

'It's nice to see you...'

Jake let her hand go. She was smiling now.

'What is it?'

'Just that... well... it's *you*... I'd never have mistaken you. You've put on weight, and the hair...' She smiled again. 'I'm glad you survived, though. An awful lot didn't.'

'I know.'

She took a breath, then, very businesslike, said, 'I'll be your guide tomorrow. Take you round and show you things.'

'There's more to see?'

'You've not seen a tenth of it. And besides, I want to talk to you. I know you have your doubts...'

'You do?' He was surprised. Had they been analysing tapes or something?

'I know you, Jake. You always had doubts. At first. When you took the job at Hinton...' She shrugged. 'We'll talk it through tomorrow. Right now I reckon you need some sleep.'

'I do.'

'I like your wife, by the way.'

It was unexpected. 'Oh? Which one?'

'Mary. You were married to her sister, weren't you?'

He nodded. Then, quietly, 'Kate died, you know. They killed her.'

Alison nodded sadly. 'I know.'

Jake blew out a breath. 'Well then...'

The words seemed to galvanize her. 'Right. I'll leave you now. The steward will see you back to your rooms. And I'll see you in the morning. Ten, shall we say?'

'Ten sounds good. Sounds *civilized*.'

She smiled again. 'Then ten it is.'

Jake slept like the proverbial log and woke to find the steward in the room with him, bearing a full cooked English breakfast on a silver tray, complete with coffee and a chilled glass of freshly squeezed orange.

Alison's doing, he thought, remembering how she'd used to treat him, at College, back when they were students. *She remembered.*

It was a nice touch – the first of many that day.

She was there at ten precisely, and he was waiting for her, showered and changed and ready for the off.

'First off I'll take you to see "the Farm",' she said. 'It's a bit of a circus, but then it is our showcase. This is where we bring all the big clients. We give them the tour. Show them what's possible.'

The Farm was even more impressive than he imagined. It was situated in a separate stack, into which they entered via a 'seal', a massive portal, half airlock, half safe door. There were only six such entrances to the whole of the stack, all of which were operated under the strictest guidelines. Guidelines drawn up by Tsao Ch'un himself. If anything escaped, the whole damn thing would be shut down, the special edict granted to GenSyn for this purpose revoked and their creatures destroyed.

It was like entering a high-security prison. There were masked guards everywhere, and, high up on the walls – which Alison pointed out to him – the jets through which the sterilizing gases would be pumped into the facility, should it ever prove necessary.

'It was a lot smaller when I first came here,' she said, almost wistfully. 'Just a single deck, that's all we had. And less than a hundred different creatures. Now this is one of four such facilities, all of which take up a whole stack. And we number the creatures we produce in the tens of thousands.'

The first section they looked at was named simply 'Extinct', the word striking Jake as being as ironic as you could possibly be, considering that Tsao Ch'un, if he had his way, would make the whole of nature extinct.

'This is our most popular range,' Alison explained, as they stood there, staring through a one-way mirror at the most famous extinct bird of them all, the Dodo. 'It's mainly creatures who've become extinct before the last hundred years. Totemic creatures that they can impress their friends with.'

'The rich, you mean?'

She nodded. 'And you have to be very rich indeed to afford one of these, because it's not only the cost of purchasing the animal, you have to sign on for the aftercare service. And then there's the construction and maintenance of the creature's environment.'

She looked to Jake and smiled. 'Well, we can't have them running around loose, can we? So whoever buys them has to guarantee to keep them isolated. We have a "look but don't touch policy". If they break the agreement then we take the creature back. And no refunds.'

Jake nodded. The Dodo looked real. It didn't look like a manufactured creature. But then, why should it? It was, to all intents and purposes, the real thing. Only it couldn't breed. None of these creatures could. That was part of the deal. Once it died it was dead and you had to buy another one. If you had that kind of money.

There were mammoths here, too, and sabre-toothed tigers – these last the most expensive item in the section. Jake asked what expensive was in round figures, but Alison wasn't going to say.

'Not unless you join us,' she said, smiling. 'Then you get to know everything.'

'Everything?'

'Well, almost everything. You'd be senior management, Jake. A decision-maker. We'd put you on the board, if you wanted.'

He wasn't sure he did, but it was nice of them to offer.

'What's next?' he asked, as they stepped through into the connecting corridor – a small airlock in itself – and waited for the door behind them to be sealed.

'My personal least-favourite. Creepy crawlies.'

'Insects?'

'And other things. Quite inventive, some of them, as you'll see.'

The door ahead hissed open and they stepped through. Into a massive hall, filled with glass cases.

'Each one is a tiny environment,' Alison explained as they walked up to the nearest of them. 'Most contain only a single species, but others... they're complex little ecosystems. Some contain over a hundred different types of insect.'

Jake crouched down, resting his fingertips against the glass of the case. It was like an exhibit in a zoo; a cross section through the earth, showing the insects' tunnels and nests. As he watched, something scuttled away into the dark of the interior – something winged and clawed and black as night itself.

'Are these all taken from nature?'

'Some are. But we like to customize, for our richer patrons. We can have their company logos imprinted on the tiny creatures. Built into them, if you like. On their wings, for instance. And we can play about with the colour of them or the shape. Truth is, there's little we *can't* do.'

'But that "little" worries the Eberts, right? They want to be able to do it all, yeah? That's why I'm here, right?'

She stared at him, surprised that he'd worked it out so quickly.

'Partly.'

'One question,' he said, straightening up, then turning to look at her. 'What exactly are you going to use the datscape for?'

She looked down, the gesture ancient in his memory. People didn't change. Not in their essentials, anyway.

Alison looked up, meeting his eyes again. 'Much of our work here – the research work, that is – is done at a microbiological level, using electron microscopes and the very finest gauge waldoes.' She smiled. 'To put it crudely, Jake, we play about with proteins. Only... what we want to do – and we're not even sure yet that it'll work – is to duplicate what happens at the nanotechnological level on a much larger scale within the datscape, so that we can, quite literally, walk around it and through it and view it from every possible angle.'

Jake smiled. 'I like that. It's a good idea. Who thought of that?'

'Gustav, of course. He bought the datscape at auction. There are only four of them left. The rest were all destroyed.'

'Ah...'

'Oh... it'll be a lot more complex than the original datscape, if Gustav has his way. He wants to replicate nature in there.'

'And his brother?'

She smiled. 'Wolfgang only worries about the cost, the likely profit.'

'Will I get to meet them?'

'If you join us, yes.'

'I see... And my role will be what? To train people up? I know that... But what else?'

'To be an enabler. And a consultant and... well, whatever else takes your fancy.'

'Carte blanche...?'

'Not entirely. But pretty free. Providing you're on call all of the time.'

'They're very demanding, then, your bosses?'

'Very. But then that's the challenge.'

He hesitated, then asked what had been nagging him, at the back of his mind. 'Did you approach Lahm?'

'No. Lahm came to us.'

'And before that?'

'I didn't even know you still existed. It was a very pleasant surprise, Jake.'

Jake looked at her briefly. She seemed to mean that. There was certainly a warmth there in her eyes.

'And your bosses... what do they want?'

'They want things up and running. So the sooner I sign you the better.'

'Ah...' He changed tack. 'Can I ask you something. Something personal, I mean...'

She shrugged. 'If you must.'

'Why did you never marry?'

'I did.'

'But I thought...'

She smiled. Faintly amused by his query, it seemed. 'You've been looking me up, haven't you?'

He nodded. 'So what happened?'

'He died.'

'Oh, I'm sorry. I...'

Alison looked down, fragile suddenly, more like the Alison he'd known, long ago. 'He was on a craft that got shot down. Terrorists. Not surprising, really, the places he went.'

'I don't understand.'

'He was in Security. A Police General.'

'Ah...' That surprised him more than anything else she'd said. 'But no children, right?'

'Wrong. We have a son.'

'But it said...'

She met his eyes, a certain hardness in her own. 'Don't believe everything you read, Jake. My son isn't in the record for good reason. Because it would make me vulnerable. If he were taken hostage...'

The tightness in her face betrayed her fear of it. But then she smiled again. 'He's eighteen next week. And very like his father. Tall and dark-haired. A bit like you were, Jake, when you were his age.'

He studied her a moment, re-evaluating her. Then, very softly, 'And you didn't remarry?'

'No.'

She looked to him, then looked away again. 'I guess I didn't want to take the risk. Not after that. It's hard enough having your heart broken once, let alone twice in one lifetime.'

Two hours later, they had worked their way up to the topmost level of the stack. There, in an elegant First Level mansion that would have been the pride of any billionaire, were the real stars of the Farm: Gustav Ebert's world-famous talking goats – man-sized creatures who stood upright on their hind legs, wore clothes, drank wine and smoked cigars, just like normal human beings.

Jake had heard of them – he couldn't remember what the story was, but they had been on the news quite recently. But encountering them face to face and with no one-way glass partition was quite intimidating. There was nothing to make him feel safe and something feral and inhuman in their eyes. When he shook their hands – tiny, trotter-like hands that could still hold a glass and use a pen – he was surprised by the sheer strength of aversion he felt towards them.

A shrinking back into his skin.

They were politeness itself, but he... he could barely say a word. All he wanted was to be out of there.

Afterwards, as they waited for the seal to open, he looked to Alison and shuddered.

'Am I the only one...?'

'To loathe the creatures? No. It's a common reaction. Gustav thinks it's rooted at the most primal of levels. We look into those eyes and something's triggered. But it's not only that... it's the smell of them.'

Jake frowned. 'I didn't think...'

'The perfume masks it. But again, at some deeper level, it registers. Their animal scent. Some people say the goats remind them of the devil... or rather, the King of Hell.'

'And yet they buy them.'

'And maybe even for that reason.' As the door ahead of them hissed open, she looked to him. 'You hungry, Jake?'

'Yes.'

'Then let's have some lunch. I've a couple more things I want to show you, but they can wait. Besides, we need to talk.'

'Haven't we been talking?

She glanced sideways at him. 'I mean *talk*. I'm still suffering from the shock of finding you're alive.'

Lunch was roast beef and Yorkshire puddings, courtesy of Alison's own chef.

Jake sat there, in her old-fashioned farmhouse kitchen, looking about him, recognizing what she'd done there, and thinking that he was probably the only one in the world who did.

'Your mum and dad's place... in Chobham.'

She smiled but didn't meet his eyes, concentrating on opening the bottle of 1982 Chateau Cissac. 'You remembered,' she said.

'I couldn't really forget, could I? Those were good times.'

'They were.'

He hesitated, then, 'You know... this could be awkward.'

'How d'you mean?'

'You and me. Working at such close quarters.'

This time she met his eyes. 'That's presuming I want you in my life again. In *that* way.'

Don't you? he thought. Only he didn't say it aloud.

She poured two glasses of the blood-red wine, then handed him one. 'No, Jake. Whatever relationship we're going to have, it's going to be a business one. We can be friends, sure, but it would be foolish and mistaken to think it could be anything else.'

She smiled. 'Put simply, we fucked that up years ago. We don't need to do it all over again.'

He raised his glass, toasting her. 'Spoken like a woman who doesn't need a man in her life.'

'But I have a man in my life, and here he is...'

She was right. Her son did look like Jake when he was younger. For a moment he wondered if the boy *could* be his. Only he couldn't. He was only seventeen.

Jake stood, offering his hand. 'I'm Jake...'

The boy's smile disarmed him. He looked to his mother, then put out his hand, clasping Jake's firmly. 'Nice to meet you, Jake. I'm... Jake...'

'Jacob Paul,' Alison said. 'Paul after my father, of course.'

And Jake? Only, again, he didn't say a word.

'Ah...' Jake looked down at the young man's hand within his own, then released it.

'You keep wrong-footing me,' he said, looking to her, seeing how the situation amused her. 'Why didn't you say?'

'That he'd be here? I didn't think he would. He ought to be at the academy.'

'They've given me the rest of the week off,' the boy said hastily. 'To revise.'

'You've got exams?' Jake asked.

'History and Social Studies.'

'Oh.'

He wondered what they taught today's youngsters. Not the truth, that was certain. But did they believe it? Or did they know it was all a fiction?

Later, back in his rooms, Jake pondered that question. Was it true what Lahm had said? Was it only a matter of time before the likes of his Peter and Alison's Jake would accept it all for gospel? Or would the truth still be there, handed on in whispers, like a seed in the earth, waiting to sprout again sometime in the future? Could Tsao Ch'un and his servants really erase it all, book by book and fact by fact?

He didn't know. But they were having a damn good try. And just as long as something didn't go dramatically wrong, a century from now it would all be academic. Because no one would care. There wouldn't be anyone left alive who'd *want* to change it back.

That afternoon, Alison had shown him the future.

Food was part of it. Feeding the ever-growing masses of Chung Kuo. For there was no doubt that after the massive depletions of the past three decades, there would be an equally massive growth, and GenSyn wanted a share of that market. To that end they had developed all manner of clever creatures; animals that were safer and healthier to eat. But their greatest achievement – one for which they got a lot of press coverage – was the *jou tung wu*, the very plainly named 'meat animal'.

The *jou tung wu* was basically a cow, though it looked as little like a cow as a rocket resembled a kite. Partly the result of breeding, partly of biological reconstruction, the great beast was a living slab of meat, without bone or sinew. Its huge weight and size were maintained artificially by the machines that lay beneath it and surrounded it on all sides. Looking down from the balcony above, Jake grimaced. Apart from the stench, it was visually repellent; a single, pulsating mass of pink flesh.

'I know,' Alison said, laughing, in reponse to his expression. 'But think how efficient it is.'

'It's not aware of what it is, is it? I don't see any heads.'

'There is one, normal size, underneath there somewhere. We tried making one without a head, but it simply doesn't work. That pulse is where we're pumping air through it. And there are slurries on all sides.'

'What do you feed it?'

'Garbage.'

He looked at her, saw she was serious.

'Oh, there are things it can't eat, but anything organic is fine. You've heard of the Thousand Eyes? This is the thousand stomachs. Like the air, the garbage gets pumped in somewhere over... there!'

Alison pointed to where a huge flexible pipe hung down, disappearing into that great mound of living flesh.

'Do you have to kill it, then, before you eat it?'

'No. It gets carved once a week. We remove something like 20 per cent of its body weight, and then it grows back.'

'So it's endlessly renewable... once you've got it up and running?'

'Not endless. It has a life span of something like eight years. But it'll feed five stacks throughout that period. At least, give them the meat intake they require.'

Jake shuddered. So this was what they'd been eating.

They moved on, down a corridor and into a lift that went up and up until Jake was sure it could go no higher. And yet it did.

'Where are we?' he asked, as it slowed and stopped.

'The Airy. It's Gustav's place. He isn't here now, but he said I could use it.'

The lift door opened.

They stepped out into luxury and style. There were paintings on the wall that Jake knew at once were worth millions. He stopped before one.

'This one's a fake.'

Alison came up alongside him. 'Really? How d'you know that?'

'Because I used to have it in my bedroom. The original, that is. This one's been doctored. Tampered with.'

He pointed to it. 'This figure and that one there – the *Hung Mao* – they aren't in the original. In the original they're Han, like the rest in the painting.'

Jake concentrated, brought the name up out of dim and distant memory.

'It's Emperor Hui Tsong's copy of *Lady Kuo Kuo's Spring Outing*. The original was painted by Chang Hsuan in the eighth century.'

Alison spoke to the air. 'Chang? Is that right? Is this a fake?'

A Han voice answered her immediately. 'It is, Mistress Alison. The gentleman – *Shih Reed, that is* – is quite correct. Only we won't mention that to anyone outside, neh?'

Alison smiled. 'Yes, Chang.'

They went inside, into an apartment that made Jake's recent accommodation seem small and scruffy.

'You like?'

He looked to Alison, saw how at ease she was here.

She must come here a lot.

Maybe she was even Gustav's mistress.

He set the thought aside, looking about him. Everywhere he looked there were treasures. Fakes or not, Gustav's taste was exquisite.

'I need you to sign something, Jake,' she said, coming back across to him, holding out a sheet of paper and an old-fashioned fountain pen. 'It's a confidentiality statement. It says, basically, that you'll not speak about anything you see while you're here.'

Jake took it, signed it without looking and handed it back.

'You should have read it.'

'I trust you. Besides, you'll have me on camera. My retinal print...'

She smiled. 'I sometimes forget who you were. *What* you were, rather. At Hinton.'

'I forget myself. But why the secrecy? Is he afraid someone will come and steal all his paintings?'

She shook her head. 'The paintings would be easy to replace. No, it's his servants. Would you like to meet them?'

Jake frowned. She was doing it again, teasing him. 'Sure,' he said. 'Wheel them in.'

The first to come into the room was a middle-aged Han. He was dressed soberly, in purple robes with a black silk edging. He smiled and bowed.

'This,' said Alison, 'is Tsu Shih. He's Gustav's steward.'

Jake bowed, acknowledging him. 'Tsu Shih.'

'And this,' Alison added, as a young girl entered the room, 'is Tai Yu, or Moon Flower, as she's also known. Tai Yu is Gustav's maid.'

Jake waited, expecting more, knowing that a man like Gustav Ebert could afford a thousand servants to do his bidding. But these two, it seemed, were all.

He frowned, then looked to Alison. 'I'm sorry. I don't understand.'

'Tsu Shi... Tai Yu... bare your arms.'

At once they did as they were asked, exposing the flesh of their forearms for his inspection. Jake went across and looked.

'I still don't...'

And then he did. He understood all too well. These were more of GenSyn's creatures. That was what the logo imprinted into their forearms meant – the small S within the G. They hadn't been born, like he or Alison, they had been grown in vats, like spare-part limbs. Only these were whole, intelligent.

Alison spoke to them. 'Tsu Shi... how old are you?'

'I am four, Mistress.'

'And you, Tai Yu?'

'I am seven, Mistress. Nearly eight.'

'And you know what you are?'

Both Tsu Shi and Tai Yu smiled, as if perfectly content, then spoke as one, their words perfectly coordinated.

'We are our Master's hands.'

'Hui?'

'Yes, Shih Reed?'

'Could you get my wife, Mary, on the line?'

Jake sat back on the sofa, closing his eyes. It had been a strange day. An interesting day. All those things he'd seen and heard. It ought, by now, to have been clear in his mind what he was going to do. Only it wasn't. He was still no closer to making a decision. If anything, he had taken a step backward, because the truth was he wanted to be part of this. Because if he wasn't...

He stood, frustration making him feel restless. Why didn't he just say yes?

'Jake?'

He turned, looking up at the screen.

'Mary?'

She smiled. 'Had a good day?'

'A brilliant day, I...' He was going to say that he'd met an old friend, only he didn't want to tell her at a distance. He wanted to be there, next to her, when he told her that. He didn't want her jumping to the wrong conclusions.

'They showed me everything,' he said. 'Things I can't even talk to you about.'

'And has it made up your mind?'

Jake hesitated, then shook his head. 'I need to talk it through, Mary... with you. I need...'

He shrugged. He didn't know quite what he needed – a sounding board, maybe. Someone to tell him he was being ridiculous and that he ought to jump at the chance.

'I'm coming back,' he said. 'Tomorrow morning.'

'And they want an answer before then?'

'I don't know. They didn't ask. I guess they're giving me time to think it through. They've certainly pulled out all the stops to get me.'

Mary smiled. 'I'm glad. You're worth it, Jake.'

'Am I?'

They talked some more, then said their goodbyes. It was still relatively early – much too early for him to go to bed – and in other circumstances he might have called Alison up and gone to see her, to talk about old times. Only that seemed fraught with difficulties. Whatever she said about the two of them, there was still that connection, that history.

And maybe that was the best reason for not accepting the job.

Why, after all, had she called her son Jake? That wasn't the father's name. At least, as far as he could work out, it wasn't. And that comment she'd made about having her heart broken twice. That had to refer to their days together.

That said, she had made it quite explicit that any relationship they'd have would be strictly business. But Jake knew women. They didn't always mean what they said. And what Alison *meant* to do might not work out in practice. Not if they had to work closely together.

Yes, and what would Mary think of that? Of him working with his ex? The woman he'd almost married.

Against which was the excitement of working for GenSyn. It was genuinely a job to die for, just to be there, once more, at the cutting edge.

He spoke to the air. 'Hui?'

She answered him immediately. 'Yes, *Shih* Reed?'

'Have you a film? Something from the old days. Something by Drew Judd, maybe? The TV version of *Ubik*?'

There was the briefest of delays – a brevity that made Jake ask whether

Hui was quite as human as she claimed – and then she answered.

'I'm afraid there's nothing listed under either of those names.'

He sighed. *Nice try, anyway...*

'Then how about John Wu's *Red Cliff*...? The uncut version if you have it.'

Something to take my mind off the problem, he thought. *And what better than Wu's epic tale?*

A big Chinese historical. Something they couldn't possibly complain about him watching.

And that, perhaps, was another reason for joining GenSyn. Because today he had seen just how important they were to Tsao Ch'un. How, by being an employee, he might avoid all the constant watching, the constant censorship. In fact, the more he thought about it, the more he understood why Alison had been so relaxed. She knew that she wasn't being watched. It was why she'd been able to refer back to things that had gone. Forbidden things. Like the wine she'd chosen to serve him. At this level one was trusted. And why not? At this level it didn't matter if you made the odd slip now and then. No one was going to pick you up on it. Because at this level one was sewn tightly into the fabric of Tsao Ch'un's new world, *owned* by it, body and soul. *Complicit.*

At this level one could look down from giddy heights. As once before.

But did he *want* all of that back, even if he could get it?

'Shih Reed... I am afraid we can only trace the abridged version of the film...'

'That's okay. That'll be fine...'

So only the two-hour version, not the five...

The room lights dimmed. Up on the screen the ancient city of Ch'ang-an came into view, its watchtowers towering above its mighty walls. Jake smiled and settled back. He would decide in the morning.

Chapter 15

FULL CIRCLE

'Are you all right in there, Jake?'

Jake looked back at the Chief Tech and nodded. Or tried to. Only the suit wasn't responding.

'I'm fine, Kurt, it's just...'

And then the suit *did* nod.

The whole thing needed fine-tuning. They all knew that. Only the problem was a lot bigger than they had anticipated. Jake knew that was partly to do with him. He was almost fifty now and his brain didn't function the way it had when he was twenty-six. It had lost a lot of its sharpness. As for his senses, they were a *lot* duller than they'd been.

Which wasn't to say that it was a *complete* waste of time, only that they might have to lower their expectations. That was, until he could train up a few young bloods and pass on what he knew to someone who could really use that knowledge.

Three months had brought him this far. He had lost over thirty pounds in weight and was fitter than he'd been in over twenty years. Mentally, too, he had worked hard, pushing his brain to the limit to try and get back the edge he'd lost. All in all he had done well. Very well. Only it wasn't enough. You couldn't turn back time.

Jake tried to turn his head to see what was going on. He sensed that someone was fiddling with his suit, checking the connections. Only he knew now that that wasn't the problem. No. He could feel what the problem was. There was a signal delay. A time lag which meant that he lost immediacy, and immediacy was *everything* inside the datscape. Without it he couldn't lose himself, couldn't step between states and tap into his *instinctive* self – adopting that thoughtless, purely reactive state where he had done all his best work.

For a man his age his reactions were pretty damn good. He had surprised himself at how good they were. Only they weren't good enough.

'Kurt?'

The Chief Tech looked up. 'Yes?'

'Let's go in. Maybe it'll improve with use.'

'Okay.'

They didn't argue with him. He was the expert, after all. The one who knew about all this stuff. And the team respected that. Only he knew, for all their trust in him, that this wasn't going to work. Not the way GenSyn wanted it to work. But he was going to try.

Besides, the thought of doing this again made his pulse race. That was what none of them understood. This had always been a high. The biggest fix a man's senses could take and still be alive afterwards.

Kurt stopped fiddling. He stepped back, letting his two assistants take over.

'All right... let's get Jake out on the rail. We linked in at the desk?'

'Linked and ready!'

'You ready, Jake?'

Ready as I'll ever be. Aloud he just said, 'Ready!'

'Okay... start the feed.'

Jake braced himself. This was always the point where the rush hit him; where the whole thing exploded on his skin. Only this time it didn't. All he felt was a kind of disjuncture; a sharp jolt as his surroundings vanished and the datscape appeared all around him.

What the...?

He tried to look about him, tried to turn full circle and take it all in, only the data lapse was worse here inside than it had been outside. Instead of the smooth, even flow of movement, he found himself moving slowly, jerkily, like he was some poorly realized avatar on a damaged disc. And when he spoke...

'K-k-urhh-t-t...'

'What's up, Jake? You don't look happy.'

No. And he didn't feel happy, either. This wasn't good.

He kept still, studying the slice of virtual reality that lay directly ahead of him.

Christ! Look at this stuff...

He knew what was wrong instantly. It lacked depth, lacked the power of the original datscape. The datscape he remembered had been information rich. Its sheer detail had bombarded the senses. This, on the other hand...

It's a first attempt, he reminded himself. *No one knows yet how to use it. How to replicate it. Give them time and it'll be a lot better.*

Maybe so. But he was disappointed. He had expected much better than this. GenSyn weren't second rate after all...

He spoke again, this time clearly, no stutter or echo in the words.

'Kurt... It's not working... the datscape...'

'What about it?'

'How many spinners have we got feeding in?'

He could hear Kurt consult. Then, 'A dozen. And another dozen or so channels on auto-feed.'

No wonder...

Jake tried to make a step, counted a full five before the suit responded.

Worse in here than outside. Now why's that?

'Kurt?'

'Yes?'

'Have we got no one who worked on the original? Technicians, I mean...'

'Not a single one. You're it, Jake. The last vestige of this old technology.'

Then we're fucked, because I only know how to use it, not how to get it up and running.

'You know what I think?'

'What's that?'

'I think we need more spinners. At least ten times as many. And this suit... It's getting slower and slower.'

And for once that isn't me...

'Well, we've followed all the manuals... it *ought* to be working...'

Maybe. But it isn't.

He turned to his left and waited. A moment later – a four count this time – the suit turned with him.

'I don't understand this,' he said. 'There's no reason why it should be so slow. A fraction of a second maybe... and even that would be critical, but four, five seconds? Something's not connected.'

'Everything's connected, Jake. Exactly as it was in the manuals.'

'Then maybe the manuals are wrong. Where did you get them?'

Again there was the sound of distant voices as they consulted, then Kurt's voice filled his head. 'We're looking into that.' Kurt sighed. 'You want to come out or stay in a bit longer?'

Jake considered that. Was there any point in staying in? If they'd set the datscape up wrongly...

It wasn't the colour or the shape of things, he realized suddenly. It was the smell. This virtual landscape had no smell to it, whereas the original...

'This isn't right,' he said. 'Where's the olfactory feed?'

Kurt answered him at once. 'There isn't one. We didn't think it necessary. Gustav wanted to simplify, so—'

'Gustav?'

'Yes, he didn't think—'

'You don't think chemical reactions *smell*?'

'Well, maybe, only—'

'Only what?' Jake was getting angry now. He had begun the day afraid that he was going to fuck up. 'Gods, Kurt, is there no real understanding of what this is? This isn't just a toy, a computer simulation. It's an RR, a reality replicant. Everything has to be there in the mix, whether it seems pertinent or not. Because, if you're going to work these simulations properly, then you can't leave any factors out. Stripping down isn't the answer. It doesn't make things more efficient. Not one tiny bit. What it does is falsify things. Look, if we're going to use this technology, we need it to be perfectly mapped – one-to-one. And this fucking suit! For fuck's sake... ! Have we *no one* in the company who can do something about it?'

There was a moment's embarrassed silence at what he'd said, and then Kurt chuckled. 'Okay, Jake... we hear you... loud and clear...'

'Good. Because I'm done here for now. Get Alison on the line, will you? I need to speak to her, right away.'

'Whatever you say, Jake. Whatever you say.'

★

Mary found her stepson, Peter, out on the patio, drinking *ch'a* and watching the news on the big screen that hung from the end rail.

'What's this, another victory?'

Peter turned to her and smiled. 'Yeah... It broke late last night. I'd have woken you, only...'

Mary smiled. Tom was teething and she wasn't getting much sleep, so they were all under orders not to wake her unless for something urgent.

She went across and sat, taking in the scene on the screen. 'So where's this?'

'Richmond... it's the surrender ceremony. Look, there's Marshal Jiang.'

Jiang Lei stood there, tall and regal, resplendent in his marshal's uniform, at the top of the steps of the world-famous Jefferson Hotel. He had made it his campaign quarters.

'And those others, with the bared heads?'

'They're the conquered generals. He took eighty-six of them this time. Surrounded them at Greenville, just outside of Dallas, and made them kneel to him. Right now they're surrendering their colours.'

Mary nodded, then put her hand to her mouth to stifle a yawn. She had been following the campaign only vaguely.

'So it's the Kingdom of Texas who've surrendered?'

'And the Little Rock Enclave. They'd joined forces at the end. Both capitulated at the same time.'

'Ah...'

The camera closed in on Marshal Jiang, as the first of the Americans' colours began to be carried up the steps to be laid before him. As ever, he seemed to epitomize all that was admirable about the Han. Looking at him, one saw how, in his singular person, he was the very image of Chung Kuo: the archetypal Confucian scholar-warrior. The light to Tsao Ch'un's dark. Though that would never be said aloud.

'It's strange, isn't it?'

'What's that, Ma?'

'Seeing that man. Who would have thought...?'

It was true. Marshal Jiang had become the second most famous man on the planet, and not for his poetry, though sales of that were in their millions now.

The camera focused on his face, so calm and dignified. It had become a familiar sight on their screens these past three months as kingdom after kingdom had fallen to him. Disregarding today's victories, he had conquered all of the land between the Eastern Seaboard and the Mississippi River. All, that was, apart from Washington.

Mary looked down. That made no sense to her. Why couldn't they just go in and end the siege? That's what they did elsewhere, so why not Washington? She'd heard the arguments, of course – that the rebel armies would not have joined with them had he made his headquarters in Washington. How, by basing himself in Richmond, he had touched upon old enmities and won himself a dozen banners from the old Confederate states. She was sure that was so, only why maintain the pretence that Washington was holding out of its own accord? What purpose did it serve?

'How's the siege going?' she asked. 'Anything new happening?'

Peter shook his head. 'There have been skirmishes, but nothing serious.'

He changed the subject. 'How's Tom, by the way? Is he all right? I heard him grizzling in the night.'

'He gets fretful, that's all. All the girls were like that...'

'Were they?'

She nodded. 'I feel sorry for them, you know.'

'Who? The girls?'

'No. The Americans. It must be hard for them.'

'But necessary. And when it's done it's done.'

She looked to her stepson, surprised by the hardness that had come into his voice. She had heard the phrase before, of course. It was one of Tsao Ch'un's sayings and the media had taken it up. 'When it's done it's done', as if it were merely a case of finishing the job. The fact that they were killing all the blacks, the mentally deficient, the politically active and the old was never mentioned. But when Peter said it, it was the hardness in his face that troubled her.

Her daughters were the same. Where she saw suffering, they saw necessity. If the world was going to be at peace, they argued, then America had to be subdued and its people brought within the walls of Chung Kuo's City. It couldn't be left to chance.

But part of her still inwardly rebelled against what they were doing.

'Aren't you going in to College today?'

Peter smiled. 'I've got the day to revise. I'll just finish my *ch'a*, then I'll get down to it.'

'I'm waiting for a call from Jake. He was supposed to be going in this morning.'

'What... into the datscape?'

'First thing... I've been expecting the call for hours.'

Peter looked disappointed. 'He didn't say... when I spoke to him the other evening...'

'He probably didn't know. Not for sure. I only found out yesterday. I thought he was coming back for a few days, but he had to stay on.'

'You don't think anything could go wrong, do you?'

'No, it's just... I know how much it means to him. If something *were* to go wrong...'

And not just to him.

Peter shook his head, a half smile on his face. 'It's weird, thinking of him using all that old technology, after all this time...'

'He'll be fine.'

But after Peter had gone upstairs again, she sat there, worrying now that something *had* gone wrong. That was the other reason why she hadn't slept. Because today was what Jake had been working towards these past three months. The reason why they had seen so little of each other lately.

Switching off the screen, she looked about her. Everything was so neat and tidy, the lid closed over the swimming pool, the garden fresh and orderly.

They were high up where they were; their apartment one of only twenty-four on the whole of this deck. It wasn't quite First Level, but it was more than Mary had ever dreamed of owning.

There was just so much room here, compared to where they'd come from. A lot more room. She should have been happy that they didn't have neighbours crowded in on all sides, only strangely enough she missed that. And the house... well, it was lovely, luxurious most would have said, and the kids each had their own rooms. Only sometimes it felt as if they didn't fit. Most of the time, if she was honest about it. And the people!

Most of their neighbours were Han; successful businessmen and their wives and trophy children. They were bad enough, with their arrogant, aggressive ways, but the *Hung Mao* – those of them who aped the Han, anyway – were a lot worse. Snobs, the lot of them. New money, as they used to call it, and with the manners of pigs. She had stopped accepting dinner invites, only you couldn't help but bump into them from time to time, in the corridors or in the lifts. And the kids... She felt sorry for her girls. Sorry for Peter, too, because they'd lost most of their friends when they'd moved up here. It wasn't even as if they could go down the levels and see them from time to time. Peter and Meg lived the other side of Europe to their friends now. It was just too far.

Mary went back into the kitchen. She ought to have been preparing the evening meal, or getting a feed ready for Tom, only she was feeling a little depressed now. It was a feeling that visited her more and more recently, especially those times when the screens showed vistas from outside – rolling landscapes and mountains and rivers and the like. When she saw those, it created a longing in her that was almost a pain. Jake's absence didn't help. She missed him being there at night; missed their whispered conversations, the smell and touch of him, especially since he'd lost all that weight.

She smiled. As she did, the comset began to buzz.

'Hello?'

There was the briefest delay and then Jake's face appeared on the screen.

'Hi, sweetheart...'

'Hi, darling. How'd it go?'

'Not well. Not well at all. Like Tom, we've got teething troubles here. The bloody thing's so slow.'

'But you're okay?'

'I'm fine. But I'm going to have to stay on a day or two longer. It can't be helped. We want to try and iron things out. I'm sorry. I know you'll be disappointed by that, but...'

'No, no. I'm fine.'

'You sure? I can always have you flown out.'

She smiled at that. 'No... I don't want to distract you. And if I was there...'

'You would distract me.' Jake smiled. 'I've missed you.'

'Missed you too. You seen the news? Our friend Jiang Lei again. It was the Texans this time.'

'Who'd have thought it, eh? At this rate it'll be over by the year's end.'

'You think?'

Mary paused. She wanted to say so much, only she knew it was all being monitored. And besides, she didn't want anyone to know how she'd been feeling. Particularly Jake. No, she'd keep that to herself, until he was home.

'Look,' Jake said, glancing around as if someone had entered the room. 'I've got to go now, but I'll call you again tonight. Once things are tied up here. Have a good day, yes? And I love you.'

'Love you too.'

The screen blanked.

Mary looked down. Was it worth it? Was all this really worth it?

Some days she felt that maybe she had driven him into doing this. That her desire for a better life had made her pressurize him into taking the GenSyn job. Because now that she had it, she wasn't sure she wanted it.

She took a long breath, then, determined not to let it get her down, went to the cupboard and pulled out the wok. There was a lot to do before Tom woke, and she'd sure as hell get nothing done when he was awake again.

That was another thing. Jake kept telling her to get a maidservant. Like the house, they could afford it now. Only she didn't want someone else bringing Tom up. Hard as it was sometimes, she wanted to be there for him at every step. If she'd had another girl, maybe she'd have felt differently, but as it was...

She stood at the window, looking out at the garden. The view of distant mountains and a clear blue sky was artificial. She knew that. She was conscious of it every waking second. Only it was better than what she'd had. Those endless walls, close up and in your face. The crowded corridors and the constant buzz of noise.

Maybe they had climbed a bit too high. Maybe that was it. If they were a deck or two lower, maybe she'd have felt different about it all.

She pushed the thought aside, not wanting to dwell on it. There would be time enough to talk about it when Jake was home.

Lahm was busy pruning the tiny oak when the comsat in the corner flashed.

'What is it?' he asked, not glancing up.

'They've called a meeting, Master. Gustav Ebert's flying back in from Shanghai to attend.'

'Anything I should know?'

'Seems there's a signal delay, too few spinners, and... oh yes, our man lost his temper, especially about the lack of smell. He read them the riot act.'

Lahm looked up. 'Reed?'

'That's why Ebert's flying back. Their woman wanted to delay things another week.'

'I see.'

Then Reed's career – his second chance – was in the balance. Because Gustav Ebert was a perfectionist and, from past experience, if it didn't work 100 per cent, it would be ditched. Gustav didn't like imperfection and he didn't care about the expense.

'Send me the tape,' he said. 'And keep me advised as to when and where the meeting takes place.'

'Yes, Master.'

Lahm straightened, then set the tiny watering jug aside. He ought to have been getting ready. The reception was in an hour, and it was important that he be there, what with the new elections to the Council taking place next month. Only he felt out of sorts. Not in the mood to spend the afternoon pressing flesh and smiling at his enemies.

And there was no doubt he had enemies.

He spoke to the air.

'Wu Chi... have my craft ready for me on the roof. And tell Steward Jung to lay out my robes for me when I'm back.'

'As you wish, Master.'

Wu Chi was his AI, both here in his office and at home.

'Oh, and Wu Chi... see if you can find out what the initial thinking is at GenSyn over this morning's trial. Whatever you can... yes?'

'I'll report back to you, Master.'

'Good.'

Only Lahm had been having doubts about Wu Chi lately. About AIs in general. Not that they weren't the perfect servants. One couldn't fault them. After all, who knew him better than Wu Chi? Wu Chi never forgot a thing.

Only *that* was the problem. For if his AI fell into the wrong hands, what could incriminate him more?

Not that there were that many skeletons. But there were *some*, and, as he knew so well, a little could go a long way in discrediting a man. He knew it for a fact: the higher he had risen, the more rivals he had gained, and every last one of them would delight in pulling him down.

In certain hands, Wu Chi would make him vulnerable. Especially when it came to things he had sanctioned; things he might claim were the products of necessity.

Yes, those especially.

Lahm spoke to the air.

'Lock everything, Wu Chi. I'm out of here.'

As he climbed the stairs up to the landing pad, he found himself dwelling on it. Maybe it was time to speak to the First Dragon about this. Maybe they should shed their reliance on such things. Because what could be used against an individual could be used equally well against a Ministry, and if it were...

Lahm pushed the thought aside. Right now it was time to play another game. To dress up in his finery and put on his falsest smile.

For necessity. To keep the vultures from picking on his corpse.

Alison looked up at him as he entered the room and smiled apologetically.

'I know, Jake. I know. You're not a happy bunny, are you?'

He took a chair, facing her across the desk. 'The suit... what in the gods' names went wrong?'

'I don't know. But we're taking steps. I'm drafting in two of our electronics whiz-kids. See if they can't come up with some answers.'

'And Gustav?'

She met his eyes. Her own were cold, blue steel. They'd always reminded him of that Joni Mitchell song.

'If Gustav wants in, Gustav gets in.'

'Fine. But as a scientist he must surely know—'

She interrupted him. 'You'll get a face to face with him, Jake. That's as much as I can promise you. But he's got a personal interest in this one, and he overrules you every time.'

Jake huffed, his frustration evident.

'Was it *that* bad?'

'It didn't come close. And unless it gets markedly better... Well, I don't think we've got a chance of using it. At least, not as Gustav wants to use it.'

'Do you think the answer is to throw more money at it? If it needs more resources, that's not a problem.'

'No?'

'No. But only if you think that's an answer. If you think we're wasting our time here...'

'You think I'd give in that easily?'

'Not for what we're paying you.'

'It isn't the money.'

'I know...' Alison looked down, then met his eyes again. 'I want this to work, Jake, every bit as much as you do. You could have a good future here at GenSyn. Follow your own research, if that's what you wanted to do. I could set you up in your own department. *If* this works.'

Jake sat back, grinning. 'Hey, slow down... Let's not think of running before we can walk. Money could be part of the answer. It'd mean we could get more spinners, and make the input side of it that much better. Sharpen things up and get some depth to it. But a lot of work needs doing on the suit. That more than anything. That's where we start.'

'And you, Jake?'

He was quiet a moment, then, 'I don't know. I still don't know. And until we get the rest of it right, I'll keep on not knowing. But I know one thing now. I'm not afraid of it any more.'

'Good. Then tell Gustav that when you see him.'

Peter set the revision folder aside, then climbed off the bed and went across to where he'd hung the map, on the noticeboard over his desk. There were twenty-four of the tiny dragon flags on the map now, all of them clustered on the eastern seaboard. Each one represented a state of the old US of A.

As yet the left-hand side of the map was empty. Out there, long trails of refugees were heading west along the old abandoned highways, in their hundreds of thousands, crossing the deserts because there was nowhere else to go. Not because there was any hope of a new and better life, but because they were afraid of what life under the Han would be like.

And because they were Americans.

If he'd been older he would have volunteered. Millions had. Mary and his father would have tried to talk him out of it, but he'd have gone, because he knew this was the final war. The war to end all wars. Quite literally so. For once Jiang Lei had finished, earth would be a single state; at peace, the dream made real. A perfect, orderly world, better than the old. A world free of imperfections.

It had taken him a long time to see it, but now he did. The campaign had helped. He understood now, and that new understanding forged all his future decisions.

Once he had his exams he would apply to GenSyn. He liked what he'd heard of them, especially first-hand from his dad. He already had the forms in the drawer of his desk. And he would spend a lifetime working for them, if he could. If GenSyn would have him.

As for Meg, he planned to marry her when he was twenty-one, as the law set down. They would have children together and climb the levels. That was his ambition now. That was why, twice a week, he spent the evening at the Institute for Linguistic Studies, polishing his Mandarin. Because that was what mattered now. The kind of thing that would help him get on.

For a time he had suffered. He had been locked into the past, unable to escape the weight of past memories, but now he was free of it. Now he saw that even the worst of it had meaning.

Like the death of Boy...

That too he understood. There had been a place for Boy, back in the old world, but in the new... no. Boy would have suffered here. And it would have been wrong to let him suffer. Even so, the thought of it still saddened him.

There was a knock on the door.

'Peter? Do you want some tea?'

He went across and opened the door. Mary stood there, Tom snuggled in against her shoulder.

'I'll come down... You want me to take him?'

'Would you? I don't want to disturb your studies.'

'It's fine. I'm taking a break. Here... come on, you rascal...'

Tom reached for him, clung on, all warm and snugly.

'Mary?'

'Yes, my love?'

'I can't wait to have my own.'

She smiled, then reached out to ruffle his hair. 'You'll be a good father, Peter. I think my girl is very lucky to have you.'

★

Jake looked about him, impressed by the changes that had been made.

'Now this is better...'

The datscape he was used to had a floor. This, because of the nature of the experiment, was more like a giant fish tank.

'You were right about the smell,' Ebert said, drifting up alongside him. 'It's small things like that that we need to get used to. Experimentally, we're used to simplifying to get an answer, but this demands the exact opposite, just as you said.'

Gustav Ebert was a tidy little man, with brushed-back steel-grey hair and the lithe muscular figure of a man who maintained himself at the peak of fitness. So he was in life and so he was in this avatar. 'No frills' as he said. He had no desire to be anything other than himself.

A mere three days had passed since that first abortive attempt. In between times Ebert had thrown both men and money at the project, making them work twenty-four hours a day to get the thing up and running as it ought.

And this was the result.

Ebert looked to him. 'So how does it compare?'

Jake turned. This time the suit moved with him. Not exactly – there was still the very slightest of delays – but it was workable. A few final adjustments ought to do the trick.

But it was the datscape itself that was strikingly different. Before it had been a cartoon of itself, but now it had texture and richness. *Depth*.

'It's almost there,' Jake said, reaching out to brush the surface of a nearby object, a veined, flesh-coloured thing which pulsed and glowed. 'What is this, by the way?

Ebert edged alongside him again, reaching out to touch the thing, his gloved hand sinking into the surface a little way.

'This, Jake, is an enzyme.'

'Ah...'

Jake had done his homework. Enzymes were the biomolecules that catalysed the rate of chemical reactions in the body. Like all catalysts, they worked by lowering the activation energy for a reaction. They were, however, very specific – the keys to biochemistry's locks, so to speak – and their activity was governed entirely by their shape. They were known to catalyse roughly four thousand different biochemical reactions. In fact, no complex chemical reaction occurred in life without them.

It was all a long way from stocks and shares. A long way from futures and the markets he had been used to.

Jake edged back, away from the enzyme, taking in the complex mass of shapes that surrounded it. From a little way back, it looked like a giant explosion of brightly coloured wood-shavings. Living, pulsing shavings, true, yet the impression stuck. Right now he couldn't tell it from any other cluster of living shapes, but he would, given time. And not just by its shape. It had, he realized, a very distinct smell.

Jake smiled. For the first time he felt really positive.

'This is good,' Ebert murmured. 'Very good. I can see already how we could use this.'

He turned, drifting out slightly, gazing towards Jake again, his plain black clothes making him look like a ninja.

'What do you think, Jake? Biochemistry's very complex. More complex than any market. Do you think this system – this datscape – can handle that order of complexity, or are we going to have to beef it up? Take it to the next level?'

Jake laughed. 'You know, I was thinking... the simple act of programming this is going to take forever. But... once it's done, you won't have to keep feeding it new information. Just use what's already stored. And you would be able to be specific about what you used. What you're looking for, I take it, are things you don't expect. Reactions you couldn't have predicted.'

For the first time that morning, Ebert smiled. It was a frosty smile, as brittle as glass, but a smile all the same.

'That's precisely what I'm looking for. The unexpected. Not the usual metabolic pathways, but whole new ones. Things we can then go on to use commercially.'

'Then you have your answer already. This, good as it is, would be totally inadequate. Think about it. You're planning to map out biochemistry itself. To put every last tiny bit of it in the mix. For that you're going to have to take this system apart and refashion it. You've got to make it a lot more subtle; to make it a much more accurate reflection of reality. Yes, that's right. Reality. Only giant size. Reality you can walk around and through, yes?'

Ebert nodded. His eyes were glowing now as he looked at Jake. 'That's *precisely* what I want. And you'll help me get that?'

'Yes.'

Jake looked back at the complex shape that hung there pulsing before his eyes, and smiled. 'You know what? I'd forgotten what a high this was.'

Prince Ch'eng I was twenty-two and, being the fifth son of the Head of Minor Family, he was to have a grand ball that evening to celebrate his betrothal to the beautiful Princess Teng Liang, with only the elite of the elite invited.

Ch'eng I's father, Ch'eng So Yuan, was not a real prince. His ancestors had not even been aristocrats. But they had been high-ranking members of the Chinese Communist Party, and in the final years of their power, when they had made the deal with Tsao Ch'un that had spelt the end of their own kind, he had granted them the title. He let them keep their accumulated wealth while offering them protection from the common law that ruled all other citizens. They were thus a special class, affluent and refined, but powerless, like winged drones on the hottest day of summer.

Powerless, yet still influential.

Ch'eng So Yuan was an avuncular big man, well-liked among his own class. That in itself was unusual, for there were many camps within the court and many potential reasons therefore for disliking such a high-ranking prince as he. Nevertheless, he was liked, partly because he never carried a grudge and partly because he gave the best parties in the whole of Chung Kuo. Parties that went on for days. Legendary parties, famous for their debauchery.

Of camps something should be said. How many? More than a dozen but less than fifty was the informed guess, but only four of them really mattered, and everyone, it seemed, was a member of at least one.

That morning, even as Prince Ch'eng I stood at his mirror trying to decide whether to wear the peach silk or the turquoise, Lahm was stepping down from the jet-black Ministry craft, walking out onto the windswept landing pad. He smiled and then bowed respectfully to Ch'eng I's father, who stood just across from him.

Ch'eng So Yuan smiled, then returned the bow.

'Tobias... I am so glad you could come, dear friend. How are you?'

Lahm embraced the older man, then stepped back. 'I am well, Prince Ch'eng. I still get the headaches, but...'

Ch'eng So Yuan nodded, as if he understood, then turned, indicating that they should go inside.

Leiyang, Prince Ch'eng's palace, was not as impressive as Tongjiang, nor was it anything like as large, but it *was* outside. That was another thing the Minor Families shared with Tsao Ch'un, Shepherd and the Seven – the right to live outside the City's walls. Less than two *li* from where they stood, the City rose from the plain, running clear into the distance where, in the east, at the extremity of vision, one could see the peaks of the Lo Hsiao Shan, misted in the dawn's light.

'I'm glad you came early,' Prince Ch'eng said, as they walked slowly down the path that threaded its way through the water gardens. 'I wanted to talk to you. About the project.'

Lahm nodded. The comment seemed vague, but Lahm knew precisely which project Prince Ch'eng meant. He was talking about the clones. About GenSyn's attempts to breed viable human copies.

Not *'breed'*, Lahm corrected himself in his head. *Grow.*

'I've set aside an hour for our discussions.'

'An hour?' Lahm was surprised. Particularly on a day like today, when all manner of things needed to be attended to. 'Just you and I?'

'And a few close friends...'

'Ah...' *Other princes, he means. Members of his so-called 'golden brotherhood'. All of them hoping to benefit in some way from this.*

'But first... breakfast. You haven't eaten, I take it?'

Lahm smiled, letting the big man put an arm familiarly about his shoulders, smelling the scent of peppermint on his breath.

'Breakfast would be good, Prince Ch'eng. I have the appetite of a fox.'

Halfway around the world it was night. In the grand suite of the Jefferson Hotel, two men were sat playing *wei ch'i* on a carved oak board.

The game was halfway through, but already it was decided.

'Do you want to play on?' Jiang Lei asked, smiling, knowing for a certainty now that he was beaten. 'It seems... how should I put it... fairly obvious that you've won.'

Shepherd looked up from the board and returned the smile. 'I was thinking,' he said.

'Thinking?'

'About the next phase of the campaign. I think we should switch things. Do the unexpected.'

'Which would be?'

'To establish a new bridgehead, on the north-western seaboard. Three separate armies. Vancouver, Seattle and Portland. We take those cities and spread out, linking up to form a single block, from the Pacific to the Rockies.'

Jiang sat back a little, the game forgotten. 'Why the change of plan?'

'To allow us to consolidate, here in the east. And to keep things fresh. Our men need a challenge. And a change of air.'

'Let me think about it...'

'Fine. But not for too long. Chung Kuo's public expects...'

Jiang Lei looked down, not seeing the board, staring instead at the map in his head. It made good sense to change things about. To slow things down here and distract their enemies with a new front. And they did need to consolidate. There'd been an increase in acts of terrorism this last month, so that too needed to be dealt with. But three separate armies...

As if reading his mind, Amos answered him. 'Three separate attacks will make it far harder for them to call on their neighbours for assistance. It'll mean they'll be watching their backs, looking to see whether the others are still fighting on or have capitulated. In short, it'll put the shits up them. Three new bridgeheads... they won't be expecting that.'

Jiang Lei nodded. He could almost sense the despair in his enemies' camps. Their time was up and they knew it. Even so, they were determined to fight on. To the last man.

'Okay,' Jiang said, after a moment. 'But one alteration to your scheme. We send a force inland. To Spokane. A fourth bridgehead, to which the other three might link. While the others are fighting their way inland, that fourth force could push inward from the east. We could squeeze our enemies between them.'

Shepherd smiled. 'A good old-fashioned pincer movement, eh? I like it, Jiang. It'll put the pressure on. We could drive them south. Imagine it... refugees flooding California from the north as well as the east. It'll stretch them thin, see if it doesn't!'

Jiang Lei nodded. Only he wasn't smiling now. He was thinking of the suffering this new phase would create. Of all the families driven from their homes, and their young men dying by the hundred thousand. And for what?

For the idea of America.

'Okay,' he said quietly. 'That's what we'll do. I'll notify Tsao Ch'un.'

'P'eng Chuan... how delightful to see you...'

The great hall at Leiyang was packed. So much silk and jewellery had not been seen for many a year.

Lahm bowed as P'eng joined their circle.

'Master Lahm...'

P'eng Chuan was no friend of Lahm's. As Sixth Dragon in the Ministry, he was nominally Lahm's superior. What's more, he was connected. His wife was a Minor Family princess and two of his brothers had married similarly. But it was his nephew, P'eng K'ai-chih, who was the thorn in Lahm's side, for P'eng was looking to get his brother's boy elected in Lahm's place. He was using his family's considerable wealth and influence to try to prise it from Lahm's grasp.

P'eng looked about him at the others, then addressed Lahm again, his manner sneering, arrogant.

'I'm told GenSyn are having problems with their latest project, Master Lahm.'

Lahm bristled. It was not the kind of thing one said at such a gathering. The arsehole clearly meant to provoke him.

'Really?' he answered, smiling, as if at a friend. 'How so?'

'The man they've hired... one of yours, I'm told... has proved too old, too slow... all rather a waste of time, neh, cousin?'

Lahm looked down. It was outrageous! To discuss his business, out in the open! What did P'eng mean by this? Besides, it wasn't true. Not if what Wu Chi had said was so. And why shouldn't it be?

'Forgive me, P'eng Chuan, but I fear your source is quite mistaken. Things are well. Master Ebert is now involved and—'

P'eng interrupted him brutally. 'I think you've backed a dud, Master Lahm. It's Ebert's money, I know, but if I were him...'

He made a gesture of pulling the plug. The others in the circle laughed.

Lahm took a long breath, then met P'eng's eyes again. 'But you are *not* him... fortunately...' He bowed, then stepped away. 'Forgive me, *ch'un tzu*, but—'

Again P'eng interrupted. 'And the suits... immersion suits, I believe they're called... old, worn-out technology...'

Lahm checked himself. P'eng had a reason for this. He *wanted* to draw Lahm into an argument. Wanted him to make a scene.

'Another time, P'eng Chuan,' he said, with an air of great civility. 'Why don't you come and see me. I would be glad to talk of such matters.'

P'eng watched him bow, then bowed in return. 'Time will tell, neh, Master Lahm? Time will tell.'

As Lahm made his way across the crowded hall, looking for Ch'eng So Yuan, so the Sixth Dragon's words took on the shape of a threat.

You're up to something, you bastard. You and your agents.

Should he warn Ebert? Or was he just being paranoid?

Later, he told himself. *I'll speak to him later.*

As for P'eng Chuan, the man could fuck himself, long and hard.

'Kurt... slow things down. One-tenth speed... and Kurt?'

'Yes, Jake?'

'Cut the sound. All but the discreet channel. I'll lift my arm and wave when we need to be retrieved.'

Jake smiled to himself. He knew Kurt hated being out of touch. He was one of those Chief Techs who liked to talk everything through. It reassured him. But Jake wanted to concentrate, and how could he do that with the Chief Tech's voice in his ear all the time?

Besides, harsh as it was, what Gustav had said earlier was right. They really could do with a new Chief Tech. Someone who could juggle things a lot better than Kurt did. Someone with a lot more mental agility.

Jake turned slowly. Now that they had fine-tuned it, it was like being in free fall, a non-gravity environment. But that would have to change, because gravity was yet another of those factors they couldn't rule out. It existed in the outside world, so it had to be in here, too.

Only he liked this. Liked how it made him feel.

Ebert was on the far side of the giant bio-morph, checking to see if it mapped. Making sure they had left nothing out. Jake could see the bottom of his legs, drifting beneath the outrageous shape.

He made to speak, then realized that Kurt had closed the channels down already. It was silent in the datscape – eerily silent.

At one-tenth speed, the pulse within the living cells was slow now – more a gradual change of colour than a pulse.

Slow it down some more and you'll be able to see the precise nature of each chemical reaction.

Which is just what Gustav wanted, and the reason why he spent half of his time now inside the immersion.

Jake smiled. For all his coldness, he liked Gustav Ebert. Liked the purity of the man, his obsessive streak. Ebert wasn't one for half measures. When he went for something, he went for it hook, line and sinker.

Which was why, only two hours back, he had allocated a further billion *yuan* to the project.

The figure staggered Jake. After all, what was this but some kind of super-toy?

That was unfair, of course, because who knew what seeing biochemical reactions like this might do? And if a man as outrageously talented as Gustav Ebert thought it might work – might stimulate whole new branches of study – then who was he to argue? He was just a web-dancer, after all.

Right now Ebert was very still, watching something very carefully. Jake had not been with him inside that often, but he knew how still he went when he was concentrating. Like he was hibernating, his burning eyes the only sign of life.

Slowly Jake drifted round, following a lazy curve that arced behind Ebert's back.

This one was like a giant jellyfish, its skin thick and translucent, threads of ever-changing red and blue running through it.

He and Ebert had talked it all through, earlier. Of the need to have two or three, maybe even a dozen of these datscapes up and running, with teams of experts, each specializing in some separate branch of biochemistry, working the immersions.

It was a huge commitment. A massive investment of time and money.

GenSyn could afford it. Of course they could.

Only it's a gamble. A huge fucking gamble.

Ebert knew that too. He'd said as much to his brother.

Wolfgang Ebert was the cautious one of the two, the businessman, but after a gruelling four-hour meeting, even he was convinced. This could well be the future, and GenSyn couldn't afford *not* to invest in it.

Jake opened the discreet channel.

'Is it all there?'

Gustav made the slightest movement. For a moment he didn't answer, then he gave a little grunt. 'I don't know. Something's missing. Something's nagging at me, but I don't know what.'

The bio-morph was incredibly complex. Much more complex than the enzyme they had studied days before. It was one of Gustav's experimental biomechanisms, an adaptation of the Hox gene clusters which were found in the genes of creatures with segmented body plans. They were a universal thing, so Gustav said, but he had given them a tweak or two to make them specific. He claimed that he was trying to reinvent evolution by coming up with different answers to common biochemical questions.

Only something was missing.

He drifted level with Ebert, studying the huge, glaucous object that hung there. He couldn't read it. Not yet. It would probably be months before he could. Only that wasn't the point. He was here to train up those who could. To turn budding young biochemists into athletes – the gymnasts of the datscape.

There was the faintest flicker, to his left.

Jake turned his head to look. A delay. He felt it. Like grit beneath a sliding door, hampering its movement.

'Gustav...?'

The sudden surge jolted him. The whole datscape pulsed.

Jake made to lift his arm. Couldn't.

Cut the fucking thing now!

He felt the left arm of his suit go numb, the left side of his body, down to the hip. Jake tried to speak, but that too was shut down.

The fucking suit's malfunctioning!

It couldn't be. They'd had it checked out. Debugged it.

There was another flicker. Faint, barely noticeable. And then the power surged through him again, like a burning in his veins.

Oh, shit!

He blacked out. When he came to there was a chatter in his head, Kurt's voice close to panic. Across from him two black-suited techs part jerked, part swam towards him, their movements awkward.

Jake sniffed. Nothing. He couldn't smell a thing. But his skin felt strangely dry. It tingled, like he'd been too long under the ultraviolet.

'What the fuck...?'

Kurt answered him. 'Jake? Are you conscious?'

He ignored the obviousness of the answer.

'What the fuck happened?'

Some movement had returned to the suit. Only he felt like a cripple, able only to jerk himself round a bit at a time.

'Kurt? Are you all right?'

Christ! Was the man crying?

'He's dead, Jake. Gustav's dead!'

There was no arguing with it. Gustav was dead. Someone had put 50,000 volts through him and fried him like a piece of pei ching duck. That flicker, the moment before the power surge, Jake recognized it from before, from that day years ago when it had all fallen apart. Someone had intruded on their system. Created a wormhole somehow and jumped right in there with them, then opened up the power tap. Jake had only survived because the surge had been directed straight at Ebert.

Jake lay there now, in the sterile suit, suspended in the hammock-like emergency web, pumped full of painkillers. His skin was crisped black in places, a bright unhealthy orange in others and his eyes hurt, like the onset of a migraine. But compared to Ebert he had got off lightly.

Which of GenSyn's rivals might have done this? Which of them would have benefited most?

Dozens of them. Every last biochemical company there was, in fact. Only Jake wasn't sure that this *was* a simple case of industrial espionage. Whoever had done this hadn't underestimated GenSyn's capabilities. They had wanted Ebert not merely dead but unreconstructable.

GenSyn's own security had arrived within minutes, shutting things down and hauling people off for questioning, a distraught Wolfgang Ebert supervising every last detail of the investigation.

While that was happening, the medics had seen to Jake; had dosed him up and let the neurosurgeon take a look at what the surge had done to his brain. Now he waited for the news.

Mary arrived an hour later, masked up and wearing a sterile suit. She winced as she saw the extent of Jake's injuries.

'Oh, Jake...'

'I'm fine.'

'Is he dead?' she asked. 'There have been rumours... on the news channels...'

'Yes.'

'Ah...' She took a step towards him and then stopped. 'I'm not supposed to come any closer.'

He gave the faintest nod.

'What's going to happen, Jake?'

'I don't know.' He paused, looking past her. Mary turned. It was Alison. She stood there in the doorway, masked up, her sterile suit identical to Mary's.

Her cold blue eyes were concerned. 'Are you okay, Jake?'

'Yeah, I... Mary, this is Alison... Alison...'

The two women nodded to each other.

Alison switched her attention back to Jake. 'Does it hurt?'

'I can't tell... I'm feeling numb right now. What's happening out there?'

'Things are bad.'

'How d'you mean?'

She was quiet a moment.

'*What?*' he asked.

'I suppose you'll hear it sooner or later...'

'Hear *what?*' Mary asked, a hardness in her voice.

Alison kept her eyes on Jake. 'It's Wolfgang. He blames you. I know, it's irrational, but he's been saying that if you hadn't shown Gustav the potential of this he'd not have been so vulnerable.'

'How the fuck did we know he was vulnerable? I thought this was a closed circuit. I didn't think anyone else *had* access!'

'Well, they clearly did. And more to the point, it's not the first time it's happened, is it?'

'I didn't warn him at all. I thought...'

Jake stopped, took a breath. Alison was looking at him strangely. She clearly had more news, and none of it good.

'So what's he going to do? Sue me? Look at me. Do I look as if I had anything to do with it? I could have died in there, too!'

Alison looked down again. 'He wanted to sack you, Jake. Cast you off without a single *yuan* in compensation, but I got you a package. It's not enough to maintain the lifestyle you've got, but...'

'You think I should take it, yes?'

Alison nodded. 'I think you should. You don't fight a man like Wolfgang Ebert. You can't possibly win. But I did what I could for you, Jake. I got you the best deal possible, in the circumstances.'

Jake looked to Mary. 'What do you think?'

She hesitated. 'I think you should take it.'

'So that's it, then? Finished. Just like that?'

'I'm sorry, Jake. I really am. But things are bad right now. Losing Gustav... it wiped 40 per cent off our share price at a stroke. We'll survive. Only it'll take some while for us to recover. It was a massive blow. Whoever did this knew what they were doing.'

'You have no idea who it was?'

She hesitated, then shook her head, only there was something in her eyes that argued otherwise – that she knew *precisely* who had done this.

Which meant that she couldn't say, not with the cameras watching.

Jake took a long, shuddering breath. He was tired now. He wanted to sleep. A deal... yes, he'd take their deal. Take it and get out of there. Once he was better. Once the skin grafts had taken and he could move again.

Lahm was sitting in the back of the craft and humming an old Polish folk tune to himself as he returned home, when the news came through.

He sat there for a long while afterwards, stunned, unable to come to terms with what this meant for his plans.

His enemies had struck a damaging blow. The deals he'd hoped to make had unravelled in a moment. Without GenSyn he had nothing. Or as good as nothing. For who would oversee the project, now that Gustav was dead?

No. GenSyn without Gustav Ebert were no better than a dozen other companies in the same field. They might have a slight advantage now – what with their more *specialized* items – but how long would that last?

Not long, if what the market thought had any influence on it. Rumour had it that two of their major rivals had already made bids to try to buy GenSyn out, while they were at their weakest.

And Reed?

Reed now was simply an embarrassment. He was the man who had delivered Ebert up to his enemies. Not that he'd known that. Not that any of them had known.

Not true, he thought. *P'eng Chuan had known.*

Lahm nodded slowly. Yes, that was what lay behind all of his unpleasantness earlier. He had known about this. Someone had tipped him off. But who?

Lahm considered it a while, identifying three possible men who might have ordered it, then let it go. What was done was done. Even so...

'Wu Chi...?'

Wu Chi's voice answered him at once, filling the darkness of the craft.

'Yes, Master?'

'Reed... have someone deal with him. And be discreet. I don't want any trails leading back to me, understand?'

'Yes, Master. It is as good as done.'

Lahm leaned back and closed his eyes. He would have to begin again. To rebuild, slowly, patiently, as was his way. It was no good panicking. No good letting men like P'eng Chuan get to him. He had not come this far by making over-hasty decisions. He would sit back and wait for those he knew to come to him, to ask him what to do, now that things had changed.

It was a setback, true enough, but it was not a defeat.

That said, it was a shame about Reed. He had genuinely liked the man. But it was no good being sentimental. To let Reed live – to leave any loose ends – would be merely careless now, and he was not known as a careless man.

Intrigues. The world was a web of intrigues.

He smiled, hearing the AI's voice in memory.

As good as done.

Jiang Lei had just bathed and dressed for dinner when word came through from Pei Ching.

It was his old friend, Hsü Jung.

'Cousin Lei!' Hsü said breathlessly. 'I have urgent news!'

Jiang waved his hand to dismiss the two servants who hovered nearby, then settled before the screen.

'Speak, dear friend. What could possibly have made you so flushed?'

'It is Reed, Jiang Lei.'

'I heard. The accident.'

'Yes, but...'

Jiang frowned. Why did Hsü Jung hesitate? It wasn't like him. He usually came straight out with things.

Hsü Jung bowed low, then, 'I fear to say this, Jiang... this being an open channel and therefore accessible to certain eyes and ears... only I must take the risk this once or see a good man die.'

'A good man?'

Hsü nodded. 'You asked me to keep an eye, remember?'

'Ah...' And now Jiang saw. 'Reed is in danger?'

'Of the worst kind. They have sent out a squad from the Thousand Eyes.'

'An execution squad?'

'The same, friend Jiang... the order was given ten minutes back.'

Jiang Lei grimaced. 'To have Reed killed? Who would do so?'

Again Hsü Jung hesitated. Again he took the risk.

'It was Lahm.'

'Lahm?' That in itself surprised him. He hadn't even known that Lahm had any interest in Reed. To instruct his men to have Reed killed – that puzzled Jiang.

Jiang Lei knew Lahm of old. Lahm had made his reputation as Director of the IHA, the Institute for Historical Accuracy – rewriting history for his Han masters. Now that he was a great man, he had made a new reputation enforcing that same history. But what had he to do with Reed?

'Are you sure of this, Hsü Jung?'

'Absolutely.'

'Then I must act at once.' Jiang smiled tightly. 'Thank you, old friend. Oh, and let me say this, for the benefit any listening ears. I, Tsao Chun's marshal, guarantee your protection. If anyone should dare touch a single hair on your head, I'll hunt them down. Is that clear?'

Hsü Jung bowed, smiling his gratitude. 'Marshal...'

As the screen blanked, Jiang Lei considered. Lahm, eh? How strange. He would not have thought Lahm interested in Reed, let alone stirred up enough to have him killed.

He clicked his fingers in the air. At once his aide appeared, bowing low in the doorway.

'Yes, Marshal Jiang?'

'I want a squad sent at once, to GenSyn's facility in Bremen. Specifically to the medical unit. They are to protect a man named Jake Reed who is a patient there.'

'He is in danger, Marshal?'

'In very great danger. The Ministry has sent a squad of their finest to eliminate him.'

'Ah...' The young man hesitated, then ran off to do the marshal's bidding.

Alone again, Jiang sat, steepling his hands together, as he often did when he was thoughtful.

Lahm. No. It made no sense. Why would Lahm be interested in Reed?

The truth was, he didn't know. But he would find out, now that he'd been alerted to the fact.

He stood, then walked through into Amos's suite.

Amos looked up at him from where he was seated in the corner, playing the three-dimensional *wei ch'i* game he had been sent only the day before.

'What is it, Jiang? You look troubled.'

Jiang quickly explained.

Shepherd nodded. 'I see... and you don't know why, neh?'

Jiang frowned. 'Should I?'

'Not at all, dear friend. Only... well, it pays sometimes to know a little of what's going on behind the scenes. Lahm... he's a major player. A very ambitious man. Pretends to be German in origin, but his father was a Pole. A devious sort. But then, aren't they all?'

Jiang stared at Shepherd a moment. 'When I went home that first time... before Tsao Ch'un appointed me... it was like that. A viper's nest, one of my friends called it.'

'And so it is. But Lahm... he was Reed's sponsor. It was his influence that got Reed the job at GenSyn.'

'Ah... but then why...?' Jiang paused. 'Ah, I see. And now he has no use for Reed... now that Gustav Ebert's dead.' He blew out a breath. 'But why not leave Reed be?'

'And have him fall into other hands? No. Lahm's a tidy man. He doesn't like loose ends. Besides, I think he enjoys it. Likes to think he has the power of life or death over men. I hear he watches tapes of his "executions". And he doesn't want to risk having anyone he's discarded fall into the wrong hands.'

'Then he is going to be disappointed this once.'

Amos stared at his friend a moment, then smiled. 'I guess he is. This once.'

Lahm touched his head to the floor for the third time, then raised himself to his feet, brushing down his dark grey cloak with his right hand.

'Master...'

'This business with GenSyn,' the First Dragon said, almost scowling as he said it. 'What has it cost us?'

Lahm had received the summons while he was still in the air. He'd had to turn right around and fly back to the First Dragon's palace. There, alone with the great man, he waited to learn his fate. But first these questions.

'The cost...?' Lahm totted things up in his head and almost shrugged. 'Fifty million *yuan*. Sixty tops.'

'Good,' the old man said, his voice a growl. 'Not too much wasted then. And the man? The web-dancer?'

'Dead, Master.'

This time the First Dragon smiled. A sickly, death's head of a smile. 'Not so. At least, not at this moment, anyway.'

Behind the First Dragon a screen lit up. On it, in clear view of the camera, was Reed, secure in his web-like hammock, a tangle of drips snaking down from the ceiling and entering his body at a dozen separate points.

As the camera drew back, Lahm could see soldiers, standing in a half circle about the room, facing the doors. Proper soldiers, not Ministry assassins.

'What the...? Where are our men?'

'Dead.'

'*Dead?*' Lahm could not believe it. 'Who would dare?'

'Marshal Jiang.'

'Marshal Jiang?' Lahm laughed. But the laughter died in his throat as he saw the First Dragon's face. He wasn't joking.

'But...'

The First Dragon nodded. 'It surprised me too, Tobias. Who could have done this? I wondered. Who would be interested in protecting such an insubstantial fellow? And then, when I learned it was Jiang Lei, I asked, what kind of hold has this man over the marshal?' .

'And?'

'And nothing. It seems Jiang Lei intervened once before, when Reed was in the camps. Saved him then.'

'Ah...' And now that he thought of it, he remembered. 'But how did he find out?'

The First Dragon leaned forward. 'That I don't know. Yet. But I shall. And when I do...'

'Can't we send in another squad?'

'And fight our own army? You think Tsao Ch'un would sanction that?'

Lahm lowered his head. Perhaps not. But why had Jiang intervened? What did he stand to gain through his actions? Was he, perhaps, in P'eng Chuan's pay?

He looked up again, pretending to be humble before the old man.

'What should we do, Master?'

'Do? We do nothing, Tobias. We let the man live. Chances are he knows nothing about the project anyway. And that's all that matters, isn't it?'

It was. But, travelling back once more, Lahm could not work it out. Why had the marshal intervened? Why had he sent his troops against the Ministry's? Was it old-fashioned spite? Or something else? For the truth was, no man acted in a purely altruistic fashion. Not at the level on which they both functioned.

Leave it now, part of him insisted. *You did what you should and, even if you failed, it was through no fault of your own. Besides, your Master does not blame you for that failure.*

It ought to have been enough. Only this once it wasn't. Being outmanoeuvred by P'eng Chuan was one thing – and he would have his revenge for it – but this second, more trivial matter...

Lahm hated being robbed of his satisfaction. Hated even the slightest hint that he had lost his touch. It did not matter that his special relationship with the First Dragon protected him from criticism. He was his own worst critic. And to be outflanked by Jiang Lei of all people. It was unthinkable.

He would have the man, hero or not. He would fucking have him, see if he didn't. Once all of this bullshit had finished in North America.

He let out a long, shivering breath, unclenching his hands and letting the tension drain from him.

He could wait. Wasn't patience his byword, after all?

Lahm smiled. And he would have Reed too while he was at it. Reed and all his precious fucking family!

There, where the Great Wall ended and the sea began, Tsao Ch'un had his palace – the Black Tower as it was known, an impregnable fortress built from black marble. It was a massive building, dominating the landscape for miles about, like a vast outcrop of basalt jutting out into the sea.

Right now, Tsao Ch'un sat in the uppermost level, leaning back in his chair, his left hand stroking his chin.

Outside, beyond the thick glass of the wall-length viewing windows, the night was dark, the merest fingernail of moon poised above the placid surface of the Po-hai Sea.

Facing the great man, surrounded by the eight huge marble pillars that supported the roof of the tower, was a bank of screens, six long and four deep, each one five ch'i to a side.

Each showed a different image.

Here one might see how Chung Kuo functioned. For here, and nowhere else, one might watch the great and the good in all their devious glory.

Long ago, in a moment of utter clarity (one might say of brilliant anticipation), Chao Ni Tsu had come up with this. He had provided his Master with the means of spying upon his inner circle, his so-called 'trusted men', using the very best in ADT – 'Anti-Detection Technology' – to achieve it. Clever stuff which, if anyone sought to detect it, would switch itself off, becoming unimportant to any probe. Cutting technology which, once it was put in place, was then 'forgotten' – its creators murdered in their beds to prevent even the vaguest hint of its existence from leaking out.

Tsao Ch'un smiled. The screens comforted him. Made him feel safe. In a world of endless betrayals, this much at least he could trust.

He eased forward a little, pressing the touch-sensitive pads on the arm rest. With a tap he could change images, or focus in on one of the massive screens, dimming the rest while one stood out clear and sharp. Just now, however, he was content to let his gaze roam from one screen to another, seeing with his own eyes how Ebert's assassination had stirred things up.

He laughed quietly. It was a regular hornet's nest tonight. Why, he had not seen so much activity for a long, long while.

Ebert's death had come completely out of the blue. Not a single one of them had known it was coming. Now they were trying to find out just what was going on, calling in their spies and consulting their advisors, anxious, in varying degrees, not to be overtaken by events.

Tsao Ch'un smiled. Let them try. They were chasing shadows. Not even the great Lord of Intrigue himself, the First Dragon, had the slightest lead as to why Gustav Ebert had been killed, much as the great man prided himself on knowing everything. But that did not surprise him, for what the First Dragon did not know – what he would never have suspected in his wildest, darkest dreams – was just how far events were shaped by Tsao Ch'un: how every single strand of their intrigues was spun from the darkness of this room, like the threads of a giant web.

Tsao Ch'un glanced across. Chao Ni Tsu was sleeping in his chair, his ash-white hair combed back from his wrinkled face. In his late seventies now, he slept a lot these days. But Tsao Ch'un still liked to have him there, useful or not, if only as a reminder of the old days, when the two of them had taken on the world and beaten it.

Yes. It was Chao who had devised this system. Chao who had given him the means by which he might control and shape it all.

It was all quite simple, really. To rule such a host of mightily ambitious men he had had to ensure that they never became his rivals. Their own, certainly, but never *his*. Which was why, over the years, Tsao Ch'un had spun intrigue after intrigue, setting one against another, keeping them at each other's throats and away from his.

What delighted him most, however, was the fact that they thought themselves completely unobserved, safe from all watching eyes.

Tsao Ch'un sat back, taking in everything.

On screen, the First Dragon yawned, then stood and came around his desk. It was his habit on most nights to send for a meal of shrimps and freshly baked bread, only tonight the old man seemed to have no appetite. He was troubled. The interview with Lahm had puzzled him.

As it ought.

P'eng Chuan, Lahm's rival, was the obvious suspect, especially after what he'd said to Lahm earlier in the day. But he too seemed greatly troubled. He paced his bedchamber, ignoring the two young boys who lay there, naked beneath the silks, whilst he spoke to his AI. Sending out queries and getting back reports, striving to discover just who had struck the killing blow, and why.

That why, of course, puzzled them all. Were BioMek the culprits? They would certainly benefit from the fallout more than any others. Only it seemed unlikely. To assassinate a rival, that wasn't their style.

Prince Ch'eng So Yuan, whose image was on the screen beneath P'eng Chuan's, was clearly not to blame. Unless, of course, he had taken something to steady his nerves, for he slept like a baby, his great fat belly rising and falling like some huge silken pillow inflating and deflating.

No. Prince Ch'eng was innocent. But then, Tsao Ch'un *knew* that. Knew what they all didn't know, Amos Shepherd included.

Amos himself was on the screen in the top right corner, the back of his head to the camera as he sketched his friend, the marshal. Another view of the same scene – focusing on Jiang Lei – could be seen three down and one in from the right.

Maybe he should call Amos and let him in on what was happening. Then again, why spoil his fun? Amos would enjoy working it out. That was, if he hadn't started already.

Tsao Ch'un smiled. Wormholes. There were wormholes everywhere, and had been for years, ever since Chao Ni Tsu put them there.

He looked back at the screen, his eyes going to Wolfgang Ebert – three squares in and two down, near the centre of the screen. Ebert had just stepped into a room, a place of white tiles and echoing voices. Tsao Ch'un frowned, trying to work out where exactly he was, then understood. He was in the mortuary. He had come to pay his last respects to his dead brother. At least, to what was left of him.

He switched cameras, wanting to see his face.

At once the angle changed. Now he was looking up past the edge of the gurney into Wolfgang's face.

That face, which was normally so hard, so uncompromising, right now was broken and vulnerable, tears dripping from those cold blue eyes as he witnessed what they had done to his brother.

'Bastards...'

Ebert knew already how it had been done. Knew now that the datscape had already been 'infected' when they'd bought it – riddled with wormholes that had been made to seem part of the machine's basic programming.

He knew how, but not why. None of them knew why.

Tsao Ch'un looked down to where his hands rested on the arms of the chair.

By such means had he neutered his enemies in the past, rendering their technology unusable. Shutting them down and controlling them, without them knowing what he had done. The Russians and the Americans... anyone, in fact, who had tried to oppose him.

But rarely so spectacularly.

Tsao Ch'un flexed his hands, then looked back at the screen.

In the bottom left-hand square, Li Chao Ch'in, one of Tsao Ch'un's seven closest advisors, was in his study in Tongjiang, seated at his desk, talking on the screen to his fellow advisor, Tsu Chen. The two were discussing the attack on GenSyn, trying to make sense of it. Only they too were at a loss.

For once that pleased Tsao Ch'un. It meant that his little ploy had worked. For if those two who were closest to him knew nothing...

He stood, tired of it all suddenly.

Maybe. But what of Lahm?

Tsao Ch'un glanced at Lahm's image on the screen, then scowled. He had grown tired of Lahm and his antics. Tired of the way the man behaved. Tired of his pompous posturing and his vindictiveness. Lahm thought himself superior to all. Thought himself a grand master of intrigue. But this once he'd been shown up.

'Clear the screens...'

At once the screens went blank. The room was in heavy shadow.

Tsao Ch'un walked over to the window and stood there, looking out across the troubled surface of the sea. A storm was blowing. If he'd wanted to, he could have gone out onto the balcony and felt its fury on his face and arms; could have listened to the waves breaking on the rocks beneath the tower. He often did, when sleep would not come. But not now.

It had been a long day.

He turned, looking back towards Chao Ni Tsu. The old man was in deep shadow. Embedded in the darkness, the mere suggestion of a seated man.

Tsao Ch'un smiled.

The truth was simple. GenSyn had been getting too big, growing too fast, becoming far too influential, especially when it came to their 'project' – that audacious attempt of theirs to clone perfect copies of living people. Not that that was a bad idea, only... he didn't want that kind of biotechnology getting into the wrong hands.

Which was why he'd had Gustav Ebert killed. Why he had stepped in anonymously an hour back, to buy up GenSyn's fallen shares on the market and save them from going under.

But that wasn't the *real* reason. The real reason was to rein them in.

Control was the key. A key that had never failed him yet.

One step ahead. That was what counted. That you were always one step ahead of everyone else. And if that meant killing a few good men, then so be it. For what was a single man among ten billion?

But Lahm... what was he to do with Lahm?

Tsao Ch'un spoke to the air. 'The Eighth Dragon... Lahm... see to it that he has an accident... something he won't survive.'

There was no answer, yet he knew it would be done. So it was. For he had power over all. And Lahm?

He would erase Lahm from the records. Erase all trace of the man, as if he'd never been.

Tsao Ch'un smiled. Amos, at least, would have appreciated the irony – that one of the great architects of their faked history should disappear, his person erased from those same pages. But then Amos would never know. No. In time they would all forget that a man called Lahm had ever existed.

Wormholes. Tsao Ch'un chuckled, thinking of it. *It was all nothing but wormholes, after all.*

PART FIVE **Daylight On Iron Mountain**

SUMMER 2087

We've learned the grief of raising sons –
Not like the quiet joy of daughters
We can marry to our neighbours.
Our boys lie under the weeds
Near Kokonor, their old white bones
Remain with no one to collect them.
Old ghosts and new complaints: you can hear them
All night long through falling mist and rain.

—Tu Fu, 'Song of the Wagons', 8th Century AD

Chapter 16

FACING WINTER

The long, carved mahogany table dominated the chamber, its massive bulk dividing the courthouse down the centre, its far end facing the raised platform of the dais and the imposing judge's chair.

On that table, stacked high along one side like some miniature cityscape from before the Collapse, were piles of dusty law tomes, their covers brown and green and black. The smell of leather and old parchment was strong in that poorly ventilated place.

Entering the chamber and seeing that great stack of books, seeing beyond them, the massed host – the Chang family and their lawyers, their ranks filling the rows of benches across from him – Jake felt his stomach clench with anxiety.

The twenty years he had worked for MicroData ought to have carried some weight. Ought to have guaranteed him his pension, only what chance did he have against such a team? What in heaven's name had made him think he could outwit and out-argue them? No. The Chang family were an old and powerful family. They had connections. And they clearly had the wealth and the will to fight him every step of the way.

Jake swallowed, then glanced round at his own legal team – at the greybeard, Yang Hung Yu and his young, beardless assistant, Chi Lin Lin. Their eyes, he saw, caught on that huge mountain of legal tomes and quailed. Advocate Yang looked down at the slender file he was carrying and seemed dismayed. He had said to Jake that this was just a formality, only it didn't look that way. The Chang family were clearly going to deal with this before it became a problem. And he – Jake Reed – would be the one to suffer the consequences.

A test case, that's what I am.

Jake looked across, as Chang Yi Wei and his three brothers – the most senior members of their clan – entered the chamber through the far door. They were dressed in the finest, most expensive silks, their wrists and necks dripping with silver and gold. From their smiling, joking demeanour, they clearly felt very pleased with themselves. In their minds the case was already decided. Decided and dismissed.

Chang Yi Wei seemed particularly smug. His face – familiar to Jake through the briefings he had had with Advocate Yang – had a sneering quality Jake found disconcerting. It seemed to imply that he was the defendant here, not they.

Yang reached across, tugging at Jake's arm. 'Shih Reed... come...'

Jake let himself be led across, taking a seat between Advocate Yang and his young assistant, the three of them lost in those massive, empty benches, facing the Chang family and their legal team.

It's like being on a battlefield, Jake thought. Like looking across the space between two armies in that final moment before the drums rolled and they threw themselves at each other.

Or like David and Goliath, he thought, only that wasn't so. What could his tiny little slingshot do against this great host of big men?

We are outnumbered, Jake thought, despairing now that his day in court had come. Hard as he knew it would be, he had imagined it otherwise. Had thought it would be more equal. More *fair*. Only the Changs were not interested in fair. They had not bought the MicroData Corporation to be fair. They had bought it to advance their family's fortunes. Yes, and to strip it to the bone.

Which was why Jake was here.

He leaned across, whispering in Yang's ear, 'We haven't a *fucking* chance, have we?'

Yang Hung Yu didn't say no, but then he didn't say yes either. He seemed... stunned. Terrified by the massed ranks that sat across from him. Cowed by them. Like Jake, he had not quite understood what he was taking on.

'Aiya!' young Chi Lin Lin murmured. 'Ai-*fucking*-ya!'

But there was barely time to get used to the situation when the Judge entered from the far end, from the huge doorway just beyond the platform, flanked by the six officers of the court, all of them resplendent in their peacock-blue gowns, big square badges on their chests denoting their ranks.

All seven of them Han, Jake noted. For that was how it was. From what Peter had told him, there was barely a single *Hung Mao* in the whole judicial system.

Which is one way of controlling it all, I guess. One means of keeping us Hung Mao in our place.

The three of them stood and bowed, even as the Judge took his seat, spreading his silks about him as if he was lord of all he surveyed. Which he was, to all intents and purposes.

Across from them the Chang clan and their lawyers had turned as one to face the Judge, bowing in unison, as if they had practised it. Which was probably the truth.

It was an inauspicious day. He had known that from the moment he had woken, hours before the dawn, not quite knowing where he was, in the grip of childhood dreams.

Up on the dais, the Judge gestured that all should be seated. Jake sat, then took the cloth Mary had given him from the pocket of his silks, wiping the sweat from his brow. He felt hot suddenly, unbearably uncomfortable.

Dreams. It was years since he'd been plagued with such dreams.

Advocate Yang leaned in, whispering to his ear. '*Their Chief Advocate... Hui Chang Yeh... he's the big fat one. He has to make their deposition now. He'll argue that there's no case to answer. It make take some while. They'll doubtless quote a precedent or two. Then I'll have a chance to speak. To convince the Judge that there is a case, and to get him to allow us to present our evidence. But as I say, it may take some time.*'

Which was true. Not only that, but Chief Advocate Hui made his presentation in Mandarin; barely a word of which Jake understood.

'It's okay,' Yang said, leaning close to whisper in his ear. '*Chi Lin Lin is taking notes. You can read a translation later. But look... it will be hours yet before Hui has finished. If you want to go and rest... I can have Chi Lin Lin come fetch you when he's winding up.*'

Jake considered that. Part of him felt he ought to stay, for form's sake, if nothing else. Then again, he had hardly slept last night, and when he had...

He looked across at the packed benches opposite. What would they think of him if he left now?

Damn what they think, he decided, smiling at Yang and standing. Fuck the Changs and their massed ranks!

'Fetch me, yes?' he said to Chi Lin Lin. *'You know where I am.'*

Jake lay there on his bed in the rented room, propped up against the wall. He had stayed in some uncomfortable places in his life, but this topped them all.

The room was barely bigger than the single bed. There was a small sink with a mirror, and a tiny screen set into the wall, its channel permanently fixed to the local news station. Only the walls...

He shuddered. The walls were the plain translucent white of ice. Normally they would have been sprayed, decorated to make them opaque, only these were not. That hadn't stopped a succession of temporary tenants from spotting the wall with all manner of foul-coloured substances, like some abstract piece of art.

I am too old for this, he thought, closing his eyes. Not that there was any real choice. Home was more than two hours by public transport, and at his age he knew it would kill him off to do that journey here and back every day. Especially if the case went on for weeks, and there was no guarantee that it wouldn't. The carriages were packed, and he'd been lucky today to get a seat.

Jake sighed. This was the Changs' doing. He had hoped they would try this case in one of the local courthouses, but they'd had it transferred here. Had used their influence to fuck him over. Why, this was barely ten minutes from their head office.

He yawned, unable to stop himself. Three hours he'd had at most last night. And then he'd woken, sheened in sweat, from the dream.

He could remember every single detail of that day. Could remember that morning, playing out in the garden with his sister, May, running about, chasing each other and giggling. The grass beneath their feet the softest green, wet from the dew, the lawn scattered with bright red leaves.

They had meant to go cycling that morning, up the narrow lanes that cut through the woods behind his grandparents' house – to the old pond, maybe, or what they called the crow's nest at the very top of the hill. Only his bike had got a puncture. A tiny nail, it was. He remembered his grandfather placing it in his palm. Could recall the cold wet feel of it. And then his parents, calling out to them, asking if they wanted to go into town to get some shopping.

May had gone but he had stayed, helping his grandfather fix the puncture, running water into the bowl from the outside tap, then carrying it across, the water slopping side to side as he walked. Watching as his grandfather squeezed the inner tube, looking for the hole, air bubbles finally rising to the surface.

There!

And then the phone, ringing and ringing, and after it had stopped, after a long and oddly peaceful silence, the birds singing in the nearby trees. Yes, he remembered. Remembered how he had turned at the sound of his grandma's choking voice, staring at her, trying to make sense of her tears as she stumbled through the door, her legs almost giving way.

He had pleaded with his grandfather. Pleaded to see it for himself. Because until he saw it he couldn't, *wouldn't* believe.

They had driven to the local hospital in silence, their faces fixed and ashen, him in the back behind them. His grandfather's hands were locked, it seemed, on the wheel of the old BMW, the smell of the leather seats strong. There in the corridor, the two of them standing either side of him, their hands gently holding his, he had glanced up and looking from one to the other, saw the devastation in their faces, the disbelief.

That corridor. How he wished he could end it there. How he wished he had woken then. Only he hadn't. He had walked on, towards that door. And inside?

Inside was his whole world. Gone, destroyed in an instant. It was there, outside the glass-panelled door, that his grandmother had lost her courage.

'Go on... go on in...' she'd said, her voice a pained whisper. 'I can't...'

Clutching his grandfather's hand, he had gone inside, into that part-lit room. There to his left, laid out on two trolleys, were his parents, their bodies stretched out beside one another. Together in death as they had been in life, their pale corpses laced with the wounds they had received when their car had hit another head-on.

Overtaking. A young man of twenty-two. Not a scratch. Not a single fucking scratch. No, and no licence either, no insurance. He was UP. A non-person.

Jake remembered how in the dream, he had turned, looking up at his grandfather. 'Where is she, Granddad? Where's May?'

And then he saw her, on the small trolley to his right, close by the doctor's desk. Covered over, only her face exposed, peaceful and marble white. He had walked across and looked. Saw how her eyes were open; how they stared out into nothingness.

Where is she?

Eight years old, he'd been. A happy child. Loved and loving. And then that. Jake shuddered and looked down.

He was sixty-eight now. A grandfather. Sixty years had passed since that autumn day, and still it had the power to unman him. To reduce him to this shivering state.

He looked about him at the shabbiness of the room. From that moment to this – where had his life gone? It seemed to have flown so fast. And this latest thing with the court case. It was never meant to be like this. None of it. Life was supposed to have been so easy. Wasn't that what they had promised him as a child?

Jake groaned, then lay down on his side, afraid to close his eyes, afraid lest he found himself back there again. In that childhood garden where things had first come apart.

God help me, he thought, bringing his hands up, placing his thin, trembling fingers against his old and shrunken face, as if to shut it all out. *God help me for the wreck I am.*

Jake woke. There was an urgent banging on his door.

'Shih Reed! Shih Reed! You must come!'

For an instant he was disoriented. Then he understood.

'Hold on, Chi Lin Lin... I'm coming.'

He hauled himself up, then sat there a moment, getting his bearings.

'Shih Reed...'

Give me a moment.

He felt dreadful. It wasn't just the dreams, it was his age, the state of the mattress, not to speak of his anxiety about the case.

Jake looked down at the timer at his wrist, then swore. He hadn't meant to sleep so long.

'Shih Reed!'

'All right!' He reached out and unlocked the door, then stood, feeling the faintest bit unsteady, the faintest bit nauseous. Wishing he were home, in his own bed. All this...

Chi Lin Lin popped his head around the door. 'Advocate Hui is summing up,' he said anxiously. 'The Judge will be deciding very soon. You should be there, Shih Reed!'

'I know, I know... and I will be there. But let me comb my hair, Chi, and put on a fresh cloak.'

'But Shih Reed...'

He turned, letting Chi see the state he was in. 'You want the Judge to see me like this? No. So give me a few moments, my young friend. I shall be there.'

Advocate Hui closed the file he had been reading from, then bowed, gravely and respectfully, before taking his seat again among his team of advocates.

Jake looked to Yang Hung Yu. 'Well?'

Advocate Yang gazed down. He was not the picture of confidence; more like a man who knows he has lost before the game's begun. And maybe he was right to feel that way, only the law was on their side. Or should have been. The Chang family had acted illegally, and they could not be allowed to get away with it.

'Your honour...' he began. But Judge Wei was having none of it.

'In Mandarin,' he barked. 'This is no peasant's court!'

It didn't augur well.

Yang cleared his throat, then began again. But he was barely three or four sentences in when the Judge interrupted him again.

Jake leaned in to Chi Lin Lin. 'What did he say?'

But Chi Lin Lin wasn't to be allowed to answer. Banging his gavel, the Judge ordered them to be silent.

Yang, standing there, looked bewildered. He began to address the Judge again, and again found himself shouted down.

For a moment there was complete silence, then, raising his chin to look about him, the Judge uttered what could have been no more than five, maybe six words in Mandarin.

This time the host on the benches opposite were up out of their seats, protesting violently, waving their files so angrily that you'd have thought Jake had won.

Bemused, Jake looked to Chi Lin Lin again. 'What did he say?'

Young Chi was grinning now. 'He says we can present our evidence. We're over the first hurdle, Jake! He says the case can go to trial!'

After that debacle with GenSyn, Jake had gone back to the levels. Made his peace with Boss Wu and tried to settle in. Only it was hard. And then fate – and who knew whose face fate wore? – intervened and he was offered a job, and a good job at that. Market advisor to an up-and-coming company quoted on the Hang Seng – MicroData, known familiarly on the market as 'Emdee'. It had been a good firm to work for, and he'd made good friends – Han and *Hung Mao*.

He had worked for Emdee for almost twenty years. Until last year, in fact, when he had finally retired on half salary. It was a good pension; enough to lead a comfortable life with Mary and the kids. Only then the old owner had died. The Chang family, who it seemed had long coveted the company, had shoehorned their way in, buying a controlling share and immediately selling off the lucrative parts to rivals.

That much was legal. It wasn't nice, but it was within their rights as owners. Only then, in an attempt to reduce operational costs, they had announced a reduction in pension payments.

Overnight Jake's income had been cut by two-thirds. It was outrageous, and *totally* illegal. Ex-employees, Jake among them, had formed an action committee, meeting to debate what could be done. Only the Changs quickly infiltrated that committee and, in the most brutal fashion, threatened and bullied some of the weaker members until they dropped out.

That had been three months ago. Since then, Jake – and a handful of others – had been preparing their cases, living off their savings while they did so. It was very much a do-or-die gesture, but the law was on their side.

Or ought to have been.

Now the three of them sat in the nearby canteen, eating noodles and trying to make sense of what had just happened.

'*You know what I think?*' Yang Hung Yu said, leaning in close to whisper to the other two, as if he did not want to be overheard. 'I think it's all a bargain-ing ploy. I think the Changs have offered Judge Wei a lot of cash to drop this case. Not to let it proceed. Only, by granting our suit, he gets the chance to ask a much higher sum.'

Jake stared back at him, dismayed. 'You think?'

Yang leaned in again. 'Judge Wei is a very rich man. That's all I say.'

Beside him Chi Lin Lin was nodding, as if he knew it for a fact.

'Then we're sunk.'

Yang smiled at that. 'Not sunk. But badly holed, neh?'

The second session began just after two, the senior lawyers for the Changs crowding the front desk, chattering away in half-whispered Mandarin, their agitation clear. Judge Wei, it seemed, was driving a very hard bargain. Jake might almost have found it amusing, the Changs being screwed by one of their own kind, only he stood to lose all he had worked for. And if he did, they'd fall, and he did not know how he – let alone Mary – would cope with that. He had to win. Justice had to prevail. If it didn't, it made a mockery of the last twenty years – of Tsao Ch'un's great experiment.

A total fucking mockery.

Out front, the haggling seemed to be over. Advocate Hui and his men took a step back, then, as one, gave Judge Wei a respectful bow. A deal, it seemed, had been made.

'All right,' Judge Wei said, looking across at Yang Hung Yu. 'Advocate Yang, you have an hour to present your evidence.'

'An hour? But, my Lord...'

'An hour,' Judge Wei repeated, his face hard and stern. 'Now get on with it. Before I rule against you!'

Jake felt his heart sink. An hour. They would barely scratch the surface in an hour. He knew it for a fact. And why? Because the Changs' legal team would eat away at most of that with their queries and interruptions. If they managed to get ten minutes it would be something!

And so it proved. Only, five minutes from the end, in the midst of yet another interruption by Advocate Hui, a messenger appeared at Judge Wei's shoulder, handing him a sealed envelope.

Wei So Yuan signalled to Hui Chang Yeh to carry on, while he slit the seal open with his long fingernails and removed a single sheet of paper.

Jake watched him, trying to make out what it was. Only Judge Wei's face did not change. Whatever was written on that paper seemed to have no power to move him in any way. He merely folded it, then pocketed it casually.

'Advocate Hui,' he said, as if tiring of the matter. 'Sit down now, please, and let Advocate Yang give his summing up.'

Yang's face lit. At least he would get to the nub of it.

Advocate Hui, however, seemed unconcerned. So maybe the letter was confirmation of some kind. A signed agreement between the Changs and Judge Wei. Maybe it no longer mattered whether Yang gave his summation or not.

Jake looked down. If they lost this today, he could always go to appeal. Only this had cost him just about everything he had, and to go to appeal would cost him another twenty thousand *yuan* at the very least, according to Yang, and where would he find that kind of sum?

Oh, he could borrow it off Peter, maybe. Only he didn't like to. In fact, he had not even told Peter what had happened. His pride forbade him. That and Mary's fear that they might drag him down with them if they lost.

No, it was best Peter knew nothing about this.

Jake looked up again. Yang Hung Yu was bowing to the Judge, his summation given. He came back to the benches, and sat down next to Jake.

'The law is on our side,' Yang said, leaning in.

Maybe, Jake thought. *But the money is on theirs.*

Judge Wei sat back a little, as if considering what to do next. Then, unexpectedly, he smiled.

'We shall reconvene... tomorrow. Until then...'

For a moment the Chang family and their lawyers clearly did not register what had been said. Then there was uproar again, and the same waving of files, the same angry faces, the same huddle at the desk, as Hui Chang Yeh and his team crowded about Judge Wei.

A half an hour later, Jake sat on the bench outside, waiting for Yang Hung Yu to return from renewing their passes. They were rescheduled for nine the next morning, when Judge Wei would hear evidence from Chang's team. Until then, his time was his own.

The proceedings had tired him. So maybe it would be a good idea to get a few hours' kip. Only he was afraid of that. Afraid he'd have the dreams again. So maybe he'd find a tea house. Get himself a paper and catch up on the news...

'*Shih* Reed...'

He looked up. The man – a *Hung Mao* – was short and squat, but powerfully built, his face hard and menacing, his hair cut razor short.

'What do you want?'

'You should not be here. You know that, don't you?'

Jake laughed. 'I know nothing of the sort.' He stood. 'Are you one of Chang's men? One of his paid thugs?'

If it came to a fight he would get trampled. The man was thirty years younger than him and fit. Fighting fit, by the look of him. Nonetheless, he would not be bullied. He had been through too much in life to be bullied by some little shit!

The man was sneering now, contemptuous. 'You are a very stupid man, *Shih* Reed. Incredibly stupid. You do not know who you have taken on. If we wanted we could crush you like a bug. You and everyone you love. Only my Masters... they would like to see this thing settled. Not to drag on. So they have sent me. To intervene. To help you see sense.'

Jake lifted his hand and poked the man's chest. 'Listen here, you little shit. Just fuck off! You understand that clearly enough? Fuck off. And tell your Masters to fuck off, too. I'll see them in court tomorrow, *understand*?'

The man looked down at the spot where Jake had touched him and nodded. 'I'll tell them, *Shih* Reed. And I'll look forward to seeing you again.' He smiled, tightly. 'Until then, neh? Until then.'

Jake didn't mention his 'meeting' with the thug. Advocate Yang was clearly overwhelmed enough as it was.

'Yang Hung Yu?'

'Yes, Jake?'

'Why did you take this on?'

They were sitting in Fu Nan's tea house, two decks up from the court complex, a *chung* of Fu Nan's finest green *ch'a* before them. It was Yang's treat to Jake.

Yang smiled apologetically. 'The circumstances of this case... they are far from normal, neh? If it were just a matter of the law...'

He sighed, then picked up his bowl and sipped from it. 'You understand... I will do my best for you, Shih Reed, only...'

'Only we're going to lose. Is that what you're thinking?'

Yang sat back, his dark, Han eyes studying Jake a moment. 'As I see it, we have come this far. Further, perhaps, than Chang Yi Wei and his brothers thought we'd come. Win or lose, you have cost them a great deal of money, Jake. Representation like that is not cheap, neh? Then again, they have a great deal to lose should you win this case. As for Judge Wei...'

'You know him of old, neh?'

'Oh yes.' Yang set his bowl down. 'And when the stakes are not so high... he can be a relatively fair judge.'

'Relatively?'

'Ah yes, my friend. Everything is relative... at this level.'

'And the Changs?'

Yang looked away. 'There I must apologize, dear friend. I was naive. I did not understand until today just what this meant to them.'

'And?'

Yang hesitated. 'I might be wrong. I truly hope I am. Only... I am afraid they will not rest until they've destroyed you. That show today... the only reason we have a hearing to attend tomorrow morning is because Judge Wei sees it as a means of hiking up his cut. Have no illusions. He will make a deal with them. We are only there, I fear, because we're leverage.'

'And if I protest?'

'You could try, my friend. You could most certainly try. Only... how should I put it? Let us just say that those to whom the matter would be referred might find it rather... awkward, things being as they are.'

'Meaning...?'

Yang shrugged. 'Just this... Were you to ask me to show you an honest man, I would show you a man who was not a judge.'

'Not a...?' Jake shook his head. 'Is there no hope whatsoever, Yang Hung Yu? Are all my efforts to get justice to be mocked by these half-men?'

Only Yang did not answer that. Yang did not have to answer.

*

Alone again, Jake went back to his room. A black mood had descended on him since his meeting with Yang Hung Yu.

He would have called home and spoken to Mary, only that would only have made things worse – to have to admit to her that he was on a fool's errand. That he had wasted their life's savings on some Quixotic attempt to get justice, when the truth was there was no justice to be had, just the force of money.

It was enough to drive a man to drink, or to murder.

Yes, he would have happily strangled that odious bastard, Chang Yi Wei. Put his hands around the bastard's throat and choked him. Only Jake knew he'd never get the chance. And even if he did, they'd nail him. Because they looked after one another, these Han. The whole thing was one giant web of connection and corruption. Of *kuan hsi*, as they called it, giving it a 'cultural' face. And he had taken them on! What kind of idiot did that?

The sensible thing was to withdraw, now, before he spent the last few *fen* he had. Why, the room alone was costing him a small fortune. Fifty *yuan* a night, and look at it!

Only he knew he couldn't. Not while there was even the slenderest of chances left. Because to go back to Mary with his tail between his legs just wasn't an option. How could he face himself if he surrendered now? If he let those cunts trample him in the dust?

This was why he'd been having the dreams. He knew that now. He had been pushing himself too hard, taking on too much, when he really should have been resting after his life's labours.

But then, nothing in his life had been easy. It had been his curse to live in interesting times. For the most part he had coped with that. Time and again he had been a survivor. And that was no small thing, for Tsao Ch'un had even sent assassins after him! Only now he was too old. To fight this further fight... just then it seemed beyond him.

No. He would call Mary later. Let her know he'd be here at least another day. But not now. Not while he felt like this.

Chapter 17

THE SEVEN

Above the ancient limestone parapet, the banner fluttered on the breeze that blew in from the east.

It was just before dawn and in the faint pre-morning light, the *Ywe Lung*, the great wheel of dragons that was emblazoned on the banner, could barely be discerned, the seven powerful forms blurred into a great circular swirl of black.

It was early, yet already Tongjiang was a hive of activity. Through the glowing windows of the palace one could glimpse servants running this way and that, making their final preparations. Grim-faced stewards dressed in sombre black robes barked out orders while lesser minions bowed and scraped and hurried here and there, bearing loads of silver and crystal and finest antique porcelain, for today was the day of Li Peng's coming of age.

In his dressing chamber, Li Chao Ch'in, the lord of Tongjiang, member of the Council of Seven, stood at the great stone window, letting his Master of the Bedchamber, Cho Yi Yi, bring his ceremonial clothes and dress him. As he was dressed, he looked out past the high walls of his palace towards the northern mountains as the light leaked back into the world and things took on form and colour once again.

He was glad this day had come; proud that his son had grown so tall and true. Li Peng was a strong, handsome young man, a credit to his family and his race. Today Li Chao Ch'in would present him to his fellow lords, and to his Master, Tsao Ch'un himself.

Today, Li Peng would officially become his heir, his right-hand man and helper, and a prince in his own right. From today his son might even take his place at Council, if need be – if he, Li Chao Ch'in, were ill or otherwise indisposed.

He smiled. It was a good day. A day to celebrate.

His thoughts drifted back momentarily, to the early days, when the whole world had been against them, and they had fought to impose their will upon the land. Back then each day had been a struggle, and he had often thought he would never see a day like this – never see a son of his grow strong and tall, the very image of himself. As solid as an iron link in a great chain. Just the thought of it made his heart swell, tears form at the corners of his eyes.

Li Peng was twenty-five years old! So brief a time, it was, and yet so long in terms of what they had achieved. When Li Peng had been born, there had been no Chung Kuo, only a thousand fractured, warring states, like a shattered bowl that needed to be mended.

For the past four years, since he was twenty-one, Li Peng had spent most of his waking hours with his father, learning the tasks which one day he would inherit, when he was one of the Seven, and T'ang. And that day would surely come, now that the world was pacified. Now that there were no more enemies to fight.

'Master...'

He turned slightly, letting Cho Yi Yi fasten the buttons of his ceremonial jacket, a long, green silk gown decorated with royal-blue medallions, each one stamped with a miniature version of the *Ywe Lung* that flapped and fluttered from the great oak pole outside.

Elsewhere, he knew, his wives and daughters would be getting dressed, putting on their finest silks for the occasion. Likewise, in the various guest chambers scattered throughout the palace, his fellow T'ang would be up and readying themselves. For this was not just a family occasion. One day Li Peng would join their sons, taking his place in Council alongside those others, like Tsu Lin, Tsu Chen's son, Fan Li, son of Fan Chang, and Wang Lung, Wang Hui So's eldest boy.

All of them fine fellows. Every last one of them proud to be their fathers' sons. Proud to one day take on the burden that their fathers daily carried; to be part of this grand venture which, in their lifetimes, had come to such fruition.

Li Chao Ch'in took a deep breath. On days like this he could think of nothing he wanted more than to serve; to offer up his life and those of his family to the great cause of unity. *To be his Master's hands...*

They had come a long distance, all of them. But now, today, they could relax and look back down that path from whence they'd come.

Twenty-five years...

Li Chao Ch'in turned from the window, looking about him at those who stood by, their heads lowered, obedient to his wishes. He grinned broadly, his smile instantly mirrored back from a dozen familiar faces.

'Such a day...' he cried, raising his arms, as if to embrace them all. 'Such a fine and glorious day!'

Li Peng stood among his cousins, staring down at the marbled floor, his face set and hard.

The ceremony ought to have started an hour back. The great hall was packed, the Seven gathered on the dais just across from him. Everyone who was anyone was there. Or almost so. For one person wasn't.

Tsao Ch'un had not come. Or rather, word was that he was delayed. He had been due two hours back. He had promised Li Chao Ch'in he would come, to give his blessing. Only the due time had come and gone and still there was no sign of him.

'*Where is the man?*' Tsu Lin hissed beneath his breath, so only his fellow sons – cousins as they called themselves – could hear.

'*Fucking some maid, no doubt,*' Wang Lung whispered, his tense body language revealing just how angry he was.

'*It is a snub,*' Pei Lin-Yi, the eldest of them, said impatiently, a scowl on his lips. '*By insulting you, Li Peng, he insults us all.*'

'Hush now,' Li Peng said, disturbed by what was being said. '*He is our Master, after all. We are but...*'

'*His hands...*' the others said, as one. But for once there was a darkness behind the expression. To be late was one thing. But to send no word of explanation...

Li Peng's head went down again. It wasn't anger he felt but disappointment. Bitter disappointment. It felt almost as if Tsao Ch'un was making a point. Keeping them waiting to remind them who was Master here.

Maybe. But was this the way to treat one's most loyal servants?

There was a sudden buzz of noise from the main body of the hall. Li Peng's head bobbed up at the sound. Had he come? Was Tsao Ch'un here?

At the far end of the hall, near the two big doors that led out to the gardens, there was a disturbance in the crowd. People were being pushed aside. Voices were being raised. At first Li Peng didn't understand, but then, as the crowd separated, he saw what it was and recognized one of the intruders, a big brute of a man who was naked to the waist.

Li Peng's mouth fell open in shock.

It was Tsao Ch'un's bodyguards! His so-called 'Honest Men' – a hand-picked little mob of murderers and cut-throats that he had come to depend upon more and more of late. Word had it that they they lorded it over the Black Tower, taking their authority direct from Tsao Ch'un. That their word – their wishes – were as his. Only what were they doing here? To bring them here was *unthinkable*. An outrage!

The heavens knew Tsao Ch'un had been unpredictable of late, but this was shocking behaviour even by his standards.

Li Peng looked across, saw at once how his father had blanched at the sight of Tsao Ch'un's men. How he now lifted his robes in one hand and hurried towards the stairs.

'Aiya!' he said, hastening to join his father, pushing past his cousins in his haste. 'Kuan Yin preserve us from such men!'

Tsao Ch'un set the bottle down then slapped his thighs, his laughter echoing across the room.

The expression on Li Chao Ch'in's face was a delight. He looked like a man who had swallowed a wasp. And that stuck-up prig of a son of his...

The very thought of it soured his mood. That they should have such sons, whilst he...

Tsao Ch'un shook his head then clambered to his feet. Three wastrels was what he had. Three good-for-nothing arsewipes barely fit to tie their own shoelaces.

That was being a bit hard, perhaps, but it was not too far from the truth. Gambling was what they liked, and drinking, and whoring. Especially the last.

Not that he himself didn't like a wench. Only he worried sometimes that that was *all* his sons wanted.

The trouble was – and he knew himself well enough to know it for the truth – he was becoming paranoid in his old age. He had begun to mistrust everyone.

There was, of course, good reason. Only last year, two of his wives – two of his favourites – had been killed in an explosion in his bedroom. He too would have died had he not spent the night in some other woman's bed. Which was why, now, he trusted no one but his Honest Men – his little band of rogues. Men he had freed from where they had been rotting in the cells. Men who owed him their lives.

And then this thing today, this... ceremony... this coming of age...

Tsao Ch'un spat, then waved at the screen.

It went blank.

To him Li Peng's coming-of-age ceremony smacked too much of their pride. Of a smugness on the part of the Seven. He wasn't sure he liked the way his advisors preened themselves; how they dressed and spoke, and raised their sons to inherit. Oh, it made a kind of sense, of course. They had been good servants in their day, and to raise their sons in that tradition seemed a natural thing to do. Only... when he thought of *their* sons and *his*...

Tsao Ch'un let out a troubled breath. He might have blamed his mood on ill health; after all, he had been sleeping badly these last few weeks and the pains in his legs had grown worse. Only the truth was otherwise. The truth was he had run out of challenges. Once you had unified a world and destroyed every last one of your enemies, what was left to do?

No. The truth was he was bored. Bored to the point of malice. Hence his little prank today.

Only maybe he had gone too far.

Tsao Ch'un narrowed his eyes, thinking on the matter. Then, raising his arms, he clapped his hands together sharply. At once a dozen servants ran to him, stopping five yards short of where he was sitting, throwing themselves down onto their knees, their foreheads pressed to the cold stone flags.

'Master...'

The word hissed out from a dozen mouths.

'Steward Ling!' he yelled, pointing to the man. 'Bring my cloak and prepare the royal craft. I am going to Tongjiang!'

'Master...'

And they crawled away backwards, on their bellies, like the dogs they were, hastening to do their Master's bidding.

At that moment, in Tsao Ch'un's capital, Pei Ching, one of GenSyn's junior executives was sitting in the anteroom of the Department of Contracts, the business arm of Tsao Ch'un's civil service.

The reception area, decorated in the T'ang dynasty style and complete with carp pond, was hugely impressive, one of the most pleasant places Reed had had to wait in these last few months – and he had waited in a great many.

A white tiled pathway led away from where he sat, through a garden filled with red plum blossom and fresh green stalks of bamboo. To the side of his seat was a small table of black carven wood, on which was a tray of sweet-meats and fruit and various delicious-scented cordials.

Hungry as he was, he left the tray alone, conscious of how important the upcoming meeting was. It would not do to go into that room with grape seeds between his teeth.

It had taken Reed the best part of a year to get this far. But this afternoon, after endless dead ends and disappointments, he would finally get a decision.

He was there to see John Buck, the Ministry's Head of Development. But Buck was only the mouthpiece. He'd be the one who did all the talking; who'd ask all the questions and answer any queries Reed had. But the decision would be made by his superior, Chen So I. Reed knew he would sit in the background, listening silently while Buck and he talked.

That was how these men did business, never sullying their hands with commonplace matters, merely giving a yes or no, without need for explanation.

The thought of it made his heart race. *To have come so far...*

Reed also knew, of course, that Chen So I would not have seen him had he not been interested. GenSyn were not, after all, a big company. Not like MedFac and NorTek. There was no real need for Chen So I to keep them sweet. Nor was Reed himself influential enough to warrant special attention. Which was why, for once, the decision would be made purely on the merits of the project itself.

It was almost unheard of, to the best of his knowledge.

More than a dozen times he'd had the door shut on him – had been thrown out of some junior official's office and told not to waste their time. But there were many doors and many doorkeepers, and he had persevered where others might have given up. Had persuaded several not-so-jaded junior appointees that to be on board such a project could only do their careers good.

And so he hoped it would prove. He was not, in that regard, spinning a line. Reed believed in the project. The fact that it had lain dormant for almost twenty years did not matter, nor that the first attempt at developing it had been a woeful failure. It was still a first-rate idea, and if he could get the Seven to agree, then both they and he – and GenSyn, of course – would benefit hugely.

A small, tidy-looking Han in dark blue silks came down the path towards him. He stopped then bowed low.

'Shih Reed... if you would like to come through...'

He followed the man, through the Moon Door and past the carp pond, over a wooden bridge and into a long, shaded office. There at the far end, in what felt to Reed like the audience room of some ancient Chinese palace, Buck was waiting. He was standing before his desk, his hand out, a pleasant smile on his face.

'Peter... at last we get to meet!'

In the shadows beyond Buck, Chen So I sat like a statue, his bald pate gleaming golden in the low, flickering light of a massive red wax candle that burned to one side.

Reed shook Buck's hand, then sat.

Buck sat down at his desk, watching Reed a moment. Then, steepling his hands before him, he smiled once more.

'Interesting,' he began. 'Very interesting indeed. Not the usual kind of proposition we get at Contracts.'

'No,' Reed answered, smiling tensely.

'Well,' Buck added, after a moment, 'the reason it's taken me so long to get back to you is obvious, I guess. I wanted to know a little more about this "project" of yours. I wanted to know its history particularly. Where it came from. Who developed it.'

Reed smiled. He had expected as much. 'And?'

'And we had to pull some teeth to get hold of that information.'

'Ah... the Ministry...'

Buck's smile faded then returned. 'It's a compelling idea, Peter. Exact copies of people. I'd say that that was the best insurance policy a rich man, or a powerful one, could have, neh? I can see how you might have developed this, let's say, outside of official channels. A lot of men would pay a great deal for what you're offering. But you were right to come to us. Contracts is where this belongs. Everything straight and above board. Controlled by those it ought to be controlled by. But then you knew that, didn't you?'

Reed shifted uncomfortably.

'One question, though,' Buck said.

'Go on...'

'Would we be dealing with you directly if we were to sanction this?'

Reed swallowed. 'I'm... not sure. Our chairman, *Shih* Ebert...'

Unexpectedly, Chen So I spoke. 'I am sorry, *Shih* Reed,' he said. He leaned forward a little, his face showing momentarily in the candle's light, like an ancient yellowed tapestry briefly glimpsed. 'I am afraid that we would insist upon it as a condition. We have been impressed by your... *discretion*, let's call it. By your sure and certain knowledge just where this ought to be placed and with whom.'

Reed's mouth had gone dry. Had they just said yes? And was their only condition that he be directly involved? If so...

'A matter like this,' Buck took up, 'involves trust at the very highest level. To clone a man is something, but to clone a great man... well... all manner of dangers are implicit in the process. We must be absolutely sure with whom we deal, and that our dealings are closely monitored. To have a man we trust...'

Reed bowed his head. 'I am honoured.'

'Good,' Chen So I said, standing suddenly. 'Then we have a deal, *Shih* Reed.'

Buck too had stood. Now he put out his hand again and clasped Reed's firmly. 'Our contract will be with you by this evening, Peter. And thanks. I'm looking forward to doing business with you.'

Back in his hotel room, sitting on his bed, waiting to be connected to his father, he knew that hc ought to have asked a lot more questions – like how much Contracts were going to pay, and how many units they were willing to purchase.

Only he knew that wasn't how it worked. You didn't haggle with those people. You could only walk away from an agreement with them.

Besides, it would all be in the contract, and Buck had promised it for that evening. It would be all right. He was sure of it. After all, they wanted this every bit as much as GenSyn.

Yes, but what if they wanted it all done on the cheap? And what if Ebert didn't like what they were offering? He could be very prickly about those kind of details.

All right. But would he dare turn down a Ministry contract? Would he dare to sully those waters and risk leaving GenSyn out in the cold, shunned by those who had influence in the markets?

For the briefest moment Reed examined the possibility. Taking it to Contracts had been a high-risk strategy. An all-or-nothing venture. That said, not even Wolfgang Ebert would turn down the chance of working with the Seven on this. *Whatever* the terms. Because even if *this* didn't turn a profit, it would at least open doors, and once those doors were open...

Yes, he thought. *We've been out in the cold far too long.*

It was time to pick up where they'd left off and start to grow again.

Even so, he couldn't help but be excited. It had been a long, hard grind and he'd been close to giving up many times. Only now he had a deal. And not just any deal. A deal with Tsao Ch'un's Ministry of Contracts.

Peter smiled. Meg would be pleased now that it was settled, and not just for the fat bonus he would make. He'd not seen a lot of her these past few weeks, and things had been a little tense. But he'd make it up to her.

The comset buzzed. His mother's face appeared on the screen.

Technically, Mary was his stepmother – his *wife's* mother. His real mother – her sister Anne – had died long ago, when he was only a boy.

'Hi, Ma,' he said, beaming back at her as she appeared on screen. 'You okay?'

'I've been baking,' she answered, indicating the flour dust that covered her apron. 'Are you coming to see us? If so, it's about time... I thought you must have gone to Mars.'

'Mars is *next* month. I've been very busy, is all. But maybe I've some good news.'

'Yes?' she said. 'Nothing to do with grandchildren?'

'Ma...' He laughed. 'You'd be the first to know.'

'Well... I've been waiting long enough. Your sisters...'

'Are dropping one a year, I know... But Meg enjoys her job. You know that.'

'Even so...'

Five minutes more of this and they said goodbye. Afterwards, Peter sat there, staring at the empty screen, musing on what had been said. Maybe Mary was right. Maybe it was time to have kids. Meg hadn't said anything, but if this new deal came off – if his bonus was enough – then maybe they could afford to have children. Yes, and to move up a level or two. Find somewhere bigger and nicer.

Not that what they had right now wasn't nice. It was just...

If this comes off, then we're in a different league.

That was partly what had driven him this past year. To put GenSyn right up there with the big boys.

Reed stood. Knowing there was nothing to do but wait, he went through and had a shower.

'Where *are* they?' Tsao Ch'un's man, Wen P'ing asked, his whole manner surly, uncompromisingly aggressive.

Li Chao Ch'in bristled inwardly. 'They're sleeping it off,' he answered. 'Come, I'll show you...'

'None of them were harmed, I hope. If Tsao Ch'un hears of any maltreatment of his men...'

'Oh, I assure you, *they* were not hurt. Not a hair on any of *their* heads.'

'And they were drunk, you say?'

Li Chao Ch'in looked down. One more rude remark and he'd have Wen P'ing stripped and flogged, and damn the circumstances. But he bit back the words that came to mind. The last thing he needed to do right now was cause trouble. No. Tsao Ch'un would be here within the hour. He had sent word. And once he was here they could get on with the ceremony.

In the meantime, he had only to put up with this man's rudeness. This puffed-up nonentity, this piece of common shit whom Tsao Ch'un had elevated way beyond his worth.

Li Chao Ch'in smiled insincerely. 'We made sure that all of their needs were seen to.'

A dozen maids had seen to that. And whilst he felt pained that he should have had to sacrifice them to such brutes, it was better than the alternative – which would have been to fight them to the death.

He led Tsao Ch'un's man through to the guest rooms where the Honest Men lay, sprawled there half naked among the silken sheets. The maids were long gone. If Li Chao Ch'in had had his way he would have slit their throats in sleep – every last one of them. Three guests were badly injured, a dozen more apoplectic from their treatment at the hands of these rogues. Were it any other man but Tsao Ch'un...

Li Chao Ch'in let out a breath. The mere sight of them made his stomach turn. And the stench!

He turned away, before he said something, or let his disgust show in his face. Tsao Ch'un was testing them. What else could it be? Testing their loyalty, their ability to tolerate such treatment.

Even so...

He swept away, lifting his cloak high above the marble flags, barely seeing the servants who bowed low as he passed, his anger threatening for once to make him do something he would most certainly regret.

We are our Master's hands.

Maybe so. Only one did not show such disregard, such carelessness, with one's hands. Not if one wished to keep them.

That thought, coming upon him unbidden, made him slow his pace then stop.

It was not the first time Tsao Ch'un had let them down. Not the first time he had tested them. Increasingly, over the last five or six years, he had acted thus – letting his baser side dictate his behaviour towards them. Only this...

This took things to a whole new level of disrespect.

Returning to his fellow T'ang, Li Chao Ch'in looked about him, seeing in every eye how out of temper this had made them. Nothing was said. Nothing *would* be said. Yet there was a quiet understanding among them.

So Tsao Ch'un was. So he had ever been. Unpredictable. Extremely unpredictable. But never this extreme. Never this thoughtless, this lacking in sensitivity towards them. To keep the cream of the elite waiting for six hours...

'Come,' Li Chao Ch'in said, swallowing his pride, trying to make the best of what had become a very bad situation. 'Let us go and greet our Master.'

As the craft set down, they kowtowed in its direction, even as the hatch hissed open and Tsao Ch'un stepped slowly out.

Slowly and unsteadily, for Tsao Ch'un was drunk. There was no mistaking it. He stood there, looking about him with the eyes of one startled awake. Then, leaning forward, he passed wind loudly, laughing as he did. As if he had made some terribly witty remark.

He smiled and gave a mocking bow. '*Ch'un tzu...*'

Tsao Ch'un sniggered, then scratched at his belly, as if unwatched at home, and not standing there before the Seven.

'Go,' he muttered. Then, when they did not move, he raised his voice, waving them away. 'Go on, go! Go away!'

Again, it was not the first time he had been thus with them, yet this once they looked to each other angrily. Wang Hui So, the eldest of them, lowered his head and took a step towards Tsao Ch'un.

'Master, we...'

'Oh fuck off, Wang Hui So... stop all this drivelling servitude. A drink... I need a fucking drink!'

Li Chao Ch'in swallowed bitterly. This was worse than he'd imagined. He knew Tsao Ch'un when he was in this kind of mood. Incorrigible. Unbearable and boorish. And deadly.

He gestured to his fellow T'ang to back off, then stepped forward.

'Come, my Lord,' he said, offering his arm to the older man. 'Let me find you a whisky. We have some vintage Laphroaig...'

It could not surely have got worse. Only it did.

For the next few hours, Tsao Ch'un behaved like the worst type of tavern bully, fondling the daughters of important men, and letting his bodyguards swagger about without a word to restrain their actions. And when the speeches were given to celebrate Li Peng's coming-of-age, Tsao Ch'un managed to talk throughout, making foul and sneering remarks. For Li Chao Ch'in it was almost too much, and when Tsao Ch'un finally departed, he was joined by the others in his study where, behind locked doors, they let their grievances spill out.

It was the first time that they had aired their opinions quite so openly. The depth of irritation, of annoyance and simple disgust, was a surprise to them all. It seemed that not a single one of them truly respected Tsao Ch'un. Not as they had before. He had been a great man once upon a time – a very great man indeed – but now?

'We will keep our own counsel,' Li Chao Ch'in said, winding things up, 'and meet again a week hence. Let us see how our Master is over the coming days. Whether perhaps he apologizes, or sends gifts, or...'

'You think he will?' Tsu Chen asked scathingly.

'I think he has much on his mind,' Li Chao Ch'in said, more generous in his words than in his feelings at that moment. 'Since his wives died...'

'Does that excuse things?' Wu Hsien said, brushing aside Li Chao Ch'in's words. 'That, today... talking throughout the ceremony, like some idle bully... it was a disgrace, cousin. An insult to your son and thus to you.'

'And therefore to us too,' Tsu Chen said, nodding his head in agreement.

'Maybe so,' Li Chao Ch'in said with a sigh. 'Yet what are we to do? He is our Lord. Without his power, what are we?'

He looked about him as he said it, seeing how, for once, eyes looked away and heads were lowered. Tsao Ch'un's actions that afternoon had embarrassed them. Worse, the incident had made them question the very source of their power.

It was Wu Hsien who had the final word. 'Let us hope our Master comes to his senses, neh? If not...'

He shrugged. But his face was troubled. More troubled than it had been in many years.

Buck phoned just after six.

'I've got the contract,' he said. 'At least, a draft agreement. You want to meet for a drink and something to eat? We can celebrate.'

It wasn't what Reed had been expecting. He'd phoned his team only half an hour earlier, to tell them to stay on; he'd have details of the contract to them as soon as possible. He'd been expecting it to be delivered to his room and that he'd spend the night working his way through it, clause by clause, until it was done. But Buck sounded as if he was expecting Reed to sign it there and then.

They had agreed to meet up at the Golden Phoenix. Reed didn't know the place, but it was apparently in his stack, three decks down from where he was staying.

'What time do you want to meet?'

'Let's say eight,' Buck answered. 'I'll have some champagne on ice ready for us and a couple of fat cigars.'

Reed sat there for a while afterwards, wondering if he should let Ebert know. Then again, Wolfgang probably knew already. He was certain to have at least one spy in Reed's team, and what was there to say until he knew the details?

But Buck's tone gave him hope.

What they'd asked for was a small fortune. No more than it cost, but still a small fortune. Six billion *yuan*. That covered research costs and development over a ten-year period, with further payments if things worked out.

The truth, however, was that he'd be happy with half that. A quarter, even. If things worked out, they'd still turn a profit.

He showered again and put on his best *pau*, the silver silk with the bamboo pattern that Meg had bought him last Autumn Festival, then he set off for the restaurant. He got there half an hour early and sat there, nursing a Scotch, until Buck arrived.

It was a luxuriously decorated place, with beautiful, hand-painted screens and meandering paths between the tables. At first he had a sense of déjà vu, then realized what it reminded him of – the Ministry of Contracts' waiting room.

Over the years, Reed had come to love the Han style of things. Had come to feel it almost his own. Some, he knew, never got used to it. They lived and died in exile, his father among them. For himself, however, he had long since stopped thinking it strange or an imposition. It was his culture now and fitted him just as comfortably as the long robe – the *pau* – he wore.

Buck was dead on time.

'Peter...'

They shook hands, then Buck handed him the folder, snapping his fingers as he did to summon a waiter and order the champagne he'd promised earlier.

'You don't need to read it,' Buck said. 'Just send it to your legal people, though I doubt they'll have much work to do.'

Reed frowned. 'What do you mean?'

'I mean the contract's fine. We've not changed a thing. If you can do what you say you're going to do on budget then we're happy with that.'

Reed's mouth had fallen open. 'You mean...' He laughed, then gave a whoop.

Six billion yuan!

'And Chen So I...?'

Just then the waiter reappeared with the champagne. Buck was silent a moment, watching the young Han open the bottle and pour.

When he was gone, Buck handed Reed one of the crystal glasses, then clinked his against Reed's.

He grinned. 'To our success! But to answer your question... Master Chen was impressed. He knew about the original project. In fact, as a younger man he'd worked on it... from our side of things, naturally.' Buck smiled, enjoying Reed's surprise, and nodded. 'Oh yes. I'm not making that up. So, as you can imagine, your approach was extremely fortuitous. Had another man been minister...'

'And our client...?' He said it quietly, not wanting to use any names, or any description that might alert some listening ear, some watchful eye. As Chen So I had said, there was a need for extreme discretion when talking of this part of things.

Buck leaned across, lowering his voice. 'Our client will not know anything. Not yet. Not until we've something to show him. But again, your timing is fortuitous. Such a scheme, right now... None of us grow any younger. Not yet, anyway. And he of whom we speak... well... men decline... even the best of them.'

Three hours later, feeling slightly drunk, Reed sat in the sedan Buck had ordered for him, smoking the tail end of a cigar and waiting for the lift that would take him back up to his hotel room.

It had been a good evening. A very good evening. He'd thought, maybe, some of Buck's team would join them, but Buck had kept it personal.

'The way I see it,' Buck had said, 'we need to keep things tight. Two small, hand-picked teams, one working for GenSyn, one for us. No more than eight in all, ourselves included. Our superiors will have to know about the bigger brush strokes, certainly, but the fine detail... well, we can develop all of that in camera. Even the researchers shouldn't know how it all fits together. That way there's much less chance of something going wrong...'

And so it had gone, until, by the time they'd finished, they'd had it all sketched out down to the last little detail. Only the contract was left to be signed.

Six billion yuan... Reed laughed, then lifted the folder to his lips and kissed it. It was a massive sum of money, and he couldn't quite believe that he had pulled it off. But Minister Chen's signature was on the draft, next to his chop. He had only to get Wolfgang to okay the deal.

He closed his eyes, imagining. His own cut would be huge. At least, he hoped it would. Big enough maybe to allow him to afford a First Level mansion. He laughed aloud, then shook his head.

'Don't count your chickens,' he said quietly. Then he frowned, wondering where that particular phrase, a favourite of his father's, originally came from.

Counting chickens... And then he thought of what it all meant, and he felt a little shiver of wonder pass through him.

They were going to clone Tsao Ch'un. To make copies of the great man. Young, vigorous copies they could grow in their vats.

And once they'd made them?

Reed smiled. That was up to Tsao Ch'un himself.

Tsao Ch'un belched, then rolled over slowly, squinting against the sunlight that poured in from the window to his right. That was the trouble with growing old. It took so much longer to recover from one's debaucheries.

He laughed, then sat up.

'Steward Ling!'

The man came running, bowing low as he ran, then prostrated himself at Tsao Ch'un's feet. 'Yes, Master...'

'I want you to send a gift to Li Chao Ch'in. Something totally ostentatious and over the top.'

'A *gift*, Master?'

Ling's habit of repeating his Master when nervous was annoying at the best of times, but added to a hangover...

'Yes, a fucking gift! And I want it sent *today*, not tomorrow!'

Ling's head went down again, attempting to merge with the hardwood floor as he made his obeisance. 'A new concubine, perhaps, Master?'

'A new...' Tsao Ch'un's face lit up. 'The very thing. That pretty one, perhaps... you know, the fourteen-year-old... the princess... send her.'

Ling's head lifted an inch or two, then went down again. 'Consider it done, Master.'

'Good. Then send for my eldest son, Tsao Heng. It's time he earned his allowance, neh? Time the lazy bastard learned to be a prince!'

Unable to sleep, Li Chao Ch'in had dressed and gone down to his study. It was there that Li Peng found him.

'Father? Are you all right?'

He turned, looking at the boy. At least that much he could be proud of; that for all yesterday's troubles, Li Peng had not complained. He'd been a rock. A pillar of untarnished virtue amidst it all.

'I've been thinking,' he said, beckoning the young man over. 'Mulling over everything that happened.'

'And?'

Li Chao Ch'in shrugged. He wished he could say he made sense of it all, only he didn't. All he knew was that he needed time and distance on this.

He hesitated, then, 'I'm cancelling all my engagements for the next few days. I thought...'

Li Peng waited silently for his father to continue, and in time he did.

'I think what strikes me most about yesterday's events, is that it was not entirely unexpected.'

Li Peng looked shocked. 'Father?'

'Oh, I don't mean it was any less disgraceful... just that it's been coming for a long time now. Perhaps I ought not to even whisper it aloud... but I believe that what happened yesterday was significant. It wasn't just that Tsao Ch'un was rude. He is often so. This once, however, he overstepped the mark.'

'And that frightens you?'

Li Chao Ch'in met his son's eyes. 'I'll tell you what frightens me. As I stood there watching him, a thought came to me. Three words of great significance. Three words I'd never thought before – not in the context of Tsao Ch'un.'

'And those words?'

'*This cannot continue.*'

'Ah...'

'Worse than that. Those three words were like a key, opening a door that had not been opened. For as I watched him lurch drunkenly about among our guests, I thought to myself "Tsao Ch'un is losing his grip. He has become a liability. And his sons..."'

The young man looked down at this, horrified. '*Aiya...*'

'*Aiya* indeed. But once started I could not help myself. I stood there, watching the old man, thinking to myself. What are his sons, after all, but troublemakers and bullies? And when they inherit...?'

'Perish the thought.'

'And yet what is to be done? We are his hands.'

'And yet...'

Li Chao Ch'in sighed, then met his son's eyes once more. 'And yet...'

He hesitated, then, more businesslike. 'We are to meet again, a week from now.'

'To meet?' Li Peng looked puzzled.

'The Seven, I mean...'

'Ah... then you mean to depose him?'

'Depose him?' It was Li Chao Ch'in's turn to look horrified. Yet what else were they talking about if not that? Either they had to tolerate Tsao Ch'un's behaviour or make him pay. And how else could they do that than by wresting power from his grasp?

It was unthinkable. After all these years of loyal service.

'*Aiya,*' he said quietly, conscious of how far he had come in speaking to his son. If anyone were listening...

He swallowed, bitter suddenly. Was that the only answer? To kill Tsao Ch'un? Was that the only way to wrest the power from him? Instinct said yes. For Tsao Ch'un would bow to no man. And if Tsao Ch'un, then sons and grandsons too. All trace of his family would need to be erased, for to leave a single shoot would be to sow the dragon's teeth.

Could he do that? Was he ruthless enough?

He looked to Li Peng and seeing him thus, so tall and straight, he knew suddenly that he must. If not now, then some day soon. For he had seen the way the great lord stared at his sons – comparing them in mind, no doubt, to his own.

Him or us...

Li Chao Ch'in shivered then looked down.

'Father? Are you all right?'

He smiled bleakly. It was where their conversation had begun.

Reed was in Ebert's office just after seven, even as Ebert himself arrived.

'Peter...? I thought you were in Pei Ching.'

'I was. I got the early rocket back.'

'Your meeting?'

'Went well. I...'

Ebert walked round his desk and sat, then looked up at Reed again.

'Well? What did they want?'

Reed took the folder from his case and handed it across, remaining standing while Ebert read it through, expecting to see his face light up at any moment. But he should have known – that wasn't Wolfgang's way.

'Good,' he said finally. 'Your patient work paid off. But I want some changes.'

'Changes?'

Ebert fixed him with a stare. 'Yes, changes. I want us to renegotiate.'

'But we can't.'

'There's no such word.' He shook the file at Reed. 'This document... now that we know they're interested... we rework it, page by page. Tighten it up. Make it more lucrative.'

'But... they're giving us what we wanted. You went through that contract yourself...'

Ebert almost – *almost* – smiled. 'I did. But I didn't think they'd bite. Now that they have...' He sighed, then shook his head. 'Don't you see it, Peter? We've asked for too little.'

'Too little? But it's six billion *yuan*!'

'And that's not enough. How do I know that? Because if it was, they'd have made an issue of it. As it is...'

Reed stared at his boss a moment, then bowed his head. It was true. In his euphoric state he hadn't seen it, but it was obvious.

'You want me to go back to them?'

'Are you up to it?'

Reed looked down a moment, then nodded. 'I think so.'

'Good. But don't get despondent. You've done a good job... so far. But the real hard work lies ahead. We need to see how much they really want this. How far they're prepared to go to get it.'

'And if they say no? If they take back what they've offered?'

'They won't.'

'Then...?'

Ebert pushed the folder aside. 'I'll draft a new agreement. We'll get it back to them by messenger this evening. Then you can fly in tomorrow night.'

Reed looked away. He felt awkward suddenly. 'Don't you think... well... doesn't it seem a bit ungrateful?'

Ebert gave a short bark of laughter. 'Ungrateful? Wake up! This is business, Peter, purely business.'

'Master...'

Tsao Ch'un looked up blearily from where he sat, watching that morning's news. 'What is it now, Steward Ling? Is the girl ill?'

Ling did not look up, but lay there, face down where he had prostrated himself.

'No, Master, the girl is fine. It is another matter.'

'Another matter? This early?' Tsao Ch'un's face was sour. All he wanted to do was go back to bed.

'It is someone to see you, Master.'

'Someone...' Tsao Ch'un stood unsteadily. He would have to take something for this. There was a pain in his head the like of which he hadn't experienced for weeks. Not since he'd gone out on that hunting party with his eldest boy.

'Who in hell's name wants to see me this early in the morning?'

'It is Ma Shao Tu, Master, he...'

But Tsao Ch'un didn't want explanations. All he knew was that this Ma Shao fellow wasn't someone whose name he was aware of. And what should such a one be doing waking the Son of Heaven from his sleep?

'Send him away!' he bellowed. 'No... throw him in the cells! How dare he!'

'But Master...'

A pleading tone had entered Ling's voice. Tsao Ch'un stared at him. It was unlike Ling to disturb him over nothings. Most unlike him. So maybe this was important. Only, who the fuck *was* this man?

One thing was sure – it had to be very important indeed to call upon his time in this manner. Even more so if Ling, who rarely let anyone into Tsao's presence, was begging him to see the man.

He took a steadying breath. 'Okay. Who is he? And why should I see him at this unearthly hour?'

Ling, who had been cringing, awaiting a surly kick from his Master, relaxed a little.

'He has come from Tongjiang, Master. From Li Chao Ch'in's household. He is a senior servant there. One of Li Chao Ch'in's most trusted men. Only...'

Tsao Ch'un was suddenly alert. 'What is his name again?'

'Ma Shao Tu, Master.'

'And what do we know of him?'

'That he is who he says he is. And that he has worked for Li Chao Ch'in for thirty years now, since he was four years old.'

'So why does he come here now, this... *loyal* man?'

'He has news, Master. News of some bearing on matters. It seems there was a meeting of the Seven, after you were gone.'

Tsao Ch'un shrugged. It made perfect sense for there to be a meeting of his advisors. They were always having meetings.

'So?'

'It was a meeting about you, my Lord.'

Ma Shao Tu had been busy, tidying and dusting in one of the small ante-rooms that led off of Li Chao Ch'in's study when the great men had come in, bristling with anger and bolting the doors behind them. Knowing that he ought not to be listening, he should have stepped out and declared himself, but his courage failed him, the moment had passed and all he could do was keep his presence secret.

Thus he had overheard everything.

Hearing Ma Shao Tu's account of it left Tsao Ch'un in a rage. The sheer ingratitude they showed to him who had raised them so high! It was staggering! What would they have been without him? Nothing!

As Ma Shao Tu finished his account, knelt there before Tsao Ch'un, his head lowered, the great man let out a roar of rage. Lunging at the servant, he grasped him by the neck, holding him up and choking the life out of him before letting him fall.

Loyal men! Thus would he deal henceforth with loyal men!

'Steward Ling!'

Ling lay there trembling, unable to keep his eyes off the dead man's blackened face. 'Y-y-yes, Master...?'

'Have Colonel Feng come at once. I have a task for him.'

Tsao Ch'un's anger had turned to a cold, slow smoulder by the time he reached Shaoyang. On the flight he had decided on what he would do. Now, as the palace came slowly into view among the surrounding mountains, misted and grey and timeless, he felt at last the hollowness of disappointment.

He had expected more of them than this.

He had come here, to Fan Chang's home in Hu-nan, unannounced. As the seven cruisers made their descent, Tsao Ch'un, looking out from the leading craft, could see how the servants of the house rushed this way and that in an effort to make ready for his unexpected visit.

Tsao Ch'un's face was hard and brutal. Fan Chang was the eldest of the Seven and his most trusted man. When he had needed help, back in their darkest days, when events were yet in the balance, it was Fan Chang who had come to him and offered his fealty, Fan Chang who had helped forge that tight little clan of helpers and advisors who had taken the great weight from their Master's shoulders and shared it out among themselves.

But that was long past. Times had changed. As indeed had Fan Chang and his fellows. They had met in secret...

Every time Tsao Ch'un pictured it he shivered with indignation. Felt that selfsame rage that had made him kill Li Chao Ch'in's servant.

Loyal men. Tsao Ch'un grimaced, hurt to the core by the thought that those he had trusted most had turned against him. For what else was it? To meet in secret to debate his future?

His pilot slowed, heading for the landing pad, but Tsao Ch'un leaned across him, pointing away towards the great green space at the centre of the palace.

'No! Put me down there!' he ordered. 'Right there, in the middle of the lawn!'

Fan Chang knew at once what was wrong. For Tsao Ch'un to turn up unannounced, without a moment's warning, accompanied by six armed cruisers, it could mean one thing alone – ill fortune for his house.

He had been in his children's quarters, coaching his three youngest in their letters, helping them perfect their brush strokes, when word came of Tsao Ch'un's approach.

As he waited for his servants to bring another robe – one of cyan blue, decorated with tiny golden butterflies – he gave the order for his family to leave, sending his wives and sons off into hiding. He might well be wrong. Tsao Ch'un might be here on other business, but he doubted it. There could only be one reason why Tsao Ch'un had come, and that was if he'd heard about their meeting yesterday, after the ceremony.

And if he had, then they were *all* in the gravest trouble.

As he kissed Fan Peng, his eldest wife, goodbye, Fan Chang wondered if he would ever see her sweet face again. Would Tsao Ch'un dare to take them on? To strip all seven of their power and demote them?

The Tsao Ch'un of old would not have blinked before doing so. He was a tiger of a man, unafraid of anything or anyone. But the Tsao Ch'un of old was gone, replaced by an old reprobate who did not know how to behave in decent company. So who knew how he'd react?

Did the tiger still have teeth?

As he pulled on his ceremonial coat, Fan Chang caught a sight of himself in the full-length mirror opposite and sighed. He was too old for this. His son, Li, should have taken over years ago. And now the years had caught up with him.

'Come,' he said, looking to his stewards and advisors, who had gathered in the room with him, 'let us go and greet our Master.'

★

As the elite troops he had brought secured the palace, disarming any of Fan Chang's men they found, Tsao Ch'un waited in the craft.

It would not do to lose his life simply through a moment's carelessness.

Fan Chang and his men had gathered on the steps below the lawn, heads bared, bowed low, waiting for him to emerge.

Tsao Ch'un was breathing heavily. 'You cunts!' he muttered, glaring at them through the bulletproof glass, his face a mask of hatred. 'You lying fucking cunts!'

How easily they played at being honest, loyal men, when all the while they despised him and wished him gone – he who had forged this world of peace and plenty.

How dare they even think of it!

Tsao Ch'un had ordered the palace's communications system jammed when he was half an hour out. It was a crude thing to do, he knew, for the rest of the Seven might think it odd that Shaoyang was silent. They might guess that it was his doing, but it was better than letting Fan warn the others. While they were in the dark he had the advantage. They might guess, but they would not know for sure. And not knowing would make them hesitate before acting, for the habit of obedience was not easily surrendered.

Not that he had any kind of plan. For now all he did was follow the burning fuse of his anger to see where it led. He was not even willing to think of consequences, only that someone should pay.

So why not Fan? Fan, who should have spoken out for him in Council. Fan who had professed to be his servant, loyal until death.

Once more Tsao Ch'un shivered with anger at the thought. His hands ached from where he had been clenching them. So too his jaws. He wanted to tear and rip and gouge – a feeling he'd not experienced in years.

As Colonel Feng returned to say that the palace was secured, Tsao Ch'un pressed the door release and even as they hissed apart, jumped down, not waiting for the ramp to be lowered.

'Fan Chang!' he bellowed, striding towards where the old man waited, head bowed among his retainers. 'You fucking insect! You lying fucking turd! I'll have your guts, you cunt!'

Fan Chang's head came up, a look of shocked surprise in his eyes, and then he sank to his knees, his head almost touching the ground.

Barely a body's length from where Fan Chang knelt, Tsao Ch'un stopped, panting from his efforts, his face set into a snarl of rage.

'This *meeting*,' he began, poison dripping from the words. 'This fucking *meeting* that you called... Is it true?'

Fan Chang groaned, then gave the slightest nod of his head.

'*Answer me!*' Tsao Ch'un yelled, his eyes almost popping from his face. 'Is it *true*?'

Fan's answer was almost a whisper. 'Yes, my Lord... only...'

'Only nothing! You *dare* discuss *me*? Dare criticize *me*, your Lord and Master?' Leaning forward, he spat in Fan Chang's face.

The old man groaned, but made no attempt to wipe the spittle from his face.

'You forget who you are,' Tsao Ch'un went on. 'You forget—'

Overwhelmed by emotion, Tsao Ch'un's voice caught in his throat. He had just noticed what kind of robe Fan Chang was wearing.

'Is this some subtle insult, Fan Chang? *Butterflies*?'

Fan knew he hated butterflies. Butterflies and all other insects.

Tsao Ch'un turned, looking to his colonel, his anger turned cold.

'Colonel Feng... strip him, down to his loincloth, then bind him hand and foot.'

Fan Chang looked up, a naked fear now in his eyes. 'But my Lord...'

A great shudder went through Tsao Ch'un. 'You are no longer my advisor, Fan Chang. I take back what I gave you. You are nothing now.'

And, with a gesture of finality, he turned his back on him.

There was a murmur of protest from Fan's servants, but it was to no avail. Colonel Feng and his men hauled Fan Chang to his feet and, ripping his clothes from him, began to bind him.

'Master!' Fan Chang cried out plaintively. 'Listen to me, Master, *please*...'

Feng slapped him hard. 'Not another word!'

The old man groaned, his voice tearful suddenly. 'But Master...'

Feng slapped him again, and then a third time, the last blow forcing the old man to his knees once more.

Fan Chang was crying now. 'Master... forgive me...'

But Tsao Ch'un was unforgiving. 'Burn it,' he said, gesturing towards the palace. 'Burn it all... and him with it...'

CHUNG KUO

Chapter 18

POSTPONEMENTS

Chi Lin Lin had come back half an hour ago, to tell Jake about the postponement. It was Advocate Yang's view that Judge Wei and the Changs were still trying to come to some agreement, not so much about the case, but about how much Wei was going to be paid to put his name to the decision. It was likely that he'd thought about it overnight and realized just how much the Changs stood to make if he gave them this. If so, it might be some while before they were summoned back to the court-room. Some while before they calculated what Wei's share would be. It was all so cynically corrupt.

In the meantime, Jake was to remain here, in this awful rented room. One of thousands, as he'd discovered. Some, Chi had told him, had been here years, their fortunes dwindling in the same measure as their chances of success.

It was fucking Dickensian.

Jake looked about him at the room, dismayed. For the money he had paid he had expected, if not luxury, then at least something comfortable. But this... It was so cheap, so tawdry, it could have easily been below the Net. Or some old world dosshouse.

The mattress was so thin and unyielding, it was like lying on a sheet of solid wood. There wasn't the slightest give in it, and as for the sheets, they were coarse and rough. Jake suspected they were made of plastic meant to feel like cloth. Because that was the way of this world. Everything was made of plastic, and everything was manufactured to seem like something else.

The screen was blank. He reached out and touched it.

Nothing. It flickered, but didn't come on. Jake touched it again, prodding it this time, letting some of the resentment he felt come out in the gesture. This time, slowly and swimmingly, it came alive.

News. Anodyne and reassuring, and, as he'd come to know, invariably untrue. A fake mirror on their fake world. Not a word unscripted. Not a word permitted to become utterance until it had been through a panel of Ministry censors.

Suddenly there was a view of hills and trees and...

Jake sat back a little, trying to take in what he was seeing.

Where the hell is this? England?

No, not England. It was China. Somewhere in Sichuan, yet so like the northern English countryside that Jake found his heart pounding.

For a moment longer it was there, filling the screen. Then it returned to the newscaster, a middle-aged Han, perfectly attired in a long blue one-piece *pau* and reading from his papers. Smiling tightly, insincerely, out at the watching billions.

Cumberland. That was what it was like. Fucking Cumberland.

Not that it had *been* Cumberland, even then. Cumberland had ceased to be a geographic region a good fifty years before *he* found himself washed up there.

Jake sat back against the wall and closed his eyes. The countryside surrounding Cockermouth, that's what it reminded him of. And Hinton's Academy, their youth training school, there in the northern wilds.

He hadn't thought of it in years.

Rough skies, and cloud and rain. And running in the mud, tired beyond belief, but keeping going whilst voices yelled encouragement, because to give up would be to fail.

Oh yes, he remembered it all too clearly.

Remembered the thickness of the walls, the old buildings built like block-houses against the winter weather, and that strange feeling of living on the frontier. Everything about it so elemental. Fourteen he'd been when he first went there. Fourteen and fragile. Not exactly a loner, just locked in; the shell he'd made for himself making it hard to socialize. And they understood that somehow. Coaxed him out of himself, bit by bit.

Church and hymns and readings from the big bible on the lectern. And the cloaks they'd worn: black for the boys, mauve for the masters.

Another world, even then. The hardships and the slow education in self-reliance. Learning to stand on his own two feet. Only one's own two feet weren't anything like enough, not when the world underwent such changes. Such seismic shifts.

Maybe. But what I learned there certainly helped. There's no questioning that. Those years in Corfe... what else was it I drew upon but that? That education in self-reliance. If I'd not had that...

Eyes closed, he could still see his friends from those times. Edward with his soft blond hair and boyish charm. Chas with his effervescent good humour and his ability to turn the worst situation into a challenge to be overcome. And Will. Perhaps the best of the lot, never fazed, never troubled, dark-haired and handsome, a leader of men.

What had happened to them all? Had they too been on Tsao Ch'un's list? And were they dead now, their fine bones rotting in the earth?

He hoped not.

It was there, in the Academy, that he had first experienced it: the datscape, or CDL – 'comprehensive data landscape' – as it was formally known. There that he'd first known the high that was total data immersion.

Yes, and it was there that he'd discovered just how good he was. How natural it felt, being inside that world of coded information. How his nerve-endings had sung in those early days.

A world of boys and bicycles, beef and beer.

'These are words beginning with a b...'

Jake opened his eyes, remembering. Wondering how it was possible he could have forgotten. Only that was the way of this brave new world of theirs. It was all one long process of forgetting.

Particularly the songs. Because songs were so evocative, weren't they? So *precise* in locating old memories.

Like that night in the Red Lion, in the high street of Carlisle Enclave. The night of his eighteenth birthday. He had been there with Will and Ed and Chas. The first time he'd got drunk. And the songs. He could still see the old jukebox in the corner. Still see the list of songs – perhaps the best selection of songs he'd ever come across, hand-picked by the landlord... what was his name now? Joe Turnbull, that was it!

Jake sat forward, surprised by how vividly it all came back. How perfectly it had been preserved, there beneath the wall-like layers of forgetting.

Elephant Talk. That was that song. Robert Fripp and King Crimson.

It made him wonder if a single copy of the song remained anywhere in the world, or whether it was only in his head now. One of those many things that would die when he died. Like in the Borges story.

He couldn't recall now who had mentioned that to him. Someone had, only...

Jake stood up, looking about him. There was only a small gap between the bed and the wall. Barely enough room to turn. No. He'd go mad with claustrophobia if he didn't get out of there for a while.

Besides, he ought to phone Mary. Let her know what was happening.

The thought brought back the conversation she'd told him about, with Peter, the previous evening. He was sure Peter was keeping something back. He had news; something he was dying to tell them, but couldn't. Which was fine, because it made it easier to keep all this from Peter.

Gods, I hope we prevail, he thought, pulling on his cloak, then reaching out to unlock the door and patting his pocket as he did, to make sure he had the room key. *Because if we don't, we're fucked.*

Jake had a quiet beer in a nearby bar, then, feeling restless, decided he'd visit Advocate Yang.

Yang Hong Yu's offices, he knew, weren't far away. Not that he'd ever visited them – they had done their business face to face on screen – but he had Yang's card. With a little help getting directions, he found himself standing at Yang's door half an hour later.

Stepping out of the lift, looking about him at the state of things, his heart had sunk. This was downlevel with a capital D. As he made his way along the corridor, beggars assailed him, pestering him until he'd been forced to yell at them to leave him be. And that was only part of it. The stale smell, the tattered look of everything. It felt like a place where people had given up all hope.

And here, amidst it all, was Yang's.

Jake reached out and knocked on the plain plastic panel of the door. There was movement inside, and then the door opened a crack.

'Yes?'

It was a woman, Jake realized. An elderly-looking Han. Yang's wife, possibly. She looked old enough.

'Forgive me, but I've come to see Advocate Yang. I am his client, Shih Reed. I...'

'Oh, Shih Reed...' Yang said, pushing the woman aside and stepping outside into the corridor, pulling the door closed behind him. 'Why didn't you tell me you were coming? I would have met you.'

Jake looked past Yang at the door. In that brief moment when he had squeezed through, Jake had seen past him.

'Is something wrong, Yang Hong Yu? Are you... in trouble?'

Conflicting emotions crossed Yang's face and then he sighed, deflating a little. 'It is... what do you call it?... an occupational hazard. Take on the big boys and you court trouble, neh?'

'Trouble?'

Again there was a moment's conflict in the old man's face. Then, sighing again, he opened the door, gesturing to Jake to step inside.

Where there was chaos, papers strewn everywhere, files torn and defaced. And over everything, the smell of shit. Of human excrement.

'Aiya!' Jake said, shocked by what he saw. 'Who did this? Do you know?'

'The local tong... Triads, you know? Probably hired by the Changs, though who is to know, neh?' Yang, looking about himself at the mess, seemed close to tears. 'I have had this before... several times... but not for years. I thought...'

Only he didn't say what he thought. Instead, he shrugged. A shrug expressive of lost hope.

Poverty and distress, Jake thought. *Signs of an honest man.*

And poor Yang Hong Yu was paying the price for his honesty.

Jake looked down. 'Do you think I should accept their offer, Advocate Yang?

Yang shook his head. 'No, Shih Reed. This makes no difference. If anything, this hardens my resolve. Such men...' There was a sudden bitterness in Yang's face. 'Such men shame us all. But the sage does not bow before adversity. And neither does Yang Hong Yu. I am still your Advocate, Shih Reed, and I advise that you reject their offer firmly.'

'Reject it?'

'Yes.'

'Whatever it is?'

'Whatever it is.' Yang looked suddenly stern, determined. 'This is a matter of principle, now. Of honour. To even think of backing down...'

Yang Hong Yu bristled with anger, then looking to Jake again, he smiled. 'You go back to your room, *Shih* Reed, while we tidy up here. I will send Chi Lin Lin to let you know when the case begins again. For it will begin, have no doubt. These scum... they can shit on us all they like, but we will have them in the end. See if we don't!'

Sitting back in the bar, Jake couldn't find it in himself to be so positive, so certain of the end result. It looked to him, rather, as if their chances of prevailing were diminishing by the hour; that there was little the Changs wouldn't do to prevent a decision from going against them in this matter.

No, they intended to set a precedent. To win the war with a single, decisive battle. To nip things in the bud, as the old-fashioned saying went. And they would be as ruthless as they had to be to get that result.

'You want another drink?' the barman asked, seeing that Jake's glass was empty. 'A Dragon Cloud?'

It was piss water. Nothing like a proper beer. But there was no choice in matters like that these days. Real ale, like real music, had been done away with.

Only what did it matter? His world was crumbling about him once again, and there was nothing he could do. Yang's bravery – his defiance – was admirable, but the truth was they were going to be crushed. Like bugs beneath some giant's thumb.

'Yeah. Give me a beer. A Dragon Cloud'll be fine.'

'You here for a hearing?' the barman asked, turning to take one of the distinctive plastic bottles from the shelf.

'Is there any *other* reason to be here?'

'You might work here.'

'Only I don't. I don't work anywhere any more. I've retired.'

The barman turned back, handed him the uncapped beer. Jake took it, smiled, then sipped.

Some other time, back in the old world, he'd have started a conversation. They'd have talked about music and events and all kinds of things. Only Jake couldn't play that game any more. If he had a beer or two he'd get maudlin for the past, and then he'd say something he shouldn't have. He'd done it before and got into trouble. So now he avoided it. Walked away, before they started opening doors that shouldn't be opened.

'Thanks,' he said. 'You got a newscast?'

The barman reached beneath the counter and pulled out a slate, handing it across.

'What do I owe you?'

Usually there was a deposit charge for borrowing a slate, but the barman shook his head.

'No charge. I trust you.'

'Thanks.'

Jake took the slate and his beer across to a table in the far corner. It was shadowed there and the screen on the wall above the table was dead. As he took his seat, Jake realized he was the only person in the room aside from the barman. Then again, it was early yet.

Thinking about his days at the Academy had made him recall all kinds of things. Things that he shouldn't, perhaps, have brought up out of those walled-in depths.

Things like his grandfather's death.

It was strange how, after the accident, he had gravitated towards his grandfather rather than his nan. Strange but understandable, for his nan had always been a much sterner person than his mother, and if he'd expected her to help him – maybe even to take his mother's place – he'd have been much mistaken. But his grandfather, with his quiet and gentle manner, had somehow helped Jake to get through, if only by being there.

Only then, when he was fifteen, his grandmother had died. She had not been well for some time, but suddenly she went down with something – a virus, maybe, there were a lot of them about back then – and within a week she was dead.

He'd been at the Academy by then, and the news, when it reached him, had been a shock. A real shock, for she had always seemed made of much stronger stuff than those about her.

Jake had gone home for the funeral, given four days leave by Mr Cahill, the Headmaster. He had travelled back, fearing the emotional fallout, knowing just how much his grandfather had loved his gran. That lovely gentle man –

Jake knew how much he must be hurting. Only, arriving home, he had seen at once *just* how bad things were.

It had been awful.

A distant relative, a great-aunt – one of his gran's sisters, Jane, whom he had only ever met once or twice – had been drafted in to make all the arrangements. As for his grandfather...

He had watched his granddad fall apart. Before his eyes. The old man had stopped eating. Stopped sleeping. Stopped showing any kind of interest in the world. At the graveside he had stood there, in his mourning suit, clay on his boots, held up by one of the funeral attendants. As he stared into the open grave, a look of such bewilderment, such agony on his face, Jake could hardly bear to look at him.

Jake had gone back to the Academy two days later. And when the news came through of his grandfather's death, eight days after that, it was no shock, for he had known. Known, from that awful moment at the graveside, that the old man could not bear to live without her. The woman he loved.

How well he knew that feeling.

After that he had put his head down, working hard to fill the emotional void, striving through work to find some kind of meaning to it all.

All dead. Everyone he'd ever loved.

Jake sighed heavily, then looked down at the slate and clicked it on. The surface shimmered, then lit up.

Talking heads, he thought, scrolling through to the channel he normally watched, then sitting back and taking a sip of his beer.

And stopped dead. He frowned, puzzled. It wasn't anything they were saying. No, if anything the news seemed even blander than usual. But something was up. He could see it in their body language, could recognize – as Hinton had taught him, all those years ago – that they were hiding something. Something big. Some rumour, maybe, or...

Jake scratched at his chin. He really ought to shave. Just in case the Judge called them back. But it was a half-formed thought. He was staring at the slate now, trying to work out just what would have put them all on edge. For there was no doubt about it. Some big news item was brewing, but they couldn't run with it. Not yet.

Only what in Christ's name could *that* be?

Jake drained his glass. His instinct was to go home. To get to Mary's side just as quick as he could. Only that was being ridiculous, wasn't it? It was not as if he knew anything. And he needed to be here, for when the case began again.

No. He'd wait. Sit in his room and keep an eye on things. And if they changed?

If they changed, he would go home. Let Advocate Yang deal with things himself.

There was one final surprise.

There, in his rented room – and who knew how they'd found him, but they had – a message was waiting for him. He sat there, the large brown envelope in his lap, staring at the logo in the top right corner.

GenSyn. It was from GenSyn. But not from Peter. He knew that, because he knew Peter's handwriting, and this wasn't his. And besides, Peter didn't know where he was. He hadn't told him, and he'd had Mary swear not to tell him.

It was twenty years since that whole business. Twenty years since Gustav Ebert had died, burned to toast in the datscape. Twenty years since he'd got his severance notice from them. So what was this?

There was only one way to find out.

Jake slipped his fingernail under the fold and drew it across, then took out the single sheet.

'Christ!'

He couldn't help himself. It was from Alison. He saw that at once. Recognized the handwriting at the bottom of the page—

Whatever you want, love Alison.

He read it through, then read it through again. Legal aid. GenSyn were going to give him legal aid – whatever he needed to fight his case.

Jake laughed. 'Unbelievable... fucking unbelievable.'

How in God's name had she known? Who had told her? Had Mary mentioned something to Peter – mentioned it and not told him that she had?

That was most likely. Only what did it matter? Help. They were going to give him help!

He wondered if they knew just what that involved; how much time and money the Changs had invested in this case.

Maybe not. Only right now, any help was welcome.

There was a contact number at the top left of the page. He had only to phone it and let them know.

Jake stood. He would do it now. Right now, before another second passed.

He smiled. And afterwards he'd phone Mary. Let her know. That is, if she didn't know already.

CHUNG KUO

Chapter 19

THE FIRST DRAGON DECIDES

It was late, and in that huge, sparsely furnished chamber, surrounded by the dark, the First Dragon sat at his desk. Staring into the faint, wavering light of a single blood-red candle.

He was dressed simply, in the plainest of black robes. Not silk, nor satin, but a rough cloth, dyed to match the night. It was his only ostentation.

He was, as all previous First Dragons had been, a Han. Only there all similarities ended. For this Han was unconnected. He had risen not through alliance or patronage but by sheer ruthlessness, ability, and a reputation for absolute incorruptibility. He was also younger than any previous First Dragon; a good twenty years younger. In his fifties now, he had a gaunt, almost severe look. Hatchet-faced, some said, though quietly, and not in his presence. Others said he resembled, in his stretched and fleshless way, what he once had been before the Ministry had recruited him: an oven man.

And so he did, yet he had one final, distinguishing feature – a birth mark, on the left of his brow; a cluster of small dark shapes that, in a certain light (as now), resembled a distant star exploding in its death throes.

He had been sitting there for the best part of three hours thinking matters through. Considering, calculating, mapping out potentiality, as if he played *wei ch'i* in his head, assessing the impact of each stone he placed upon the board, each probable response.

To his right, discarded now, lay a pile of handwritten reports. They had been useful, to a point, but something in their hasty preparation had made him question their value even as he read them. They lacked the sharpness of vision this situation merited. Nor did they take into account the uniqueness, the unprecedented character of events. For all their accuracy and intelligence, they did not, in even the smallest fashion, convey an understanding of what lay before them.

They were, and all credit to them, perfectly reasoned. Only reason would be the first thing to go in a scenario like this, and these papers had been compiled by men who had little experience of war. Not a single one of them understood just how much chance would play a part in the days ahead; how much would depend on who could improvise the best. On who could 'wing it', as the *Hung Mao* used say. Whereas he... he had 'winged it' these many years, playing it by ear, doing the unexpected, outflanking his opponents.

Which was why, right now, he needed to be alone. To hear no other voice but his own. To think things through while he still could, before all the disparate voices sullied the clarity of his thought.

Simplicity. That was the answer. Or part of it.

Maybe. Yet it did not help him come to a decision, and a decision must be made before this night was out.

His duty was quite clear. He was Tsao Ch'un's man. Hadn't he prostrated himself before the emperor and sworn the oath of loyalty?

He had. Only maybe those had been empty words. If so, then what was he? What *purpose* did he serve?

Custodian, his thoughts answered him. *You are custodian of it all.*

Yes, there was no doubting that. He was the custodian of this world. In his hands lay the fate of all, for it was he who was responsible for policing their knowledge of the past, and without that...

Without it, it would fall. For Chung Kuo was not just the City, the plantations, the orbitals and all the rest of it that was visible to the eye. It was an idea, an idea that the Ministry – the Thousand Eyes – maintained and guarded on a daily basis and which he, as First Dragon, kept watch over.

He was the glue that held it all together. And, because that was so, it was his duty to ensure that proper thought was given to the problem. For they had come to a major cusp in history – a moment when they must choose a path and follow it to the death.

For all their sakes.

For some time now he had known that it would come to this, but now that the hour was upon them, he realized that it was not anything like as simple as he'd thought. He needed to be certain that the decision he made was the right one, for if it were not then he and his great Ministry would vanish, as if they never had existed.

And that could not be allowed. That was why he must make the right decision and make it before this night was over. Tomorrow would be too late.

Only now, at this critical hour, he found himself thinking of his own small life, rather than the greater picture. Of his climb from nothing to the eminence he now commanded, rather than that abstract mesh of power and influence that had become his world.

He put his hand out, feeling the warmth of the candle's flame.

Of the twelve dragons who shared his burden, not a single one of them knew him, nor understood him. They knew his history, of course. How could they not? For that was their business, after all, to know everything they could unearth about each other – but that was very different from understanding. To do that, they would have had to *be* him, to have suffered what he'd suffered, to have lost a world and been given only shadows in return.

For what was this world if not a place of shadows? A waiting room, beyond whose door was death. And that was his secret. That he was dead inside, and had been these past twenty years and more.

Even so, he might simply have remained what he had been – another empty, bitter man, obsessed with his loss, eaten away by it – had not chance intervened.

His eyes widened at the thought. Chance was everything. And when it came one grasped it and hung on, as to the proverbial tiger's tail.

Chance, then, and loss. And no small loss at that, but the loss of everything that made a life worth living.

He had always been ambitious. Hard-nosed, his mother said, and proud of it. As a young, married man, his business had thrived. He had grown rich. A big man in the Ho-nan town where he'd been born. Only that day, when the bombs fell, the poor were made level with the rich. What Shen Fu had so carefully built had been destroyed in one single blinding flash.

His life, quite literally, was turned to ashes: wife, children, factory and all.

Chance had it that he had been away that day, on business. A thousand miles away. In the general chaos he had made his way back, riding on the back of an army jeep against the tide of refugees, returning to find his home town levelled.

He had not remarried. When the City came, he went through re-education, and, when the jobs were allocated in his stack, he chose the lowest of them, oven man, in charge of incinerating the dead. Why he had chosen that even he could not say. It was as if, for a time, he was asleep. And then one day he woke.

Two officials from the Ministry had come, seeking a favour. And he had known, in an instant, that there was something else he could be. Something greater.

It was purest chance. A favour they had called it, when in fact what they wanted was for him to cover their tracks. To do their dirty work for cash, and no questions asked.

Seeming to agree with them, he had arranged things as they'd wished. Only, instead of keeping silent, instead of taking their money and doing as they'd asked, he had gone directly to their offices, where he had sat for the best part of three hours, refusing to see anyone but the Grand Master himself.

That was where it had begun. The first link in the chain. For there, before that great man, he had betrayed them; had given them over, knowing the risk he took.

It would have been easy, he knew, to be rid of him. To *condone* what had been done. The Ministry had destroyed ten thousand men greater than himself. But he was lucky. Chance and audacity favoured him that day. The great man was new to his post, a recent appointment, and he had arrived with a mission to reduce corruption in his command; to deal with any offenders harshly and without mercy.

The matter itself was easy to prove. There were the four coffins for a start, and there was bound to be taped evidence.

One of the watchers – an agent of the Ministry – had become obsessed with a woman he was watching, a young, high-spirited maid who had been forced by her parents into marrying an older man. It had begun one night when, after submitting to her husband's brutal lovemaking, she had looked up past the sleeping man's back and directly into the lens. Then she had smiled seductively and blown a kiss.

After that, the observer had spent every evening watching her. Sensing she was being watched, or perhaps knowing that such behaviour would hook one such as he, she began to perform for the Ministry man when her husband was not there, stripping off her top and playing with her nipples.

And other things.

And he? He was hooked. Like a gasping fish he watched her, his infatuation growing by the hour, raging like a fire, until he knew he must have her.

So he had crossed the line; had visited the woman, starting an affair with her.

An affair that quickly grew out of control, so that one afternoon, as they lay there after making love, they talked of killing the husband and setting up home together uplevel.

But fate turned against the unhappy couple. Unknown to them, an audit had been requested from that department of the great Ministry which – in secret – watched the watchers. And, as chance would have it, our young lover was among those chosen at random to be observed.

Thus it was that their little scheme – the poisoning of the husband and the bribing of the official who issued the death certificate – was watched by the same two who later on had come to Shen Fu, begging a favour.

Too late to prevent the deed, they could only put things right in one way: by killing all those involved and destroying all record of what had transpired, for it was unthinkable to hand the matter over to their great rivals, Security. It would have meant losing face, and the servants of the Ministry hated losing face.

At any other time it would have ended there. Only the new Master listened to Shen Fu. After a brief investigation, he decided he could make capital of it, could use it to build his reputation as a stern yet honest man.

And so the two were tried by a panel of their peers and sentenced to die.

And Shen Fu?

Shen knew that the opportunity would not come again, so when they offered him a job he grabbed it with both hands. With no word of his betrayal on his official file, he began that very week, a thousand miles from where he'd been, appointed at the lowest level, as a *fen lei*, a classifier.

The First Dragon sighed and stared into the darkness.

To be *fen lei* back then had been to watch a world – a whole culture – slowly vanish before your eyes.

He could remember how it was.

Standing there at his station in the great hall alongside a thousand other *fen lei*, spread out in row after orderly row, his job was to take one of the passing crates from the conveyor belt to his left and, breaking the plastic seal, tip it out onto the tray, a big trough a full two *ch'i* to a side. Then he quickly sorted through the contents, deciding what should be sent on to the ovens and what queried, returning all that was to be burned to the crate and, after sealing it again with a film of red plastic, placing it on the conveyor to his right.

Looking back, most of it was incinerated. Tons and tons of the stuff, every hour of every day. The Ministry's ovens, like those he had tended as an oven man, never cooled, and the truth was that very little ever got queried. Some of the *fen lei*, in fact, had simply taken off the clear seal and put on the red one without ever glancing at the contents, but that was not his way. He was *fen lei*, after all, a selecter, and his job was to select.

What he did select he would put onto the shelf beneath the tray, where it would stay until the end of the day. It was mainly things he didn't recognize, books in foreign languages, or objects he didn't know the significance of. Anything that wasn't obvious. Anything that made him think twice.

Looking back, that had been an awful job. Soul-destroying if one had a soul. Only he hadn't. He had lost his. What it did, however, was to open his eyes to the great size of the task that they were undertaking. It awed him to see so many objects being destroyed simply to serve an ideology. For ten hours a day he had laboured thus, processing what the *chi lei*, the collectors, brought in. Piles and piles of the stuff. Films and books, magazines and T-shirts, music and pictures, games and old computers, cameras and box files full of papers, old photo albums, tourist nick-nacks and endless other stuff; products of the old West, of a vast consumer society that was no more. Cast-offs from the Age of Waste.

The dead-end products of a self-indulgent culture.

They burned it all, leaving no trace.

After three long years in the sorting hall, he had been moved. Had become *chi lei*.

To be *chi lei*, now that had been an adventure, and if he'd had the capacity for enjoyment, he would have enjoyed it. As it was, his two-year stint in Collections brought him a certain infamy.

Chillingly ruthless, he had led raid after raid upon First Level mansions, or into the Clay, that darkness beneath the City where most of the forbidden material came from.

He demonstrated a lack of concern for his own safety that was almost heroic, coming away with items that other, less determined men would not have unearthed.

'The Burrower' they called him, or simply 'Black Hands' for his habit of wearing black cloth gloves, a habit he still maintained.

Men grew to fear him, both those who had collections and those who worked alongside him as *chi lei*. For his ruthlessness extended to his colleagues, and at the least sign that any one of them was taking bribes, or hiding away any of the treasures that they found – and as the days went on and the ovens kept alight, so each individual item grew in value – he would kill them with his own hands. Then he would feed them to the ovens personally, with never a by-your-leave from his superiors. For they too, seeing his purity, feared him.

As for those who had collections, especially those among the new *Hung Mao* elite who had a taste for special, ancient things, they barely slept for fear of him. Several of them – men whom he had raided – put out contracts on his life. But he led a charmed life, and besides, by now there was a small band of followers. Men faithful to him alone, inspired by his behaviour, men who were close by him all the time, vigilant against such attempts.

Many had predicted that he would soar above the next three rungs of the ladder, becoming secretary to some great man within the Thousand Eyes, but it was not to be. Maybe it was his sheer unlikeability, that austere nature of his that let him down, or maybe some prejudice against the humility of his birth.

Whatever it was, Shen Fu did not advance.

Fear him they might, but many also hated him. Hated his puritanical manner, his absolutist stance. They might be the City's eyes, its conscience, yet they were also men and they understood men's weaknesses, whereas he...

He seemed barely human. And they were right.

It was thus that he found himself *yen ching*, an eye, that is, a watcher and given his own bank of screens to supervise.

And for once he did not excel. The job was too narrow, the people that he watched too dull. When he tried to punish them for minor misdemeanours, he received no encouragement from his superiors, only a warning to back off and leave them be.

On the surface, it was a bad time. A frustrating time. Or would have been, had he not taken the opportunity to learn his craft: to discover how to evaluate what people said, to analyze and sift, to read a body like a book and, in the last resort, how to trick a man into saying more than he intended. All these skills, learned at this time, would come in useful later when he had risen further.

From *yen ching* he was promoted to *fu*, literally 'next in rank', the title given to an Assessor – one of those bored-looking officials who helped run the great sorting halls. Three years had passed in the limbo of *yen ching* when Shen was made *fu*. By then he had spent more than eight years in the Ministry and some of his early promise seemed not to burn so brightly. Even so, there were still those who believed in him. After a mere four months as *fu* he was recruited by the Institute.

Nominally independent from the Ministry, the Institute for Historical Accuracy was, in effect, the very heart of the organization. Manned entirely by the elite of the Thousand Eyes, it was responsible for creating and enforcing – and *revising* – the history of Chung Kuo.

For Shen Fu it was the job he had wanted since leaving the *chi lei*; a chance to influence what people thought, what they believed, how they saw their world.

In a very real sense, the Institute was the single reason why the Ministry existed – why they burned things and watched people and sifted every word, every phrase that people uttered. It was all done to safeguard what the Institute had created. For at the Institute they made history. Literally so. Manufactured it and disseminated it. A fully consistent history in which the Han were dominant and the West... the West was nothing, its states and tiny kingdoms at best a gaggle of barbarians, vassals to the East.

It was strange how even he, who had experienced the world before Chung Kuo, found it hard now to believe it had been so, because the fiction they had set up in its place was so strong and powerful. It was consistent in its detail, it undermined everything he knew, replacing it, such that for the majority of the time he was in a state of blissful ignorance, blissful acceptance. Only rarely, when he was tired or when some event had re-awoken something, did he recall the old world he had known. For the briefest moment, he would find himself stranded in a state of half-belief, a limbo of uncertainty.

Though never for long.

What's more, it was true what many of the experts had predicted – it had indeed become easier as the years passed and many of those who remembered the Past – the *real* past – had died. The young who replaced them, newly born into the world, simply embraced things as they were, or rather, as they appeared to be. They had no reason to doubt what was told to them of their world. Whereas the old...

Increasingly they watched the old, fearing they'd hand their secrets on, coming down ever harder on them for any relapse, any slip of the tongue, any flouting of the rules. 'Making the break clean', as they called it.

He had been two years at the Institute, making his reputation anew. Just as he had begun to think that opportunity had passed him by, that he had attained the highest level that ambition and hard work might bring him, there was a chance meeting. Chang Li Chen, the Junior Dragon charged with drafting the proposed new Edict of Technological Control, was impressed enough to offer him the job of secretary to the great man.

It was a chance he could not possibly say no to. Only he did. Why? He wasn't sure. Only that his instinct was against it; that in the brief time he was in the great man's company, he felt wrong somehow – that his destiny lay elsewhere.

And so he began a period in his career when things went awry: when chance no longer favoured him; when, for the first time, he began to question whether he had been right to shun the great man's offer. For one whole year his luck seemed to desert him and wrong decisions haunted him, until he arrived at his desk one day to find the whole office buzzing with the latest news.

Chang Li Chen had been indicted. He was to be executed that night, along with seven of his closest aides, for taking bribes from several of the major companies – all of whom had stood to lose a great deal if the Edict had gone through in its proposed form. The scandal was so great that, for once, the media had got wind of the story. They were to run news items that very evening.

Shen Fu was the one who was asked to deal with the media – to make sure that those who knew were quickly warned not to breathe a word; that it would be in their worst interests – their *very* worst interests – to pursue this. His death-like presence, there in their offices, convinced them. Say a single word, he told them, and your lives will be made a living hell. He, personally, would make sure of it. And they believed him.

Not a word *was* said. Thanks to Shen Fu, the scandal passed, reduced to an internal problem by his timely actions.

The rest was history.

Three days later he was summoned to meet the First Dragon himself. There, at the meeting, he was offered Chang Li Chen's job.

Again he refused. This time not from any instinct, but because – as he said to the First Dragon himself, prostrating himself humbly as he did – he lacked experience.

But the First Dragon would not listen. He was to be a junior minister. He would gain experience. Given time.

Thus, against his will, he became a Dragon. And not just any Dragon. The Edict was perhaps the single most important document ever drafted, and he would be in personal charge of it: forging it clause by clause, paragraph by paragraph, word by word, until it expressed the will of those who had envisaged it, the seven great lords, Tsao Ch'un's chief ministers, known simply as the Seven.

And so, step by inexorable step, he had risen, until, after the untimely death of the First Dragon five years back, he had found himself thrust into that role, young and inexperienced as he was.

He remembered how it had been, that first day. How he had looked about him at the luxury, the sheer opulence of this chamber and vowed to himself that it would change – that his would be a simpler, purer reign than that of those who had preceded him. And so it had been. Puritan by nature, he had swept away all of the clutter, all of the misplaced pomp and ostentation that had grown like barnacles on the great hide of the beast. At the same time he had set himself the task of hunting down every last trace of corruption and, in so doing, had built a new pride in the Ministry; the same pride that had existed when the Thousand Eyes was but eight men, operating out of two rooms in Tsao Ch'un's palace, all those years ago.

He had rebuilt it well, in his own severe image. And now it would be tested. Both he and it.

Shen Fu stood, the sudden movement making the candle flame dance, the shadows waver.

Who are you? the voice inside him asked, as it so often did.

I am Shen Fu, who lost everything.

It was that loss – of his wife and children, of all his hopes and dreams – that had made his rise possible, for a man with nothing more to lose could achieve a great deal, especially within an organization like the Thousand Eyes, where emotional detachment was the greatest of virtues. But chance too had played a hand, and at those crucial moments in his career when he had gambled, he had invariably made the right choice. Luck, some called it, others said audacity, but it was neither. It was chance that favoured him, for chance favoured the dead.

This night, however, would be the greatest gamble of them all. 'Double or nothing', to use the old, forbidden parlance of the West.

Sitting back, he spoke to the air. As he did, a screen came down to the right of where he sat, its sudden brightness filling the chamber. For the next half hour he called up image after image from the past, from before Tsao Ch'un's great City – things that were forbidden to other, lesser men.

He watched Picasso paint, bright colour falling upon the whiteness of the canvas; saw Hitler standing in his staff car as it drove beneath the Eiffel Tower, his arm held upward in a stiff salute. Kennedy's assassination, the Moon landing, Hiroshima, all followed in quick succession, those and a hundred more, some in black and white they were so old. But most of them in colour. And then the sequence slowed, showing a young boy, eight or nine at most, shaven-headed, walking slowly through a Russian cornfield, as in a dream.

Shen Fu sighed. Dead as he was, this single image could yet touch him.

Tarkovsky...

He stared at it, fondly almost, then whispered to the air. 'Blow him away... Blow them all away.'

Shakespeare and Beethoven, Michelangelo and Einstein, Planck and Tolstoy, Nietzsche and Mozart, Bob Dylan and James Dean, Muhammad Ali and the Beatles, Churchill and Stalin, Newton and Copernicus, Van Gogh, Monet and Chaucer, Erasmus, da Vinci and Columbus, Voltaire, Chaplin and Edison, Martin Luther King and Xerxes, Hitchcock, Cortez and Darwin, Gandhi and Lord Byron, Werner von Braun, Elvis Presley and Nelson Mandela, Washington, Napoleon and Marilyn Monroe, Henry Ford, Luther and Mercator, Michael Jackson, Wordsworth and Neil Armstrong, Julius Caesar and Karl Marx, Faraday, Roosevelt and Tchaikovsky, Freud, Wagner, Tolkien and Jimi Hendrix, Benjamin Franklin, Wittgenstein, Dostoevsky and Charles Dickens, Lenin, Alexander and Lincoln, Judy Garland and Neil Young, Cleopatra and Moses, Cromwell, Turner and Lord Nelson, Charlemagne and Jesus... and all the rest.

Names that had once meant something in the world. Names he had come to know in the performance of his duties. *Yin fa chi*, they were... *Triggers*.

Let them all disappear; let them rot in the desert sands of Time.

Yes. Let it all vanish, as if it had never been.

He understood now. People could not be left to choose their destiny. They must be guided by those who knew better. Those who were willing to make the sacrifice on their behalf. Men like himself.

Two hours had passed. Outside the night was slowly drawing on to morning. For Shen Fu, who had sat there most of the night, those last two hours had seemed interminable, unendurable, and yet they'd had to be endured, for there was a need – a very great need – to ensure that he was right.

He had considered a great deal in that time: the role of the Minor Families; how fit the Seven were to fight a war; whether the companies would commit themselves and get involved, or whether they'd just keep their heads down. And then there were the Banners and the New Confucians. Where would *they* stand if push came to shove?

The Seven, it was obvious, would need to fight or go under, but the rest?

The Banners were almost certainly Tsao Ch'un's. They would remain loyal to him. Only if Jiang Lei came out of retirement might there be a question.

The rest? Well... the rest were ineffective. They might seem powerful, yet when the chips were down...

Shen Fu almost laughed. Here he was, contemplating war, and for once he was thinking in cliché. And Western cliché at that!

'Push and shove'. 'When the chips were down.'

Shen Fu stood. The time for consideration was at an end. The First Dragon had come to a decision. It was time to let his fellows know. To seal their fates with his.

He spoke to the air, knowing they were at their desks right then, awaiting his decision.

'Things are finely balanced,' he began. 'Indeed, as things are, Tsao Ch'un will win this war, despite his disadvantages. Why? Because he is one and they seven, and who among them will make those crucial, momentous and utterly vital decisions? Yet even if he wins, what then? The Seven, of course, will die – they and all their families, to the last generation. But Tsao Ch'un too will die. Not now, perhaps, but some day soon. Ten years from now. And what then? Who will rule after him? Which one of his three bone-idle, useless progeny?'

He went on. 'We have seen this many times before in our long history – how new dynasties have been formed through the strength and vision of a single man; how chaos has been turned into order through such a channelling of power. Yet when that great man died, what then? Did his sons build upon what he had achieved? Or did they fall upon each other like hungry wolves?

'We must not let that happen to our world. We have worked too hard to let it happen. That is why our role in this cannot be passive. We must act, and act now, *against* our Master. In fact, we must use every last shred of our influence to rally opposition to his rule.'

Shen Fu paused, looking about him at the darkness.

'I know what you are thinking. That we have all sworn oaths of loyalty. That if we cannot be trusted, then who can? But there are precedents. History teaches us that when a Son of Heaven forgets his responsibilities, when he steps beyond just and acceptable behaviour and stumbles into tyranny, then the Mandate of Heaven is broken and... well, I do not have to say. The Mandate *has* been broken. Tsao Ch'un's treatment of Fan Chang cannot be borne. We cannot cover our eyes and keep our heads bowed. Not in the face of this.'

Afterwards, alone, the First Dragon sat at his desk, his fingers steepled beneath his chin. Already six of those he had addressed earlier were dead – killed by Ministry assassins to prevent them from going straight to Tsao Ch'un. Not only that, but contact had been made with three of the Seven, as well as with Amos Shepherd, declaring that the Ministry would support 'those whose righteous actions against an act of tyranny will prevent our world from sliding once more into chaos'.

The words were Shen Fu's. Now, alone again, he sat in the darkness, looking at images of his darling wife and children, wondering if they would have understood what he did here today. As their image faded, so a voice sounded, informing the First Dragon that his cruiser was awaiting him on the roof.

Shen Fu stood. It was two hours until dawn and the die had been cast. He was to go to see Li Chao Ch'in at Tongjiang – that is, if Tsao Ch'un had not anticipated his treachery and already sent cruisers to blast him from the air. But he was not afraid. Let the heavens fall, it did not matter now. Nothing had really mattered since the bomb went off. The rest had been a game; a filling-in of time until he too was crated up and offered to the oven man.

As his cruiser lifted from the roof, Shen Fu watched the newscasts as the first few skirmishes took place. All seemed normal. Most people, waking, would think this another ordinary day. But it was far from ordinary. Even as he sat there, in the comfort of that cushioned space, the sound of the engines a constant dull vibration, countless life-changing decisions were being made.

Forces were being rallied and deals made. Already, almost certainly, hundreds had been killed, maybe thousands, and more – many more – would die violent deaths in the hours to come. But Shen Fu, one-time oven man, was completely unperturbed. For he knew what few others guessed – that Death, not Tsao Ch'un, was the only true Master.

He who had not smiled but once in twenty years, now smiled again at the thought. Did Tsao Ch'un know? Or was he yet ignorant of his Dragon's flight? And when he learned of it, would he rage and curse him for his ingratitude? Or would he take a calming breath and appreciate the move, as one Master to another across the board?

Shen Fu hoped it was the latter. Hoped that in this, his most trying hour, Tsao Ch'un would prove the man Shen thought he was. It was rare for Shen to like any man, but he revered Tsao Ch'un.

Shen Fu looked up at the camera, as if addressing the great man directly. 'No hard feelings, neh?'

He looked down again, then nodded. A week he gave it. One week... then one or other of them would be dead.

Chapter 20

SCATTERED MEMORIES FROM
THE AGE OF WASTE

hey got the message from the court last thing at night, just after eleven. At ten past, Chi Lin Lin was knocking on Jake's door once again, hammering hard, not caring who he woke.

'Shih Reed! Shih Reed! We've news!'

Inside, Jake sat up slowly, rubbing his eyes. *News?*

Then he remembered. The case. Young Chi was talking about the case.

Jake had been having dreams again, and Chi had woken him from one. A dream in which he'd met Alison for the first time, outside Blackwell's, on a sunny day in late September, a million years ago.

He edged across the bed, then stood, blinking his eyes, trying to get fully awake. Then, and only then, did he unlock the door.

'Chi Lin Lin... what's to tell?'

'We are to be in court, *Shih* Reed. First thing.'

'First thing?' For a moment he was confused, then, 'You mean at eight?'

'And not a second later. Earlier, if at all possible.'

'I'll be there... and Chi...'

In that pause between words he had changed his mind. He would tell Advocate Yang about GenSyn in the morning. After all, there was nothing he could do right now, and it would be nice to see his face when he found out.

They had promised him a team of three lawyers. Specialists in company law and pensions agreements. He would have to let them know, of course, but he had the funniest feeling that they probably knew already. They had seemed to know everything about the case.

'Yes, Shih Reed?' Chi asked, when Jake had said nothing for a full five seconds.

'Nothing. Just thank you for coming to tell me. And see you in the morning, neh?'

When Chi was gone, he went back inside and locked the door. He had been told earlier, by the barman, that gangs of thieves operated in these levels preying on the gullible and careless, and he did not intend to fall into either of those categories.

He reached up, turning the screen back on. If he couldn't sleep – and he couldn't, now that Chi had woken him – he might as well watch some news. Only once again he noted that uncertainty that seemed to lie behind everything; the way the media's reporters seemed to be only half attending to what they were saying. As if some whole other story was going on. One that the general public were not to know about.

Getting that message from GenSyn had made him forget. But now that he saw it again, he knew he was right. Something was happening, something big.

Only what?

His instincts, backed up by experience, told him to start at the top. What was the biggest thing that could be happening right now?

War. War between Tsao Ch'un and the Seven.

He laughed. Ridiculous. Absolutely ridiculous. Because they wouldn't be able to cover up something like that. Everybody would know. Or would they? Especially if it had only just begun. What if they didn't know quite how to report it? Or, more likely, what if the Thousand Eyes had put an embargo on reporting it?

Jake spent the next hour switching channels, trying to find some small speck of evidence that something was going on behind the scenes, but there was nothing. Only the edginess of the newsmen and women, the way their habitual glibness had a certain fragility to it. And their eyes. They were scared. He could see it wherever he looked.

But... scared of what?

'War.' He said it softly, quietly, fearing to say it out loud. 'They're having a fucking war out there!'

★

Jake met Yang Hong Yu in the forecourt outside the courtroom at five to eight. Advocate Yang looked anxious, flustered.

Like a man who has been up all night, clearing up.

Jake felt sorry for Yang. He had got in way out of his depth. Only things would surely change now that GenSyn were involved.

'Where's Chi Lin Lin?' Jake asked.

'I left him to scrub out the office. The stench...'

'I'm sorry.'

'It's not your fault, *Shih* Reed. Shall we go in?'

Inside, Advocate Yang took three steps, then stopped, gesturing towards the three men who sat in the previously empty chairs on their side of the courtroom.

'They've got the wrong courtroom, surely?'

On the big, central table the huge pile of dusty tomes on the Chang side were now matched on Jake's side by an equally impressive stack of newer, shinier leather-covered books. Matched one to one, in fact. As if, in the night, a new mountain range had been thrown up in opposition to the other.

Yang turned to him. '*Shih* Reed?'

Yang Hong Yu's face was a treasure to behold. Jake laughed, then gestured that Yang should continue on down. 'It's okay,' he said. 'They're on our side. GenSyn sent them to help us out.'

'*GenSyn?*' Yang looked totally confused.

Right then the Chang clan and their lawyers made an entrance, smiling and laughing as they came in. And stopped dead. Seeing the books, seeing the three new lawyers in their impressive silks, they fell silent for a moment, and then a hissed whispering began, mouth to ear, as they sought to understand this new development.

Jake took his seat, then turned to face the newcomers.

'I'm Jake Reed. Alison said you'd help us out.'

The three – two middle-aged Han and one bright-eyed youngster – introduced themselves, bowing to Jake and then to Advocate Yang, as if he were their equal. But a single look at them told Jake that these were the best money could buy. GenSyn, for some unknown reason, were pulling out all the stops for him.

GenSyn, or Alison?

Oh, no doubt she had instigated it, but... well, it was crazy to think that she would commit them to this without some reason.

Guilt, perhaps. Guilt at how shoddily they treated me, after Gustav's death.

Only corporations like GenSyn rarely suffered guilt.

The most senior of the three was Meng Hsin-fa. A robust, highly intelligent-looking man, he had decided to play things quietly, to unnerve the Changs and their team through a display of sheer unflappability.

The next hour proved very interesting. Judge Wei, appearing almost a quarter of an hour late, was also shocked by the new development. He had clearly settled with the Changs, only to find his best laid plans spoiled by this new presence in his court. He tried to have the newcomers barred, only Meng Hsin-fa had anticipated that tactic and come armed with sealed documents from Wei's superiors, forbidding such.

The look on Wei's face when they'd presented the documents was worth all of the previous day's suffering. Yang Hong Yu looked set to expire with joy.

And that was just the start.

When they broke for lunch, just after one, things were swinging their way. The Changs' lawyers had presented various compelling precedents to justify reducing Jake's pension, which amounted, when all was said and done, to their right to do what they bloody well pleased as new owners of the Micro-Data corporation. But Jake's team – his three new men – were ready for them. They presented their own precedents – precedents that were not merely more recent but considerably more compelling.

Jake, sitting there and looking on, didn't understand one-tenth of it, but he could see the consternation in the opposing camp as, one after another, the carefully laid planks of their case were torn up and thrown aside.

As for Yang Hong Yu, he sat there like he was in a daydream, enjoying every last second, the smile on his face widening from time to time as the GenSyn lawyers went about their subtle and ruthless work.

Jake knew he would have to contact Alison and thank her. Only how could he ever repay her? For he understood it clearly now. They would have been ripped to shreds without them. Chewed up and spat out, for all Yang's indignation.

Outside the courtroom, too, things had changed. Before now there had been only a single security guard – an old *Hung Mao*, in his sixties if he was a day – but now there were six of them, armed with lantern-guns, their faces masked.

Jake touched Yang's arm. 'Will you do something for me, Yang Hong Yu? Will you look after our friends while I make a call or two? I won't be long.'

There was a room at the end of the corridor where he could make the calls. He went there, getting himself patched through to Mary.

'How's it going?' she asked. 'Are you winning?'

'I think so,' he said, deciding that he'd explain it all later, when he was back with her. 'But listen... has there been any mention on the news of trouble?'

'Trouble? Not that I know, but... well, I did notice that some of the news channels had gone off the air.'

Then it was true. There *was* something going on. That and the additional guards. All the signs pointed that way. Only when would some proper news break? When would they find out what it was?

'Mary. I've got to go. Things to discuss. Only if there's anything on the news... anything at all, then let me know. Send me a message, all right?'

'All right.'

He said his goodbyes and signed off, then dialled again.

'Hello?'

It was her. Unmistakably. Twenty years had passed, but she remained unchanged.

'Ali?'

Her smile was warmer than he remembered. 'Hi. How did it go?'

'Very well. And thank you.'

'You're welcome. And before you ask, it was Ludo's idea. Ludo Ebert, that is. He's Gustav's son. He feels you were treated badly by his uncle. It's him you have to thank.'

'Ah...' Only Jake wondered how he'd known. Had Alison tipped him off? Explained, perhaps, what had happened to Jake?

'Look, Jake, I'm busy right now. But let's speak later, yeah?'

'Okay. I'll talk to you then.'

'Okay. Bye for now.'

Jake sat there a moment, lost in his thoughts. He could still remember the first time he had ever seen her, there on the pavement outside Blackwell's, in Oxford. She had been talking animatedly to two female College friends. It was pure chance, because he had been intending to walk on past and meet a friend in the pub nearby, only the window display had caught his attention and he had stopped to look, and there she was. For the briefest moment their eyes had met and she had smiled...

And that was it. Five years of his life. That's where it began. On the pavement outside Blackwell's.

Jake stood, then looked about him. It was such a shabby little room. It made him wonder just how many shabby little deals had been made in it.

More than enough.

These last few days it felt as if a wall inside him had been breached; that, under the stress of the court case, he had re-awoken all of this old stuff, this *difficult* stuff. All those things he had learned to wall in and deny these past twenty years. All of it come back to plague him. Only that wasn't strictly true. It wasn't a plague. Not at all. The truth was that he *liked* it. Liked that feeling of having let go. Of having relaxed the constraints he'd set in place to stop him thinking of it all. All the things he'd lost. All those wonderful, beautiful things. Things that *they* didn't want him to remember.

Oxford. He had only to close his mind and he could see it all again, all of those images, imprinted on his brain. Scattered memories from the Age of Waste. Yes, he could see it now. How this world they inhabited had its roots back then, in their neglect, their wastefulness. How the West had thrown its future away, like some undervalued piece of trash.

'Shih Reed?'

He turned. It was Chi Lin Lin.

'What is it, boy? Is it about to start again?'

'No, Shih Reed. But my Master... well, he felt we should talk things through. Agree upon a strategy.'

'Of course.'

His mind wasn't in it. His mind wanted him to stay there, on the pavement outside Blackwell's, in that bright late autumn day.

So long ago. So very long ago.

The afternoon session proved a lot more lively.

The Changs, it seemed, were not going to roll over and take things lying down. They had retrenched and reconsidered things during that long lunch break and had returned to court with a whole new tactic.

Advocate Yang leaned in and whispered to Jake's ear. '*The bastards are playing the delay card. If they can't get the case dismissed, then they mean to see you die before you collect.*'

He had been warned it might be so, for that was apparently how big corporations played it sometimes. If they couldn't win they would delay. Keep the case in court for thirty years if they had to, wearing the opposition down until they were forced to make a deal.

Or died.

But the team GenSyn had sent him had anticipated this. Advocate Meng had risen to face the Judge, clearing his throat.

'My Lord, I would like to...'

Judge Wei brought his gavel down hard. 'Advocate Meng... would you like a ruling now?'

For the first time that day, Meng looked surprised. 'My Lord, I...'

'*What is this?*' Jake whispered to Yang.

'I don't know,' Yang answered, as much in the dark, it seemed, as Jake.

'Do you want me to rule?' Judge Wei insisted.

Meng hesitated, then asked, 'Might I consult with my client, my Lord?'

Wei nodded. 'You may. We'll have a short adjournment. Be back here in an hour.' And with that he got up and left the courtroom hurriedly.

'What in the gods' names was that?' Jake asked, alone in one of the anterooms with his team. 'I didn't think he *could* rule. Not without hearing all the evidence, and we've barely begun that.'

'He *ought*,' Meng answered. 'Only I think our Lordship is playing another game. If it weren't so outrageous, I'd think he was trying to start an auction.'

Jake looked to him for explanation.

'Well... I can't be sure, but... I think the Judge is waiting for our offer.'

'Our offer? But I thought it was between us and the Chang family if we wished to settle?'

'If we wanted to settle out of court, yes. But I don't mean that. Judge Wei has as good as said he'll rule for the party that pays him the biggest bribe.'

Jake should have been shocked, only he wasn't. It was no worse than what the Changs had done in denying him what was legitimately his. In this rapacious world, the only wonder was that such behaviour wasn't officially sanctioned.

'So how do we answer him?'

'You don't want to pay the Judge, then, Jake? It would be cheaper for us all. Cheaper and less bother.'

Jake bristled. 'I most certainly *don't* want to. But what happens if he rules for the Changs?'

'Then we appeal.'

'But that just plays into their hands, surely? It would take months to get a case re-scheduled.'

'Not necessarily. And in the meantime we could find out a few facts about Judge Wei. Like how much the Chang clan have paid him, for a start, and whether they have any *other* kind of hold over him.'

Yang, sitting there and listening, beamed at the thought. 'And the Changs... could we investigate them too?'

Jake interrupted. 'But this all takes time and money, surely? Why can't we force Judge Wei to behave as he ought?'

Meng smiled patiently. 'Why do you think the Changs had the case moved to this court in particular? Any higher and they'd have had trouble finding as corrupt a judge as our good friend Wei. Any lower and any decision the Judge made would be laughed... well, out of court.'

'Yes, but...' Jake huffed, hating the fact that he had to deal with such rogues and pickpockets. It all seemed so *unclean.*

Just then Chi Lin Lin came back. He looked troubled by something, but he said nothing, just sat there on a chair at the back of the room looking on.

But Jake had noticed. He went across, leaving the advocates to discuss how to proceed.

'Chi Lin Lin? What's up? You don't look the ticket.'

Chi Lin Lin looked down. He seemed reluctant to answer Jake. Then he started to cry.

Jake reached out and took his shoulders gently in his hands. 'Aiya... what's the matter?'

Chi looked up at Jake through his tears. 'I went home. To have a shower and get a change of clothes. And while I was there... well, there have been rumours, Shih Reed. Awful, terrible rumours.'

Jake felt a strange dread. 'What kind of rumours?'

Chi looked past Jake at the wall-mounted camera, as if afraid to say what he was about to say, then said it anyway.

'They say that Tsao Ch'un has killed one of his closest servants. One of the Seven. They say...' His lip trembled. 'They say it's war.'

'What's that?' Yang said, coming across. 'War? What nonsense is this, Chi Lin Lin? You've not been spreading rumours have you, boy? The gods help us all if you have, because—'

Jake cut him off. 'It's war. I thought it was earlier. And now I'm sure of it.' He looked to Chi again. 'What else are they saying?'

'Nothing. At least, nothing that makes sense. There have been deaths, it seems. Random assassinations. Awful things, apparently. But no one knows anything for sure. The news channels... they're hiding it. Trying to make out that all's well and nothing's changed, only...'

'I knew it,' Jake said. 'I thought it had to be that. Tsao Ch'un and the Seven, finally at each other's throats.'

'Gods!' Yang said, appalled. 'Don't even say it!'

'What's that?' Advocate Meng asked, coming across.

'War,' Jake said, thinking suddenly just how small a matter his case was in the circumstances. 'Tsao Ch'un has declared war on his trusted servants.'

Jake returned to his room and lay down. He had not slept well the previous night and now he felt exhausted. Even so, he changed the screen onto one of the more reliable news stations, turned the volume down low, then lay back. But sleep quickly overtook him and, when he woke, his head was filled not with thoughts of the war, but with the dreams that had come to him.

Dreams? Or memories?

Unsurprisingly perhaps, the dreams had been of Alison and his days at College. They had never actually gone punting, yet while he slept that was what they were doing, Alison lounging in the long, narrow boat while he pushed them through the water, as the luxuriant green banks of the Isis flowed past.

Somewhere south of the city they had stopped off at a pub and from its balcony they had looked back at the dreaming spires, framed by his own night-time imaginings in a perfect sunlight that was roseate pink, making the whole thing seem to glow with warmth.

'Home from home', he'd used to call it. Which was not surprising, after the spartan austerity of the Academy. That you could have framed in mud and ice and rain. In heaving lungs and aching legs. And other 'let's not mention it' things.

Only it hadn't all been bad. He remembered how he had enthused to Alison about the datscape. About the smell and feel and touch of it. About the *rush* he got every time he went inside. Addictive, even then.

But that day they had talked about the death of loved ones, and she had sat there, her head slightly tilted to one side as she listened to every word. About the crash, and after. About... well, simply about being. And that evening – in the real world that now seemed like a dream – she had taken his hands and led him to her bed, where they had made love for the first time. Eighteen she was, he nineteen. Destined, she'd said.

Destined.

Here they were, at the tail ends of their lives, and destiny had led them different paths.

He had tried to get her earlier, but she had been too busy to take his call. But now she called him back.

'We should get you better accommodation,' she said, looking past him at the state of the room he was in. 'That can't be comfortable.'

'It isn't, but listen... the case...'

'I've heard from Advocate Meng.'

'Right... so what's to be done?'

Alison smiled, somewhat wearily it seemed. 'It's already done, I've spoken to Ludo and he's authorized a beefing up of our presence in court. Five new advocates. And I've agreed to finance an investigation into Judge Wei and his connection to the Changs.'

Jake stared at her, astonished. 'How did you manage it? I mean... how the hell did you get this past Wolfgang?'

'I didn't. Again you've Ludo to thank. He knows how to placate his uncle. He's the son Wolfgang never had, and he'll be running things one of these days. You might say that what Ludo wants, Ludo gets. And you're Ludo's hero.'

'*Me?*' Sheer disbelief made him laugh. 'You're spinning me a line, girl!'

'Not at all. He *loves* the datscape. He's in it all the time. Once this is over he wants to meet you and...'

The words seemed to die on her lips. She looked down, her face changing suddenly. 'Jake...?'

'What?'

'These rumours...'

He could see she wanted reassuring. That for all that she seemed in control, she was still a little girl. Her father's daughter. The same little girl he had met all those years ago. So tough on the outside, but inside...

'It'll sort itself out,' he said. 'See if it doesn't.'

'You think?'

'I know.'

She smiled, grateful to him. 'I'll speak to you later, yeah?'

'Yeah. And thank Ludo for me.'

Afterwards he sat there, his back against the thick plastic of the wall, staring at the news screen. Wondering if that were so, if it *would* sort itself out, because things were already escalating. There were reports of trouble in the local stacks, appeals for calm.

And then Mary called.

'Hi, sweetheart, I...' And then he stopped, taking in her face. She was as white as a sheet. 'What's happened?'

He saw how hard it was for her even to begin to say. She was on the verge of breaking down.

'Some men...' She took a long, shivering breath, then continued. 'Big men, thugs... they came here, Jake. Threatened us. They...'

A tear rolled down her cheek.

'Did they hurt you?'

She shook her head. 'They... *warned* me. Said...'

'Said what?' he asked gently, when she didn't continue.

He ought to go home. He knew it now. What with all that was going on. Only if he did, the Changs would have won.

'Listen,' he said, trying to keep in control. 'I'll speak to GenSyn...'

'*GenSyn?*' She looked up, staring at him, not understanding. But then she wouldn't have. He hadn't told her yet.

'They're helping us... I'll explain it all later. But I'll try and get protection.

I'm sure we could work something out. Until I'm back.'

Mary looked close to tears again. 'Can't you come back now, Jake?'

'Tomorrow. Once things are settled. I promise you. Only I have to be here now. There're things need to be decided.'

'But can't you do that from here, Jake? I'm... *afraid*.'

That got to him. In all of their life together, she had never been afraid. Not enough to say as much, anyway. Only if he wasn't in court what kind of signal would that send?

'Look,' he said. 'I'll sort something out. Okay? And then I'll call you again. But don't be afraid, sweetheart. Things will be fine. I promise they will.'

Only what were his promises worth? It wasn't as if he was an influential man.

He called Alison again and told her what had happened.

'I'll get onto it at once,' she said, clearly pleased that there was something she could do. Some task to keep her busy and stop her worrying about the bigger picture.

Good old Alison, he thought, as he cut connection. *What would he have done without her?*

Only he didn't have time to think about it, for right then Chi Lin Lin arrived, to tell him he had to get back to court at once.

He arrived, late and breathless, taking his seat even as the Judge began his address.

'*Who the fuck is that?*' he asked, leaning in to whisper to Yang.

Yang gripped his arm. '*Didn't Chi tell you? Judge Wei had an accident. This is Judge Yo. He's in charge of things now.*'

Judge Yo was tall and skeletal in appearance. He looked like a hanging judge: his features, particularly his eyes, exuding a humourless disdain for the proceedings.

'I will have *silence* while I speak!' he said coldly, glaring at Yang and Jake. 'And before we begin, let me make it clear... any attempt to influence my decision will be punished to the full extent of the law. You understand me, ch'un tzu? Good. Then let us proceed.'

'So tell me, ' Jake said, three hours later, when they took a break. 'Is Judge Yo a good thing or bad?'

Meng Hsin-fa looked up from where he was studying some papers he had just received by courier.

'I'm hoping good. But it's hard to say. Judge Wei's accident, it would seem, was far from accidental. And if it *was* the Changs who were to blame, then why would they take such action without knowing who would replace him? No. I would reserve judgement for the time being. But listen. I've been instructed to delay things – to seek a postponement until tomorrow. Help is on its way, it seems. Reinforcements.'

The way he smiled made Jake think that there was something he wasn't telling them.

'This help... is it something special?'

'Oh, very special,' Meng answered, his smile widening. 'But let's not spoil it for you, Jake, neh? This is something I want you to see with your own eyes.'

There was a note waiting for him when he went back to his room. Or rather, an envelope, in which there was a note and a key and other things, including a picture of them both when they were young.

Alison and I, he thought, remembering the day it had been taken. Graduation day. And the year? 2040. August the eighteenth, to be precise. His twenty-first birthday.

They had been the perfect couple, perfectly matched. Only now that he looked at it, across the space of forty-seven years, he could see just how brittle they had been. How shallow the soil in which their love had grown. Like two actors, pretending it was fine, when deep down they both knew it wasn't.

Destined. How could she ever have thought they were destined?

Looking back across a lifetime, he understood it clearly now. She had always struggled to be sociable, to fit in. There was always some defect in her. A lack. Which was why, perhaps, she had made the change from old world to new so easily. Her indifference to music and to culture in general – something that had been a weakness in the old world – had proved a strength in Tsao Ch'un's City.

Only it wasn't fair to single her out. It wasn't only her, after all.

No, as a Hinton web-dancer he had lived a schizophrenic existence. In the datscape he had been one thing, a magnificent creature of instinct:

sensitized to taste and smell and touch; his brain rewired to do his job; parts of him stripped away by the drugs he took. Devolution to a purpose, they'd termed it. All to improve his web efficiency. But outside...

Outside he had been every bit as shallow as her. Unsentimental. A creature of surfaces, keeping nothing and travelling light, afraid to make too deep a contact with life, because life had this nasty habit of betraying you. When you made attachments it would rob you of them, suddenly and viciously. Hadn't he learned that much from life? Hadn't that always been the way of it? Such that, when Alison came along, she had made it easy for him to live like that. Unattached. Pretending everything was fine. Because that was what society had wanted.

And even afterwards, with Kate.

He looked down, saddened by the realizations he had come to.

Yes, even with Kate there had been a part of him that had faked it. He had loved her, true enough, but that love had been a shallow thing, all in all. Shallow enough that he had forgotten about her for years at a stretch. Those years when, in adversity, he had found true love. Had learned to take the risk and love someone as she had deserved to be loved. His sweet darling, Annie.

Yes, and had her taken from him. As if to remind him what the rules were.

Jake smiled, remembering her. How just the thought of her would always make him smile.

Jake set the photograph aside and picked up the key. According to her note, she had found him better quarters, fifty levels up, away from the shithole he was staying in.

Which was kind of her, only what was all of this about? What did Alison want from him? Because she must have known he would never leave Mary. He was much too old for all that...

Or was it just residual fondness?

He thought of the anxiety in her eyes the last time he had spoken to her, and felt a disquieting sadness. That was the trouble with this world. That you couldn't protect all those people you wanted to protect.

Jake packed up his things and made to leave. But first he checked the news once more, the screen lighting up to show a familiar media face.

Chiu Fa had been on earlier, rubbishing the rumours. Chiu was one of the more famous newscasters, popular in the Mids, and his calming reassurance seemed to have done the trick there. But down here in the Lowers there was unrest, as the word-of-mouth rumours spread of military activity and a whole spate of assassinations.

If it wasn't a war, then *something* was going on. A campaign against the Triads? That was one rumour. Only that couldn't be true, because if it were the Ministry would be working its propaganda channels for all they were worth.

No. This was something that *involved* the Thousand Eyes.

Jake was returning the key to the desk clerk when Chi Lin Lin found him again.

'*Shih* Reed... you must come at once.'

'Is there trouble, Chi?'

Chi almost smiled. 'There is always trouble, *neh*, Master?'

Jake noted that 'Master'. Chi had clearly reassessed things.

But this once Chi didn't lead him to the courts, but to a bar in the Mids, close to Jake's new quarters. Meng Hsin-fa and his team were waiting there, along with Yang Hong Yu.

Meng indicated to Jake to take a seat.

'So?' Jake asked. 'What's happening?'

Meng smiled. 'I went to see Judge Yo. Privately, you understand.'

'But I thought...' Jake stopped. 'Go on...'

'You understand then. I told him you weren't interested in a deal.'

'And what did he say to that?'

'He said he might be forced to rule for the Changs. Which is when I threatened him. I told him I'd let the dogs loose on him. To which he said he'd hold me in contempt, only I threatened him some more. I told him that I'd uncover enough evidence to drag him down to join the very lowest of the low. To which he told me to go to hell.' Advocate Meng paused. 'I'd guess they're paying him a small fortune.'

'Can they afford that?'

'The question is, can they afford *not* to? Think about it, Jake. What would you be down if you lost this case?'

'Five thousand a month. Six, maybe, depending on the ruling.'

'Per month for the rest of your life. Well, multiply that by ten thousand or so and you get a rough idea of the stakes involved. It's tens of millions, Jake.

Payable month after month. Just think what that would mean to them, not having to find that kind of money.'

'So what's next?'

'We meet tomorrow morning, in court, to try to resolve things.'

'Isn't that just back to square one?'

'If square one is at the top and to the left, rather than down the bottom and to the right, then yes. All we need is your agreement, Jake.'

'Which you have. But I don't see...'

Meng smiled. 'You want to know the truth, Jake? The truth is, I don't know either. You see, I won't be in charge of things tomorrow.'

Jake looked about him. They all seemed amused by something.

'What?'

Meng smiled. 'Let's not spoil it for you. Let's worry about all that tomorrow, neh? I've just one question.'

'And what's that?'

'What'll you have to drink? Oh, and don't worry. It's on the firm. It's *all* on the firm.'

The new room Alison had found him was spacious, bordering on the luxurious. It had executive class stamped on everything, and Jake knew it must have cost GenSyn a small fortune. Tired and slightly drunk, he set his bag down. Then, plumping down on the huge double bed, he asked to be connected to Mary.

'Hiya,' he said, as her image appeared on the big screen facing him. 'Is everything all right?'

She smiled. 'Your friends were as good as their word, Jake. We've got two armed guards outside, and they've given me a number to call if I need any more.' She laughed. 'I just don't know how you managed it.'

'Look, I'll tell you all about it when I get back. I just wanted to let you know that things are going well. In fact, there's a good chance it'll all be settled tomorrow.'

'Tomorrow?'

'So I'm told.'

'Oh gods, let's hope so, eh?' She hesitated, then, 'Jake...?'

'Yes, my love?'

'This woman... this Alison... she's the one I met, right, after the GenSyn accident?'

'That's her.'

'Then...?'

'Tomorrow,' he said. 'When I'm home. But don't worry. It's all going to work out fine, okay?'

Mary hesitated, then gave a little nod. 'Okay. And Jake...?'

'Yes?'

'I miss you. So keep safe, huh?'

He smiled. 'I shall.'

Dreams. Dreams of the last day before it began. Dreams of Hugo and Chris and Jenny, sitting about the big wooden table in his penthouse apartment, looking out across the river at Hinton and the massed skyscrapers of the City. His dear friends laughing and joking, the deathly pallor of their faces laced with dark, thread-like scars, their eye sockets burned black from the torturer's poker.

Laughing and talking about Drew Ludd and Ubik, while at the far end of the table sat the Jory avatar, its shovel-like teeth bared in a ferocious smile.

Dreams? Nightmares, more like.

Jake woke, his heart racing, his body sheened in sweat, the screen just across from him murmuring its low-volume commentary on the world.

Poor bastards, he thought. *Their only crime was to know me.*

He lay there a while, letting his heartbeat slow, the sense of panic diminish. But at some deeper level he knew that it was all happening again. That for the third time in his life, it was all about to change.

Jake got up, padded across to the bathroom and stood there, peeing, wondering whether he should call Mary and check everything was all right.

He was sure it was. Sure that GenSyn would have called had anything gone wrong. Only if *he* had been organizing things for the Changs he'd have taken Mary and the kids and held them until he'd got his way. That is, until he had a signature.

Jake went back through. On the big screen everything seemed fine and calm. In the warm glow of the bedside lamp, the room seemed a perfect haven.

All's well in the half-life universe.

Only he knew it wasn't. Because that was what the dream meant. That was why *he* was there, in the dream: the Jory avatar, looking on and laughing at them all.

Jake shivered, chilled to the bone by the thought, then climbed between the sheets, praying sleep would come.

CHUNG KUO

Chapter 21

WAR IN HEAVEN

Li Chao Ch'in reined in his horse and waited for his sons to catch him, looking about him at the wild, uncultivated terrain.

If one looked to north or east, the land was beautiful, framed as it was by the distant mountains of the Ta Pa Shan, but to the west, far away, hidden by the early morning mist, was the City, its pearled whiteness sepulchral.

Lord Li took a long, calming breath, then reached down to pat the flank of his mount, a grey he had bought from Fan Chang's stables just a year ago.

They had been riding hard this last half hour, stretching their horses, plunging across shallow streams and through hidden, mist-wreathed valleys. They were pushing north, climbing all the while as the sun rose to their right in a clear blue sky, coming finally to this place. As a boy, his own father, a senior Party member then, had often brought him here.

Close by, on the crest of the hill, were the ruins of an ancient Buddhist temple. Built in the time of the Sung dynasty, the great three-tiered building had been badly damaged by the Red Guards during the Cultural Revolution, its roof tiles broken, its statuary smashed. Even so, it retained a great deal of its original beauty, its timeless elegance and serenity.

The ruins lay at the very edge of his estate, fifteen li north of the palace of Tongjiang. Inaccessible by road, Li Chao Ch'in did not come here very often, only today he had needed somewhere safe. Somewhere that he knew he would not be seen by watchful eyes, overheard by prying ears. Somewhere in which he could talk openly with his sons.

And here they came, spurring their horses up the slope. The eldest, Li Peng, leading the way on his jet-black Arab, dressed in a bright blue silk, his five brothers following close behind, their heads bared, their dark hair flowing back in the wind.

Seeing them, Li Chao Ch'in felt his heart swell with pride. A man never had six such fine sons as his. Tall and strong they were – intelligent, handsome young men. He watched them approach, noting how they, like he, wore white trimmings on their arms and legs, in mourning for their cousin Fan.

The mere sight of them made his heart ache.

Had Tsao Ch'un had such sons there would have been no problem. He might have handed over power to them, letting them rule in his stead, like pillars of the finest jade, the future of Chung Kuo guaranteed by their mere existence.

And then today would not have come.

Only he hadn't. Tsao Ch'un, blessed by the gods in war, had been cursed in love. As a younger man he had been married to three wives, and each had given him one living son before they succumbed, either to illness or assassination. And recently, when he had married once more, in his 'dotage', again he had been undone, his new wives – each a treasure – murdered in his bed.

Li Chao Ch'in looked down. How had it ever come to this? What sickness had overtaken their Master to have made him do what he did?

Yes, and what was Tsao Ch'un doing at that moment? What was he thinking? Was he scheming, even then, to undo them all?

His six sons slowed their horses, forming a half circle just below him on the grassy hillside. Li Chao Ch'in sighed. He did not want to fight Tsao Ch'un. His instinct was to serve, not to oppose, but what choice had he?

'My sons...'

He looked from one to another, meeting their eyes briefly. Their horses steamed beneath them, snorting after their long ride, yet each one kept its place, obedient to its master's will.

Things had moved too far, too fast. For the first time in his life he had no answers.

'My darling boys...'

His eyes settled on his youngest, Li Chang So, fifteen only last month, yet fully grown. Six two in his leggings, he was, and his mother's favourite. Her 'baby boy' as she called him. Yet her baby looked quite fierce today.

He looked away, conscious of how patiently they waited for him to say what must be said, their heads slightly bowed, their whole demeanour showing the utmost respect, the utmost obedience to his will. Like the mounts they rode.

Good sons. The very best of sons.

Only this once, and maybe only this once, he could not ask for their blind obedience, for obedience itself was in question here. He needed to hear what they had to say. For this did not affect him alone. This affected them all. It would not be fair to make this choice without first sounding them out.

'I have brought you here this morning because we must come to a decision. You all know what has happened. To say it was a shock understates the matter... but it is done, neh? And we must live in the ruins of that act.'

He looked to his eldest.

'Li Peng and I have already spoken of this. Of what might lie ahead. It barely needs saying, yet I must ask you what I asked him. What might we do to rectify matters, short of war? And if war is our only option, then how do we go about that? After all, we are peace-loving men. The very notion of committing violence against our Master...'

One or two of them looked down at that. The sight of it sobered Li Chao Ch'in. It was not just he, then, who was terrified of the prospect of fighting Tsao Ch'un. Yes, he could see it now in their eyes.

'Li Chang So?'

The boy looked to him, meeting his father's eyes, a rock-like certainty in his own, young as he was.

'I will do what must be done, Father.'

'And you, Li Kuang? Have you anything to say?'

Kuang, his fifth son, eighteen now, hesitated. Then, in a rush: 'Had he merely burned Cousin Fan's palace... had he stopped there...'

Li Chao Ch'in nodded. Those were precisely his thoughts. To punish them was one thing – and who knew, maybe they even deserved it for harbouring such thoughts as they'd had – but to kill them...

'Li Shen?'

His second son, who was built like an ox and sometimes seemed as slow, this time was quick to answer.

'We must kill him, Father. Before he kills us.'

'Ah...' Li Chao Ch'in made to answer, only Li Shen had not finished. He spoke again.

'The only question, Father, is how we go about it. We are unprepared. But then so is he.'

Li Chao Ch'in stared back at him, surprised.

'How so?'

'If Tsao Ch'un had a plan, we'd be dead already. No... the Great One's actions have smacked thus far of carelessness. There is no great master plan behind this, only a wilful disregard for anyone's feelings but his own.'

It was true. But though things had been wrong for some time now, the Seven had never met to discuss what they would do in these circumstances, never drawn up a plan to deal with it. Why, to even *begin* to think of it... that surely would have been the ultimate disloyalty.

Until now the thought of usurping Tsao Ch'un had never occurred to them. They had, until these last few days, been his most loyal supporters – his most trusted men – but that had changed.

War was, he knew, inevitable. Yet still he would postpone it.

And meanwhile?

Tsao Ch'un, he knew, would pre-empt them. Unprepared as perhaps he was, the great man knew enough about waging wars to beat them with the minimum of effort. And if that were so...

'Perhaps I should seek an audience with him,' he said, tentatively, not sure what reaction he would get. 'Prostrate myself and offer up my life if he would spare you all...'

There was a strong murmur of protest, but it was Li Fu Jen, his third son, who answered him. He leaned forward in his saddle as he did, his face dark with anger.

'*Never!* Why, I would rather have my eyes gouged out, my body cut open and my organs burned before me on a grill, than kowtow to that man! Forgive me, Father, but the man has lost any right to our respect! What he did... first at my brother Peng's party, and now at Fan Chang's palace... it is intolerable! There is only one choice, to fight him to the death! And if we die... we at least did not grovel on our knees before the tyrant!'

The horses moved skittishly at the words, as if they understood.

Li Chao Ch'in looked about him, seeing how they were stirred by Li Fu Jen's words – how they had lit a fire in their eyes.

He raised a hand.

'If we fight Tsao Ch'un we will lose. I have no doubt of it. We are administrators, whereas he... Well, we all know what Tsao Ch'un is. Everyone knows. And rightly fears him. Yet if we *must* fight... if we *really* must... then we must begin at once.'

He looked to Li Weng, his fourth son, the only one who had yet to speak.

'Weng... have you anything to add?'

Li Weng, while no less sturdy than his brothers, had always been teased for his bookish ways. Of the six of them, he was the intellectual, the thinker. Now, he showed that his reading had not been in vain.

'One thing before all, Father. History teaches us that we should sound out who is for us and who against. Once we know that we might rally our support. Tsao Ch'un is powerful, yes, and the Banners will probably obey him, but he has made many enemies these past years. If we can persuade those enemies to become *our* friends...'

Li Chao Ch'in raised his chin, nodding thoughtfully. For the first time that day, he felt the most slender glimmer of hope. Li Weng was right. It was not they alone who had fallen out with Tsao Ch'un. He had offended many. Only how far did their hatred go? Would they fight alongside the Seven, or would they be afraid to join a war against Tsao Ch'un?

He looked to his fourth son and smiled.

'And so the bookworm turns...'

There was laughter, then smiles all round as Li Peng leaned across and ruffled Weng's hair. Only Li Chao Ch'in, seeing it, felt his heart break again, knowing that this was possibly the last time he would see them so. For it was war. There was no doubting it, after all. A war in Heaven itself. Li Chao Ch'in swallowed and looked down.

'Father?'

He looked up, meeting Weng's eyes again. 'It's all right, Weng. I'm okay. I was just thinking... maybe we should leave the horses here and get a cruiser to come and pick us up. If we're to begin...'

He left it unsaid, but now that it had been decided, then there was nothing left but to act. To wait any longer... no... they must begin at once.

Yet still he hesitated. Still he longed for things to be the way they'd been two days ago. Before the sky had changed. Before the days of ease had ended.

★

Li Chao Ch'in bowed low, welcoming his unexpected guests, the great audience room cleared for once of servants.

'Fan Peng... Prince Li...'

He and his sons had arrived back only minutes earlier, to find the estate in turmoil, details of Tsao Ch'un's preliminary strikes fresh, uncensored, on all the news channels. When he'd subsequently heard that an unidentified cruiser had entered Tongjiang's airspace he had expected the worst. Even so, he had not panicked; had not had the craft shot out of the air, as another might have done. That restraint had, for once, paid off.

'Forgive us for imposing on you,' Fan Li said, kneeling and bowing low, taking Li Chao Ch'in's right hand as he did and placing the iron ring that rested there to his lips. 'We beg you, my Lord, to have mercy on us and give us shelter...'

'Fan Li... please... you are my guests...'

There was grief in the young man's face as he glanced up; a grief that was mirrored in his mother's countenance. The sight of it moved Li Chao Ch'in deeply, for Fan Chang had been like a brother to him.

'Please, Prince Fan... you do not have to bow to me.'

But Fan Li remained kneeling, his head bowed. 'We were attacked, Lord Li. He sent two of his attack craft out after us... we shot them both out of the sky, but not before one of them knocked out our communications. If it had not been for our pilot...'

The young man stopped, composing himself.

'It was awful,' he said quietly. 'We could see it from the sky as we flew away... That cunt torched the whole fucking palace, and the servants... they threw the poor bastards back into the flames...'

That cunt... Li Chao Ch'in noted that; noted the venom in the young man's voice when he'd said it. Until that moment, he had still been contemplating making some kind of peace with Tsao Ch'un. But that was impossible now, he realized, for he had taken in as guests Fan Chang's wife along with his son and heir. That was an irreversible act. Unless, of course, he handed them over to Tsao Ch'un. But how could he do that? How could he face his sons – how face *himself* – if he acted thus?

No. It was war.

Li Chao Ch'in groaned, knowing that, for all he had said to his sons, he had not really decided until that instant. He had wanted to keep it all safe – he and all his friends and family – but that simply was not possible. Tsao Ch'un wanted them all dead, and what Tsao Ch'un wanted Tsao Ch'un usually got.

He pulled Fan Cho to his feet, then placed his hands gently on the young man's shoulders.

'Cousin Li... Lady Fan... my house is as yours. You are my kin, and I promise to protect you, if I can...'

Li's head dropped, then he began to weep. 'My father...'

Behind him, his mother began to wail, her voice rising and falling in torment.

'Your father was a good man,' Li Chao Ch'in said, the slightest tremor in his voice. 'A brave man, too. I will miss him greatly. But I would be as a father to you, Fan Li, if you would have that?'

Fan Li fell to his knees again, clutching at Li Chao Ch'in's knees. 'I would be honoured, my Lord...'

'Then come,' he said, raising the boy to his feet a second time. 'I need you to stand beside me, Fan Li, while I call our cousins.'

An hour later, Li Chao Ch'in sat at his desk, alone. The arrival of Prince Fan and his mother had set off a spate of calls between the Seven that had ended abruptly ten minutes back, when Tsao Ch'un had cut their communications.

It was an ominous portent. But much had been decided before the lines went down. He knew, for instance, that they were of one mind in fighting Tsao Ch'un, whatever the result. Fan Chang's death had achieved that much, to weld them into a single force. Tsao Ch'un had crossed the line.

Looking back, he could see it clearly now: the slow decline, the descent from greatness into paranoia. Tsao Ch'un had always been whimsically unpredictable, and thus always dangerous, but always clever with it too, knowing whom to hurt and whom to praise. Whatever his excesses, he had always been loyal to those who were loyal to him. How else could he have achieved what he'd achieved. Only recently...

It was the death of his wives, Li Chao Ch'in decided. It was that that had pushed him over the edge. But it barely mattered now. All that mattered were the hours ahead.

He let out a long breath. They had to overthrow him. To wage total war against him. But how in the gods' names did they fight that war? How stop the primal force that was Tsao Ch'un in his anger?

The truth was, none of them had the least idea. Kill him they must. But how did they go about that? Dozens had tried and not a single one of them still lived, while Tsao Ch'un...

Li Chao Ch'in stood, then walked over to the window. He had assigned each of his sons a separate task. But now, with the network down, they were idle, like him. Until they could find another means of contacting each other...

One thing he knew for certain. He could not sit here in Tongjiang and wait for Tsao Ch'un to come to him. To do so would mean certain death. No. He had to organize somehow.

Shepherd was the key. He was sure of it. If he could only get Amos Shepherd on their side they might have a chance. Only Shepherd was Tsao Ch'un's man, and besides, he was half a world away.

Outside a craft was setting down. Li Chao Ch'in watched it a moment, then turned away. Friends were arriving all the while now, rallying to his call, but it was not enough. None of it was enough. Unless they could turn the Banners, unless they could find some way of getting to the man himself...

There was a knocking on the outer door.

'Who is it?' he called, his voice sounding old and frail even to his own ears.

'It is I, Father. Li Peng.'

'Then come...'

Li Peng came several paces into the room, then bowed low. 'Father, we have a guest.'

Li Chao Ch'in gestured towards the big window at his back. 'I know. I saw...'

'No, Father. He's incoming right now. We've told him that if there's any funny business we'll blow him out of the sky.'

'Him?'

'Forgive me, Father. I mean Shen Fu... the First Dragon... he'll be here in just ten minutes.'

★

The First Dragon set the map aside, then looked up at his host. Li Chao Ch'in looked drawn and pale, like a man who'd had no sleep.

'Things are looking bad. But not as bad as they might have been.'

'How so?'

'You might, for instance, have been blind.'

'But we *are* blind. Tsao Ch'un is jamming all our communications.'

'Not all. You have my eyes.'

'Your eyes... ?'

'Oh, we don't like to speak of it, but the Ministry possesses a discreet communications network. It was designed precisely for times like this.' The First Dragon looked up, meeting his eyes coldly. 'You may use it if you wish.'

Li Chao Chin stared at him a moment, then his face split into a wide grin. 'Are you serious, Shen Fu? A proper communications network? One Tsao Ch'un knows nothing of?'

'Well, if he does, we'll soon find out. But as far as I know—'

'But that's wonderful! If we could get that up and running...'

Li Chao Ch'in stopped, noticing the look on the First Dragon's face.

'What?'

Shen Fu nodded. 'I'm sorry, Lord Li, but there is bad news as well as good. Tsao Ch'un has acted quickly. He has sent in one of his Banners, under the command of his eldest son, Tsao Heng.'

'A whole Banner army?'

'Yes. Half a million men. They went in an hour back... to Manhattan Island...'

Li Chao Ch'in looked down, his whole manner suddenly downcast. Manhattan Island was where Wu Hsien had his palace.

'Has he been captured?'

'Not yet. At least, not according to our sources. But who knows how long he will evade their forces? Tsao Ch'un, it seems, means to divide us then pick us off one by one.'

Lord Li stared at him. 'You know... that still sounds very odd. That "us". You of all people... I would have said you were the most loyal of all his servants.'

'I was. Until he crossed the line.'

'But there must have been doubters... in the Ministry.'

'There were. And now they're dead.'

'And you are here.'

'Yes. Together with my hands... my *shou*...'

Shen Fu stood, looking like a great gaunt crow, his black robe dragging behind him on the floor. 'Let me say what I must, Li Chao Ch'in, without wishing to cause you any loss of face. At present you don't know what to do, am I right?'

'We were trying to contact our friends...'

'And then Tsao Ch'un put a stop to that, neh? And now what? You are here and he is... well... you simply do not know, neh? He might be fifteen minutes away, at the head of another Banner army. You simply wouldn't know.'

'But now we have your eyes...'

'Maybe so. But that is not the point I'm trying to make. What will win this war or lose it is information... knowledge of what your enemy is doing... of when and where and why.'

Shen Fu had been pacing slowly up and down as he said this. Now he turned, looking directly at the T'ang.

'Right now we have one single, small advantage, and that is that Tsao Ch'un did not plan this war. If he had it would already have been over. You would have been dead, and your cousins along with you. As it is...well, we have a chance. A very slim chance, but a chance nonetheless.'

'I'm afraid I don't see that, Shen Fu. If Tsao Ch'un has all the armies.'

'Ah... but he doesn't. When the last of the American states surrendered to Jiang Lei, Tsao Ch'un disbanded the majority of his Banner armies. Now only six remain, and those, for the main part, will be loyal to Tsao Ch'un.'

'So?'

'So this... When the American campaign was stalling, Tsao Ch'un brought in mercenaries – trained soldiers from the old Northern European States – Danes and Swedes, Finns, Norwegians, Lithuanians, Poles and Russians – to form new Banner armies. It was those new Banners that finally swung the balance. The American empire fell and with it the last opponents of Tsao Ch'un.'

Li Chao Ch'in shrugged. 'Every schoolboy knows as much.'

'Maybe... but what they do not know is how much bad feeling there was among the mercenary ranks. Oh, they were paid off, and paid well... Only many felt that Tsao Ch'un was not grateful enough... That he was, perhaps, embarrassed by the need to call on them.'

'I see, and you think...?'

'That maybe they would form those Banners again. If we asked them to. If the cause was right. And if, at the end of it, we were to make the Banners permanent.'

Li Chao Ch'in drew in a sharp breath at that. Was that the cost of this? To make the *Hung Mao* armies permanent?

He looked away, troubled. 'I would have to consult my cousins.'

'Of course... but you yourself would have no objection?'

Li Chao Ch'in hesitated, then looked to Shen Fu again. 'What choice have we? To fight a war without armies... how is that possible?'

Shen Fu smiled tightly. 'It isn't. So make those calls. Speak to your cousins. And Lord Li...'

'Yes, Shen Fu?'

'Tell them that they must decide right now. Tomorrow will be too late.'

While Li Chao Ch'in went off to make his calls, the First Dragon made a call of his own, on a secret line one of his predecessors had set up twenty years ago but never used.

'Marshal...'

Aaltonen, Head of Security for City Europe, was seventy-six now, the same age as Tsao Ch'un. Only the years had treated him with greater kindness than his Master, and though his hair was grey, his face was ruddy with health and his eyes sharp and vigorous.

The old man bowed respectfully. 'First Dragon... how unexpected.'

But Shen Fu was not fooled. He knew Aaltonen had been waiting for a call, if not from him then from one or other of the Seven, for he had kept an eye on the old man these past few months, noting who he'd been in contact with. If anyone were the key to this, it was Aaltonen, for of all the old North European mercenaries, only he had retained any kind of position after the disbanding of the Banners.

Shen Fu smiled. 'You're looking well, Marshal. You've kept yourself in fine health, I see.'

'I can't complain. And you? Are you well, Shen Fu?'

'As well as I might be in these troubled times.'

'Ah yes... these times...'

'I am at Tongjiang.'

'*Tongjiang?*'

He saw how Aaltonen's eyes widened at that. Saw how he weighed it up and almost – almost – smiled.

'I am here with Lord Li, and Fan Cho...'

Aaltonen gasped. 'Fan Cho... But I thought...'

'You thought he was dead. He and his mother. So the newscasts would have it. Only they escaped. And now they've taken refuge here, at Tongjiang.'

Aaltonen hesitated. He had already heard enough to make him a deadly enemy if he chose. No one else knew as much as he right now, and were he to pass that knowledge on to Tsao Ch'un...

Shen Fu waited, then saw the man smile.

'So what might I do for you, First Dragon? How might I be of service?'

It was all a matter of experience.

Or, as Shen Fu realized only too well, inexperience.

The Seven were great ministers, great peacetime leaders. Under their practical guidance, Tsao Ch'un's great City had grown and grown, its citizens prospering, their number growing ever larger, ever richer by the year. As servants of the great man they had no equal. Only the fact was, not a single one among them had ever been involved in the business of warfare. Tsao Ch'un had made it his policy to keep such matters strictly within his own compass. And now they could see why.

The cards, it seemed, were stacked heavily in Tsao Ch'un's favour.

Fortunately for Li Chao Ch'in and the others, the First Dragon had thought long and hard about how to wage a campaign against his Master. In these early hours, when things were still in flux, his advice would, he knew, prove invaluable. Would be, perhaps, the difference between success and failure.

The key to it all, of course, was Aaltonen. For it was Aaltonen, and Aaltonen alone, who had influence over three men, all members of the North European mercenaries who had brought in their hired men to swing the balance when the campaign in North America was faltering.

Those three – each one a retired marshal – were now swiftly recruited to the cause, along with what remained of their forces.

The question was, would it prove enough?

'Shen Fu...?'

The First Dragon turned from where he sat, facing the great window. Lord Li was standing there in the doorway, his eldest son beside him, the young man's head bowed, showing Shen respect. It made him wonder what his own boy, Chien, would have been like had he lived. Chien would have been twenty-nine now. A man. Maybe even a great man. After all, look at what his father had achieved.

Shen Fu pushed the thought aside, then stood and went across, bowing to the pair.

'Lord Li... Prince Peng... what news?'

'It's not that, Shen Fu... it's...' Li Chao Ch'in took a breath. 'I have come to a decision.'

'A decision?'

'To go to Europe. To see *Shih* Shepherd.'

'Shih Shepherd...?' Shen Fu almost laughed. Only he was a man who never laughed. 'Have you considered the risks, my Lord?'

'I have. But I think I ought to go. If we can convince him of the justness of our cause...'

'Maybe so. But it is a long way, Li Chao Ch'in. More than four thousand miles, and much of that over hostile territory.'

'I know. Only we have discussed it, my sons and I, and... Well, there seems no other way. We must take a gamble now. Besides, how can we ask others to take risks if we are not willing to take them ourselves?'

'Well spoken, my Lord. But let me suggest one refinement to your plan. Why not fly instead to Bremen? Have Amos meet you there. And while you're at it, why not ask your Head of Security, Aaltonen, to join you?'

'Marshal Aaltonen? You think he'd come?'

'I know it for a fact. And a few of his friends, I warrant.'

'Then Bremen it is. But do you think Shepherd will meet us there? After all, if Tsao Ch'un were to hear of it...'

Shen Fu shook his head.

'Shepherd is his own man. Speak to him. Ask him to meet you. He can only say no.'

Li Chao Ch'in considered that a moment, then nodded. 'All right. I'll speak to him now. But Shen Fu...'

'Yes, Lord Li?'

'Do you think we still have time?'

Before boarding his craft, Li Chao Ch'in gathered his sons about him for one final word.

'My sons... take care of things in my absence, and do not despair. We will come through. With the help of our good friends, we shall win this war against the tyrant. I leave Li Peng in charge in my stead. He and the First Dragon will arrange things from henceforth, while I am in Europe. As for the rest...'

He embraced them, one by one, all but the youngest, Li Chang So, who was to accompany him on his perilous journey. Looking at them this last time he felt a dark and secret fear gnawing at him. He didn't want to leave them. It felt like abandonment. But he had to go. This wasn't a game, it was a war for their very survival. Tsao Ch'un would take no prisoners, therefore failure was not an option. Tsao Ch'un *must* be overthrown, he and his sons destroyed, so that a new, more just rule – that of the Seven – could be established.

But the hours ahead held hidden dangers. Who knew what Tsao Ch'un was up to? Maybe he was out there already, beyond the periphery of Tongjiang, waiting for Li Chao to emerge, ready to blast his craft out of the air.

Six heavily armed cruisers were to accompany his craft, to guard and protect him against attack. But he knew what Tsao Ch'un could put into the air, and beside it his own force was insignificant. He would need luck as well as daring if he were to reach Bremen.

He went inside and strapped himself into his chair, steeling himself against the anguish he was feeling at that moment. Only the thought of it would not go away.

I will never ever see them all again...

He looked across at Li Chang So. His youngest son was sitting back in his seat, his eyes closed, relaxed, or so it seemed.

Li Chao Ch'in swallowed, his mouth gone dry. How had it come to this?

There was a clunk as the outer hatches closed, then a low growl from the engines. A moment later they began to lift.

Kuan Yin... keep them safe...

But a small, still part of him knew his wish was quite forlorn. They were dead. He knew it for a fact. They were all as good as dead, and he among them.

My loves... My pretty ones...

But it was all too late. The die was cast. The gods alone could aid him now.

'Forgive me, First Dragon, but what exactly is it that you're doing?'

Shen Fu turned to the young prince and bowed politely.

'We are doing what we at the Ministry are best at. Using the media to communicate our message.'

Li Peng nodded, then looked about him once again at his father's study. It was unrecognizable. There were big screens and camera equipment everywhere, along with mixing desks and stack after stack of massive signal-boosting equipment.

'Ah, I see... but...'

'How are we getting the signal out when Tsao Ch'un is supposed to be jamming us? That's very simple. We have our own feeds. Oh, he'll find out how to shut us down in time, but before then we plan to make an impact.'

'But if it's your word against his, who will they believe?'

'They don't have to believe anything. They just have to bear witness.'

'What do you mean?'

'I mean, we just show them the truth for once. The total, unvarnished truth.'

Li Peng laughed. Then he saw that the First Dragon was being absolutely serious.

'The *truth*?'

'That's right. I know... it goes against our tradition, neh, Prince Peng? But what more powerful weapon could there be than to show Tsao Ch'un's tyranny as it is, without exaggeration? How better win the hearts and minds of Chung Kuo's citizens than to show them just what it is their Master has in mind for them?'

The young prince stared at him a moment longer, then shook his head.

'It won't work.'

'Won't it? You should see the footage we have. Innocent men killed in their beds. Grieving widows. And more. Much more.'

'He'll fight back.'

'Of course he will. And fight dirty. That is his way. But they'll know the difference. They'll *know*. See if they don't.'

Exhausted, at the end of a long day haggling over contract details, Reed sat at the corner table in the Red Lantern tea house in one of the West Bremen stacks, staring up in total shock at the news reports coming in from North America.

He had never seen the like of it. Up on the screen, in vivid, garish detail, Tsao Ch'un's elite troops could be seen kicking their way into a locked bedroom. Using fists and boots, knives, knuckledusters, iron bars and clubs, they laid into the unarmed occupants, beating them savagely, sadistically before finishing them off with their handguns.

There was no commentary, just the images. And no sooner was one thing finished than another – equally horrifying – took its place, all of it uncensored, like it was being streamed in from the darkest heart of nightmare.

From time to time a printed message on the screen would give the images a context, date, time and location, but otherwise there was no attempt to provide any kind of intermediary comment. None of that bland, whitewashing crap they usually fed the people. And that, for some strange reason, made it all the more compelling. Because this was happening right now.

The levels were buzzing with rumours. But one thing was crystal clear. Tsao Ch'un was at war with his own chief ministers. Everyone knew that much.

Rumour was that several of the T'ang were already dead. Killed for plotting against Tsao Ch'un. But many said that that was a lie, that it was simply Tsao Ch'un trying to hold on to his power by any means, and the images seemed to bear this out.

Reed looked away, feeling sick. The day, which had begun so well, so brightly and hopefully, had ended in disaster. The contract he'd been working on was worth nothing now. He might as well just tear the fucking thing up! As for his dream of a First Level mansion, that had just popped like a soap bubble, because Tsao Ch'un, with the Banners and Security on his side, was bound to win this struggle. Only a fool would back the Seven.

He sipped at his *ch'a* bowl, then spat it out. It was cold.

Reed looked about him. This whole situation made him feel uneasy. If Tsao Ch'un *did* win it would mean crackdowns and purges, yes and endless executions. Because that was how they were, these Han. They didn't mess about. Tsao Ch'un least of all.

Purification, that's what they'd call it. An excuse to get rid of their enemies – of anyone who in the smallest degree had opposed them.

Yes, along with anyone who'd had dealings with their enemies.

Which put him squarely in the firing zone.

He stood, his hand searching in the pocket of his *pau* for some change to leave for the *ch'a* when all the screens went suddenly blank. For a moment they seemed dead. Then, with a little fanfare, they came on again, showing the familiar image of Bremen Central – not five *li* from where he sat. There stood a group of six men on a platform, staring uneasily into camera.

'*Kuan Yin...*' he said, his mouth falling open, recognizing suddenly who they were.

Jesus Fucking Christ!

Bremen, it seemed, had officially declared itself for the Seven. And there, on screen, as if to emphasize it, were Li Chao Ch'in, Marshal Aaltonen, Amos Shepherd, and three very grizzled old soldiers in their ancient Banner uniforms, men whom Reed recognized from the campaigns in America.

It was a particular shock to see Shepherd there among them. But a further shock awaited him, for as Li Chao Ch'in turned to greet and embrace each of the three old soldiers, so Reed saw his own boss in the background, among a group of other Company Heads. Wolfgang Ebert standing there, looking grimly on.

Reed whistled to himself. It was a coup. It was a fucking coup! The Seven wanted Tsao Ch'un out. That's what all this was about. And a number of very important people were joining them.

Not that they had a hope in hell, but it was good to see.

Bremen... for the Seven.

Actually, now that he thought about it, it was quite a big thing. Because Bremen was the centre of a whole lot of stuff. The Ministry had their head-quarters here, and Security. And if Amos Shepherd had thrown in his lot with them...

That last particularly made him think. Shepherd wasn't a stupid man, far from it, and if he thought they had a chance... Well, maybe they did. Maybe there was stuff going on that none of the City's many citizens had heard about.

Amos Shepherd, he knew, only backed winners. When Jiang Lei had conquered North America, who'd been his right-hand man? Shepherd. And before that? When Tsao Ch'un himself had conquered half the globe, there again was Shepherd, right alongside the great man, giving advice.

But not this time. This time he'd abandoned his Master. This time he'd backed what at first sight appeared to be the odds-on losers.

So what did he know that they didn't?

The soundtrack crackled then cut out. A moment later the screen went blank. Only this time it didn't come on again.

Home, Reed told himself. *Get your arse back home, and make it quick now. Before it all starts up once more.*

Tsao Ch'un stood before the screen, raging at the scene that was being transmitted from Bremen Central. His chair had been thrown back, the footstool kicked away in a fit of rage. Looking on, the handful of servants that were present bowed low and backed away, terrified of what their Master might do in his anger.

There had been *some* good news. Wu Hsien's palace in Manhattan had been taken, but Wu Hsien himself had escaped and his capture was the primary aim.

Tsao Ch'un shook his fist at the screen, cursing his good-for-nothing sons. More troops were to go in within the hour – to attack his enemies in their own strongholds – but such things took time to organize, and in the meantime the Seven were digging in, entrenching their positions.

What concerned Tsao Ch'un most, however, was the re-formation of the North European mercenary armies. How big a force would they be able to get together? And how long would it take? Days? Weeks? If the latter, then he needn't worry, for it would all be over long before then.

He slowed his breathing, calming himself. And then he laughed, realizing just how much he had missed this. The excitement, the challenge of it. For the first time in years he felt alive, a sense of purpose coursing through him.

It felt almost like his blood had slowed, become silted like a river, but now...

Turning, he looked to his Chief Steward, Ling Yu.

'Steward Ling... have my marshals report in to me, within the hour! And I want to know what the latest word is on each of the remaining T'ang. Where they are, what they're doing, who they've spoken to. And my sons...'

Tsao Ch'un smiled; a smile that might easily have been misinterpreted as a snarl, so fierce it was. For a moment he had forgotten. For the briefest moment he had let things slide, underestimating his enemies. But now he knew. The scene from Bremen had reminded him. There was still much to be done if he was to destroy them.

Alive. Yes, he felt suddenly alive again.

As his men ran this way and that to do his bidding, Tsao Ch'un gave a great roar of laughter and, rubbing his hands together, began again to mould events, like he had once before, back when this world was young.

Back when it was all fresh and new.

Chapter 22

TIGERS AND BUTTERFLIES

Judge Yo leaned forward in his chair, his sculpted, skull-like head tilted towards his right, where the Changs and their lawyers sat.

'Advocate Hui,' he began, his voice cold and clear and emotionless. 'I understand you have moved to have this case thrown out.'

Hui Chang Yeh heaved his massive bulk out of his chair and stood, head bowed, before Yo Jou Hsi.

'I have, my Lord.'

'May I ask on what grounds?'

Hui remained as he was, head bowed, as if Judge Yo were the Son of Heaven himself.

'I would refer my Lordship to the decision of the *Ta-li ssu* in the case of Chu versus Chi. My Lord has the papers. There the precedent is firmly established that any contract entered into by the past owners of a registered trading concern is not necessarily binding to the new owners.'

'And on what basis was this claimed?'

'It is claimed on the basis of the *Ko-hou ch'ih*, my Lord... the Edicts Subsequent to Regulations, which ruled...'

Jake leaned in to Advocate Yang. 'What is he talking about?'

Yang glanced fearfully at Judge Yo, then whispered back.

'*The Ta-li ssu is the Supreme Court of Justice. And the case of Chu versus Chi has stood for more than a thousand years.*'

And this was the first time he had been told of it! Jake looked past Yang at Advocate Meng, as if something should be done to counter what he was hearing. Only Meng appeared to be dozing, as if he had no interest in the case whatsoever.

What in God's name is going on?

Out in the space below Judge Yo's chair, Advocate Hui was busy piling precedent upon precedent, citing case after case, while Judge Yo nodded from his position up on the dais, the faintest rictus of a smile animating his face.

We're having our arses kicked, Jake thought. And where's the reinforcements GenSyn promised?

Detained somewhere else, he answered, his spirits sinking. Tied up on some other case while the world falls apart!

That morning's news had not been good. Rumours were that at least three of the Seven were already dead. After the uncensored images that had been screened the previous day – images Jake himself had missed – people were terrified that things would escalate and everyone get dragged into the conflict. It wasn't helped by the fact that the news channels had been shut down most of the day. And even when they were broadcasting, the news from them was mixed. The Bremen declaration was decidedly so, and whilst part of him silently cheered on the Seven and hoped they'd have the victory, another part feared the outcome. For if Tsao Ch'un were to triumph, anyone who had been associated with GenSyn and the Eberts in any way was likely to get it in the neck, his son Peter and himself included.

Jake had been surprised that the hearing had continued, when there was every reason to postpone it until the troubles were over. But the Ministry, it seemed, had decreed that all government functions be maintained, and so here they were sitting in court, as if nothing in the outside world had changed.

'Advocate Yang...' he began, only this time Judge Yo turned to him, his eyes blazing with anger.

'Shih Reed! You will be quiet or I will have you removed from the court-room!'

Jake bowed his head. 'Forgive me, my Lord.'

Yo glared at him, then turned back, smiling at the fat man who stood before him in his expensive silks. 'Continue, Advocate Hui.'

Before Hui could say another word, the doors at the far end swung open.

'My Lord...'

If Hui was big, the newcomer was huge, twice Hui's size at the very least. Only unlike Hui, the newcomer had a distinct air of elegance. His long dark hair was braided with pearls, while his flowing silks were a beautiful olive green, bordered in black. Most distinctive of all, however, was the golden staff he carried.

Jake stared at the man, astonished by the sight. Yet when he looked back at Judge Yo, he was surprised to find not derision, but a kind of shocked awe on his features.

Yo Jou Hsi was afraid!

Beside him, both Yang and Meng had suddenly woken up. Their faces shared an expression of delighted expectation.

Who the fuck...?

Was this what they had promised him? Was this what Meng Hsin-fa had meant when he'd told him 'Wait and see'?

Judge Yo swallowed, then gestured towards the newcomer.

'Shu Liang... have you an interest in this case?'

The big man – Shu Liang, he presumed – looked puzzled. 'An *interest?*' He came down the steps, then smiled at Jake. '*Shih Reed...*' He bowed respectfully, then turned back to face Judge Yo.

'I understand Judge Wei is dead. An *accident*, I'm told...'

There was no hint of threat, yet Judge Yo looked like he'd been struck.

Shu Liang walked slowly on past Jake and Yang and Advocate Meng, until he stood just below the Judge, with his opponent, Hui, a mere arm's length away.

'Has he cited Chu versus Chi?'

Yo nodded.

'And the New Code, the *Hsin-lu*... has he quoted from that, too?'

Again Yo nodded.

'Hmmm... I thought as much. And you've *allowed* this, Yo Jou Hsi?'

Yo didn't answer. He seemed to have shrunk back into his skin.

Shu Liang slowly shook his head, as if disappointed. 'No doubt our friend here will be quoting from the *Wu-te* code next. Or is that too *modern* for him?'

Beside Jake, both Yang and Meng laughed.

'*Too modern!*' Yang repeated delightedly, then nudged Jake, as if he too should get the joke.

But Shu Liang wasn't done. Suddenly the gentle, mocking tone was gone, and in its place...

Jake felt a tingle down his spine. Suddenly it was as if a snarling tiger stood before them. The look on Shu Liang's face was predatory and his voice...

'Yo Jou Hsi...'

Judge Yo quailed before him. 'Yes?' he said, his voice faint, apologetic.

'Are you going to listen to this drivel, or are you going to call a recess? Because if you really *are* going to waste our time in this fashion...'

Yo swallowed again, then, as if he'd made the decision unaided, reached for his gavel and brought it down hard.

'An hour's recess,' he said, looking to Shu Liang, who smiled and nodded. 'But be back here in good time.'

Then, as if he couldn't get away fast enough, he was gone.

For a second or two, Shu Liang watched the space Judge Yo had vacated. Then he turned back to them, smiling broadly, his mouth the tiniest of slits in the middle of those folds of flesh that were his chin and neck. '*Shih* Reed... forgive me for my lateness... As you've probably gathered, I am Shu Liang, your Senior Advocate.'

Jake took the massive scented hand, his own dwarfed by it. 'Shu Liang...' Only as he looked up, meeting the big man's eyes, he caught his breath.

A Han with green eyes! It was unheard of. Or were these fake? Lenses, perhaps?

'My own,' Shu Liang said, smiling, as if he'd read Jake's thoughts. 'Or rather, my mother's. She was *Hung Mao*.'

'Ah...' Even so... it felt wrong. Wasn't there something about dominants and recessives? Shouldn't his eyes be dark?

Shu Liang looked about him. 'Advocate Meng, Advocate Yang... friends... is there a room we can use? If we're to have a strategy...' He paused, then laughed. 'Did he really cite Chu versus Chi?'

'He did,' Meng answered, grinning.

'Then maybe we won't need to use anything stronger than irony.'

Seated in one of the smaller anterooms, Shu Liang faced Jake across the table, while the rest of them looked on, Meng holding Shu Liang's staff.

'Doubtless you want to know who I am, is that not so, *Shih* Reed?'

Seen close up, Shu Liang really was something. Precious stones had been sewn into his olive-green silks – stones that looked like tiny tiger's eyes – interspersed with tiny butterflies made of golden thread. From his clothes one might have mistaken him for a dandy, a dilettante, except for those eyes. Behind the green, *embedded* in the green, was an intelligence that was somehow cold and machine-like.

Jake smiled. 'You must be someone very special, Advocate Shu...'

'Oh, I *am*, friend Jake. You might also think that I think a great deal of myself, saying that. Then again, there is a great deal of me. Appearances might suggest that I have a whole school of lawyers in here, fighting to get out!'

Shu Liang let the laughter die, then spoke again. 'But let me be serious a moment. This case... it *interests* me. The very fact that the Changs should pursue it through a court at this level says a great deal about their motives. They wish to establish a precedent, I imagine. To win two or three such cases. Enough to establish them in law. As for what Advocate Hui was doing back there... it stank of obfuscation, neh? Chu versus Chi...' He laughed. 'Only, if he thinks he can play such games with me, then he's very much mistaken.'

Shu Liang shifted a little, as if uncomfortable on the small chair he was sitting on. 'Your case, *Shih* Reed... the truth is, it should not have needed to be heard. The Judge should have ruled, at once and without need to have considered anything but your original agreement with MicroData. A contract is a contract, after all, and anyone who buys into that contract does so as if they stepped into the shoes of the previous owner.'

He sighed. 'Only the fact is this... we live in dark times. Our sense of *yi*, of social rightness, upon which all of our law is based, has been worn down, our social conscience abraded. As a result, self-serving lackeys like our friend Yo Jou Hsi have proliferated, like bugs on a bloated corpse. Judge Wei's death – his "accident" – surprised me somewhat. It was somehow too bold, too... *direct*. Perhaps Wei simply got too greedy. Or, more likely, Judge Yo promised to undercut him. To deliver the verdict at half the cost. Whatever... the one thing we can be certain of is that Yo is *their* man, and that given the chance, he will rule for them.'

Jake frowned. 'Then that business of the auction?'

'Was, I believe, to test your resolve to continue with the case. To see whether you would not rather prefer to settle than to fight on. Judge Yo may be venial, but he is not stupid. I can't believe he would have accepted a higher bribe from you, even if you had offered such. He is, I am sure, conscious now of just how ruthless his employers can be. Wei's accident will have told him as much.'

Shu Liang smiled. Then, lifting himself up out of the chair, he walked over to the far end of the room, where shelf after shelf of leather-bound volumes filled the wall from floor to ceiling. Idly, he pulled one down and studied it a moment, then put it back.

'You see, the problem is not in winning this case, but in making it stick. Making it... *unchallengeable*. Making it so that the Changs – and others like them – will be discouraged from bringing a similar case against someone new. Someone who, unlike you, *Shih* Reed, is not so willing to fight for what is theirs.'

Advocate Meng spoke now for the first time. 'So what next, Master Shu? You spoke of a strategy...'

Shu Liang turned back, facing him.

'I think our first task is to expose Advocate Hui for the fake he is. To shoot down all his ducks. All of his Chis and Chus. To blow the dust away and get down to the facts.' He smiled. 'I'll enjoy that. It'll be fun.'

'Fun?' Across from him Meng laughed. But Jake could see from his expression that he was clearly in awe of the big man, and if Meng was in awe, then Shu Liang *had* to be something special.

'Well, maybe fun is overdoing it,' Shu Liang said, coming back across and taking his staff back from Meng. 'But I do enjoy watching men like Hui Chang Yeh shown up for the fools and charlatans they are, don't you? I just love to see them squirm.'

While Shu Liang and the others went to get some breakfast, Jake took Advocate Yang aside.

'Shu Liang,' he began. 'The man's impressive, I agree, only...'

'Only what?' Yang said. 'This friend of yours at GenSyn... he must like you a great deal, *Shih* Reed. Shu Liang... he is, how d'you say it? A "one-off". His reputation... well, I was honoured just to be in court with him.'

'He's good then?'

'*Good?*' Yang laughed. 'Why, the man has an eidetic memory. There's nothing he doesn't know. Twenty-four centuries of Han law... he has it all, up here, in his brain, from the *Ta k'ao* – the pronouncements of the sage kings – to the most current legislation on genetics and nanotechnology! Chi and Chu... he could quote you Chi and Chu, word perfect, and all the subsequent cases built on it! Don't you understand? The man is a walking, talking encyclopaedia. Why, I almost feel sorry for Advocate Hui. Only the man deserves what's coming to him. Deserves the humiliation and loss of face... Oh, and speaking of which, I have to thank you, Jake.'

'*Thank* me? For what?'

'For this.' Yang pulled a slip of paper from the pocket of his silks and handed it to Jake.

Jake read it, then looked up. 'I don't understand. I thought you said your offices weren't insured.'

'They weren't.'

'But this is...'

'An insurance cheque, I know. I called them. They said it had been authorized by their clients, GenSyn.'

'And you thought...' Jake shook his head, then handed the cheque back. 'I didn't know a thing about this. But look... I'll thank them on your behalf. I'll go speak to them now, before we have to go back in.'

'Thank you, *Shih* Reed. Only one last thing before we go back in...'

'Go on?'

Yang looked about him, as if to check no one was listening, then leaned close, speaking softly, so only Jake could hear.

'I probably worry far too much, but... well, it occurs to me that, if Shu Liang is as good as we hope he'll be, then... well, it will not be Advocate Hui alone who'll suffer loss of face. The Changs...' He swallowed. 'I guess what I am saying is that I would consider asking GenSyn for protection. And your wife... well, if it were me, I would consider bringing her close, where no one could threaten her.'

Yang saw how Jake looked down at that and blinked. 'You mean... they have already?'

Jake nodded.

'Then do not delay, dear friend. Bring her here at once. Under armed guard, if necessary. Judge Wei must have thought himself safe from them, only look where that got him. Sharing a drink with the God of Hell!'

Ten minutes later, Jake was back in his room, speaking to Alison's assistant, a young Han named Tu Mu.

'She should be in any minute now,' Tu Mu was saying. 'But I'll pass your message on, all right? And you really mustn't worry about your wife, Shih Reed. We've a team of four looking after her, twenty-four hours a day. And if there's any problem at all, we'll contact you immediately, even if you're in court.'

'Thank you,' Jake said, reassured. Deciding, there and then, that it made no sense to drag her out here. That it made better sense for him to go there, even if it meant travelling back and forth. 'And tell Alison I'll speak to her later. After the morning session.'

Jake cut connection, then looked at the time at the bottom of the screen. It was just after nine. Normally, if he'd been home, they wouldn't even have got up yet, only he knew Mary hadn't been sleeping well lately; that she'd been getting up early to make a cup of ch'a and watch the news.

He called her, then stood there, waiting to be connected. Only this time he wasn't.

A face appeared on screen. A young male Han, not so very different from Tu Mu. It was preprogrammed, he realized, not real-time. The slightest lack of sync betrayed its nature.

'Forgive me, Shih Reed,' it said, bowing to him, 'but there are problems with the communications grid at present. If you would like to leave a message, I can record one for you and send it on later, when the grid is back up.'

Jake frowned, not understanding. One moment it had been working, the next it was gone.

Someone had clearly pulled the plug.

He left a message, then cut connection again. He really ought to be returning to court, to join them for Shu Liang's 'performance', only there were a couple of things he wanted to do before he went back.

The first was to check on the news.

But when he tried to get the screen to work, it didn't. It was just blank. He changed channels, hoping to find one that was still up and running. There was nothing.

Had everything been switched off? Or was it, perhaps, just a local fault?

Whatever it was, he felt a deep unease. Was Tsao Ch'un using this oppor-tunity to purge his enemies? To cleanse the levels of those who'd sided against him? If so, it was not beyond belief that he and Mary would be on his list.

Jake counted to twenty, calming himself, trying to think things through. It was going to be all right. And how did he know that? Because it was different this time round. If it *was* war – and it clearly was – then it was a war to establish who controlled it all. A war between the big people. A 'War in Heaven', as they liked to call it. He and his like – the *hsiao jen*, or 'little people' – wouldn't be affected. Not in any serious way. They might be *inconvenienced* a bit, only...

Jake bit his lip. No. It was no good lying to himself. If the Seven lost this war – and surely they must – then his life and the lives of those he loved best were all in danger. Not immediately. Perhaps only once things had settled again. But Tsao Ch'un would make it his business to deal with those who'd opposed him *in any fashion, whenever.* For that was Tsao Ch'un's way. It was why he was still in charge.

The screen lit up again. But it wasn't the news channel. Nor was it Mary. It was Advocate Meng, calling from the communications room in the court-house, sixty levels down.

'Jake? Are you all right? Look... in view of what's going on, Judge Yo has suspended the hearing. They're going to reassess things tomorrow, midday local time. I can handle that, if you want. In the meantime you might as well go home.'

'D'you think that's wise? I mean... is it safe to travel?'

'As far as I know. Why? Have you heard any different?'

'They've shut down the communications network. Did you know that?'

'No...' Meng looked thoughtful. 'Look, I'm sure it's temporary. And if you're worried, we can try and arrange something. Rent a cruiser, maybe.'

On GenSyn's bill, no doubt, Jake thought, wondering whether he should try Alison again.

'Okay,' he said. 'And thanks... 'Til tomorrow, neh?'

Meng smiled back at him. 'Until tomorrow. And Jake... keep safe.'

The screen went black, like it was dead.

Meng was right. He ought to go home. Sit this out there, with Mary at his side. As for the case, that could wait until things were settled.

Jake went over to the bed and sat. The best thing would be to go and see them at reception. See what could be arranged. Maybe he should do that now. Only he found he was loath to move. What if Mary called him back and he wasn't here? No. He'd give it ten minutes. Then, if nothing was happening, he'd go and see them at the desk. Try and organize transport home.

If anything was still running.

He spoke to the screen. 'Hello?... *Hello?* Is there anybody there?'

The room was silent. Or almost so. Underneath the silence was the slow and steady pulse of the big circulatory fans, pushing the air through the levels.

Jake stood again. What was he waiting for? He ought to go and see them now. Only right then the screen lit up again.

'Jake?'

'Mary... thank fuck...'

'*Jake...*' Only for all her surface disapproval, she was smiling, pleased to see him. 'What's happening? The TV keeps blacking out.'

'I know,' he said, not wanting to get into that. 'Look, I'm going to come home. The Judge has suspended the hearing temporarily, so there's no real point being here. I don't know what's up and running, but I'll try and get back ASAP. You just sit tight, okay?'

'Okay... but Jake... don't take any risks. And Jake... I love you.'

He smiled. 'Love you, too.'

And she was gone. The screen was blank again.

Alison... he really ought to phone Alison.

Later, he thought. *When I'm home. I'll phone her then.*

Jake stood, looking about him. Then, knowing there was nothing else to do, he threw his holdall onto the bed and started gathering all his stuff together.

War in Heaven... Pray God it stayed that way!

Mary went through to the bedroom, then stood there, looking about her. How good it had been just to see his face. How comforting. Only now she feared for him. The world was at war and he would be travelling back through it. The thought of it ripped at her guts.

Oh, Jake... be safe...

She had woken that morning with dreams of home. Of her and Annie as children, playing in the fields behind the house. And of Tom and Jake... husbands both, the two of them in bed with her in her dream, one either side of her, her arms about them both.

So calm, those dreams. So strangely calm, and once again so comforting.

Jake too had been visited by dreams lately. He had told her of them. At least, those that *could* be spoken of. Only Jake's dreams were much darker than her own. Dark, threatening dreams that mirrored the sheer awfulness of those things that had happened to him, back in his past lives.

She went over to the dressing table and sat, studying herself in the mirror, examining the ruins of her face. She had been so pretty, and now so old.

Strange how he never dreamed of Annie. Or maybe he did and never spoke of it to her.

For a moment longer she sat there and remembered her sister's face, seeing her there, laughing in the sunlight, smiling at the memory.

And then it was gone.

Silence, and then... the screens were on again, the chatter of excited voices filling the air.

The bolt had stopped. For the best part of an hour it had run along its tracks, chewing up the miles, on through the stacks, bringing him closer and closer by the minute. But now it had stopped, and further up the station there was a disturbance. People were shouting and there were screams.

Jake looked about him at the packed carriage. They were afraid. Every last one of them. Terrified that here, in a place none of them knew, it would all come to an end. With a mob of rampaging thugs who had been freed by the situation to indulge themselves. To break and smash and maim.

Across from him an old lady had begun to cry. Beside her a mother held her two children close, while the father stood protectively in front of them.

Jake looked down, swallowing. Why couldn't the bastards just let them be? What God-awful quality in men made them behave like this? If he'd had a gun...

If I had a gun, what?

No. There was no fooling himself. It was a young man's world. A Yang world full of aggressive little shits who just loved to trample on their fellows and kick the crap out of them, or beat them with lengths of metal piping. Young men who never saw the consequences.

Back in Corfe they'd have known what to do.

Only this wasn't Corfe.

Outside the noise had grown. Down there, at the far end of the platform, they were fighting now. He could see the blur of struck blows, the yells and cries of pain.

And then there were whistles. Suddenly, from one of the entrances to the left of the platform, armed soldiers – Security by the look of them – began to pour. At least thirty or more of them, armed with guns and batons. A gun went off and then another, and suddenly the mob broke, making for the exits, even as the soldiers grabbed hold of some of them, grappling them to the floor.

Thank Christ, Jake thought, never happier to see the Security forces at work. Ignoring, for that moment, all that he knew about the way they operated. How corrupt they were. How they would beat up prisoners in their cells. No, right then he wanted to hug them. Because without them…

There were cheers and applause, and as their officer turned to look back down the platform, big beaming smiles.

'Please, get back inside, ladies and gentlemen,' he said, his voice amplified by the loudhailer in his hand. 'We will have you under way again in just a few minutes.'

Jake looked to the old woman just across from him. She was smiling now, smiling and wiping her face with her hankie, relieved that things had turned out as they had. He smiled at her. Old? She was no older than him. No older than his Mary.

'Are you okay?' he asked, leaning down to her.

She nodded, but clearly the incident had shaken her.

'It'll all be fine now,' he said, wanting to reassure himself as much as her. 'We'll be home soon. Safe indoors.'

Only even as he said it, he wasn't convinced. Indoors. What single one of them was safe indoors?

CHUNG KUO

Chapter 23

BEAUTIFUL AND IMPOSING

The sky was a solid lid of grey above the drill yard, a fine mist of rain falling steadily through the tall lighting stanchions that flooded the ancient cobbles with actinic light.

It was barely ten in the morning, but more than a thousand had already gathered. They stood there now, their kitbags – containing four days' provisions – slung over their shoulders, looking on as the slow trickle of arrivals became a flood. A great queue of men lining up to sign the huge, leather-bound roster ledgers that lay open on the trestle table in the far corner of the yard, beneath the awning.

There, on an old campaign chair Jiang Lei himself had left him, a grizzled sergeant watched as each man bent to sign the ancient book. He knew each one, greeting them by name and grinning fiercely, pleased to see so many of the old guard responding to the muster.

Even he had to admit that they were a motley-looking bunch, some long-haired, some shaven, some – and in this they showed their years – looking more like monks than hardened fighters. But he knew better than to go by appearance. There were no men he would rather fight alongside than these. No one he would trust more. When things had got tough in America, these men had delivered. Twenty years ago now, but that didn't matter. They were still some of the toughest fighting men the world had ever produced. Finns and Danes. Norwegians, Swedes and Russians. Big men. Hard men. Men whose distant ancestors had once struck terror throughout Europe, voyaging, *a-vykingr*, in their long boats. Now they would have their day.

Word was coming in of attacks on some of those who were making their way in. Of ambushes and attempts to scare men off, but they seemed to be having little effect. The men had waited years for this call, and now they came, throwing together their kit and hurrying off to Bremen by the quickest means possible.

Many a one who had not seen his old comrades in long years now greeted them with open arms. Yet behind the laughter, behind those heartfelt smiles was a grim sense of purpose. They were here for a reason. To finish what they had begun all those years ago.

Which was why they stood there now, raindrops glistening in their hair, the men forming up in their old Banners and awaiting orders. Some had not come, those who were sick or who had died in the intervening years, but they were very few. If they could limp or hop or crawl they were there. For duty's sake.

Where the big roster ledgers had been these past twenty years was a mystery. Many had thought them destroyed, after the Northern Banners had been disbanded. But here they were, and as each new arrival signed their name, so, in their eyes, something was reborn. Banned by law from being soldiers, they had found other occupations that had complemented soldiering. They had become cooks, or medics, had joined Security or taken jobs in engineering; even so, the years between had been like a dream.

This was what they'd been created for. This.

Each man knew what a risk he took with his life, just being there, but not one among them would have thought not to come. They were there because they had to be. Because it was ordered thus. It was why most of them had kept in shape all these years, spending long hours in the gym. Looking around at them, there was nothing flabby, nothing middle-aged about the men.

Tsao Ch'un... There had always been a problem with Tsao Ch'un. It wasn't he they had fought for all those years ago. They had fought for their marshals, and for their pride – because they were who they were. Only once it was done they had felt let down. They had been paid, certainly, but they hadn't been *rewarded*. What Tsao Ch'un owed them had never been acknowledged, and that had rankled with them all these years. When they'd met, in twos and threes, they had often said as much. Yes, and got into trouble with the Ministry over it, but now it was out in the open. They were here to air their grievance in the only way they knew how.

This was what they were good at. What they did best. And the devil take the man who underestimated them.

To fight Tsao Ch'un. That was why they'd come. To put things straight. To get their just reward at long last. And to free Chung Kuo from tyranny.

From the balcony, high above the drill yard, the six great men looked on.

'See... I told you they would come.'

It was one of the old marshals, the grey-headed Svensson, who said it, his eyes burning with pride at the sight of the men gathering down below.

'I never doubted it,' Shepherd answered him, 'in fact, I *counted* on it.'

Li Chao Ch'in glanced at him at that, then looked away again. The T'ang seemed fascinated by events, and genuinely surprised by how many had already come. It was, after all, only an hour since they'd sent out the summons.

'I was with them... in America...' Shepherd said.

It was an obvious thing to say, for they all knew of his role as advisor to Jiang Lei, but he felt he had to say it. To *remind* them.

'I was surprised,' another of the marshals, Raikkonen said, his steel-grey eyes fixing Shepherd. 'I thought you were his man.'

'And so I was. Yet I always knew this day would come. It was why I helped establish the Seven. To ensure stability.'

'Is that why you're here?' Li Chao Ch'in asked. 'For stability?'

Shepherd laughed. 'What you really mean is, do I think we can win? Well, the truth is, I don't know. But the Northern Banners will give us a chance. That is, if they all turn out.'

'They will come,' Raikkonen said, and his fellow marshals nodded.

'Good... Then, as I said, we have a chance. The thing is this... whatever happens now, this day could not have been avoided. It's a mistake to think it could. Whatever might have triggered it, we would always have had to fight Tsao Ch'un eventually, because a single man cannot rule an entire planet, no matter how many sons or loyal servants he has. Eventually it would have proved unviable, for a single man is mortal, while seven families...'

Li Chao Ch'in stared at him, horrified. 'You mean, you *knew* this would happen?'

Shepherd rested his hands on the balcony wall, looking down at the thousands who had already gathered. The queue before the roster ledgers seemed to have grown even in the last five minutes.

'Of course. But if you had known that, you would have done everything in your power to avoid it. Isn't that the truth?'

Li Chao Ch'in hesitated. 'Maybe...'

'Seven families, ruling by consensus. That was always my intention.'

'And Tsao Ch'un?'

'Was a means of getting to that. Perhaps the only means. His ruthlessness... it was the necessary factor. That uncompromising nature of his. Kinder, more rational men – men like yourself, Lord Li – they don't have what it takes to conquer a world. But they do have the qualities necessary to rule it.'

'And is that what we're doing here?' Marshal Bakke, the youngest of the four marshals asked. 'Fulfilling your plan?'

'If you like... only...' Shepherd turned, looking back at them. 'Well... it was all quite vague. I must confess I was wrong-footed by this. However, like our friend, the First Dragon, I have thought long and hard about this eventuality. My only *real* surprise was that it hadn't happened before now. I had begun to think that maybe Tsao Ch'un would weather the storm, that we would face this crisis ten years down the line. That we'd be forced into a war against his sons. But now that it's come...'

'You don't have a plan,' Bakke said, grinning at him. 'Right?'

Shepherd nodded, smiled. 'I thought we might just... *improvise.*'

Li Chao Ch'in looked from one man to the other. 'But I thought...' He stopped, then nodded. 'He'll send his armies against us, won't he? The Seven, I mean... because if he kills *us*, it's over...'

'Yes,' Shepherd said quietly. 'So we have to prevent that. Have to prolong the struggle. Because the longer it goes on, the better chance we have of winning. And right now we need to come up with a strategy. We can't keep the troops here, in a single block. That's far too vulnerable. So decisions need to be made.'

'And will be,' Raikkonnen said, looking about him at his fellows.

Shepherd looked to Li Chao Ch'in. 'Did you know that he sent you a present? Or rather, that he meant to. A new concubine. It was his way of saying sorry. Only then your man went to see him.'

'My man?'

Shepherd explained. When he had done, Li Chao Ch'in had a solemn look.

'So close...'

'True. But look at it this way. His anger has given us a chance. That and the incompetence of his sons.'

'And the Northern Banners?' Raikkonen asked. 'How are we going to deploy them?'

'That's up to you, *ch'un tzu*. Only we must survive these first twenty-four hours. That's crucial. After that...'

He shrugged expressively.

'*Shih* Shepherd?'

'Yes, Marshal Svensson?'

'Are you not afraid of him? Of what he might do if he gets his hands on you?'

'Terrified. But he won't.'

Li Chao Ch'in looked at Shepherd again, then looked away, giving a little shudder. The thought of what Tsao Ch'un might do to him quite clearly unnerved the man. His hands shook at the thought of it.

Shepherd looked down. In that brief instant he had seen that Li Chao Ch'in was not as brave as he. It was there, in his eyes. The man lacked courage. Or was that being unfair? Wasn't it simply good sense to fear Tsao Ch'un? He was, after all, a complete psychopath. Whatever, he would have to watch Lord Li. If he, or any of them, lost their nerve...

'Lord Li,' he said, reaching out to touch his arm, 'take heart. We *shall* prevail.'

Only he could see that Li Chao Ch'in did not believe him. That, in his head, he had already lost.

The thought appalled him.

So much for all my vain ambitions...

Maybe. Only he for one would not give up. Not until there was no hope left whatsoever. Because it was true what he had said. They did not have a choice. They could either fight Tsao Ch'un now, or his sons later.

'Come,' he said, looking to the others. 'Let us go down. Our men are awaiting their orders.'

★

Yet even as they spoke, even as the veterans mustered, the war was escalating. In the skies to the east of Bremen, Security air forces loyal to the Seven found themselves fighting Tsao Ch'un's air forces in a battle for the skies. Outnumbered three to one, they nonetheless fought off their adversaries, and, though a few craft got through and inflicted damage on the North European stacks, as yet Bremen and its surroundings were unscathed.

The first round had gone to the rebels.

On the propaganda front, Tsao Ch'un had appointed a new First Dragon – his own man, Chang Yu – who quickly re-established control over the media. But the impact of those first few hours, when the news had been reported openly, had left their mark, and there were riots and mass demonstrations in a number of places; disturbances that the Security forces for once were loath to put down. The most serious were in America where native resentment over their defeat and consequent subjugation had never quite died out. There were major revolts in Memphis in the south and in Portland in the north-west, along with minor outbreaks in Chicago, Boston and Monterrey. Intent on tracking down Wu Hsien and his family, Tsao Ch'un would in other circumstances have ignored these, only he knew that not to deal with them would in all likelihood have major implications. Since Wu Hsien himself was clearly not going to intervene, he had sent in several elite battalions to firefight.

None of which had helped.

It was late morning now, and Tsao Ch'un was at his command centre in the Black Tower. Normally he would have summoned his advisors, only his advisors were now his enemies; thus he sat there, alone, mulling over what needed to be done.

It was while he was sitting there, brooding over the matter, that news came in of the capture of Tongjiang.

He stood, looking up at the screens, which were filled with images of the palace burning; of servants and family members being loaded onto cruisers, their hands bound, their heads bowed.

Tsao Ch'un grinned ferociously, then ordered that the images be sent on – for Li Chao Ch'in to see.

Then, from the same source, came even greater news – visual evidence of the death of Fan Li and his mother, the two of them butchered in the cellar in which they'd been hiding.

Tsao Ch'un whooped, elated by the news.

By the end of the day he planned to have reduced them even further. To have whittled them away to nothing.

'I will erase you one by one... all trace of you... see if I don't...'

Spurred on by the news from Tongjiang, he sent an order to his eldest son to increase his efforts to find Wu Hsien and his brood. He knew they could not have gone far, and if he could eradicate *them*, then the pressure would be immense on the remaining five.

He smiled at the thought. Yes, he would have them brought here, to his dungeons and make them pay personally for their audacity. He would pluck off their fingernails and burn out their eyes... and other things.

Right now, however, he had other problems, chief of which was preparing his Banner armies to fight.

He let a long, sighing breath escape him. At any other time he might have raged at the situation – have thrown a fit and cracked a head or two together. Only the fault was his. He had been too soft in recent years. Too complacent. He had not prepared for this, and now he was paying the cost.

Back in the old days he would have had his Banners out there within the hour – two hours at most. There in the field, fully supplied with sufficient food and ammunition for three days and the means to resupply at short notice. Only these weren't the old days, and his Banners had grown fat, his officers corrupt. As for his troops, they were poorly trained and totally inexperienced. He ought to have purged the Banners years ago, only it had slipped his mind, and now it was too late.

They had not fought in twenty years. In fact there were barely a handful who had fought at all. He had read the reports, just this morning, and it was not pleasant reading. Even his elite teams, which he'd sent in to try to prevent the muster, had failed.

Peace... to an army it was like rust on metal.

But what was done was done. He was sure that sheer numbers would out. The very most those *Hung Mao* could raise was fifty thousand men, and what could they do with so paltry a force? He outnumbered them by sixty to one at the very least.

Even so, he wasn't happy. He wished there was someone to share the burden with – and he didn't mean his sons. Someone like Chao.

Yes, only Chao Ni Tsu was dead. Ten years dead, and no one to replace him.

Between them they had subjugated a whole world – he with his will, Chao with his computer skills. And what skills they'd been!

With Chao at his side they would have cracked it in a morning. As it was...

'Master...?'

Tsao Ch'un turned, looking to his Chief Steward, who had prostrated himself in the doorway.

'More messages of loyalty?'

'More than five thousand newly arrived, *Chieh Hsia...*'

Tsao Ch'un spat. He had been sent over twenty thousand messages of loyalty already this morning! Only it didn't fool him. He was convinced they had sent similar messages to the Seven, hedging their bets...

Only one betrayal had surprised him, and that was Shepherd. He had brooded long and silently over why his old friend had abandoned him. Oh, Amos had always been a cold fish, but to join with his enemies against him... that had been totally unexpected.

He looked to his steward again. 'And what else?'

'Your trusted men, Master... they are dead, just as you requested. There was a struggle, but...'

'It is done, neh? Good.'

Their deaths had been precautionary. Just in case any of them had thought to profit from the situation.

'Anything else?'

'There have been attacks on Ministry offices, Master, in all of our cities. Agents have been injured, many killed.'

Tsao Ch'un shuddered indignantly. That was the worst of it; the way the *hsiao jen* climbed onto the bandwagon, taking the opportunity to even the score.

'Stamp down on it! Order Security to crack down on whoever was involved and deal with them severely!'

Tsao Ch'un turned away, looking back up at the screens. There was a view of Bremen now – of the drill yards and the gathering mass of soldiers. He stared at it a while. Maybe he should nuke Bremen. It would certainly deal with the problem. But something like that might come back to haunt him later on, and besides, he did not have to decide at once. It would be hours yet before he'd need to deal with them. No, first he would increase his efforts to locate Wu Hsien. That was the key, after all. Yes, he'd take them, one by one, and in the process he'd unnerve them.

He laughed. Then, going over to his desk, he sat and began to write out fresh orders for his eldest son.

The old man lay on his bed, the pale silks covering his emaciated frame. He was dying, yet from the nearby garden came the sounds of children playing; sounds that made the old man smile.

For a moment he had forgotten where he was. He had been back there again, in the country of the past, before they had iced it all over. Before China had come and put the world into a box.

Sometimes he saw it all quite lucidly.

He grew conscious of a presence there beside him. Turning his head he looked up. And smiled. It was his granddaughter, Lo Wen.

She smiled down at him. 'Yeh-yeh Jiang...'

Her hand was holding his, hers warm, his cool.

His smile blossomed. 'Sweetheart...'

She was the prettiest thing, eight years old and the image of her mother. 'You've been sleeping, Yeh-yeh...'

'Sleeping...' And he laughed his gentle, old man's laugh.

It was almost as if he could see himself from above. Some days he seemed to leave himself completely.

The big screen in the corner was murmuring something. He looked away from Lo Wen, his weak eyes struggling to focus, to make sense of it. He couldn't quite make out what they were saying, but it sounded urgent somehow. Something was happening.

He gently squeezed her hand. 'Darling girl... turn it up, will you?'

Lo Wen jumped up and went across. At once the noise grew clearer, sharper.

Just then his daughter, Ch'iao-chieh, appeared in the doorway. Seeing the images on the screen, she put out her hand, calling Lo Wen to her.

'Sweetheart... go into the garden for a while with the others. I just want to talk to Grandpa...'

As Lo Wen vanished outside, Ch'iao-chieh closed the door after her.

'Help me sit up,' he said, putting his hand out to her.

She sat him up, plumping the cushions behind him, then sat beside him, where Lo Wen had sat a moment before.

She took his hand. 'Are you all right, *fu chin*?'

He stared past her at the screen. 'Is it war?'

She nodded.

'It is the Seven, neh? Fighting Tsao Ch'un for control over things?'

Again she nodded.

He leaned back, closing his eyes, then sighed. 'I always thought it would be so. It was merely a matter of time.'

She squeezed his hand tenderly. 'What was he like, Tsao Ch'un?'

Jiang laughed. 'He was a tyrant even then. What other kind of man could have unified a world? But he wasn't wrong, was he? Mankind could not go on being at its own throat.'

Opening his eyes again, he could see at once that she was not convinced.

'Isn't that exactly where we are right now? At each other's throats?'

But Jiang Lei merely shrugged. 'I'm tired now, Ch'iao-chieh. Let me rest.'

'Shall I...?' She gestured towards the set.

'Yes, yes... turn it off... I don't need to see what's happening.'

And that was true. Besides, even that smallest effort had worn him out.

He heard her footsteps leave the room, heard the door close quietly after her.

So who was it to be? Tsao Ch'un or the Seven?

Jiang Lei sighed, then closed his eyes once more. After a moment he began to snore.

Karl looked about him at the men in the cruiser with him. It was twenty years since he had seen some of them; others he had been drinking with only a week ago. Now they were comrades again, 'rebels' as the media termed them, and in just over an hour they would be going into action once again.

That is, if they weren't shot out of the air.

They were heading for New York – right into the heart of the storm. Two thousand men, hand-picked by Marshal Raikkonnen, sent in to locate and protect Wu Hsien. And, if possible, bring him safely back to Europe.

It was one hell of a fucking task.

Karl checked his gun for the third time, then looked across the aisle again. Anders and Dag were talking, leaning in to speak to each other's ear over the roar of the cruiser's engines. A bit further on from them, Einar, who he had fought beside in the Californian campaign, stared into the air in the way he always did. Beyond him was Ragnar and, right at the front of the craft, near the cockpit, Henrik and Sven. Old friends. Men you could rely on.

Even so, some doubts remained. Two thousand of them, and what did they face? Almost half a million men.

Karl took a long deep breath. He was sure Raikkonen knew what he was doing. He always had in the past. They'd been outnumbered before and triumphed, only they'd never faced such odds before. Not to speak of their lack of preparation.

It was a gamble. Everyone knew that. But one worth taking. If they lost Wu Hsien...

Anders leaned towards him. 'Karl! You remembered the grenades?'

Karl grinned. It had happened once before, in Monterey, but only the once. Even so, Anders liked to tease him by reminding him.

Karl patted his kitbag. 'I have spares if you need them!' he yelled back.

'Oh, we'll need them all right!'

There were savage grins from all the others. They would find Wu Hsien and bring him back. After all, when had they ever failed to complete a mission?

'And after that, we'll kick Tsao Ch'un's arse!' Dag said, scratching at his neck, his face hard.

And all the while Einar stared into space, just like he always had.

Reed stepped into the shadowed hallway and set his bag down, then closed the door quietly behind him.

From somewhere inside the big house he could hear a TV. It would be tuned to the latest news, if he knew his father, though for once he could understand the old man. Things were developing fast out there.

He walked through, the newscast getting louder and clearer as he stepped into the kitchen.

Jake was sitting with his back to the doorway, cradling a cup of *ch'a* as he watched the screen intently. Standing nearby was his wife, Peter's stepmother, Mary. She too was captivated by what was happening on screen.

Peter hesitated, then cleared his throat.

The two of them turned as one. Seeing him, their faces lit up.

'Peter!' Jake said, getting up and coming over to hug his boy. 'We were worried...'

And for once they were right to be, he thought. Bremen wasn't the place to be right now. He let Mary embrace him, then stepped back, looking towards the screen again.

'What's been happening?'

'A battalion of the Northern Banners have gone in...'

'The Northern Banners? Already? But I thought...'

Peter shook his head. Things *were* moving fast.

'Where?' he asked. But his question was redundant. His answer was up there on the screen. They'd gone in to the New York stacks. Two thousand men, armed to the teeth. To find Wu Hsien and bring him out.

'What's going to happen?' Jake asked, standing alongside him, looking at him now rather than the screen, as if he knew any more about it than the news media.

'I don't know,' he answered truthfully. 'But I couldn't stay there. It wouldn't surprise me if Tsao Ch'un makes a strike at Bremen.'

'We're just glad you're home, Peter,' Mary said, her eyes looking at him with concern. 'Home and unharmed. You should let Meg know you're back.'

'I called her on the way back. She should be on her way...'

'Good.' But Mary looked like she was going to cry. 'Gods, this is frightening. I just wish the girls were home...'

'They'll be okay,' Jake chipped in. 'They'll be safe on the plantations.'

But Peter wasn't so sure. For once he agreed with Mary. If things were going to fall apart, he'd rather they were all here, facing it together.

On the screen there was a big explosion, followed seconds later by another.

'Look,' Jake said, 'they're going in...'

The camera close-upped on a small group of *Hung Mao* soldiers as they blasted their way into a ventilation shaft and disappeared out of sight.

'I thought we'd done with wars,' Mary said quietly.

Jake stepped across and put his arms round her. 'It's gonna be okay. Right? Whoever wins... All we've got to do is keep our heads down and wait things out. There's food in the pantry and...' He sighed. 'It's not the first time, neh?'

Only Peter could see that for all his reassurances, Jake too was scared. Because no one could see where this was going. This could bring the whole thing tumbling down again.

As for his own dashed hopes...

No, he wasn't going to say a thing about the contract. He'd lost it now and it was gone for good. He was pretty sure about that, because even if his side won – and what chance was there of that? – it'd be a different world after this.

'Who d'you want to win?' Jake asked, looking to him again. 'The Seven or... you know who...'

'Tsao Ch'un?'

He looked up at the camera on the far side of the kitchen, and shrugged. He wasn't going to say – not while there was still a chance someone was watching – but even not saying was an answer. He wanted the Seven to triumph. He wanted that new order they were sure to bring. Only realistically they didn't stand a chance. Tsao Ch'un had all of the firepower, after all, and firepower was important. It outranked wishful-thinking every time.

Only right then, even as he thought it, something happened. There was a fanfare up on the screen and then, suddenly, a newscaster was reading a statement they had received fresh over the airwaves.

'News is coming in from City Australasia that one of Tsao Ch'un's Banner armies... the Fourth Banner Army, we understand... has mutinied. We understand that its commander, Marshal Ku, has been killed, along with seven of his most senior officers in a coup by junior officers, the leader of whom has declared for the Seven...'

'Fucking hell....'

Mary looked to her husband. 'Jake...language...'

'But Jesus...a whole fucking Banner army. Tsao Ch'un only has six of them.'

'Had,' Peter said, wondering what effect this would have on events. The Fourth Banner was the smallest of the six and City Australasia the least of the seven cities, only... if this had a knock-on effect. If the other Banners heard of this...

Jake looked to him and grinned. 'D'you think...?'

But Peter didn't answer. Crossing the kitchen quickly, he crouched over the comset and, tapping in the code, waited to be connected.

'Who're you calling?' Jake asked, coming alongside him again.

'GenSyn... Your old friend, Alison... my boss!'

Tsao Ch'un sat at his desk, contemplating the news.

Fortunately he had put his most important forces into the personal charge of his sons, and as far as he could make out, there was no question of their loyalty. But this betrayal had shaken him. He had not expected it at all.

He would have to change his strategy. Forget Wu Hsien. Forget picking them off one by one. He needed to be decisive. To deal with this at a stroke.

Bremen was the key. If he could take Bremen... Only the news from his agents in Bremen was that Bremen was impregnable. They had turned it into a citadel.

So what next? Assassins?

Tsao Ch'un sighed irritably. He had already tried assassins, but none of them had got through.

Well then, he'd send a fresh wave and then another. As many as he could spare. One surely must get through. And maybe that was all it would take to shake them and weaken their resolve.

And if that failed?

Then he would nuke them. And fuck the consequences.

Alison blanked the screen then sat back.

The contract Peter had been working on was on the desk beside her. Worthless now, of course, for why would the Seven want to clone themselves, even if they won? They had sons, good ones. And Tsao Ch'un... he'd not be interested now in anything that had GenSyn's imprint on it, thanks to Ebert declaring for the Seven. He'd probably put the lot of them up against a wall.

But it had been sweet of Peter to call her. Sweeter still to hear from Jake, even if it was only to say goodbye, good luck.

She stared at the blackness of the screen a moment. Then she leaned forward and, pulling open the drawer, took out the neat, pearl-handled gun she kept there. It was a ladies' gun, from the time before the City. An illegal item, stamped with its maker's mark.

Remington.

She smiled, a sad, partly bitter smile. It was over. She had known it from the moment she'd had the news from Fan Chang's palace. They could not win. They could only prolong the end.

She took a cartridge from the box and loaded it.

She paused a moment, thinking of her son, and of what he'd think when he heard the news. It would break his heart. Only she could not live through all that again. Could not see it all come down another time.

'*Goodbye,*' she whispered. Then, placing the gun into her mouth, she pulled the trigger.

'Is there still no news?'

Li Chao Ch'in looked up from the report he was reading and gave a roar of delight, jumping to his feet. 'Tsu Chen! Hou Hsin-Fa! Cousin Wang! When did you get here?'

The three T'ang beamed back at him. 'We've just got in,' Wang Hui So answered, embracing him. 'Under the umbrella, you might say.'

'Does Amos know you're here?'

'It was he who arranged it,' Tsu Chen answered him, grasping his hands. 'Hence the uniforms...'

Standing back a little, Li Chao Ch'in saw now what he'd failed to notice straight away – that they were garbed in the uniforms of common soldiers.

'Good disguises, neh?' Hou Hsin-Fa said. 'But our question... is there any news of cousin Wu?'

Li Chao Ch'in shook his head. 'None yet. But that, I feel, is a good thing. If he were dead, that bastard would be showing off his body and rubbing our noses in the fact.'

'But no word from Raikkonen about the rescue mission?'

'Only that it continues. They've suffered heavy losses.'

'I'm not surprised,' Tsu Chen said. 'It was an audacious thing to do.'

'We had to do something, and a proper campaign would have taken weeks to organize.'

'And the news from Australasia?'

'Is good. Chi Cheng Yu is in firm command. The new marshal has sworn personal fealty to him. He and all of the Fourth Banner.'

'And the muster? How many finally turned up?'

'More than ninety thousand...'

The three T'ang stared at him. 'Are you serious?' Tsu Chen asked.

'Not enough to form a proper Banner, I know...'

'No, no... it's good. It's very good. They're excellent soldiers. None better. And it's better than nothing, only...'

'You'd hoped for more...'

'Yes. Twice that number.'

'They're battle-hardened, experienced men,' Li Chao Ch'in went on, 'and that experience will count when confronting forces who have no experience of open warfare.'

'Maybe. Only will it be enough?'

Li Chao Ch'in shrugged. 'I don't know. Only time will tell. But there is one thing in our favour. Tsao Ch'un could not have expected them to muster quite so quickly. The speed with which they've done so will certainly have taken him by surprise. From what our spies have learned, his own forces have been unaccountably slow in their preparations. And that might prove decisive.'

'In the short term, maybe,' Wang Hui So said, 'but the war's still his to lose, not ours to win.'

There was a momentary silence. No one challenged Wang Hui So's statement. Each of them knew they were walking a fine line. Wang spoke again.

'But come now, cousins. Let's not despair. Let's see what *Shih* Shepherd has to say for himself.'

They went through, into the Strategy Room. Shepherd was waiting for them there. Seeing them, his handsome features creased into a smile.

Amos Shepherd, like his long-time Master, Tsao Ch'un, was in his seventies now. But he was well preserved for his age, his face and arms tanned from the sun, his green eyes bright with intelligence.

'My Lords...'

The greetings over, they sat, looking up at the great map, conscious of the historic context of the place.

Much of the logistics of the North American campaign had been worked out in this room. All of the 'follow-up stuff' as Shepherd called it. The fine detail. The big decisions, of course, had been made by Shepherd and Marshal Jiang in a hotel room in Richmond, over a *wei ch'i* board. But this chamber had played its part. As now it would again.

'Okay,' Shepherd said, addressing them directly. 'We've little time, so might I suggest this... with ninety thousand men at our immediate disposal, it makes no sense to use them as a single force. What I'm suggesting is that we split the Northern Banners into smaller units of two thousand men – much like the assault force that went in to New York earlier. That'd give us forty-five tiny armies, fifteen to a Banner, that can be flown in to hot spots, and that can be used to turn the tide against Tsao Ch'un.'

Li Chao Ch'in looked about him. His fellow T'ang clearly liked the idea.

'Moreover,' Shepherd went on, taking their smiles for agreement, 'we move them out of Bremen as swiftly as we can. And ourselves. The more we concentrate our forces here, the more likely we are to become a target. It would not surprise me if Tsao Ch'un decided to try a nuclear strike against us. So let's not be here for that. Let's spread ourselves a little wider, a little thinner, and make it difficult for Tsao Ch'un to pick us off.'

Wang Hui So spoke up. 'And the disposal of the troops... who decides on that?'

'I thought we'd leave that to the individual marshals. We can provide guidance, of course, and identify priorities. But it's important, I feel, that they be given the power to fight this war the best way that they can, unhampered, without one hand tied behind their backs all the while. Tsao Ch'un believes he has an advantage over us in that regard. The fact that there's but one of him and several of you. He thinks that'll make it easier for him – that his decisions will be faster, more responsive to the situation, whereas, if we do this, it'll give the advantage to us. His sons against our marshals... I know who I'd back to win...'

'If our forces were even...' Tsu Chen said. 'But two thousand men...?'

'Trust me,' Shepherd said, looking from one to the other. 'Sometimes sheer weight of numbers can prove a handicap. Just think. There's the problem of feeding all those mouths, of finding transport to move them swiftly from one point to another. The larger the force the bigger the problems, whereas our much smaller forces won't have any of that. We can drop them in and pull them out again. Use them precisely where they're needed. And no need to worry about lines of supply.'

'I like that,' Li Chao Ch'in said. 'It seems...'

'An elegant solution,' Wang Hui So finished for him.

There was sudden laughter. The laughter of relief, at the thought that this might yet work. That they might, after all, survive the day.

'So what do you need?' Tsu Chen asked. 'You want us to sign a document, empowering the marshals?'

'Not at all,' Shepherd said, getting to his feet. 'Just your word of agreement.'

Li Chao Ch'in looked about him, then back at Shepherd again. 'You have it. But you said about us moving away from here...'

There was a sudden hammering at the door. Shepherd walked across and threw it open. One of the Ministry's agents stood there, head bowed, what looked like a small parcel in one hand. There was a whispered exchange between the two, then Shepherd came back across to them. He had the parcel.

He held it out to Li Chao Ch'in.

'It is for you, Lord Li. From your "Master", Tsao Ch'un. Our agents have checked it for poisons and explosives.'

Li Chao Ch'in reached across and took the parcel from Shepherd. He looked inside. 'What is it?'

Shepherd looked down. 'A tape. From Tongjiang...'

Li Chao Ch'in's face changed. All colour blanched from it. And the parcel... he held it away from him now, as if he held some dead thing.

'Do you want to be alone?' Tsu Chen asked gently.

Li Chao Ch'in hesitated, then, in a small, quiet voice. 'No... we'd best all see this. I...'

He groaned, closing his eyes, knowing what he was about to see. His worst fears made real.

Wang Hui So reached across, put his hand over his cousin's. But he said nothing, for there was nothing to be said.

Li Chao Ch'in thrust the parcel towards Shepherd again. 'Put it on...'

'Are you sure?'

The T'ang met Shepherd's eyes. There was anger in them as well as hurt. Uncertainty too. Maybe Tsao Ch'un had spared his family...

Only the tape showed otherwise. Tongjiang was burning, and there, in the gardens where he had stood but half a day ago, lay three of his sons: dead, their eyes sightless, their naked bodies smeared with blood.

Seeing that, Li Chao Ch'in made a strange, half-choking noise. '*Kuan Yin* preserve us all...'

But worse was to come. Panning away from that awful sight, the camera showed another – showed his wife, baby daughters, and Li Peng, being led in chains, up into the back of an unmarked cruiser.

And there, just in the background, visible for a moment beyond his family, was the First Dragon, Shen Fu: his wrists and ankles bound, being carried on a stake, up into another of Tsao Ch'un's craft.

Li Chao Ch'in groaned again.

The camera jerked round, reacting to the sound of shots. There, near one of the doors at the back of the east wing, soldiers were waiting, guns raised, picking off whoever emerged. Laughing as they shot the poor devils who staggered out, their hair and clothes on fire.

Li Chao Ch'in buried his face in his hands. He could bear to see no more.

'Enough!' Shepherd called, his face, usually so hard, touched by Li Chao Ch'in's suffering.

The tape stopped.

'*Aiya*,' Wang Hui So said softly, staring at his cousin who sat there now, sobbing in the sudden silence of the room.

But there was nothing to be said.

In the seventh subterranean level of the Black Tower, in a cellar which had been adapted for the task, lay the chamber. There, naked on the slab in the centre of that white-tiled room, lay Shen Fu, his hands and feet bound tight. Taut wires attached him to the brightly polished electrodes that gleamed in the scouring white light from overhead.

Tsao Ch'un had stripped off. All he wore was his butcher's apron. In the heated iron brazier close by were the implements, ready for his use.

He had promised himself this, from the moment when he'd heard that Shen Fu had sided with the Seven. The First Dragon deserved to die. Only he, Tsao Ch'un, had no intention of letting him die. He was interested only in giving him pain, endless pain.

Right now Shen Fu lay there, as if at his ease, his chest rising and falling slowly, his eyes closed. He seemed almost relaxed. But that would change. And as for closing his eyes...

Tsao Chun reached out for the heated clippers and smiled.

He'd be fucked if the bastard was allowed to close his eyes.

*

Wolfgang Ebert stood by the board, looking on as his team of hackers responded to the latest assault.

They were trying to shut Bremen down, to infiltrate its computer systems and switch the whole thing off. Only his men were preventing that; tracking each new attack and deflecting it. For the last three hours they had tried, just as Shepherd had said they would, and now their attempts were getting more and more desperate. What had begun as a kind of dance, a trial of intelligence and agility, had turned into smash and grab raids.

Ebert smiled. They could try smashing and grabbing as much as they liked, only it was a stalemate. And the longer it went on...

Something on one of the screens caught his attention.

'What's that?' he asked, pointing to it.

'What do you...?' his man began, then let the query drop. 'Shit...'

Pixel by pixel, it seemed, the screen was turning black. Like an old mirror, flecked with black spots, the darkness on the end screen slowly grew.

Ebert looked along the line. Every screen was now affected.

'What can you do?' he asked, looking to the team leader.

The young man shrugged. 'If we had any idea what it was... it's not a virus...'

The end screen was completely black now, while the others...

Everything blinked, like there'd been a power surge. A moment later there was a fanfare, a faint, tinny little tune, like you'd get from a child's computer game when you'd made another level. One second later the whole damn place switched off.

In the sudden dark, voices yelled and people knocked against each other in the room. If they'd shut the big circulation fans down then they were all in trouble. Without air they couldn't breath. Not for long, anyway.

Ebert touched out a code on the communicator inset into his wrist. A moment later a voice sounded in his head.

'Wolfgang? What's happened? The whole fucking lot's closed down!'

'I know. And I can't explain it. One moment things were fine, the next...'

'Are none of your machines working?'

'Not one. Something closed them all down...' Wolfgang paused. He had an idea. 'Amos... can you get hold of Alison? She had a team working on this kind of thing and—'

'Alison's dead.'

'*What!*' The news shocked him. But Amos didn't go into detail.

'Get out of there at once,' Shepherd said. 'We're giving Bremen up. The troops are out and the T'ang are elsewhere, and as for the new First Dragon...'

The voiced in his head vanished, like it had been switched off.

Ebert swallowed. Then, calming himself, gave the order to withdraw.

Shepherd crouched over the body, staring at it in shock.

Wang Hui So had been shot twice, once in the heart and once in the head, the second bullet taking the top of his skull clean off.

The assassin had been one of his own. A groom called Yu Ch'o, a Wang family retainer who had served since childhood, which was almost thirty years. Why he'd done it they would never know, for he'd used the third bullet in his gun on himself.

The others had gone on already, to the Domain. He could think of no safer place right now. But was anywhere truly safe when something like this could happen?

It was an ill omen. Things had been on the turn, but now...

Amos stood back, letting the medics take the body away. He was tempted to keep this a secret for a time. Because when news of this got out there would be another great surge of fear.

He could sense it in the air. Could see it, there in the eyes of those that surrounded him. People were afraid. And with every new event that fear grew. The uncertainty of it all ate away at them. It bored into their psyches like acid. Out there, in the levels, they were running scared. Literally so. He had seen for himself news item after news item showing the riots and the protests, and the endless mass hysteria.

Only a quick and decisive result could end it, and that was precisely what he didn't want. Only Tsao Ch'un could benefit from a rapid resolution of events.

But as for Wang Hui So...

He walked through, into the communications room and, giving his code, had himself pasted through to the Domain.

It was Tsu Chen who answered him.

'Lord Tsu... I have bad news...'

Tsu Chen's face barely reacted. 'What other kind is there?'

'There is bad and there is *bad*. And this...' Amos swallowed, then came straight out with it. 'Wang Hui So is dead. Assassinated by his own groom.'

'*Aiya!*' Tsu Chen looked horrified. 'Who else knows?'

'A handful of men. But they've been sworn to secrecy.'

'We're not announcing this, then?'

'Not yet. I thought...'

Amos stopped. There was a news screen just across the room from him. The sound had been turned down but he could see, as clear as day, just what had happened.

'Oh Christ... Oh Jesus Christ...'

Tsao Ch'un stood at the sink, washing the blood from his arms.

'This had better be good,' he said, snarling threateningly at his steward, who knelt there, his head pressed to the tiled floor.

There was a faint moan from the man on the slab. He was still alive, though the gods knew how.

Tsao Ch'un grabbed a towel, then left the room, with barely a glance at his prisoner.

'This better be *really* fucking good.'

Li Chao Ch'in let his head fall into his hands. Beside him Hou Hsin-Fa groaned.

On the screen, Wu Hsien was dragged towards camera, his arms held by two guards who showed him less respect than a common criminal. Wu Hsien's left eye was missing, the socket black and swollen, while his face and shoulders showed signs of a severe beating. But he was still alive, still defiant.

Defiant, sure, but dead. Whenever Tsao Ch'un ordered it.

As Tsu Chen returned to the room, Li Chao Ch'in turned to him. 'Have you seen?'

'I have. I was on the line to Shepherd and...'

The two T'ang turned to face Tsu Chen, surprised by the tremor in his voice.

'What is it?' Hou Hsin-Fa asked quietly. 'What now?'

'It is Wang Hui So. He's dead. His groom...'

'Aiya!' Hou looked to Li Chao Ch'in, then back at Tsu Chen. 'Three of us gone...'

'We are cursed,' Li Chao Ch'in said, looking back at the screen. 'The gods are repaying us for serving that demon loyally all those years. We'd have had better treatment from the Lord of Hell.'

Tsu Chen stared at his fellow T'ang, astonished by his outburst.

'Cursed? No, cousin Li. But we are at war, and we must win or see everything we built lost.'

Li Chao Ch'in turned to him, his face fierce yet also anguished. 'Is it not all already lost? For myself—'

But Tsu Chen shouted him down. 'For yourself? Do you wish to stand down, cousin?'

'No... No, I...'

'Then take heart. Until he has us all, he has but part of us. We are Seven, neh? And Seven is stronger than One. We have but to kill him and it is done.'

'And how do we do that?' Hou Hsin-Fa asked.

'I do not know. And yet I must believe we can. Or else, what hope is there for any of us?'

'None at all,' Li Chao Ch'in said, in a low, defeated voice.

'You must stop this, cousin!' Tsu Chen said, getting angry now. 'If you do not show strength, then how do you expect—'

He stopped dead, not finishing the sentence, his jaw dropping at the sight that now greeted his eyes.

'Gods...'

The other two turned to look... and groaned. For there, centre screen, was Tsao Ch'un's eldest son, Tsao Heng, grinning into camera, Wu Hsien's bloodied head on the stake he held in his hand.

'Barbarians...' Hou Hsin-Fa said quietly. 'They're all bloody barbarians...'

But then we knew that, Tsu Chen thought, staring bitterly at the sight of his dead friend's damaged face. We knew that from the first day we worked with him.

Tsao Ch'un looked a ghastly sight as he stared up at the giant screen. He was naked beneath his apron, the pure white of which was spattered with blood and gobbets of flesh. But it was not that which caught his servants' eyes as they looked on at their Lord and Master, it was the erection he sported; an erection which a man fifty years his junior would have been proud of.

They tried not to look, but it was impossible not to see it. Besides, Tsao Ch'un himself did not care. All he cared for was the fact that another of the Seven was dead, his head on a stick.

'At last!' the great man said, a ferocious smile lighting his features. 'At fucking last!'

With Fan Chang and Wu Hsien dead and Shen Fu on the torture slab, all was well in Tsao Ch'un's world. Five more – six, if you counted Shepherd – and he'd be done with it. Until then...

'Send in the Third Banner,' he barked, looking to his marshal who stood by the great double doors, his head bowed. 'I want Bremen destroyed! Issue the men with ice-eaters...'

'Is that wise, *Chieh Hsia*,' the man began. But Tsao Ch'un shouted him down.

'I don't *care* if it's fucking wise! I want it done!'

The marshal fell to his knees. 'Yes, *Chieh Hsia*.'

Tsao Ch'un turned back, forgetting the man instantly. He rubbed his hands together and laughed. 'That's my boy... And I thought you'd lost your touch.'

The dungeon keeper stood beside the slab, looking down at his charge.

With that much damage done to him, the First Dragon ought to have been dead. Any other man would surely have succumbed. Then again, it was said that Tsao Ch'un knew ways of keeping a man alive – of hurting without harming. Harming permanently, that was. Not that there wasn't evidence enough of real harm. Why, there was barely a bone that was not broken, barely a nerve-ending unpunished by the electrodes. And the man's eyes...

Had he not seen it before, he might have felt nauseous at the sight, only in the years he'd worked as dungeon keeper, he had seen many like this one. Tsao Ch'un's 'special guests' as he liked to call them. Men whose conduct had annoyed the great man sufficiently to warrant his special attentions.

Many would have called the great man a sadist. But he felt differently. To him, Tsao Ch'un was, in this one respect, an artist; a man immensely skilled in the art of creating pain. Just as a great and talented woman might have learned the arts of lovemaking, in order to enhance and intensify the pleasure of sex, so Tsao Ch'un had practised his arts across the years, until he could make a man sing on the slab; could make him beg and gibber and betray.

Especially the last.

Shen Fu seemed to be sleeping. He seemed as if in a dream. Whatever pain he had suffered – and he surely must have suffered much – seemed now to have left him. He seemed quite beyond pain. And yet how could that be so? When his Master returned it would begin again. He knew that without doubt, and surely Shen Fu knew that too? Only he seemed calm now, untroubled.

The dungeon keeper reached out, his fingertips gently touching the sleeping man's face, as if to bless him. Then, knowing his Master would soon return, he hurried from the room, back to the tiny cell he called his home.

Karl let his head rest against the wall. They had been fighting for the best part of a day now, skirmish after skirmish, and he was exhausted. Across from him Dag sat where he'd sat for the last two hours, staring into space with a vaguely surprised air about him, the hole in his forehead where the laser had burned him puckered and black now.

A lot of their men were dead, and even those that still lived – men like himself – were barely so. Cut off from reinforcements and steadily running out of ammunition, it was only a matter of time. As soon as the enemy had taken out their cruisers on the roof he'd known the game was up. Jump in, jump out had been the strategy, but without aircraft...

These Han were not as dumb as they looked. At least, their junior officers weren't.

He could hear them, further up the corridor, whispering to each other. They'd be making another assault real soon now. It had been at least twenty minutes since the last, and they had to know now that they were pushing against an open door. But they were being cautious. And who could blame them? They had time and numbers on their side.

Ragnar lay out there somewhere, dying, his left leg blown off. He hadn't made a sound in some while, so maybe he was dead. Who was to say? As for the others...

Karl slowly turned his head, looking at the handful who'd survived. They were all sitting there, their backs against the wall, waiting.

Henrik didn't have a gun. He'd lost it earlier, but he had a grenade – his last – and he cradled it now like a child. Beside him, Sven had his head tilted back, his eyes closed, his big automatic balanced across his left knee. He had one clip left. After that he'd have to use the gun as a club. As for Einar...

Einar looked like he'd been sprayed in a fine mist of blood. His face was dark with it, like a demon's, his eyes showing bright and white amidst that caked mask. His handgun lay on the deck beside him to his left, his big hunting knife in his right hand.

Karl smiled. If he was going to die, it was good to die alongside these men. And die they would, because Tsao Ch'un wasn't taking any prisoners. They'd learned that early on.

Yes, and they'd badly underestimated them. He knew that now. Whatever Marshal Raikkonen might have said, the men they'd been facing weren't raw recruits. And they certainly weren't pushovers. As for their tactics – well, that had surprised them, as well. How clever they were. How brave, too. He'd have taken his hat off to them, only they'd probably have blown the top of his head off if he had.

No. It was a lost cause, they all knew that now. If he had any regrets it was that he wouldn't see his wife, Margaret, nor his boys again. But this was his time, and they would understand.

Some day.

Maybe, he thought. Only he wished he could have seen the end of it. Wished he could have known whether this had made any difference at all. Whether their efforts had freed the world from that bastard Tsao Ch'un's grip. Now he'd never know.

From further down the corridor the whispering grew in intensity. A moment later there was the distinct noise of safeties being removed, the sound of clips being fitted into guns.

Sven had sat forward. Henrik and Einar, too, were suddenly tensed.

'You ready?' Karl asked, smiling at them fondly, knowing it was the last time he would see them.

It was Einar who answered, his bloodied features stretched into a grin. 'You bet we fucking are!'

Tsao Ch'un stood beneath the shower's flow, washing the blood from his chest and limbs, even as his men reported to him.

He had finished with Shen Fu for today. Had had his way and purged himself. For the moment. Now he took the time to listen to what had been happening in his absence.

First up was the news of Wang Hui So's death, shot by his own servant. Tsao Ch'un was pleased with that. Very pleased. But not as much as by the news that they had managed to hack in to Amos Shepherd's systems.

He hadn't been sure his team were up to it – that they could in any way match a man like Shepherd for intelligence and guile, but they had, and the beauty of it was that Shepherd – and the remainder of the Seven – would not even be aware of it. From this point on he could track their every move, hear every order they gave the moment it was given. It gave him a tremendous advantage.

Only what Tsao Ch'un didn't know – and he didn't know because no one wanted to give their Lord the bad news – was that there were rumours of unrest, even of revolt, in the ranks of Tsao Ch'un's Third Banner Army; the army that was camped out around Bremen, waiting for the order to go in.

It was an order he was just about to give, only right then news started to come in from North America that four of the Seven's newly formed two-thousand-man units had attacked Tsao Ch'un's forces there, hitting them out of the blue and withdrawing almost immediately, inflicting heavy damage. These attacks were not decisive militarily, yet their effect upon morale was huge. They had been dealing very well with the situation up to that point. Now...

He got Tsao Heng on the line.

Seeing his father on the screen, Heng bowed low. 'Father...'

'You must hold firm, Heng. Things have changed. From here on *we* dictate what happens.'

'But I thought...'

Seeing his father's face Heng fell silent again, his head tucked in to his chest. He had learned not to argue with his father.

'As I said,' Tsao Ch'un said, slowly and deliberately, as if dealing with a recalcitrant servant and not one of his marshals, 'from now on *we* dictate what happens. Await my orders, Heng, but spread the word among your officers that something is happening – that something has changed and that we now have a massive advantage over our enemies.'

'Can I know what that is, Father?'

'Best not,' Tsao Ch'un said, 'but you will see with your own eyes how things fare from henceforth.'

He cut connection, then turned towards his grooms, throwing the towel he was holding aside and letting them bring his clothes to him.

It was time to up the pace of things. To take a few risks and show them who was boss.

Three were dead now. Four alone remained.

Tsao Ch'un pulled on his trousers, then nodded to himself.

Assassins. He would send in another round of assassins. And then another. As many as it took. Just to show them he was serious.

Big Wen swung from the rope, his feet dangling, his face black and his tongue lolling from his mouth. Below the landowner the crowd cheered and laughed and those who had been his tenants, who had hired shabby rooms from him at exorbitant rents, laughed and cheered more than any.

Earlier, when the news had first broken, they had been afraid. They had thought this the very worst of news. But now... well, now they understood. It was their chance. For this brief moment, while Tsao Ch'un's eyes roamed elsewhere, they could take their vengeance on bastards like Big Wen. Men who would as soon have spat on them as give them a *fen* in charity.

And right then, even as their excitement threatened to die down, there was a surge in the crowd over by the big lift and a sudden roar of delight.

'Boss Yang! They had captured Boss Yang!'

Roped-up and struggling, a dozen men carried him through that great press of people, across to where Big Wen dangled from the ceiling beam. There, as the crowd bayed and Boss Yang struggled, his great bulk pressing down on his captors, they strung him up beside his fellow exploiter. The whole crowd chanted out the numbers – 'One! Two! Three!' – and they heaved him up into the air, where his small white feet kicked and kicked, then grew still.

The crowd went mad. Great smiles adorned their faces. Even young children were celebrating, dancing around and laughing at the sight of the two fat villains strung up side by side.

'Who next?' was the question on everyone's lips, but the answer wasn't difficult.

'Chi Fei Yu!' someone shouted, and the cry went up from a thousand mouths – 'Chi Fei Yu! Chi Fei Yu! Chi Fei Yu!' – even as a group of them rushed off to try and find the man who had lent so many of them money in time of need, only to demand huge interest payments when it came due.

And so it went on, late into the night, in level after level, stack after stack, the world gone mad, gone vengeful.

Amos Shepherd stood there beneath the crescent moon, looking out across the darkness of the water.

Inside, in the brightness of the cottage, the three T'ang were talking, debating matters and deciding what to do next.

After a day of setbacks, he knew what they needed to do. It was exactly what they'd had to do from the start. They had to kill Tsao Ch'un. To throw everything they had at him until he succumbed. Until there was no breath in his body, no thoughts coursing through his brain. Until he was dead, as in gone.

All else was sophistry.

They even knew where he was. Only how to get at him?

Yes. That was the problem. It always had been. And it wasn't as if they were the first. Great men were natural targets for the demented, the ambitious and the vengeful. And Tsao Ch'un had survived them all. A dozen of each, and more besides. Why should *they* succeed where so many others had failed?

A voice cut into his thoughts.

'Shih Shepherd?'

He turned. It was Haavikko, the young major Marshal Raikkonen had sent as his intermediary.

'What is it, Knut?'

Haavikko came across. From his face Shepherd could see that it was not good news.

'The last unit we sent in... to Baltimore, to counter Tsao Heng's move south... They were waiting for us. Blew our ships out of the air.'

The news shocked Shepherd. 'But they...'

He stopped. He was going to say that they couldn't have known. But why not? What if they had a spy in the system? Someone feeding back information?

'How many people knew where they were going?'

'Aside from the pilots... and they had sealed orders... just six of us. And I'd vouch for every one.'

Shepherd nodded. So would he. But this still suggested that their security systems had been breached.

'We lost them all?'

'Every last man.'

Shepherd pondered that a moment, then, looking up, addressed the young major again.

'Knut. Go tell your marshal that we're done with North America. We must let it go for a time. It's time for new strategies. Time for something audacious. While there's still time for it. I want...'

He stopped. The back door of the house had just opened, spilling light out onto the lawn. Through that bright rectangle the three T'ang stepped, like figures from a dream, their Han robes looking totally out of place in that setting.

'Gentlemen,' Shepherd called to them, giving the briefest nod to Haavikko, before walking slowly towards them. 'What has been decided?'

It was Li Chao Ch'in who answered him.

'We have decided that the normal period of mourning for Wang Hui So must be set aside. His son must inherit. Which is why, at noon tomorrow, Wang Hui So's oldest son, Wang Lung, will be made T'ang in his father's place.'

Shepherd opened his mouth, meaning to say that there were more important things to be doing with their time. Killing Tsao Ch'un for one. But these were very formal men. And they were Han. Ruthless they might be at times, but they were real sticklers for tradition. And besides... to bring the numbers back up again – that would be one in the eye for Tsao Ch'un!

'What an excellent idea,' he said, smiling, then bowing low to each of them in turn. 'In the meantime let me share my thoughts with you...'

*

Marshal Aaltonen, Head of Security for City Europe, stood beside the generator, looking on as the searchlight picked out body after body.

It looked as if someone had dropped them from the sky. And maybe they had. Only there were too many of them, and besides, most of them were wrapped in plastic, like flies trapped in a spider's web.

Aaltonen let out a sharp breath. The bastards! They'd used ice-eaters. Sprayed them down onto the levels and then watched as the levels turned to sticky pap, collapsing, taking the bodies down with them.

Bremen. This big gap in the City had once been called Bremen, after the north German town that had stood beneath the super-plastic the Han called ice. Now it was just a hardened, transparent mess. A see-through tomb for half a million souls.

Tsao Ch'un really did not give a shit who got in his way. Ruthless was not the word for this. This was demonic. These were just families, getting on with their lives. To kill them...

Aaltonen was a hard man, yet he felt for once like crying for the waste, for the simple tragedies of all those lives that had ended as suddenly as that.

He clicked his fingers. At once his aide approached. 'Yes, Marshal?'

'Schwartz... get word of this back to the Domain. Most important, let Shepherd know, because if they could do this here...'

Schwartz waited for something more, but Aaltonen shook his head. 'Look... just tell him, okay?'

Shepherd sat at the communications board, looking up at the bank of screens, wondering who could be leaking information to Tsao Ch'un. They had to be, because for the last few hours the old man had anticipated their every move, and that simply wasn't possible. The two units he'd sent in to hit him at the Black Tower, for instance. The speed with which Tsao Ch'un's troops had locked on to the two small fleets made no sense – not unless he *knew* where they were coming from and where they were headed. One thing was for certain – it wasn't guesswork.

The big question was who... and how?

Or was it?

Amos stood, then turned away from the board. It was after three in the morning now on the second day of the war.

Yes, and we're still alive. But for how much longer?

The problem with his leakage theory was that there was no one he could think of whom he didn't trust. All of the technicians and guards here were hand-picked, and besides, they had no direct access to what was going on. As for the main players, not a single one of them stood to benefit from aiding Tsao Ch'un. Quite the contrary.

So what then?

The truth was, he knew the answer. Had known this last hour but refused to acknowledge it. Why? Because he didn't think it possible. Because he'd been so careful all these years to safeguard it, and if what he was thinking was true, then all those years of watchfulness had been in vain.

They had hacked into his system; climbed over all of the spiky mile-high firewalls he had constructed with such care, sneaking past all of his best detection systems – systems he had put months of his genius into – and in so doing had not shown a single trace of their existence. They hadn't stumbled over a single tripwire!

It was an affront to his pride. But he had to face it. His so-called discreet system had been breached, and now Tsao Ch'un was looking on, over their shoulders, watching their every move the moment that they made it.

He went back inside.

'Shut it down! Shut the whole thing down! It's been corrupted!'

Heads turned, disbelief in their eyes.

'But *Shih* Shepherd...'

He raised a hand, silencing the sudden clamour. 'No, *wait*... rescind that order. I need to think this through. But listen... don't process any instructions until I tell you it's safe.'

Shepherd walked through into his own office, a tiny space sectioned off from the rest of the basement, then sat, mulling it over.

This was the kind of thing that Chao Ni Tsu had been good at. It had his touch. Only Master Chao was dead, and as far as Shepherd knew, no one of that kind of ability had replaced him.

Tsao Ch'un had a team of hackers, true, working out of Pei Ching. And they were good. Only not this good.

Okay... So maybe Tsao Ch'un's been keeping secrets from me...

Maybe. He wouldn't put it past the old bastard. But surely word would have got out if Chao had had a successor. Rumours of it, anyway. As it was he'd heard nothing.

Then maybe it was a team of lesser programmers and hackers. Maybe they'd been working on this for some while.

If so, then there was an aspect of Tsao Ch'un he'd not anticipated. To be that devious.

Okay, so let's assume he has penetrated my system. That he's watching it right now.

That didn't mean he could see everything they were doing. Only what was on their screens. What they were actually doing and saying was still a blank to him. All he was seeing was the results of their discussions; the end product of their deliberations.

Which meant that as of that moment Tsao Ch'un didn't know that they knew he'd hacked in.

Shepherd smiled, realizing what that meant.

He's responding to what he's seeing on our screens. To where we say our troops are heading.

But what if they're heading somewhere else?

For a brief window – an hour, maybe two hours – they could feed him misinformation. Could make him react to ghost messages. But only for a brief time. Once he didn't see results any more, he'd guess that they knew. That they'd worked out he was watching them.

So they had to use this while they could. Give him something to reassure him that his trackers were still up and running, while hitting him hard elsewhere.

Handwritten orders, that was the key to this right now. Something Tsao Ch'un couldn't see on the screens in front of him. Something only an old-fashioned spy might discover.

And then not in enough time to make any difference.

Shepherd's smile broadened. He could see it already. Three armies, each comprising five units of two thousand men. The first would attack the Third Banner Army in Bremen. Only that would be a feint, up there on the screen where Tsao Ch'un could watch. The other two... they'd be the real assaults. One on the nest of programmers in Pei Ching, the other on Tsao Ch'un, attack craft swooping in over the Po-hai Sea to attack the Black Tower itself.

Shepherd nodded to himself. He would organize it all right now. Before they lost the initiative.

He paused, wondering whether it was worth waking the three T'ang to let them know what was happening, then decided to let them sleep. After all, there was no real point. It would be hours before their forces could be readied.

Besides... this was a matter of professional pride.

Shepherd's smile faded; became a look of pure determination. He would track those prying bastards down and roast them online. Fry their brains and burn out their cerebral nerve-endings, even as his elite troops fell on them from above. But not yet. Not just yet. Let them think they had the upper hand a little longer. Then he would turn on them. They and their Master both.

Tsao Ch'un yawned, then pulled himself up onto his feet. He ought to take the chance to rest while he could. Tomorrow, he knew, would be the decisive day. Only, tired as he was, he didn't feel like sleeping. There would be time to sleep when this was done. When his enemies were all dead.

He walked over to the big picture window and looked out across the bay. In the late morning light the sea was grey, the sky the palest blue, like the eyes of one of the long-noses, the *Hung Mao* as they had come to call them.

Had he been right to let the *Hung Mao* live? To let them share the world with the Han?

The truth was he didn't know. Only that back then he'd had no option. His scheme would not have worked without their compliance. To have had to fight them all, that would have been a step too far. His certain undoing. Chao Ni Tsu had thought as much, and what Chao thought was usually very near to the truth.

Tsao Ch'un turned, looking to the ancient chair he'd kept as a reminder of his one-time companion. If only he'd had Chao to call on now.

He sighed. How he missed those days, when things had not yet been cast into their final form. How he missed the uncertainty, the *hazard* of each day. All of his schemes and intrigues since had been but games, to make him feel as if he were doing something. It was only now that he realized just how little it had satisfied the need in him.

That need to be alive and active. To be a man. Fully a man. Yes, and at the same time a power greater than any the world had seen. Greater than all their Hitlers and Napoleons, their Caesars and Alexanders. To be Tsao Ch'un. Why, even the mention of his name had struck terror into hearts.

And maybe that was why, now, he delayed before finishing them off. Why he prolonged the struggle, not wishing for it to be over too soon. It wasn't something he could tell his sons, nor his advisors, but it was so. He enjoyed this. Like a great *wei ch'i* player, he longed for an opponent who could match him, stone for stone.

Oh, there was Shepherd, true. And there had been the First Dragon. Only Shen Fu had let himself be taken far too easily. Surrounded not in the end game, but in the opening gambits, before the shapes could be determined on the board.

But as for the others...

These T'ang... these erstwhile friends of his... they were good adminis-trators, good men to have in peacetime, but in war?

Tsao Ch'un spat contemptuously. Without Shepherd and Shen Fu on their side, they would have lost to him in hours.

There was a knock on the outer doors.

Tsao Ch'un turned, looking towards the sound, distracted by his thoughts. 'Come...'

One of his servants entered, carrying a tray, his head bowed.

'Master, your breakfast...'

Tsao Ch'un glanced at the man, then gestured towards the low table at the side. 'Put it there...'

He was thinking about Chao Ni Tsu. Wondering what Chao would have made of all this. So caught up in his thoughts that he was barely aware of how close the man had come.

The clatter of the tray hitting the floor woke him, made him half fall, half jump to the side, even as the assassin's blade caught and cut his shoulder, tearing silks and flesh with equal ease.

He rolled and came up, clutching the first thing that had come to hand.

It was a chopstick. Tsao Ch'un laughed, amused by how fate had played its hand.

Laughter which, he could see, unnerved the other, who now threw him-self carelessly into a new assault.

The blade cut air. Tsao Ch'un, though seventy-four, was no longer there. He slipped down, under, and with a subtlety of limbs that belied his age, had come up directly behind his attacker.

He brought the chopstick down hard into the fleshy part of the man's neck, between ear and spinal cord, feeling the blunt stick wedge then snap.

As his attacker stumbled, clutching at the broken stick embedded in his neck, Tsao Ch'un fell on him savagely, sinking his teeth into the man's upper cheek, then wresting the knife from him.

It was over in a moment.

Tsao Ch'un stood there, looking down at the dead man, his chest rising and falling violently, the breath wheezing from him.

His shoulder ached, but it was nothing. What shocked him most was the identity of his attacker, for yet again this was someone he had trusted implicitly. A man who had been with him since he'd been a child.

How had they turned him? Or had the man harboured some deep, resentful grudge against his Master? Something he had kept hidden, waiting for this moment to express?

Tsao Ch'un cursed. He should have kept the man alive. Bled him on the slab as he had bled Shen Fu. But it was too late now.

Servants were running to him now, crowding in the doorway to the room, anxious for their Master but afraid to enter, lest they receive the same treatment as his attacker.

'Take him away!' he ordered, stepping back, away from the body. 'And send a medic. Someone we can trust, neh?'

But the heavy irony in that last request was not lost on any there, for they knew their Master's moods and how randomly his rage could fall. Especially when, like now, he seemed so calm, so in control.

Then, as they knew, he was at his most dangerous. You might as well pick a tiger's teeth, it was said, as serve Tsao Ch'un at such moments.

Yet one there – a young groom of only eighteen years – dared to speak up. 'Should we burn the body, Master?'

Tsao Ch'un's eyes fell on the groom. For a moment all there averted their eyes, fearful for the young man, but then Tsao Ch'un smiled.

'Yes, burn him. He and all his family.'

★

As night gave way to day over the ruins of Bremen, so Tsao Ch'un's youngest son, Tsao Ch'i Yuan, gathered his officers together to discuss the situation. He had his father's orders in the pocket of his uniform. Orders that were most specific. Only they didn't make any sense. Not now that Bremen no longer existed. If the idea had been to break the rebels' stronghold, then that was done. Only the rebels had gone elsewhere. They ought to have been attacking Shepherd's place, the Domain, for that was the enemy's heart now.

Tsao Ch'i Yuan could not understand why his father delayed. Why he didn't throw everything he had at the remaining T'ang and finish it. Shepherd had nukes, it was said, but so what? He didn't have enough to fight even a limited campaign. Only sufficient to defend himself.

What worried him more, however, was the effect this delay had on his men. There had been rumblings of discontent among the ranks even before yesterday's assault on Bremen. Those rumblings had grown overnight – a product of their inaction. Now he would have to deal with them.

He had his father's permission, of course. Much as the old man had promised him that *he* would be in command, he liked to meddle. Liked to hold the strings, even as he allowed his sons the illusion of being in charge. But Tsao Ch'i Yuan was not fooled by his father's masquerade. Tsao Ch'un feared his sons. Or, at least, he feared them becoming independent of him. Rivals to him.

But this needed to be attended to. Needed to be stamped out in the bud, before it got serious.

As he stepped into the chamber where his officers were waiting, the buzz of conversation died. As one the men turned to him and bowed, their heads bared.

'Ch'un tzu,' he addressed them. 'We have a problem...'

Later, when he was alone again, seated in his cruiser, waiting for the craft to be given clearance to take off, he wondered what his father really wanted. Long term, that was. Was his plan to share the world out between the three of them, or was it all to go to Tsao Heng, the eldest?

It had never been discussed. Whenever the matter had been raised, their father had crushed all mention of it instantly. But it wouldn't go away. Eventually they would have to face it squarely. And then?

Then this, between them and the Seven, would be a mere rehearsal. For there was no way he would bow to Tsao Heng.

So why not hit him now? He and his other brother. Take them both out and end the debate before it happened.

It was a tactic his father surely would approve of, for wasn't he always talking about simplifying matters? And this would simplify it all.

Tsao Ch'i Yuan smiled. Maybe, only first he had to purge his own ranks. To round up all the troublemakers and put them to the sword.

Then, and only then, would he make his decision.

Tsao Ch'un had showered again and dressed, now he stood beneath the screens, watching as his forces took out the latest wave of rebel craft.

The Seven were using up their troops with a speed they could really not afford, and that was not like Shepherd. Not like him at all.

Maybe they've overruled him.

Only that wasn't likely. The T'ang might be pompous, but they were not stupid. None of them had any experience of warfare, and they were sure to defer to Shepherd every time than trust to their own flawed instincts.

Unless Shepherd himself were dead...

Only he'd know that, surely? Word would have got out.

Tsao Ch'un spoke to the air.

'Find out the precise time when we can last verify that Amos Shepherd was still alive.'

The thought of Shepherd's death ought to have excited him, and yet it didn't. If anything it disappointed him, for it would mean he was facing them alone – those three incompetents.

There, even that betrayed his thinking, for there were four of them still. Only he didn't really count the T'ang of Australasia. He could deal with him in a morning if he had to.

Tsao Ch'un reached up, touching his shoulder. The GenSyn patch was already at work, healing the wound, generating new growth, but it was sore still, and would be for days.

They say I have a charmed life...

He chuckled. If he had died, the Seven would have had a chance. Because the moment he was dead his idle, good-for-nothing sons would have been at each other's throats. As it was...

Tsao Ch'un spoke to the air once more.

'Get me Tsao Heng. Tell him I have new orders for him.'

He had decided, there and then, to wind down the campaign in North America. To de-prioritize. He'd get Tsao Heng to shift his forces east – to Europe. Most of them, anyway. They'd need to keep a presence there, in case anything flared up again, but the rest of his forces could be thrown against the Seven.

Not that that was his purpose here. Oh no. It would take his son days, maybe even weeks to redeploy his forces. To get the best part of half a million men across an ocean and into position was no easy task, especially if they were being constantly harried and attacked. Tsao Ch'un knew that it wasn't the most efficient use of his forces, not when he already had a Banner army established in Europe, but it would keep Tsao Heng busy, and that was the point.

'Ah, Heng,' he said, as his eldest son's face appeared on the screen above him, 'listen carefully. This is what I want you to do...'

Li Chao Ch'in watched as Wang Hui So's eldest walked down the sloping lawn towards them. He was dressed, like all of them, in his ceremonial robes. Though only twenty-two, the ancient silk garments gave him an air of great authority, of great distinction.

Amos Shepherd stood nearby, next to his wife and daughter, looking on, his eyes, as ever, taking in everything.

Li Chao Ch'in looked to his fellow T'ang, Tsu Chen and Hou Hsin-Fa. Like him, they seemed greatly moved by the moment. By the simple sight of Wang Lung, who, dressed as he was, looked the image of his father when he'd been younger.

When we first met, back in Nan-ching, all those years ago.

Back then, none of them would have imagined such a moment. Why, even to live in such a world was beyond their wildest thoughts. Yet, ineluctably, it had come. And now they were on the verge of ruling that world.

If we can survive that long.

But this was an important step towards that goal. To make Wang Lung one of the Seven. A T'ang.

Li Chao Ch'in shivered. Why, even the word moved him today. *T'ang.* 'Beautiful and imposing' was its literal meaning. And to be a T'ang... from henceforth it was be the equivalent of Son of Heaven. For this ceremony would be different from those which had given them their titles. This would be the first of a new ceremony, where the new T'ang would give his oath of loyalty not to a single man, greater than he, but to his fellows.

Beautiful and imposing... So they would be from this day on.

Against all sense, against his better nature, and certainly against the great streak of cynicism that ran in his blood, Amos Shepherd watched Wang Lung become a T'ang. He felt a strange, impassioned longing that this dream, that currently looked so hopeless, so incapable of being fulfilled, should yet come about.

A world, ruled by the Seven and at peace.

For even as he stood there, even as Wang Lung said his vows and bowed before each of his fellow T'ang in turn, kneeling and kissing the black iron ring of power on each one's right hand, so the two strike forces were in the air, winging out across the greatness that was Asia, towards their targets.

An hour from now we shall know.

Word was that Tsao Chun's son was packing up in North America; boarding his men onto whatever troop ships he could muster and flying them back here for one final confrontation. But they would know long before the first of them returned. It would be settled long before then.

Shepherd looked to Wang Lung. The young man was speaking to Li Chao Ch'in now, equal to equal.

'I shall have him, Chao Ch'in. I swear to you. I shall hold that man's heart in my hand before this is finished.'

Maybe so, Shepherd thought, moved by the young man's words, but they walked in darkness right then, their destinies uncharted.

Jiang Lei woke suddenly, the taste of ginger in his mouth. Or so he thought. For when he licked his lips he realized that it was not ginger but the memory of ginger, from a meal so long ago, so distant that he had forgotten it 'til now.

That first meal with Chun Hua.

The old man lay there, staring almost silently at the whiteness of the ceiling, the faintest smile colouring his features.

There had been a poem... ah... something vague... something about...

No. It was gone.

The smile slowly faded. Ginger... what was it now? Something about ginger... something about... ah, yes.

Chun Hua. His beautiful Chun Hua.

Jiang lay there a moment after that, thoughtless, his eyes slowly blinking.

And then... her smile. It was there suddenly, there in his mind, in his memory, as sharp as the day he'd first seen her. Her smile. Like the dawn itself.

Her smile.

Chapter 24

CONSEQUENCES

J ake woke. For a time he lay there in the dark, the whole of him trembling as he tried to recover from where he'd been, adrift once more, lost on the floodtide of memory.

It was just after five. From the living room he could hear the faint murmur of the news channel. He closed his eyes, ignoring it, shutting it out. Only the dreams were in his head. He couldn't shut *those* out. And so he lay there, remembering that circle of spitting faces, their eyes filled with hatred, their thin and ugly mouths accusing him, tearing him to shreds.

Back in the beginning. When they'd first come to the levels.

They had called them 'tzu pao kung i' – 'self report, public appraisal', part of the process of 'passing through the gate', of purifying yourself by exposing your weaknesses to those who lived and worked with you.

They argued that the old self had to be stripped away before the new self could be built. It was a technique the Communists had used, under Mao Tse Tung, supposedly a way of making citizens more sociable, more compliant. Which was all well and good, only what was never said was just how vile it was. To experience a *tzu pao kung i* was to have one's soul flayed publicly. It destroyed one's trust in one's neighbours. Twenty years on and Jake could still see those awful, hate-filled faces. Still feel the flecks of their spittle on his face as, one by one, they had leaned in to criticize him, pecking away at him like crows, making mountains of the pettiest little faults. Condemning him for being who he was. And not a word of praise. Not a single utterance in his favour.

People had been known to kill themselves after such sessions.

He had been stronger than that. Or so he thought, for even now, twenty years later, he lay there trembling. Afraid of those memories. *Terrified*.

And it wasn't only that. Some mornings he forgot. Some mornings, when he woke, it really felt as if he were back there. That all this was a dream. Only then he'd remember, and with it he'd think of everything he'd lost. All of those things that made life bearable, which, here in this other world, were converted into shadows of themselves.

The Big Lie, it touched it all – every last sentiment, every cherished recollection – until, in the end, you began to doubt that any of it had ever really happened; began to accept Tsao Ch'un's crazy rewrite as the truth. And then you were in trouble, because that was when you began to fall apart inside. When none of it made any sense. When there was no coherence, no logic – rational or emotional – behind the rewritten story of your life. No reason for having done all the things you'd done.

On such mornings he would wake before the dawn, in the fevered grip of some recollection turned to dream. And there, in those waking moments, he would face it – the abyss. That great, gaping nothingness that underpinned his existence. That absence where there should have been a healthy, happy presence.

A continuity.

His life. All the things he had ever done. All of them turned into a lie.

They had told him that what he felt was natural. That things *would* get better, once they settled down. Once he'd grown accustomed to the life. But simply being there, *inside*, in the levels of their vast, earth-spanning City, was a kind of torment. For Jake it had always felt like an imprisonment, like he'd been *trapped*.

Some people slowly fell apart. He'd seen it with his own eyes, countless times, and whilst most went quietly, some went out in a blaze of violence. Ticking bombs, they were. Ticking fucking bombs.

Reconstructed, they said of him. Only that wasn't really how he felt. No, he felt like an actor who had forgotten his lines.

Beside him Mary woke. She reached out, taking his hand in hers.

'What's up?'

The simple touch of her fingers, entwined against his own, warm and familiar, lightened his mood. She was the sunlight of his winter years.

What's up? It wasn't something he could properly answer.

'I'll make some *ch'a*,' he said, giving her hand a squeeze. 'Just wait there. I'll bring you a cuppa in bed.'

Jake sat there at the kitchen table, waiting for the kettle to boil, looking up at the muted screen and watching the silent images of Security forces going about their business. Calming things down, making sure there was order in the levels.

He'd checked his messages and as yet there was no word from Advocate Meng. Then again, he'd not expected anything. Not until later. But there was a message from Beth, letting them know that she'd be over in the afternoon.

He was about to make the tea, when the door buzzer sounded.

Jake looked up, speaking to the house screen, 'Switch the view to the external corridor.'

The image changed; showed a figure in the corridor outside. It was a courier by the look of it.

Jake went out, standing there a moment. No, he thought. *You're just being paranoid. If they wanted to get you, they'd get you.*

The buzzer went again.

'Jake?' Mary called from the bedroom. 'You getting that?'

'It's okay,' he called back. 'Just a delivery.'

Only his heart was racing now. He reached out and unlocked the door, then pulled it open.

The courier – a young Han – smiled at him. 'Sorry to be so early, *Shih* Reed. If you'd just sign...'

Jake signed, then took the parcel from the boy.

'Have a nice day...'

'And you.'

Jake closed and locked the door, then went back through.

Christ, you are being paranoid.

But he had every reason. There was the case, and his involvement – Peter's involvement, come to that! – with GenSyn, and the fact that he'd been on Tsao Ch'un's 'list' all those years ago. And the war, and...

He put the parcel down, then went across and made the *ch'a*, setting

Mary's blue china *ch'a* bowl – the one she liked – there on the tray, beside the steaming *chung*.

Green tea, no milk, no sugar. The way they both liked it these days.

More Han than the Han, that was the expression.

He took Mary's tray through to her then came back. The screen was still showing the corridor outside. He changed that, then put the volume up, so he could hear.

The cameras were showing Bremen now, or, at least, where Bremen had been until yesterday. Then the view switched and showed Tsao Ch'un's eldest son at the head of his troops, surrounded by endless generals, stern-faced and very military, Han every last one of them. For a moment longer it dwelt on them, and then it cut again, this time to Mars and one of the great domed cities of the Martian Plains. There were riots there, it seemed, as there had been all over. But things had settled down.

Let's hope so, Jake thought, then turned, looking at the parcel and wondering who could have sent it.

Jake picked it up and examined it. There was no clue from the outer wrapping. Going over to the drawer he got out the scissors then came back, sitting down to slit the package open.

Inside were two small tapes.

Again he was surprised. There was no note, no labels on the tapes. Nothing to indicate who these were from or what they were.

Unless they were from Meng and he'd forgotten to put something in with them.

He slipped one of the tapes into the slot at the bottom of the screen.

For a moment nothing, and then the view on the screen switched suddenly, to show a room – a bathroom by the look of it. Downlevel. A small, very ordinary-looking bathroom, with a sink and a big water jug nearby.

For a thirty, forty count there was nothing. And then, completely naturally, without any sense he was being watched, a figure came into the room. Went across and stood before the mirror, raising his chin to locate a spot, there on his neck...

It was Chi Lin Lin!

But even as the young man began to squeeze at the spot on his neck, so the door buzzer went. Once. Again. And then a third time. Urgent, it seemed.

Chi Lin Lin turned at the first buzz, clearly irritated that he'd been disturbed. Then, as it buzzed and buzzed again, he turned from the mirror.

'Okay! Hang on!'

Jake swallowed. He had a bad, bad feeling about this.

The bathroom was empty now, but he could hear sounds from the other rooms. Could hear Chi Lin Lin unfasten the door chain and begin to speak.

And then a shriek and urgent footsteps, and the sound of furniture being knocked over as Chi Lin Lin tried to get away. For a moment the room on the screen was empty, and then Chi Lin Lin burst in, trying to push the door shut behind him. Only someone else was in the room with him now, pushing at the door with their shoulder. And then, as suddenly as that, they were inside, two of them. Han by the look of them, masked and violent. One of them pushed Chi Lin Lin back against the wall and punched him full in the face, once, twice, cutting his lip open, while the other put the plug in the sink and then filled the sink from the big water jug.

Jake groaned. He watched now, horrified, as the first thug hit Chi Lin Lin again, breaking his nose. Poor Chi, his eyes were glazed now, his legs close to buckling under him. But they were not done with him. Dragging him over to the sink, the first thug plunged Chi's head into the bowl, the two of them holding Chi down as he struggled desperately to get loose. He was no match for them. One of them was forcing his mouth and nose beneath the water while the other punched the back of his head and neck.

Chi Lin Lin struggled a little longer, his movements weaker by the moment, then he was still.

The two thugs stepped back, looking down at their handiwork, then exchanged a few words in Mandarin, making some joke or other. Laughing and grinning now, pleased with their work. And then they went, leaving Chi Lin Lin slumped there, his face still in the water, his buckled legs wedging him against the casement of the sink.

A *Security tape*, Jake realized, understanding at once the significance of that.

And the two thugs? *Tong* runners, probably. Only how were the two connected? Through the Changs, most certainly, but...?

Jake cleared the screen, finding the sight of Chi Lin Lin slumped there unbearable to watch.

He would contact the courier company; find out who had sent this.

And then what?

No, they clearly thought that current circumstances would let them get away with this. They thought...

Jake's thoughts stopped dead. *Oh God! There was another tape!*

He turned, looking at the tape that lay there on the kitchen table, his stomach clenching at the sight.

'Oh fuck... Oh Jesus no...'

Mary set the tray down on the table and came round to where he was sitting.

'Jake? Jake? Whatever's the matter?'

He looked up at her, not hiding the fact that his face was wet with tears.

'Oh no,' she said. 'What is it? You're frightening me now. Is it one of the girls?'

He shook his head, then, taking a long shivering breath, explained what he had seen.

Chi Lin Lin's death had been horrible enough, but that of Advocate Yang and his wife was worse somehow. The little cunts had set a fire in their apartment while they were inside, sleeping, then had sealed the apartment door so that they couldn't get out. The sight of the two of them banging desperately at the door, clawing at it and screeching for help, was seared now in his memory. How could they have done that to them? How could those bastards sleep, knowing they had done that?

Because he was certain they'd have seen it. Certain that they'd have had their own copies made. To gloat at. To watch, time and again, while they considered what big men they were.

Mary sat, all of her strength drained from her, it seemed. He saw how her eyes went to the tapes, then jerked away. How she shivered, then looked down.

'You have to give up the case, Jake. You know that, don't you? If they could do this...'

'You want that, Mary? You want me to give up?'

'I want...' She stopped. 'If it were just us, Jake, then... only it isn't. How many more tapes do you need to see before you understand? It's their world, Jake, and if they can get away with that...'

Jake bristled. 'They *haven't* got away with it. Nor are they going to. They only think they have. We've still got Shu Liang on our side, and GenSyn, and—'

Mary interrupted him. 'Haven't you been watching what's been happening, Jake? We picked the wrong side. Don't you understand that? We picked the wrong fucking side. The Seven... they've lost this war. It's only a matter of time now. And once it's over... then they'll come for us. You know how it is. Tsao Ch'un will be rubbing his hands with glee at the thought of settling old scores. Yes, and making a few new ones, too.'

Jake was silent. He knew Mary was right. Only how could he let them get away with it? Poor Yang. Yes, and poor Chi Lin Lin, too. How could he let that go unanswered? How could he just sit there and let them shit on those people like that?

He looked to Mary again. 'I'll call Advocate Meng,' he said. 'Let him know what's happened.'

If he's alive. And if he hasn't seen the tapes already.

While Jake showered and got ready, she watched the tapes, forcing herself to, the sound turned low. Jake had asked her not to, only she had to see for herself, because this involved her just as much as it did him. And because this was her family that was being threatened here.

Even so, it was hard, and as she sat there afterwards, she felt the sheer weight of it pressing down on her.

What in God's name had they taken on?

Jake was still in the bedroom when a message came through from Meng Hsin-fa. He at least was still alive.

'Fu Jen Reed,' he greeted her on screen, bowing respectfully. 'I am glad you are safe and well. This business with poor Yang and Chi... *Aiya...*' Meng shook his head, clearly pained. 'Suffice to say, I have placed the matter in the hands of some friends. Though whether circumstances will overtake us...'

Meng swallowed, then looked down. His tone had changed, becoming less formal. 'Tell Jake this... We are not giving up. Shu Liang agrees with me. We're to meet this morning and devise a new strategy. The Changs think they've won, only... well, we will not give up. But look, Jake doesn't have to be there. We can keep him advised, consult with him by this means. No...

thinking about it, you must keep Jake there with you, *Fu Jen* Reed. Keep him safe and out of their hands, neh? Because who knows what these bastards are capable of? I thought… well, let's not speak of common decency. These are evil men, and it is our duty to see them brought to justice. It goes beyond the case now. Beyond contracts and agreements. If those bastards want a war…'

Meng stopped. His chest rose and fell. 'Forgive me. I didn't mean…'

But Mary was nodding now. 'You are right, Advocate Meng. I didn't see it until now. I was… afraid. But what you say is true. We thought the war was happening elsewhere. But it's right here, among us, neh? And we must choose sides. Before it's too late. Before those insects eat us all from within!'

Meng smiled. 'Then I will let you know what is decided, neh? Until then, take good care and be safe. Kuan Yin preserve you!'

And with that he cut connection.

Mary sat back, taking a long, calming breath, even as Jake appeared in the doorway, towelling his hair.

'Who was that?'

She turned to him and smiled. 'It was Advocate Meng. He's safe and well.'

'And Shu Liang?'

'Is alive.'

'Good…' Jake looked relieved. 'What did Meng say?'

'He says we're to fight on. And he's right. I understand that now, Jake. We can't just lie down and let them trample on us.'

Jake went across and, pulling her up out of her seat, held her a moment.

'Jake?'

'Yes, my love?'

'Can we destroy those tapes? Take them to the oven man to burn?'

Jake smiled sadly, then kissed the top of her head. 'I'll do it now. Before the girls get here.'

Jake paused, there in the corridor outside their apartment, listening. Maybe it was his imagination but sometimes he thought he could hear it all, there like the faintest murmur, the whole thing masked by the sound of the fans, pumping the air about the levels.

Ten thousand murmuring voices.

He had thrown the tapes into the ovens for himself, then had stood there afterwards, chatting with the oven man, conscious of the huge stack of plastic coffins – each one containing an unburned body – that filled the corridors outside his quarters. Victims of the latest rioting.

He hadn't thought it had been so serious, so costly in lives. But there it was, the brutal fact of it, stacked up along the walls of the corridor.

So much violence. And for what? Only he knew it was wrong to seek any kind of sense in it. People were people. They weren't logical, sensible machines. Not even the best of them. No. This had been coming for a long while. All of that repressed anger, repressed fear. This 'War' had found an outlet for them.

Jake let himself in then paused, smiling, hearing Beth's voice. At least she'd got here safe and unscathed.

'Mary, Beth, I...'

He stopped. Oh God... What now?

Because Mary had been crying. She got up and came across to him. 'Jake... Ludo has just been on...'

'Ludo?'

'At GenSyn. He asked me to get you to call him.'

'Did he say why?'

She nodded. 'I think you should speak to him. I...' She looked to Beth. 'Look, we'll take the kids and go and do some shopping. Leave you be.'

'Mary?'

'No. Just call him. Okay?'

Jake waited, while they tried to find Ludo and connect him.

Jake knew it wasn't good news. Good news wouldn't have made Mary cry and behave as she had. The question was, what kind of bad news was it? Were GenSyn pulling the plug? Had they decided not to fund Jake's case any longer? Or was it something worse than that? Only what *could* be worse?

He quickly found out.

'*Aiya*... Does her son know?'

Ludo Ebert was very like his father, Gustav. He nodded, his grey eyes moist. 'I called him first, before I called you. He's... devastated.'

Jake let out a long breath. 'I don't know what to say. I... I thought she was okay. I thought... well, I thought she could handle it all. She seemed so tough. So...'

Self-reliant. But he knew, even as the phrase came to mind, that it wasn't what he had thought. Not when they'd been together, anyway. There had always been something brittle, something fragile about her.

Besides, maybe she was right. Maybe she understood better than any of them what was to come. For if Tsao Ch'un won – and it seemed now that he had – then they were all for it. Lined up against the wall.

If they were that lucky, and didn't end up on the torturer's slab.

Like Chris and Hugo and Jenny. Because nothing had really changed. Tsao Ch'un was still in charge.

He met Ludo's eyes again. 'What's going to happen? Is there going to be a service of some kind, or... I guess everything's up in the air right now, right?'

Ludo nodded. 'It is. But if anything happens I'll let you know. And Jake... I hope I can meet you, once all of this is over. In better times. I...' He shrugged. 'Well... keep safe, neh? And keep your head down.'

Then he cut connection.

Jake stood there, holding on to the edge of the table. Kate, and Annie, and now Alison. All the women in his life, dead. All except one.

He took a breath, then spoke to the screen. 'Get me Peter. Tell him I need to speak to him right now.'

Meng Hsin-fa paused outside the restaurant, regaining his composure. That morning's news had shaken him. He had come to like Advocate Yang a very great deal. And as for Chi Lin Lin... What a darling boy he'd been.

Shu Liang was waiting for him inside, on the far side of the dining area. Meng looked about him, surprised by how empty it was, how few diners there were. Only why should that be strange? The world was at war. And only fools and madmen acted as if nothing had changed.

So which was he?

Shu Liang greeted him, then gestured towards the meal that was spread out before him.

'Help yourself, Meng Hsin-fa. Big as I am, there's plenty for us both.'

Meng sat, then looked about him, surprised by the sheer amount of food that filled the table. It was a nine-platter meal, at the centre of which were the three meat dishes: pork, stir-fried; Pei Ching duck, glazed a golden red, with the head left on; and pangolin – anteater – boiled and skinned, cooked in ginger and garlic and surrounded on the dish by tiny crabs, turtles and sea slugs. Arranged around these were six other dishes: spicy bean curd; pine-apple, to strengthen the stomach; two kinds of noodles; a huge bowl of boiled rice; some small meat dumplings; and as a starter, tiger and phoenix soup.

Seeing all this, Meng stared in wonder. Barring celebratory feasts he had attended, he had never seen such a spread. No wonder Shu was the size he was.

Only he had no appetite right now. The tapes had robbed him of his hunger. The only hunger he had now was for revenge.

'Shu Liang...'

Shu Liang raised a hand. Then, taking a plate, he began to pick from this dish and that, talking as he did.

'My reasoning is this. That, things being as they are in the greater world, our friends the Changs will think themselves unassailable. The mere fact that we are associated with GenSyn will, so they'll believe, drag us down. And yet the law is the law. And we are mere hirelings. It might be argued that we are not to blame for the sins of our clients. Even assuming that we are, how could we get around such a problem?'

Shu Liang paused, took one last rather large spoonful of rice, then set his plate down in front of him. That done, he looked to Meng again.

'Let me suggest the following solution. That you and I – and I mean not to railroad you into this, forgive me if it seems like such – but that you and I... well... we take this case on separate from GenSyn. That is... that we do the thing without charge.'

'Without charge?' But Meng didn't mean it to sound quite like that. It was just that he had been thinking the same coming over here.

'If you wish to withdraw, Meng Hsin-fa?'

'No, no. Not at all. I think that it's a splendid idea. I think...'

He paused, as Shu Liang raised his chopsticks to his mouth and swallowed down a huge portion of duck and rice.

He leaned towards Shu Liang. 'To be blunt about it, Shu Liang, I want to nail these fuckers. I want to make them crawl and beg for mercy for what they've done. And even then... well, justice is not enough, don't you think?

I want more than that. I want to humiliate them and make it impossible for them to show their faces in polite society ever again.'

Shu Liang swallowed another huge mouthful of food, nodding as he did. He swallowed, then gestured towards Meng with one of his chopsticks.

'Then we are of one mind, Meng Hsin-fa. For I shall not rest until I see those bastards humbled and hung out to dry. Curse their evil black souls. I mean...'

He leaned forward, taking another huge pile of duck and rice.

'...buying judges is one thing, but what they did to Chi Lin Lin... to involve the brotherhoods...'

Shu Liang frowned, then put one hand to his chest. 'Forgive me, I...' He belched, then made to smile at Meng apologetically, only the smile became a look of surprise.

'This duck...'

Shu Liang dropped his chopsticks and grabbed the edge of the table. His face was a strange colour suddenly, his eyes...

He tried to get up, to haul himself up onto his feet, his chest convulsing now, his eyes seeming to pop out from his face.

Meng stood, going round the table to try to help him, but it was already too late. Shu Liang's hand went to his throat, and then he fell. Sideways and backwards, his huge weight pulling the chair down with him, the tablecloth catching in the big man's hand, pulling all the dishes down on top of him as he crashed to the ground.

'Aiya!' Meng cried, knowing that he too had been meant to be a victim of this; seeing how Shu Liang gasped for air now, his face an ugly purple, his huge chest heaving like some animal were trying to force its way out of him.

'Shu Liang! Shu Liang!'

Only Shu Liang was dead. He lay there now, staring up at the lanterns overhead, his swollen, sea-green eyes stranger yet in the plum-coloured bruise that was his face.

'Kuan Yin preserve us,' Meng said, falling to his knees. Only he knew now it would take more than the Goddess of Mercy to protect him. Because this had ceased being a court case. This now was war. And no judges to rule on what was right or wrong.

★

Judge Yo stepped through into the hushed silence of the courtroom, looking to his left as he did and smiling to himself, seeing that it was empty. No presence at all on any of the benches.

He took his seat, smoothing out his silks.

'Advocate Hui,' he began. He looked to his right, where the Changs and their advocates sat, five deep on the benches there, and the Judge felt a deep satisfaction that matters had been settled finally. 'I understand that *Shih* Reed has decided not to pursue his case.'

Hui stepped out into the space before Judge Yo then bowed low. 'It is so, my Lord.'

'Then it is my ruling...'

But Yo Jou Hsi never completed his ruling. Right then the doors at the far end burst open and Security officers flooded the floor of the courtroom.

For a moment there was uproar, and then Judge Yo banged his gavel.

'What in the gods' names is meant by this? By whose authority do you invade my courtroom?'

One of the Security men – a full major by the look of the leaping tiger on his chest patch – confronted Judge Yo.

'Yo Jou Hsi,' he began, reading from a scroll he had unfurled. 'I am arresting you for conspiracy to prevent the just outcome of the case of Reed versus the MicroData Corporation.'

Judge Yo was outraged. He stood and then turned, looking towards the Changs, as if for some explanation. But Chang Yi Wei, the eldest and most senior of the clan, was being handcuffed right then, while another of the soldiers was reading out the charge against him. A charge of murder and conspiracy to murder.

As for Advocate Hui, he had been forced to the ground and was being read his rights, the big man squirming as he tried to free himself, all dignity gone from him.

'This is outrageous!' Chang Yi Wei yelled, as he was half-pulled, half-shoved, up the steps and out of the courtroom. 'You'll pay for this! Just you wait! I'll have you stripped down to a common soldier, see if I don't! You think GenSyn will save your arse? Not if our great Lord, Tsao Ch'un has his way!'

War. Yes, this was war. Only things weren't decided yet. And until they were...

Looking on, using a screen further down the corridor, Meng Hsin-fa wondered how long it would be before Chang Yi Wei bought himself a judge and got his freedom again. Not long, perhaps. But it bought Meng time. And in that time he could find other reasons to incarcerate and slow them down. To buy decisions, the way they were wont to do. And to use the law the same way that they did, to make things swing his way.

After all, what did it matter now if he were ultimately disbarred? Unless he fought them now there was no chance. And besides, he no longer cared. Not since they'd killed his friends.

Yes, they had missed a chance when they hadn't simply put a bullet through his head. They'd thought that they'd get him along with Shu Liang. Only they hadn't. And now that small omission would come back to haunt them.

And to litigate against them, Meng thought, smiling grimly. For whether Tsao Ch'un won or didn't win seemed irrelevant now. He could not wait for the world to find its balance once again. He had to act now. To bring them low. To make them...

Meng Hsin-fa smiled broadly at the thought. To make them pariahs, smeared by so many accusations that they could not go out in public for fear of lost face.

Why he almost laughed. But laughter wasn't appropriate. Not after what they had done. If he'd had a gun...

Only he hadn't. Nor would he get one. Not yet, anyway. He would do this his way. Using his mind. Oh, it wasn't as fine a mind as Shu Liang's, but it was sharp enough to cut and wound a thousand Changs. Let them line up against him, he would defeat them all!

But first he would deal with Judge Yo. First he would see that hatchet-faced bastard squeal and beg for mercy.

Jake was sitting there quietly in the corner of the living room when Mary got back. She had come back alone, leaving Beth and the kids with a neighbour.

'What is it?' she asked, seeing his face. 'What have those bastards done now?'

Jake looked down into the glass of Scotch he'd poured himself. 'They killed Shu Liang. And they would have killed Meng, too, only...'

He explained it all to her. And then, strangely, he laughed.

'What?' She went across and sat, facing him.

'The case. We won. At least, a court of appeal has reversed Judge Yo's decision.'

'I didn't know he'd made one.'

'Well, he did. But now he's been arrested, for conspiracy. Him and Chang Yi Wei.'

Mary stared at him, shocked. 'Who…?'

'Advocate Meng,' Jake answered her. 'It seems he took offence when they tried to poison him. Seems he's pulled all kinds of strings. An influential man, our Meng. And besides, there are a lot of people who admired Shu Liang. To take such a big man down… well, they did not anticipate the adverse reaction to their act. Shu Liang was much loved and much admired.'

'But if Tsao Ch'un triumphs…?'

'Then he triumphs. But the law will go on. Tsao Ch'un cannot rule without the law. How could he? He is but a single man.'

'Even so…'

'The Changs assumed too much. They tried to set themselves above the law, and that has angered a goodly number in that profession. It seems they are not all like Judge Yo. Far from it.'

Mary looked down. 'So you think we are safe, Jake?'

He took another sip, then shook his head. 'Safe? No. But in no immediate danger.'

There was no news. In fact, there was a total news blackout. But was that good or bad?

Meng Hsin-fa stepped down from the sedan he'd hired. Taking five coins from his purse, he paid the chief runner.

The truth was, he had stirred up a regular hornet's nest. If he had called in all his favours, then so too had the Changs.

Which was why he was here now, at the lowest level of the City, brought here at the summons of his old friend, Shao.

He and Shao had been at school together, but then Meng had gone into law while his friend had joined the Academy, training to be a soldier. And now he was a major in Security.

At least, he was until all this business was resolved.

Meng had shown his friend the tapes. Had shown him first-hand the contempt the Changs had for legal process. To get warrants for arrests – that had been pretty easy. The Changs had taken on the law itself when they had murdered two of its officers, for small as Yang Hong Yu and Chi Lin Lin had been, they were still lawyers.

The rest was timing.

Meng ducked inside, through the plastic sheet, to where Chang Yi Wei sat on a chair with his wrists and ankles bound, in the middle of what looked like some kind of warehouse. Seeing and recognizing Meng, he began to yell at him, swearing and threatening his life.

Meng walked right up to him, then leaning close, slapped the man's face hard.

'Shut up!'

Chang Yi Wei stared back at him, shocked. 'What is this?' he said, his voice quieter than any of them had heard it before.

'This,' Meng answered him, 'is a trial. And a far fairer trial than any you have bought.'

'But I...'

Meng raised his hand and Chang fell silent.

'Good. I see you get the idea. You speak when you are spoken to, or not at all. You understand that, *Shih* Chang?'

Chang nodded.

'Good. Then I'll ask you one question. Did you instruct your men to have Advocate Yang and his assistant killed?'

Chang blinked, but he did not answer. He turned his head away, looking away from Meng.

Meng walked round the big man until he stood within his eyeline once again.

'I don't think you understand what's happening, do you?'

Chang's eyes flared at that. 'Oh, I think...'

Meng's slap surprised him. Chang looked down, murmuring to himself. 'I'll have you, you fucker...'

'Oh, you might. Although I doubt it. Not *you*, anyway. But I want an answer. Did you or didn't you...?'

'I didn't.'

'Oh? Is that the truth now, Chang Yi Wei?'

Chang turned his head. Again he did not answer.

Meng turned, looking to his old friend Shao. 'Major... you found the two men in those tapes, is that right?'

Major Shao stepped forward. 'I did. It was all rather easy, actually. We enhanced the retinal prints on the tape and tracked them down.'

'And where are they now?'

'Why, they're here.'

Shao turned, gesturing towards the darkness at the end of the big room, from which came four of his men, two of them escorting each of the accused men.

'These are the men?'

'They are.'

'And do we know who gave them their orders?'

'We do. Unfortunately the man is dead. But we do know who gave him his orders. We have that on tape.'

'And who was that, Major Shao?'

'It was Chang Lai-hsun, the nephew of our friend here.'

Chang Yi Wei snorted. 'If you think you can...'

Meng leaned in close. 'If I think *what*? That I can prove you had my friends killed? That you gave instructions to your nephew, who then hired these men? Do you think I could prove that?'

'Not in a court, no.'

'Then what is this?'

Chang Yi Wei sniffed dismissively. 'This is kidnap. This is—'

Meng slapped him again. 'This,' he said, straightening up, 'Is justice. And better justice than you allowed any of your enemies.'

Chang met his eyes, defiant now. 'You wouldn't dare.'

'Wouldn't I? Not if I knew for certain it was you?'

Chang shook his head. 'I know your sort. Liberals...' He spat at Meng's feet. 'Go on... do your worst! You simply wouldn't dare!'

Meng turned. 'Major Shao. Give me your gun.'

Shao unholstered his gun and, after checking it was loaded, handed it across.

Meng hefted the gun in his hand, getting used to it, then walked across to where the two Tong runners were being held. 'These are the men, right?'

'Without a shadow of doubt.'

Meng stared at the two men for a second, seeing how brave they were at the end, for all their lack of compassion. Admiring that if nothing else about them. Then, stepping closer, he put the barrel to the temple of the first of them.

'Guilty.'

The detonation shook Chang. His eyes widened with fear, watching as Meng Hsin-fa stepped across to face the second of the two.

'And you,' he said. 'Guilty.'

This time Chang's whole body jerked at the sound of the shot. As if he knew what was next.

'And you?' Meng said, coming back across, the gun glinting in his hand. 'How do you plead? Or are you going to claim some mitigating circum-stances for your actions? Was it, perhaps, merely good business practice?'

Chang Yi Wei seemed to grit his teeth. Then he spoke. 'Kill me and you might as well put the next bullet in your head. They'll come for you, you know. My whole clan. They won't rest 'til I'm avenged.'

Meng smiled. 'Then maybe that's what I'll do. To save them the bother. Only you're not going to die. Death's far too good for you.'

'What do you mean?'

Meng walked back over to Major Shao and handed him back the gun. Turning away, he spoke to the darkness once again.

'Surgeon Pa... step forward, if you please.'

A man stepped from the darkness. An old man, a greybeard, dressed in a green medical one-piece.

'Surgeon Pa... you have your equipment with you?'

'I have.'

'And you know what is required?'

'I do.'

Meng turned to Major Shao again. 'Major... could one of your men tape this for us. I would like this distributed as widely as possible.'

Chang Yi Wei looked about him, a look of query and alarm in his face now. 'What in the gods' names are you up to?'

Meng turned to face him again. 'My dear friend, Shu Liang, whom you had poisoned... oh, and before we quibble about that, I *do* have evidence... he told me a wonderful story the other day. About a court case from centuries past... one that set a precedent that still stands to this day. One very few people know about.'

Chang tried to get up, tried to pull his hands out of the restraining cords, but he found he couldn't do either. His face was red now from his exertions.

'You will release me now!'

Meng smiled acidly. 'Aren't you interested, Chang Yi Wei?'

Chang swallowed and looked down.

'Cut his clothes from him!' Meng ordered, as two of Shao's officers made their way across, one holding Chang tightly while the other took a knife from their belt.

Again Chang started to struggle, only he was no match for the two elite soldiers. In a moment his silks had been cut from him and he sat there, naked beneath the glaring light.

'Good,' Meng said. 'How you came into the world, neh?'

'You're dead!' Chang spat, furious now, a colour at his cheeks.

'Maybe,' Meng said. 'But it is the ruling of this court that, as punishment for your actions, you be castrated.'

Chang gasped. He might have guessed, but to hear the word.

'Hold him down!' Meng barked, as the two officers grabbed Chang's arms and pushed him back in the chair. 'Surgeon Pa...'

Meng watched as Pa did his work and the big man screamed and screamed.

There, he thought. *It's almost enough.* Only it wasn't quite. He wished he could cut Chang's balls off a thousand times. His and all his clan's. And maybe he would. Maybe he could pick them off, one by one, and bring them here. Only he doubted they would let him. No. He had only managed to get this far because they'd thought him toothless – lacking in the will to do something like this. Only they'd been wrong. But they would be forewarned from here on in. And he...

Maybe Chang Yi Wei is right. Maybe I should take Shao's gun and end it, now, before they come for me. Because if I fall into their hands...

Chang's screams went on and on, even as Surgeon Pa cauterized the wound.

Meng turned, looking down at Chang Yi Wei, not feeling the least compassion for the man. 'Chang No-balls, that's what they'll call you henceforth.'

He smiled, the smile fading even as it formed as he recalled what this man – this vile piece of shit – had done to his friends.

'And now I'm done.'

Jake ended the call, then walked through, looking about him at his family, glad that they were there – most of them, anyway – at hand and close by, not half the City's length away.

'What did he say?' Mary asked, looking up from where she was sewing.

Jake smiled. 'He said it's done. It's over. He didn't give any details, but he thinks they'll not pursue the matter.'

Only Jake didn't really believe that. He knew what they were like.

He sat himself down beside her on the sofa, studying her face as she worked, seeing how from time to time she would turn to him and smile. She was still there, beneath the wrinkles and the odd touch of grey. And if her face had become thinner and her neck more lined, he did not love her any the less for that. Of all the women in his life, she had been the best.

'What...?' she asked.

'Alison's death,' he answered. 'It got me thinking... about Annie.'

'And?'

'When I think of her... it doesn't hurt any more. It's as if I've come to peace with that.'

'But you think of her still?'

'From time to time.'

She looked down again, starting another row of stitches. 'I think of Tom sometimes. Of how lucky we were. To have that time together. And then you...'

Mary looked up, met his eyes and smiled.

'It's been a hard day,' he said.

And it had only just begun. The fate of their world lay in the balance. Out there, somewhere, it was all happening. The last decisive moves of the game.

He knew the odds. Knew that Tsao Ch'un ought to win. Ought to crush them, in fact. Only the day's events had brought him some small hope. Hope that there were still good people in their world. People who were strong as well as kind.

It reminded him of a film he'd loved, back in the old world – a black and white movie that was over a hundred years old when he'd first seen it. Gary Cooper had been the star. The same actor as had been in *High Noon*. He'd played this man from the country who'd inherited a fortune and had come up to New York to sort things out. A love story. Only a love story that was to a certain liberal cast of mind as much about the woman in it.

He let his head fall back and closed his eyes. It was hard, living in utopia. And some days it was far from perfect. Sometimes it was just plain tough.

And today?

Today felt like it was the end of something. Like they were waiting for something new to begin. Only no one was sure quite what.

Sometimes he felt like he had lived too long, seen too many changes. But not today. Despite everything that had happened in the last week– and five deaths were no small thing in a person's life – he felt strangely optimistic. As if, from these death throes, something better might transpire, a phoenix from these ashes.

'Jake?'

'Huh-hmm?'

'I'm sorry about your friend, Alison. It must have been hard.'

He opened his eyes, looked at her again. 'You had nothing to be jealous of, you know?'

Mary's smile was warm, open to him. 'I know. Even so... you're a good man, Jake. It must have touched you.'

He thought about that. About all those he had lost. Presences in the landscape of his memory.

'It was hard,' he said finally, 'I mean, just living through these times. Harder than I ever thought it would be. But rewarding, too.' He smiled. 'I'm glad I did. Glad I had you beside me.'

He reached out, taking her free hand, lacing his fingers into hers.

'Jake?'

'Yes, my love?'

'Let's pray for a miracle, yes? A good old-fashioned one. Touch wood we all get through.'

CHUNG KUO

Chapter 25

DAYLIGHT ON IRON MOUNTAIN

Shen Fu lay on the torturer's slab, where he'd been left by Tsao Ch'un, alone beneath the unsparing light, a dim consciousness flickering in his head. He was in pain and yet beyond pain. So many of his nerves had been burned away that it no longer hurt. Not that this troubled him in any way. Nor did the smell of shit and burned flesh worry him. He was in a state of sublime indifference.

The truth was, he had lived in his own private hell since that moment when his world had quite literally vanished in an instant, vaporized in the flash of a nuclear explosion. Blind as he was, he could still picture it vividly.

And later, serving as an oven man, there had been that chance meeting, the offer of a job. All of which, step by step, had led to this moment of nullity, of meaningless physicality. Of pain.

And the world? Chung Kuo?

He did not care about the world. In truth he had never cared.

Shen Fu lay there, his mind utterly detached from the battlefield of pain that was his body, waiting for the blackness.

It was in that state that they found him, the Seven's mercenaries. In a palace littered with corpses he – who looked as if he should be dead – was the only one alive. All the rest had fled, or committed suicide, or been killed where they stood. They took care of Shen Fu and, having bathed and dressed him, carried him on a litter to a waiting cruiser.

Oblivious, the First Dragon dreamed.

*

Li Chao Ch'in stood beside Shepherd on the sunlit lawn as the ship came down, just below them on that long, grassy slope.

It was a beautiful morning, made more so by the news coming in.

Tsao Ch'un, it seemed, had gone into hiding, fleeing his fortress after the Banners had turned against him, murdering their officers and declaring for the Seven.

It was wonderful news. Only, relieved as he was, nothing could have made Li Chao Ch'in happy, for he knew what it meant. That he would see Tongjiang again, and he didn't know if he could face that. Not after what had happened there.

Shepherd, however, seemed distracted by this incoming flight. Who it was Shepherd wouldn't say, but Li Chao Ch'in had rarely seen him so animated.

'Li Chao Ch'in,' he said, turning to him, raising his voice over the craft's engines. 'You should send for Li Chang So. There's someone I want him to meet.'

Li Chao Ch'in gestured to the nearby guard – a full major, in dress uniform – who hurried off to find and bring the prince.

As the craft touched down, the engines whining down to silence, Shepherd went across, as the hatch lifted and a young man – mid-twenties at the most – stepped out.

The two embraced warmly, then turned, walking back up the slope towards the T'ang.

'Li Chao Ch'in,' Amos said, 'Might I present my son, Augustus.'

Li Chao Ch'in stared at the young man, shocked, not merely because he looked the very double of his father, as he might have looked fifty years ago, but that he existed at all.

'A *son*? You have a son?'

Amos smiled and ruffled his son's dark hair. 'My little secret. Kept out of harm's way, until such a day as this.'

'But Tsao Ch'un...'

'Probably knew about him, yes. Only the moment I declared for you, he went into hiding. But with the news...'

Augustus had something timeless about him. He looked like one of those ancient Greek statues, only alive, his green eyes – and again, they were

Amos's eyes – filled with an intense intelligence.

'I'm pleased to meet you, Li Chao Ch'in,' he said, bowing respectfully.

'Your voice...' The T'ang almost laughed. It was *so* like his father's.

Just then there were noises from the cottage up the slope behind them. Li Chao Ch'in turned to see his own son, six two and handsome with it, coming towards them.

'Father...' Li Chang So slowed, his eyes taking in Shepherd's son. 'But I thought...'

'Come, Prince Li,' Amos said, smiling broadly now. 'Come and meet your new advisor.'

It had ended suddenly. As suddenly as it began.

Even as the assault units were in the air, heading for Pei Tai Ho and Tsao Ch'un's fortress, everything had changed.

Tsao Ch'un, reacting to the news, had not waited to hear any more. One moment he was there, the next...

They were still trying to work out which of the fifteen craft that had sped away from the Black Tower was his. Or whether, perhaps, he was on one of the shuttles that had launched.

Whichever, they would track him down and have him. Given time.

And they had time, now that the Banners had defected; now that his sons were dead, his nest of hackers destroyed.

There was some mopping up to do, of course, a winding down of the campaign, but so little as to make the sudden peace seem strange. More like a change of weather than a great political upheaval.

One moment it had been stormy, the next...

Li Chao Ch'in glanced about him at the others in the cabin. They were flying east from Pei Ching, to see Tsao Ch'un's fortress for themselves. He and Shepherd and their sons, the two young men deep in earnest conversation, leaning across the aisle between them, their heads almost touching.

On their return from the Black Tower that evening, there was to be a feast, and afterwards, a meeting of the Seven. With the war so abruptly ended, there was much to be decided. The appointment of a new First Dragon, for a start, to replace Tsao Ch'un's man, Chang Yu. And then there was Tsu Chen's proposal that they merge the Banner armies into Security. To make them an elite force, possibly, but principally to close down their camps and establish them within the levels and not outside. It made sense, as did the legitimizing of the Northern Banners – without whom the war could not possibly have been won – to work alongside their Han compatriots, again as part of Security.

For they didn't need the Banners. Not now that the Age of Wars had ended. Security was the problem now, and to that end they planned to increase vigilance. For a time. Until things were settled again. For the war had woken something in the people.

Yes, he thought. *That part of it surprised us. The anger of the masses. The violent retribution that they took.*

He could see it now, in memory, those five bloated corpses hanging from the beam. Landlords and usurers, bullies and enforcers. Users, all of them, and all of them strung up by the people they had bled. Just one example of many.

So much had changed so quickly. For the better, he hoped. How could it not be better, now that Tsao Ch'un had gone?

Thinking that, Li Chao Ch'in looked to Shepherd. Amos was convinced that Tsao Ch'un was already dead; his body one of those charred, almost skeletal figures they had pulled from the wreckage of the cruisers they'd shot down. DNA tests would confirm it, but it was unlikely he'd survived. It would have been nice to have taken him alive, to have stood him up and tried him for his crimes – nice yet problematic. As Shepherd rightly said, to give him the chance to defend himself would not have been fair. Not after how he'd treated those who'd come before him. It was good that he was dead. Only without a body to parade rumours would circulate that Tsao Ch'un was still alive, that he gathered his forces about him, awaiting the day of his return.

Ridiculous, he thought, *but true.* It was how the masses thought.

Up ahead, in the cockpit, the pilot turned his head, looking back at him.

'We're five minutes off, *Chieh Hsia.* I am beginning the descent.'

Li Chao Ch'in nodded, noting how the man had addressed him. *Chieh Hsia.* The same words they had used to address Tsao Ch'un, a mere three days ago.

And so the circle turns, and a new cycle begins.

Chung Kuo had new masters. New masters and a new beginning.

★

Li Chao Ch'in stood over the pale, disfigured body of Shen Fu, wincing at the sight of what Tsao Ch'un had done to the man.

'Look at him,' the T'ang said, turning to Shepherd. 'That is the world Tsao Ch'un would have had *us* occupy, *if* he had won.'

Shepherd looked, his eyes taking in everything. It seemed like his interest was academic, almost artistic. Indeed, he studied it almost as if he planned to paint the scene from memory.

'I only wonder he's alive. Was there a tape?'

Shepherd's question was prurient, almost obscene. Li Chao Ch'in looked away, vowing to himself that if there was a tape, he would destroy it, for no one deserved to be seen in such distress. No one.

Yes, Li Chao Ch'in thought, and that was the difference between he and Shepherd; he and Tsao Ch'un. There were things he would and wouldn't do. Moral boundaries he would not cross. Even now, when he grieved his sons, his wife and baby daughters, his retainers and old friends. Even now, filled as he was with hatred for Tsao Ch'un, he would not have done this to the man. Kill him, yes, but keep him alive in this state of suffering... no. Only a demon would have done such a thing.

And that was how this new world would be different. It would be a world with laws and limits, a world where a man could live without fear of another's violent whims.

A world where the presence of six other powerful men – where the need for their consensus – acted as a check to tyranny.

He felt a tiny ripple down his spine at the thought. Tonight it would begin. After the ceremony. Once they had all gathered, there at the centre of the world. At the place where his kind, the Han, had gathered to ritually renew the world of their ancestors since the dawn of time. There at the Temple of Heaven.

'Come,' he said, touching Shepherd's arm, not wanting to look a second time at the shallow breathing corpse that lay there on the trolley. 'We've much to do before the meeting.'

'And Tongjiang?'

Li Chao Ch'in met Shepherd's eyes, keeping his voice carefully under control. 'Tomorrow. I will deal with that tomorrow.'

★

Tsao Ch'un was crouched down behind a rock on the mountain's side, look-ing out into the failing light, the sound of baying dogs – GenSyn-enhanced creatures, possessed of limited intelligence – filling the cold, late afternoon air.

The shot that had brought down his craft had been a lucky one, but then he too had been lucky. The pilot and his bodyguard were dead, the latter burned alive in the crumpled ship while *he* had crawled free.

Free and without a scratch. It was an omen, surely.

He was tired and cold, and his shoulder ached from where he'd lost the GenSyn healing pack, but he wasn't beaten. Not yet. If he could survive this night and hide somewhere, if he could persuade just one old and trusted friend to take him in, then all would be well. It did not matter about the Banners. It did not matter that his sons were dead. All that mattered was that he lived. For he would rebuild and, one day, not so long from now, have his revenge.

He turned, making his way down the slope. As he did he could hear distant shouts and, far off, the sound of a cruiser's engines. But safety was in sight, and, as he descended down the far side of the slope, he chuckled to himself.

Nearly, he thought. *You nearly had me.*

Only nearly wasn't good enough.

That evening, in the Forbidden City, at the very heart of Pei Ching, the sur-viving T'ang met for the first time since it had all begun, three days before. They took on their new offices there beneath the *Ywe Lung*, the great Wheel of Dragons, once symbol of their stewardship, now of their rule, each of them allocated a part of Tsao Ch'un's world-spanning empire.

There would be seven cities from henceforth, each ruled by a T'ang, one of the 'Beautiful and Imposing', with Wei Shao, once Chancellor, drafted in to fill the vacant position created by the extinction of the Fan family.

Sons of Heaven they would be, each one of them, yet their powers were to be subject to constraint – to the democratic vote of the majority of their number. So it would be, for there must be no more tyrants. Chung Kuo, that great world-spanning City of ice, was to last ten thousand years, and that was their toast as they raised their silver goblets: 'Ten thousand years!' It was the traditional salute to emperors, yet for once it had a ring of truth.

Ten thousand years...

In that length of time men had emerged from beneath the trees, to create artworks and forge language, to build great civilizations and great cultures. And to make war, endless war.

But now they had the chance to put an end to that. To make a peace of ten thousand years. What nobler, higher cause could there be?

Not one. Yet it had come at a price. That night Li Chao Ch'in, alone in his sleeping chamber, finally succumbed, lying there in the darkness, the tears streaming down his cheeks.

While there'd been things to do, he had been all right. But now that it was accomplished...

He lay there, remembering their faces. Seeing them clearly. Hearing them in memory. His darling boys and girls dead, and their father far away, unable to protect them.

That helplessness had hurt him most. How ineffective he had been. How he had failed them. How, in the confusion of the times, he had left them there, within the tyrant's grasp. If asked he would have said it was unforgivable. Only no one thought to ask, for he was T'ang now, a Son of Heaven. And one did not ask a T'ang such questions.

But lying there he asked them of himself, and felt ashamed. Had Chang So been older – had he been twenty-five and not fifteen – he would have stepped down, letting his son be T'ang in his place. But things were not so ordered.

I had six sons...

And now he had but one. His mother's favourite. And she... dead like the rest of them.

No. He did not need to imagine how Shen Fu had suffered. Had not needed to see that pale, cadaverous body, laced with unhealed scars, to know that each day from now would be a torment.

And tomorrow?

The mere thought of it; watching them being led off like that, bound hand and foot, into Tsao Ch'un's less than tender care. It was enough to drive a man mad.

Li Chao Ch'in sat up, placing his head in his hands, the anguish he felt beyond all bearing.

'It was not my fault!'

Only he knew it was. He had betrayed them. Abandoned them. Left them to their fate.

Kuan Yin have mercy on my soul. Sweet Goddess of Mercy, forgive me for what I have done.

The dawn was grey, unvarying. As for Tongjiang...

Tongjiang was a shell, the floor plan of a palace laid out in ash and fallen stone. Li Chao Ch'in had seen it, up there on the screen in the Domain, but standing there amidst its smoking ruins he groaned. The devastation touched and scarred his soul.

He dared not see the bodies of those who had been taken by Tsao Ch'un. He did not dare to see how they had suffered on the slab.

One thing, however, brought it all home. One small detail amidst that hell on earth. They had burned his horses. Burned all the mounts they had ridden that fateful morning. They lay in the stable yard, badly charred but recognizable for what they were. Seven long, blackened forms, a fine layer of ash lifting up from them in the cold morning breeze.

The palace could be rebuilt. They had the plans, after all. But how to rebuild a life? How to bring back a dead child, a dead wife? It was impossible. And yet he must. It was his duty, not merely to his ancestors but to the world he now ruled. For nothing that he did henceforth was private. He was in the spotlight now. A T'ang. Beautiful and imposing. Yes, and a model for them all. For so an emperor must be. A paradigm. Not merely wise, but unerring.

He turned away, walking back to the craft where his son was waiting.

Li Chang So had refused to see it. Had sat there staring at the floor, shaking his head, refusing to leave the craft. Not that Li Chao Ch'in had possessed the heart to force him.

Does he blame me too? he wondered, glancing at the boy as he strapped himself in again. More specifically, did Li Chang So blame him for the death of his mother? If so, then what future had they? He loved his son. Loved him fiercely. Loved the anger and the hurt he saw in him at that moment. Loved him for the sensitive young boy he was.

Li Chao Ch'in swallowed bitterly. He knew that a T'ang ought not to think such thoughts. That a man could lose his reason thinking thus. But he could not help it. For two whole days he had blocked it off. But now...

There was ash on his sleeves, ash on the hem of his gown and on his hands. Ash in his hair.

Li Chao Ch'in groaned.

'Father?'

He looked up. Li Chang So was looking to him, concern in his eyes.

'It's hard, neh?'

Li Chao Ch'in looked away, grimacing with pain. In that instance of his son's concern, all of his doubts had been blown away. Yet that moment had also exposed him. Made him vulnerable again. And now he sat there, tears coursing down his face, his fists clenched against what he was being forced to feel.

'I abandoned them... I *abandoned* them, Chang So...'

The young prince looked back at him, tears running down his own face now. 'No, Father. You are not to blame. It was that man. You could have not have acted any other way. You gave us all a chance. If you had stayed...'

His voice caught, gave way. His head went down again.

But Li Chao Ch'in shook his head, inconsolable.

He had abandoned them.

Half a world away, in a makeshift office on the edge of what had once been Bremen, Wolfgang Ebert and his team were finalizing the agreement with the Ministry of Contracts.

Amidst the chaos they had resurrected the deal. Just as it had seemed to have slipped from their grasp, Reed had brought them all together once more, labouring day and night to make it work. They went through the agreement clause by clause, all the while knowing that in a day or less they might be dead, or worse, prisoners in Tsao Ch'un's cells.

It had been a gamble, but as it had turned out, it had paid off spectacularly. The Ministry of Contracts had reported directly back to the Seven and, in gratitude for GenSyn's declaration of support, their order had been increased fivefold, to a cool fifteen billion *yuan*.

For Reed, standing there as they raised their wine bowls in noisy celebration, it was a day he would never forget – the day he had become First Level, a member of Chung Kuo's elite.

That very afternoon, knowing that the deal was imminent, he had taken an hour off to go and see the mansion he would purchase with his share. Had signed the contract there and then. Tonight, after work, he would take Meg and his parents there.

And between times the war had ended and the Seven had triumphed and...

Reed laughed at the thought and sipped from his bowl, then lifted it high, toasting his fellows.

A *change of sky*, he thought, remembering what his father had said about the old days, when they had first come to the City. *There's been a change of sky.*

Yet even as he thought it, the smile he'd been wearing faded. For a moment he'd forgotten.

Alison...

'Are you all right, old friend?'

Reed looked up, meeting Buck's eyes. Buck was still Head of Development at Contracts. They had worked so closely these past few months.

'I was just thinking... of Alison.'

'Ah, right. A sad business. How's her son?'

'He took it badly. Very badly. He'll be looked after. Only...'

Buck nodded. 'From what I've heard, she wasn't the only one. A lot of people were undone by the last few days. Pushed over the edge. The uncertainty of it... not a lot of people can live with that.'

'You can say that again.'

'In the light of which, what *you* did, Peter...' Buck smiled. 'Well, let's say we're not ungrateful. I'm sure GenSyn paid you well, but if you're ever looking to change your occupation...'

'The Ministry?' He laughed. 'Are you serious?'

'Absolutely. Chen So I loves you. He'd double your salary at a stroke.'

Reed grinned. 'Really?'

'Really. Now finish that off. I fancy a real drink.'

At that very moment, three thousand miles away, Jiang Lei lay in his bed, at rest after his life's strange journey. It was quiet in the house, the curtains drawn against the afternoon's sunlight.

Downstairs, the Jiang family was in mourning, grieving the old man's passing. Every now and then the comset in the study would chime and some-one would go to answer it. They would accept the sympathies of old friends who had just heard from other old friends, or from the newscasts which, in the last half hour, had taken up the story.

Young Lo Wen, who had known her grandfather only in his latter days, was amazed by just how famous he was. A great poet? She never even knew he wrote! And not only that but a marshal too, in charge of fifteen million men! He was a man who seemed to have a thousand friends.

Among those messages of condolence was one from an elderly *Hung Mao*, who, head bared, bowed low and thanked Lo Wen's mother for her father's generosity in sparing himself and his family. A man named Jake Reed. Lo Wen asked her mother what he meant by that, only her mother wasn't going to say. It was Jiang Lei's 'private business'. Even so, it made her curious. There was so much she didn't know about Jiang Lei. But she liked the idea of him having another name – a poetic name – and wanted to do the same. Maybe *she* could become a poet.

Later, when no one was watching her, she sneaked up to look at him again. He looked so peaceful up there in his big bed, his arms folded across his chest, his light blue ceremonial silks replacing the old satin pyjamas he used to wear. She wanted to touch him, to kiss his brow the way he'd so often kissed hers, but she had been told not to. He was an ancestor now, and to be revered accordingly.

And so there in that cool and silent room she revered him, bowing low to him before saying goodbye, remembering as she did how kind he'd been, how soft and pleasant his voice. A man whom she knew would never have hurt a fly.

'Goodbye, Jiang Lei,' she said one final time. And then, because it had been him too, 'Goodbye, Nai Liu.'

And blew a kiss. A tiny kiss. For her *yeh-yeh*, her granddad.

'Ah, Peter, darling... come in... I thought...'

'We had a little drink,' he said, stepping past Mary into the hallway. 'We just signed a big contract, so we had a little celebration. I called Meg on the way back... she's coming here direct from work.'

'Peter?' His father's voice called from the living room. 'Is that you, lad?'

He kissed Mary, then went through, stopping dead when he saw what was on the big screen he had bought them last year for their anniversary. 'Aiya... is that who I think it is?'

Jake came over and gave his boy a hug, then stood next to him, whisky tumbler in hand, saluting the image.

'Never thought you'd ever see that, eh, lad?'

On the screen was the image of a dead man. And not just any dead man, for this was once a Son of Heaven. Now he was nothing but a naked corpse, lying at the bottom of a well, his pale skin laced with his own blood.

Jake poured his son a tumbler of the old malt, then clinked glasses.

'It's over then, thank God!'

Peter winced at that last word. His father knew it was proscribed. 'Dad...'

'Ah, fuck it, lad... Do you still think it matters in the light of what's happened?'

Peter shrugged. He didn't want to get into an argument again. He wanted tonight to be a good night, a memorable night. But he knew that it *did* still matter. For this was Chung Kuo, and though their rulers may have changed, the world itself had not. If anything it would get far stricter. For a time.

The world his father had grown up in – that same world he had experienced as a child – was dead and buried. And rightly so. If it had been worth keeping it would have been kept. People would have fought to keep it.

Yeah. There were a dozen arguments to be had on the subject, only tonight he didn't want one. Dismissing it from mind, he smiled.

'Mum, Dad... I've something I want to show you.'

Shepherd watched the screen, nodding to himself and humming an old, forgotten tune. Something by Beethoven. One of the piano concertos.

He was in the same suite he'd always stayed in when he'd come to visit Tsao Ch'un at the Black Tower, with a view from the wall-length window of the sea. In that sense nothing had changed. But in all others...

On the screen, the camera moved in slowly, giving a close-up on the corpse. Now that it was much closer, you could see that the infestation had begun. Bugs crawled and bit and burrowed, they flew and hummed and laid their eggs. Only Tsao Ch'un, who had hated insects more than he'd hated anything, was unaware. His eyes, once as ferocious as a tiger's, were now opaque and dull. Whatever demon had once occupied him had now departed. The insects had moved in.

The camera dwelt on them a while, as if making some moral point about the fate of emperors. Or maybe it was just strange, what with the rareness of insects these days.

More than a few would be having nightmares tonight.

From all accounts, an accident had befallen Tsao Ch'un; he had stumbled upon the ancient well in the darkness and, not knowing that the thick wooden lid was rotten, had made to cross it.

And had fallen through.

Shepherd smiled. Poor bastard. Just when he thought he'd got away.

The camera eye drew back, showing the splintered lid, the slope down to the path behind it. Thus he had come, last night as the sun was setting. The Son of Heaven, half naked and undone. On the slopes of T'ieh Shan, Iron Mountain.

It rose further, showing the hill and, beyond it, the site of the crash. In the light of day it seemed an inauspicious place to die. Had so many not been looking for him, he would have lain there for eternity at the bottom of that well, unvisited, the flesh rotting on his bones, the insects burrowing, his rictus smile of death ironic.

But then, Shepherd thought, *the Han have little grasp of irony. Fate, yes, but not irony...*

'Mei fa tsu,' he said, lifting an imaginary glass to his one-time friend and Master. *It is fate.*

There was a knock at the outer door.

'Amos?'

It was Li Chao Ch'in. He went across and opened it.

'Have you seen it?'

The T'ang nodded, then moved past Shepherd, into the room. He was quiet for a moment, then he turned, looking to the other.

'You know... I thought I'd feel good about it, once I knew he was dead. I thought...' Li Chao Ch'in took a long breath, then shook his head. 'Well... it is done with, neh? We can move on. Let the insects have him now.'

Shepherd frowned. 'What d'you mean?'

'I mean that we're leaving him there. Where he fell. Leaving him to rot. There'll be no honouring of the dead, no ceremonials, not for him. Not after what he did. No, he can lie there till the sun grows cold.'

Surprised by the bitterness in his voice, Shepherd stepped closer, touched his arm.

'Are you all right, Chao Ch'in?'

Li Chao Ch'in shook his head. 'I thought I would be, but...' He swallowed, then, 'We'll place a cordon of iron around the site and guard it day and night.'

'You think that will stop them coming?'

'No. There will still be those who revere him. To whom he was a great man.'

'He *was* a great man.'

Li Chao Ch'in glanced at him, then shrugged. 'Anyway... are you ready?'

Shepherd nodded. 'Strange, neh, how both men died on the same day?'

He was talking about Jiang Lei now.

'Now he was a great man.'

Shepherd smiled. 'There are those who would argue with you, Li Chao Ch'in.'

'But not you?'

'No. Not me. I admired his qualities. He was a true man. And, rarest of all things, an honest man.'

'Then come... let's celebrate his life.'

As the last rays of the sun settled over the edge of the City, Li Chao Ch'in's cruiser set down on the pad above where Jiang Lei rested, in his bed, in the First Level mansion that had been his home these past twenty years.

Stepping down from his craft, the new T'ang of Europe looked about him. It was silent up here on the roof of the City. A silence broken now and then by gusts of wind which blew the gathered dust about in swirls.

He turned as Shepherd stepped out of the craft.

Shepherd looked about him a while, then grinned. 'I should have built it with more character, neh? A few more minarets and the odd bridge and decorative fountain. As it is...'

'It works,' Li Chao Ch'in said. 'It may not be beautiful, but beauty generally comes at a price, neh? Some rich man's folly paid for by a thousand poor men's graft.'

Shepherd stared at him, taken aback. 'You surprise me, Li Chao Ch'in. Such sentiments...'

'Can be expressed but once, between you and I, and never again.'

They fell silent. Across the way from them a welcoming committee was forming up, near the airlock.

'Come,' Li Chao Ch'in said. 'Let us do our duty.'

Li Chao Ch'in knelt at the bedside, Shepherd stood directly behind him, both of them bending their heads in respect to the man who lay there, serene in death.

Across from them, on the other side of the massive bed, Jiang Lei's family waited silently, knelt with their heads lowered, as the T'ang and his advisor paid respect to their Head of Family.

All, that is, except for young Lo Wen. As if she knew she would never witness such an event again, she had raised her head, looking across at the two great men who had come to pay their respects to her *yeh-yeh*. And they did indeed look like great men, the one – Li Chao Ch'in – for his impressive silks, the other – Shepherd was his name – for his great shock of hair, his beard and his fierce eagle eyes.

As the T'ang stood once more, she saw how his eyes went to her and, despite the solemn nature of the moment, he smiled.

Lo Wen liked that. Liked that he wasn't like the others, cold and haughty.

'My dear friends,' Li Chao Ch'in began, addressing them all. 'I heard with great sorrow of Jiang Lei's death, and have to come to celebrate the man. Tomorrow, it has been decided, will be a holiday, to celebrate his life. And to give universal thanks to a man who helped this great world of ours through its birthing pains. A great man. A truly great man.'

There was a great murmur of satisfaction from the family at that. Satisfaction and surprise at the great honour being done their family.

'*Chieh Hsia*...' they answered, bowing low once more, the word hissing out from every mouth, uncoordinated, so that it sounded echoey and strange.

'And you,' Li Chao Ch'in said, gesturing to Lo Wen. 'You must be Jiang Lei's granddaughter... Lo Wen, is that right?'

She grinned, delighted that he knew her, and bowed her head.

'Come here, child.'

Li Chao Ch'in picked her up and held her a moment, pleased with how pretty she was.

'I had two daughters once like you,' he said, and there was the faintest wistfulness as he said it. Only as he set her down again, he was smiling.

'You must come and visit me,' he said. 'At Tongjiang, once it is rebuilt. You and your family, of course.'

'*Chieh Hsia...*' the older members of the family uttered, honoured even further by this invitation, which spawned yet another spate of bowing and murmuring.

Li Chao Ch'in's eyes had returned to the figure laid out on the bed.

When he had first worked for Tsao Ch'un as advisor, Jiang Lei had been a figure of awe to him – someone not merely to admire, but to aspire to. It was Tsao Ch'un who had made their world, certainly. But it was the spirit of Jiang Lei, and his alter ego, Nai Liu, who had transformed it. Without Jiang Lei this world of theirs would have been a different, darker place.

Again he bowed his head. 'Master Jiang... go in peace...'

He would have a great marble edifice built for Jiang Lei. A place where his descendants could come and give honour to their illustrious ancestor; where they could sweep his grave and burn incense as of old. Counterpoint to the well where Tsao Ch'un's bones lay rotting and untended.

He looked to Shepherd. 'Do you wish to say anything?'

Amos stepped forward. He stood still a moment, looking down at the old man. Then, leaning over him, he kissed his brow and taking a single black stone from his pocket, placed it in Jiang Lei's right hand.

'For old times' sake,' he said, and stepped away.

Later, flying back in the craft, on their way to Bremen, where repairs had already begun, the two men looked across the cabin at each other.

'Why no cameras?' Shepherd asked.

'Because he deserved better than that from us. Deserved not to be used for some cynical act of propaganda.'

'Yet you meant what you said.'

'I did.'

'Then...?' But Shepherd was confused now. It had seemed, to him, the perfect opportunity to make an impression – to make a firm statement to all the citizens of Chung Kuo that they were starting anew, and that the figure of Jiang Lei was to be their template now.

'Leave it,' Li Chao Ch'in said, knowing that Shepherd would not understand. Not that he really understood it himself. Only that it had not seemed right to make that private moment public.

And the girl. Lo Wen. Such a pretty thing she'd been. So like his darling Kuei.

He looked down, a cold shadow falling over him at the thought. For a moment he had forgotten. For the briefest instance the pain had gone away. Looking up, he met Shepherd's eyes once more – saw how Amos watched him closely, intensely, but for once with an unfeigned sympathy.

'It *will* get better, *Chieh Hsia*.'

'Will it?'

'You must take a new wife. Replace the children that you lost.'

Li Chao Ch'in stared at him aghast. '*Replace?*'

'You cannot live in a void, Chao Ch'in. You survived, and that must be made to mean something. Li Chang So can take your place in Council, once he's old enough, but for now you need to go forward not back. However much you hurt, you can't afford to dwell on it. If you were any other man, maybe... only you are T'ang now. One of the Seven. It was not fated for you to be a common man and suffer common miseries.'

There seemed some truth in that. Even so, his heart rebelled against it. Shepherd had not lost what he had lost. Shepherd had not paid the price *he* had.

'If I could turn back time...'

'Yes,' Shepherd said, softer than before. 'And yet you can't.'

Li Chao Ch'in was silent for a time, staring at his hands, then looked up at Shepherd again.

'We won,' he said quietly, shaking his head in disbelief. 'I can't believe we won.'

Shepherd nodded. 'I know. But that's the easy part.'

EPILOGUE   Lilac Time

SUMMER/WINTER 2098

'Going to see the river man
Going to tell him all I can
About the ban
On feeling free.'

—Nick Drake, 'River Man', 1969

CHUNG KUO

LILAC TIME

Jake stood beneath the arch, getting his breath, looking out across the sunlit veranda towards where the children were playing.

It was late morning and he had woken from a dream. A rare dream. Of Corfe. One that bore no resemblance to his usual fogged and half-formed recollections. No. This once he had been there, looking back from the ridge-way, the castle's shape cut cleanly against the blue of the sky.

In the dream he had felt the wind tickling the hairs on his arm, felt the sun's warmth on his back through his thick cotton shirt. Late summer, back in the days, before China had come.

One of the children noticed him; saw him standing there in the great curve of the moon door, and ran over to him.

It was Cath's youngest, Beatrice. The vivacious nine-year-old was wearing a special blue silk dress for the occasion. She looked like a Han princess, her dark hair coiled in a bun, a delicate pink and blue butterfly brooch securing it.

The Han clothes the children wore these days confused him sometimes; made them all look the same, but Beatrice was different. She was her own person. A real character. Which was why she was one of his favourites.

He bent down, his ancient features creased into a smile. 'Hey, sweetheart. You been here long?'

She grinned back at him. 'We've been here *hours*, Yeh-yeh... Auntie Meg said we weren't to make too much noise. She said that you and Nanna needed your sleep, but it gets awfully boring being quiet!'

He laughed. 'Well, now you don't have to. Now you can make as much noise as you like!'

He watched her run away and rejoin her playfellows, eager to tell them the good news.

Jake stretched and yawned.

Maybe it was just the day. Birthdays always got him thinking, and Mary's birthday more than most. They would all be here later on – family and friends. Here to celebrate, before it was all gone. Before...

He stopped himself.

Savour it while you can. Before the world is nothing but ghosts.

Jake turned, looking back at the big, three-tiered house. Peter had done well for himself. Very well. Only there was something overbearing about these big Han mansions that set his teeth on edge. Grand they might be, and elegant... but they were dauntingly uncomfortable. All those big vases and formal chairs. Like living in a giant waiting room.

'Yes, but waiting for what?' he said quietly, and laughed.

He was still chuckling when Beth came out.

'Daddy... why didn't you say you were up?'

'I've only just surfaced. I've left Mummy in bed. Thought she could do with an extra hour.'

Beth smiled at that, then leaned in, embracing him and kissing his cheek warmly, the scent of plum blossom washing through his senses.

Again, it was distinctly Chinese.

As she stepped back he looked at her, studying her face.

In her fifties now, Beth was still a lovely woman. There were signs of ageing, sure, at her neck and in the skin of her arms, but the crow's feet about her eyes only enhanced her beauty. Or so *he* thought.

'What's Peter up to?'

Her smile was beautiful.

'Organizing things. You know how Peter is. He's been up since dawn.'

Dawn, Jake thought. *Lights up, more* like. But he said nothing. He'd promised Mary he'd not cause any trouble today or say all the wrong things like he sometimes did. No. He was going to be on his best behaviour. But it still rankled, beneath the surface. The fakeness of this world of theirs.

'I... had a dream,' he said hesitantly, looking away, not wanting her to see how much it had troubled him.

'A dream?'

'Of the old days. It woke me.'

'Ah...'

Yes, 'Ah...' he thought, and wondered how they managed that particular trick – the not-thinking-of-how-it-was trick. They seemed to find it easy, whereas he...

'It's okay,' he said quietly, looking to her again, conscious of the camera on the eaves nearby. 'I won't misbehave.'

'Good,' she said, as if to a little boy, then leaned close to kiss him again. 'Now I must go through and help the others.'

'You should have got caterers,' he said. 'All that work...'

But Beth would have none of it. 'You know how much Meg and Cath like to do it all themselves. And besides, it's not just about preparing the food. It's the talk. We get so little chance to catch up on things.'

'What are you cooking?'

'A nine-course meal. Lots of things you'll like, don't worry.'

Maybe and maybe not, he thought, but he'd been hoping that they'd do a barbecue, like in the old days. Only that too was fraught with danger. Anything that touched upon the past.

He watched Beth go, then, with one last wistful glance across at the children, turned and went back inside.

Jake had been sitting in the low armchair this last hour and more, half dozing in the sun. Mary, the subject of all this activity, was sitting forward in the chair to his right, laughing and joking, as full of life as she always was on these occasions and acting as though the last thirty years had changed nothing.

He didn't know how she did it, but he sometimes wished he felt more comfortable in his skin – like she did. She and her brood, all of whom were here today. When you counted the in-laws, it came to four daughters, three sons and a full seventeen grandchildren, not to speak of two great-grandchildren.

Not bad going, he thought, looking about him, *for a man who'd lost every-thing.*

It was some while since he'd thought about it, but today, for some reason, it had all come flooding back. That first day of his new life. That fated day when he had walked into the village and been taken in by them. Tom and Mary and all the rest. His friends. The best friends he'd ever had.

Maybe it was that dream of Corfe that had set this off – this brooding, sentimental mood – but he could not shake it.

Across from him, Peter was talking about how his employers, GenSyn, had survived the Collapse. How Tsao Ch'un's man, Chao Ni Tsu, had selected a small elite of companies, buying stock heavily in the weeks before the Collapse to keep them afloat; maintaining them as going concerns until the time came when they could be useful again, in the reconstruction.

It wasn't something that was generally known, not something the authorities particularly wanted known, but it wasn't forbidden. Not like most of it.

Jake's thoughts drifted momentarily.

In his head he could see it vividly: could see the slope below the farmhouse, the land stretching away to the sea, which lay there in the bright morning sunlight like a sheet of beaten brass. And halfway down, almost hidden by the vegetation, Ma Brogan's house. Sweet woman that she'd been.

He sighed, then looked to his son again. Did Peter ever think of that? Did he remember *anything* of those years? Or was it gone, no traces left, erased as if it had never been, the tape wiped?

The conversation had moved on. Now they were talking about the new biography of Tsao Ch'un that had come out a month or so ago. 'A Reassessment' as it had been subtitled, published with the Ministry's permission. A regular monster of a book, more than a thousand pages long. Jake had seen a copy of it on the kitchen table. Peter's probably. It was a runaway bestseller and several of the family had read it. There was to be a TV series. But...

May he rot in hell...

The truth was, Jake didn't want to know *why* Tsao Ch'un had done what he did. The only thing that mattered was the suffering he'd caused, and no apologist could excuse that. Suffering on a scale that was unimaginable. And the deaths...

The whispered 'truth' was that four billion had died to get Tsao Ch'un's City up and running. Four billion. The thought of it was staggering. And now they wrote books on him, reassessing his life and motives. As if one could reassess such a monster.

Jake looked down. He could do with a drink. Only his children conspired to keep him from drinking these days, lest he 'embarrass himself'.

Embarrass you, more like...

He looked across again, noting the animation in Peter's face as he talked. He'd been a good son all these years. The very model of filial piety. That was just it. Peter had absorbed this world. Had become an intrinsic part of it, from hairstyle and mannerisms down to the silken *pau* he wore. More Han than the Han.

'Peter...?'

Peter turned and looked to him, smiling. A smile of infinite tolerance. 'Yes, Dad?'

'Do you ever think of Boy?'

It was not the kind of question one should ask. Only he felt compelled. He wanted to know.

'Boy?'

Jake held his son's eyes a moment, then looked away. He didn't remember. He genuinely didn't seem to remember.

Your dog, he wanted to say. Don't you recall? You loved that dog and they shot it. Those bastards killed it without a thought. Those bastards you work for now. Those same bastards who won't let you wear denim or listen to rock music.

It was unsayable. It was all unsayable. Like in that Ray Bradbury novel. What was it called now?

He shook his head. 'It's okay, lad. It doesn't matter...'

Even if it does...

Peter watched him a moment, smiling still. A smile of infinite tolerance and respect. Not a Western smile at all. Oh, Jake knew his son loved him. There were endless little kindnesses that testified to such. But it was in a Han fashion, like everything in their world.

How he yearned for something pure, something untainted. A broad West Country accent, maybe, or a jug of ale – real ale – something peppery and strong and not the processed piss they served up as beer in this great world of levels.

One couldn't buy such things, not for a prince's fortune.

Jake eased back a little, letting his head press back into the silken cushions and closing his eyes, as if he were dozing. But he was wide awake now. Not sleepy in the least.

So just what DO you remember?

It was a game he played a lot these days. To fill the void and stop himself from slowly losing touch.

The idea was a simple one. He had to remember ten things he had forgotten. To go down into that dark labyrinth of the mind and haul them out into the glare of the sun, *remembered*.

Like the Jesuits long before him, he set himself strict rules. For a start, nothing could be 'remembered' twice. The point of it was, after all, to recover 'new' memories. To dredge up fragments that, until that moment, had been lying there hidden, discarded in the dark.

Yes, and to reverse the flow. To counter that great drift towards forgetting, if only in my own head.

To begin with, he was to allow himself only two musical referents. Beside which were four other specific categories – art, film, books and sport. That left four slots for more general remembrances. Things from history, or science maybe, or...

The first came to him at once. A memory of the US President, Barack Obama, on the steps at his inauguration, standing where Martin Luther King had stood before him to give his landmark speech. Back when there'd been black men in the world. Before the Han had erased them.

Jake sighed, for as so often was the case, the memory came to him not pure and isolated, but embedded in some other thing. That was the thing about memory.

He could recall where he'd been when he'd seen that ancient footage. Could see the big old television set in the corner of his grandparents' living room, could smell the musty smell of that house.

He had always been sharp of mind. That was what had made him such a good web-dancer. But for a long time he had not exercised those skills. The long years since had eroded something of his sharpness.

He relaxed, concentrating, letting his mind do what it did best.

A work of art... something... Dutch?

It came to him at once, and with it the memory of actually seeing it, facing him across the room, in the Rijksmuseum in Amsterdam. The canvas had been massive, the figures life-size. They had spent a long weekend there in Amsterdam, he and Alison. He remembered walking right up to the painting. Remembered standing there, staring into those thick layers of paint, as if he might step through into the canvas itself.

Rembrandt... The Nightwatch...

Which brought his third, and with it, in his head he heard the sound of an electric violin and thought of a drunken afternoon spent in the company of Old Josh, King Crimson's *Starless And Bible Black* blaring from the speakers. West Country boys, as Josh liked to remind anyone who'd listen.

Jake smiled, recalling Josh's face. That mischievous smile he sometimes had...

And focused again. A book this time, maybe. Something unusual...

He had it at once, almost as if the book itself had leapt out from the shelf into his hand.

In his mind he turned it, studying the orange and white cover. Such a slender, magical little book it was.

Chinua Achebe... *Things Fall Apart.*

He remembered finding it on one of the shelves in the hallway of the house in Church Knowle, intrigued by the writer's name. Remembered how he'd meant to sample a paragraph or two and put it back, and how he'd spent the rest of the day curled up on the old sofa in the back room, immersed in Achebe's evocative little tale of clashing cultures.

Back when Annie was alive...

He felt a hand on his shoulder, gently shaking him.

'Dad?'

Jake looked up, half startled. 'Wha...? Oh... oh, it's you, Meg. I thought...'

For a moment he had been back there. For a moment...

'I thought you might like to go inside for a bit, Dad. Have a little lie down before the guests arrive.'

It was kind of her. Thoughtful even. Only he didn't want to go back inside. He was quite happy where he was, lost in his memories. But he knew what they were thinking. If he got tired he'd get cranky. So best let him have an hour or two before the party got going.

'All right, sweetheart,' he said, letting her help him up out of the chair. 'You finished doing the food?'

She smiled and took his arm, leading him through. 'Don't worry, Dad. It's all done. Looks lovely, it does. We've really done Mum proud, see if we haven't.'

He nodded, sure that what she said was true. Except that wasn't what he wanted to ask. Looking at her, he felt something else bubble up out of the darkness.

'Meg?'

'Yes, Dad?'

'I...'

He stopped, his mouth suddenly dry. His eyes met hers briefly, wide, startled eyes that stared out of his old face.

'Dad?'

He looked away, giving the vaguest little shrug.

Inside, in the shadows of the guest room, he let her take off his slippers and get him stretched out on the bed. Then, with a peck on the forehead, she was gone, leaving him alone.

Jake lay there, staring up into the dark.

For one crazy moment he had been about to ask her how it had felt all these years, watching her sisters give birth to child after child, while she...

He hesitated to say it, even in his own head, but the words still came.

While she was barren...

Not that she seemed bitter. Of all Tom's girls, she had been closest to him, a real darling of a daughter-in-law and now that she was older, the very image of his own Annie.

When he thought about it, he couldn't believe that she didn't rage against her fate, at some deep and instinctive level, the same way he raged against his. That she masked her childlessness in the same way that the rest of them masked their past lives; hiding them away, lest they prove too damaging.

Forgetting. Yes. It was all a process of forgetting.

Jake put out his hand and found hers, there in the darkness next to him. Closing his fingers about hers, he lay there, eyes shut, listening to her breathing.

Somewhere, far off, there were noises, but it could have been a thousand miles away.

Or a hundred fathoms deep.

He wanted to talk to her, to tell her how she had kept him sane all these years; how, without her there to whisper to in the darkness, he would have gone mad.

No, he would not have survived, head games or otherwise. It would have been a slow suffocation. Death by inches.

Yes, and even the word was banned now. Inches and feet, yards and furlongs, bushels and pecks... It was all *chi* and *sheng* now. The conquest complete.

For a moment he drifted. Unaware of what he was doing, he began to hum a tune.

And stopped. Was he imagining it, or had he once sat in a bar, somewhere downlevel, listening to some weird hybrid of traditional Han music and Western rock? What had that been about? Some strange experiment, perhaps – an attempt to soften the blow? If so, it hadn't lasted long, for the music they played now on the radio was totally Han, and thus totally anodyne – a mixture of traditional music, cloyingly sweet pop and stirring martial themes.

Piss poor the lot of it!

It was like this latest business with TV. According to the authorities, next year was the four hundredth anniversary of television. Four hundred! It was laughable. Completely laughable. Only no one was laughing. According to the powers-that-be, television *had* been invented back in 1699. It was 'a fact'.

And that was it. That was what made him catch his breath. The sheer audacity of it all. The lie so huge it seemed impossible to swallow. Yet swallow it they had.

It almost made him laugh. Only what was there to laugh at? Some days it felt as if he were living in a mental institution. But it wasn't he who was insane.

Mary's breathing changed.

She was silent briefly. Then, in a whisper, 'Jake?'

He felt her fingers squeeze his own. Felt their warm presence in the dark, solid and familiar. Unmistakably hers.

He whispered back. *'What is it, my love?'*

'Are we really here, or are we dreaming this?'

He laughed quietly. *'You too, eh?'*

'Only...' She stopped. For a moment he thought, perhaps, she'd gone to sleep again. Then, *'Only my dreams seem more real sometimes than this.'*

He smiled. So it was. And this strange congruence of feeling between them – who, back then, would have guessed it would develop? More like mind-reading than conversation.

'Mary...?'

'Yes, my love?'

'I was back there today. In Corfe. Up on the ridgeway.'

'In the sunlight?'

'Yes...' He laughed. 'In the sunlight. I...' Jake hesitated, then squeezed her hand again. 'Tom was with me. He had his walking stick with him. You know... the one with the carved ram's head.'

For a moment he wondered if he'd said too much. If he ought to have kept Tom out of it. But Mary seemed to sense that too.

'It's okay,' she said, speaking quietly but no longer in a whisper. 'You didn't steal anything from him, Jake. Tom was Tom. He gave me my girls, yes, and lots of wonderful memories. But you're you, and you added to what I had. Immeasurably. I'd not have had it different.'

'No?'

'Not a thing.'

For a moment he lay there, his heart swollen by her words, feeling pride and love and a thousand other things. So life had been.

Jake squeezed her hand. 'Well, old girl... shall we rejoin the others?'

He sensed her smile in the darkness. 'Guess we should, eh?'

'Mary...?'

'Yes, my love?'

'Just kiss me. For old times' sake...'

CHUNG KUO

CHARACTER LISTING

MAJOR CHARACTERS

Jiang Lei	Also known as Nai Liu, 'Enduring Willow', Jiang is general of the Eighteenth Banner of Tsao Ch'un's army. The foremost poet of his age, he is an honest man and a strict Confucian; a good man in bad times.
Reed, Jake	Before the Collapse Jake was a login or 'webdancer', one of the best, operating within the virtual landscape of the DatScape. When things fell, he fled to the West Country where he married and had a child, Peter. Twenty years on, his past is about to catch up with him.
Shepherd, Amos	Scion of his clan, Shepherd is the architect of the great City of Ice being steadily built across the globe by the tyrant, Tsao Ch'un. As Chief Advisor to the great man he has great power and influence. His main love, however, is for his art, and for the Domain, his golden valley outside the City he created.
Tsao Ch'un	Former member of the politburo, also known as 'the Tyrant', is the single powerful man responsible for conquering the world and unifying it as Chung Kuo, the 'Middle Kingdom'. The target of assassins, he is fearless and cunning, ruling his newly-created City by means of his council of Seven.

THE SEVEN AND THE FAMILIES

Ch'eng I	Minor family prince and son of Ch'eng So Yuan
Ch'eng So Yuan	Minor family head
Cheng Yu	One of the Seven, advisor to Tsao Ch'un
Fan Chang	One of the Seven, advisor to Tsao Ch'un
Fan Cho	Son of Fan Chang
Fan Lin	Son of Fan Chang
Fan Peng	Eldest wife of Fan Chang
Fan Ti Yu	Son of Fan Chang
Hou Hsin-Fa	One of the Seven, advisor to Tsao Ch'un
Li Chang So	Sixth son of Li Chao Ch'in
Li Chao Ch'in	One of the Seven, advisor to Tsao Ch'un
Li Fu Jen	Third son of Li Chao Ch'in
Li Kuang	Fifth son of Li Chao Ch'in
Li Peng	Eldest son of Li Chao Ch'in
Li Shen	Second son of Li Chao Ch'in
Li Weng	Fourth son of Li Chao Ch'in
Pei Ko	One of the Seven, advisor to Tsao Ch'un
Pei Lin-Yi	Eldest son of Pei Ko
Teng Liang	Minor family princess betrothed to Prince Ch'eng I
Tsao Ch'I Yuan	Youngest son of Tsao Ch'un
Tsao Ch'un	Ruler of Chung Kuo
Tsao Heng	Second son of Tsao Ch'un
Tsao Wang-Po	Eldest son of Tsao Ch'un
Tsu Chen	One of the Seven, advisor to Tsao Ch'un
Tsu Lin	Eldest son of Tsu Chen
Wang Hui So	One of the Seven, advisor to Tsao Ch'un
Wang Lung	Eldest son of Wang Hui So
Wu Hsien	One of the Seven, advisor to Tsao Ch'un

FRIENDS AND RETAINERS OF THE SEVEN

Aaltonen	Marshal and Head of Security for City Europe
Bakke	Marshal in Security
Chang Yu	Tsao Ch'un's new appointment as First Dragon

Chen Yu	Steward to Tsao Ch'un in Pei Ch'ing
Cho Yi Yi	Master of the Bedchamber at Tongjiang
Ling	Steward at the Black Tower
Ma Shao Tu	Senior Servant to Li Chao Ch'in
Raikkonen	Marshal in Security
Shepherd, Amos	Chief Advisor to Tsao Ch'un and architect of City Earth
Svensson	Marshal in Security
Ts'ao P'i	'Number Three'; steward at Tsao Ch'un's court in Pei Ch'ing
Wei Shao	Chancellor to Tsao Ch'un
Wen P'ing	Tsao Ch'un's man. A bully
Yu Ch'o	Family retainer to Wang Hui So

OTHER CHARACTERS

Anders	A mercenary
Beatrice	Daughter of Cathy Hubbard; granddaughter of Mary Reed
Big Wen	A 'landowner'
Boss Yang	An exploiter of the people
Buck, John	Head of Development at the Ministry of Contracts
Chang Lai-hsun	Nephew of Chang Yi Wei
Chang Yi Wei	Senior brother of the Chang clan; owners of MicroData
Chao Ni Tsu	Computer genius; friend and advisor to Tsao Ch'un
Chen So I	Head of the Ministry of Contracts
Chi Fei Yu	An usurer
Chi Lin Lin	Legal assistant to Yang Hong Yu
Chiu Fa	Media commentator on the Mids news channel
Chun Hua	Wife of Jiang Lei
Curtis, Tim	Head of Human Resources for GenSyn
Dag	A mercenary
Ebert, Gustav	Joint Head of GenSyn; brother of Wolfgang Ebert
Ebert, Ludovic	Son of Gustav Ebert and GenSyn director
Ebert, Wolfgang	Joint Head of GenSyn; brother of Gustav Ebert
Einar	A mercenary

Feng I	Colonel in charge of Tsao Ch'un's elite force
Grant, Thomas	Captain in Security
Haavikko, Knut	Major in Security
Henrik	A mercenary
Ho	Steward to Jiang Lei
Hsu Jung	Friend of Jiang Lei
Hubbard, Cathy	Daughter of Tom and Mary Hubbard
Hubbard, Meg	Daughter of Tom and Mary Hubbard
Hui	Receptionist for GenSyn
Hui Chang Ye	Senior Legal Advocate for the Chang family
Hung	Tsao Ch'un's spy in Jiang Lei's camp
Jiang Ch'iao-chieh	Eldest daughter of Jiang Lei
Jiang Lei	General of the Eighteenth Banner; Poet
Jiang San-chieh	Youngest daughter of Jiang Lei
Jung	Steward to Tobias Lahm
Karl	A mercenary
Ku	Marshal of the Fourth Banner Army
Kurt	Chief Technician
Lahm, Tobias	Eighth Dragon at the Ministry, 'the Thousand Eyes'
Lo Wen	Granddaughter of Jiang Lei
Ming Hsin-fa	Senior Advocate for GenSyn
Nai Liu	'Enduring Willow', pen name of Jiang Lei
Pan Tsung-yen	Friend of Jiang Lei
P'eng Chuan	Sixth Dragon at the Ministry, the 'Thousand Eyes'
P'eng K'ai-chi	Nephew of P'eng Chuan
Ragnar	A mercenary
Reed, Jake	Ex-webdancer; father of Peter; husband of Mary
Reed, Mary	Wife of Jake Reed
Reed, Tom	Son of Jake and Mary Reed
Reed, Peter	Son of Jake Reed; executive employee of GenSyn
Rheinhardt	Media Liaison Manager for GenSyn
Schwartz	Aid to Marshal Aaltonen
Shao Shu	First Steward at Chun Hua's mansion
Shao Yen	Major in Security. Friend of Meng Hsin-fa
Shen Fu	The First Dragon; Head of the Ministry
Shepherd Alexandra	Wife of Amos Shepherd and daughter of Charles Melfi

GLOSSARY OF MANDARIN TERMS

Ch'un Tzu An ancient Chinese term from the Warring States period, describing a certain class of noblemen, controlled by a code of chivalry and morality known as the *li*, or rites. Here the term is roughly, and sometimes ironically, translated as 'gentlemen'. The *ch'un tzu* is as much an ideal state of behaviour – as specified by Confucius in the *Analects* – as an actual class in Chung Kuo, though a degree of financial independence and a high standard of education are assumed prerequisites.

Hung Mao Literally 'redheads', the name the Chinese gave to the Dutch (and later English) seafarers who attempted to trade with China in the seventeenth century. Because of the piratical nature of their endeavours (which often meant plundering Chinese shipping and ports) the name has connotations of piracy.

Ko Ming 'revolutionary' The *T'ien Ming* is the Mandate of Heaven, supposedly handed down from Shang Ti, the Supreme Ancestor, to his earthly counterpart, the Emperor (*HuangTi*). This Mandate could be enjoyed only so long as the Emperor was worthy of it, and rebellion against a tyrant – who broke the Mandate through his lack of justice, benevolence, and sincerity – was deemed not criminal but a rightful expression of Heaven's anger.

pi p'a A four-stringed lute used in traditional Chinese music.

San Kuo Chih
Yen I

The Romance of The Three Kingdoms is a long book of 120 chapters, covering a hundred years, from the downfall of the Han dynasty to China's reunification under the Tsin in AD 265. Based partly on fact, part on myth, it is still regularly read in public and is China's most engrossing heroic saga. Its opening words say much of the Han's attitudes towards history – 'The empire when united tends to disruption, and when partitioned, strives once more for unity.' Anyone studying Chinese history would see the truth in those words.

Wen ch'a te

'Elegance' – this is much more the expression of a concept, that of a certain sense of perfection embodied within that elegance, than a simple descriptive term.

Yin yueh 'music'

Again, the word is used conceptually, almost poetically here.

Ying Kuo

England, or, more often these days, the United Kingdom.

AUTHOR'S NOTE &
ACKNOWLEDGEMENTS

Much has happened between the publication of the first of these prequels, SON OF HEAVEN, and this second helping. One of the developments I've enjoyed most is the creation of a wonderful new home for Chung Kuo on the internet – Matt Acevedo's *Of Gifts And Stones: The Chung Kuo Website*. For anyone wanting further information on what's happening with the sequence, search it out at http://ofgiftsandstones.com. There's a lot of Chung Kuo-related material on it, and I'll be blogging from time to time.The official series website and blog can be found at http://www.chung-kuo.net.

Special thanks this time out go to everyone at Corvus, for their enthusiasm, and to my good friends – you know who you are – who've helped me with encouragement and advice.

Additional thanks go to George R. R. Martin, for writing of an exceptional level. His A SONG OF ICE AND FIRE sequence has lost me many hours of sleep these past few months. May he keep producing work of such magnificence.

Finally, a word of thanks to Larry Rostant, painter extraordinaire, for the covers.

DAVID WINGROVE
June 2011